THE HOUSE OF ROHAN

RUTHLESS
RECKLESS
BREATHLESS

And don't miss the bonus story

THE WICKED HOUSE OF ROHAN

Also by Anne Stuart

SILVER FALLS
FIRE AND ICE
ICE STORM
ICE BLUE
COLD AS ICE
THE DEVIL'S WALTZ
BLACK ICE
HIDDEN HONOUR
INTO THE FIRE
STILL LAKE
THE WIDOW
SHADOWS AT SUNSET

ANNE STUART

Shameless

MILLS & BOON

Mills & Boon, an imprint of Harlequin (UK) Limited,
Eton House, 18-24 Paradise Road, Richmond, Surrey TW9 1SR

© Anne Kristine Stuart Ohlrogge 2011

ISBN: 978 0 263 89774 6

024-0712

Printed and bound by
CPI Group (UK) Ltd, Croydon, CR0 4YY

For Lynda Ward,
who saves my butt time after time,
and Lauren A. Abramo,
the best rights director in the universe

Beginning

London, 1842

Benedick Francis Alistair Rohan, Sixth Viscount Rohan, arrived at his town house with a mission. First and foremost, find a biddable bride, get an heir and a spare on her and then proceed to ignore her for the rest of their lives.

The second and more pressing need was to get thoroughly and royally fucked.

He wanted someone so skilled in the erotic arts that he would be unable to move, talk, or think for at least four hours afterward. He didn't want a mistress—his most recent had been cheerful, complacent and only moderately inventive. He wanted variety. He wanted to shag everyone who caught his eye, young and old, fat and thin, pretty and plain. He was after mindless sensation, and he intended to find it.

London was the best place to take care of these pressing needs. In fact, there was nowhere else he wanted to be. He was tired of his house in Somerset, even more tired of his parents' house in Dorset. His brother Charles was simply annoying, with his smug wife and their smug children. And his sister's place in the Lake District was untenable due to the fact that he was certain to murder his brother-in-law if he was forced into any proximity with him.

At least he was properly enchanted with Miranda's unending succession of offspring, even if they were fathered by that spawn of Satan commonly referred to as the Scorpion.

No, at least the familiar house on Bury Street was empty of loving but interfering parents, siblings and anyone else who wanted to fuss over him. He was handling his second widowhood perfectly well. His headstrong wife had died in childbirth, as his first wife had, and he'd come to the conclusion that he was better off marrying someone made for breeding. He hadn't loved Barbara as he had Annis, but her death had still been difficult. The year of mourning was thankfully over, and he had returned to London for the two aforementioned reasons.

He'd already chosen his new bride. The Honorable Miss Dorothea Pennington would do him very well. She wasn't fresh from the schoolroom, though at three and twenty she was still young and strong enough to be able to give him the children he needed and well-bred enough not to cause him much trouble. She was everything that was proper, and once he wed her he wouldn't have to think of her again.

And if she were unfortunate enough to die after

presenting him with a couple of boys, he would take it in stride instead of mourning desperately, as he had after his first wife's death in childbed. After all, any woman unlucky enough to marry him was probably doomed anyway, two wives gone already. Lucky in cards, unlucky in love, they said, and he was an excellent gamester.

He was about to rap on the front door with his walking stick when it was flung open, and Richmond, his majordomo, greeted him with his usual repressed effusiveness. "Your lordship! We had no idea you would be returning to us." He signaled the coachman as he moved to allow Benedick to enter. "The house is, of course, ready for you, but had I known I would have endeavored to have fresh flowers brought in."

"There's no need, Richmond," he said, stripping off his greatcoat and gloves and handing them to him. "Flowers are the least of my worries. I need a hot bath and food and a nap and a little breathing space before I can face anyone."

Richmond made that discreet noise he tended to use when he wished to impart something unpleasant, and Benedick halted his stride toward the stairs, wheeling around to look at him.

"Spit it out, man," he said, trying not to sound too irritable. Richmond was one of the few people he tended to spare the brunt of his bad temper. He'd known the man since he was in leading strings, and while he hovered like the others, he did so unobtrusively and with only the occasional look of reproach.

The only other human being on the face of this earth capable of making him feel guilty was his mother, but fortunately she and his father were traveling in Egypt.

"Master Brandon is here, my lord."

"Brandon? Here?" He was flooded with both astonishment and annoyance. "We thought he was up in Scotland, fishing. How long has he been here?"

"Two months, my lord." There was something in Richmond's tone that conveyed a great deal. Brandon was in trouble. Which came as no surprise—ever since he'd returned from the Afghan Wars he'd been a changed man, no longer the cheerful boy who'd entered the army expecting a great adventure.

"Where is he?"

"Abed, my lord."

It was four in the afternoon. The younger brother he knew rose with the birds and was out riding by the time the sun was full. "Is he ill?"

"I do not believe so, my lord." Richmond was an excellent servant—he anticipated his master's every need. "He is in the blue room at the end of the hallway."

Benedick took the steps two at a time, his long legs eating up the distance, irritation and worry fighting for dominance. Irritation won. When he reached the bedroom at the far end of the second-floor hallway he flung open the door without knocking, strode into the Stygian darkness and flung open the curtain, letting in the bright afternoon light.

The figure sprawled out on the bed didn't move,

and he knew an instant's dread, one he refused to consider. He went over and yanked back the cover to find his baby brother lying there, still in his breeches, his back rising and falling.

He was too thin. The scars on the left side of his torso were healing slowly, but Benedick knew how pity scourged a man, and he refused to feel any. "Wake up, you miserable reprobate, and tell me what the hell you're doing here."

"Go 'way," Brandon muttered thickly, his face buried in the pillows.

"Not likely—this is my house you've chosen to usurp. Why aren't you in Scotland?"

Slowly Brandon rolled over, and even in the shadowed light of the bedroom he could see the ruin of his once-handsome face. The mortar that had killed his commanding officer and seven of his comrades had only taken half of Lord Brandon Rohan's pretty face, turning it into a horror of torn flesh that even now managed to both break Benedick's heart and enrage him. For some strange reason he felt he should have been able to protect his headstrong younger brother, kept this disaster at bay. Though, if their father had refused to buy him colors, Brandon would have run off and enlisted. He had been army mad, determined to become a hero.

He was a hero, indeed. And a shell of a man.

"Looked your fill, Neddie?" Brandon used the old nickname that only his brothers were allowed. "Lovely, aren't I?"

"It's healing," he said without sympathy. "What are you doing abed at this hour?"

"Don't you think I'm better off being a night creature? Who wants to look at this in broad daylight?"

"I never thought you were one for self-pity," Benedick said scathingly.

Brandon's mouth twisted in a parody of a smile. "Trust me, brother mine, I have been experimenting with all sorts of things that are new to me." He sat up, swinging his legs over the side of the bed. "I suppose you're going to write mother and father and tell them I never went to Scotland."

"Why should I? They'll only worry, and I know full well what a trial their concern can be. If they only visited in on you then you would be well served, but I expect they'd fuss over me, as well. So no, baby brother, I shan't tell on you. Is that why you chose my house over the family manse in Bury Street? So no one would rat on you?"

Brandon's smile was without humor. "You know me well. As I do you. There's no way you're going to allow me to catch a few more hours of sleep, is there?"

"Not likely. Where were you that you returned home so late?"

"None of your damned business," Brandon said sweetly, and for a brief moment Benedick remembered when that sweetness had been real. "I have friends."

"I expect you do. Anyone I know?"

"Doubtless. But you're not invited."

"Not invited where?"

"None of your damned business."

"Are we going to keep going round and round?" Benedick demanded.

"As long as you keep asking me questions I have no intention of answering. Don't worry—I'll remove to a hotel while I find rooms…"

"Take a damper, Brandon," Benedick said irritably. "You'll stay here. In truth, I don't give a damn what you do as long as you don't interfere with my plans for the next fortnight."

"And what plans are those?"

"I plan to get engaged. And to indulge in all manner of acts of sexual gratification."

"Presumably not with the same female…and I trust you're restricting yourself only to females?" There was an odd languor about Brandon, the faint teasing in the questions almost pro forma.

Benedick fought down his uneasiness and fixed his baby brother with a haughty glare. "My tastes are narrow in that regard. And I do not think the Honorable Miss Pennington will be the type to satisfy my rather urgent demands, do you?"

"*She's* going to be your next wife?" Brandon laughed mirthlessly. "That shows a singular lack of imagination. Then again, if she's going to die you're probably better off picking someone as cold and judgmental as you are. She'll do nicely. So if she's not the one to satisfy your…er…sexual urgings, who is?"

"I rather thought I'd start with Violet Highstreet.

If I can find her. I gather she left Mrs. Cadbury's establishment." Benedick didn't like the slow, wicked smile that crossed his younger brother's ravaged face.

"Excellent choice," Brandon purred. "I can give you her new direction. I expect she'd be more than happy to come to you this evening. And I'm afraid Mrs. Cadbury's excellent house is no more. You'll have to find some new source for your tame excesses. In the meantime, I'm going out. And don't ask me where."

Benedick resisted the impulse to protest. His planned excesses felt far from tame. "My interest in your activities was simply a momentary lapse, baby brother. You may go to the devil any way you please."

"Decent of you," Brandon replied. "I intend to."

2

Six o'clock in the evening was not the most conventional time for sexual congress, but Benedick, Viscount Rohan, didn't give a damn. Living in Somerset had required a certain amount of sexual circumspection on his part, and ever since his latest mistress had departed in a wounded huff, some six months before, he'd been depressingly celibate. He intended to take care of that matter immediately, and Violet Highstreet and her talented mouth would prove more than up to the task. Of all Mrs. Cadbury's highflyers she was the one who specialized in that particular variation, one of many he was extremely fond of. She would take the edge off him, so to speak, and he would then enjoy himself more traditionally or perhaps head over to his club to discover who exactly was in town. At the moment, however, all he could think of was La Violette's carmined lips enclosed about him.

If Emma Cadbury had closed her doors, he would

have to find a new source of enthusiastic—and healthy—companions. The women of London fell into a number of categories, starting with the virtuous wives and widows, which were of no interest to him, followed by the virgins, who were only worth marrying and turning into virtuous wives and widows and nothing more.

Then there were the far from virtuous widows and married women who only wanted pleasure without accountability, his favorite breed of bed partner. Followed by courtesans and mistresses, highflyers living under the protection of a distant, beautiful abbess like Mrs. Cadbury, women whose establishments could range from crystal chandeliers to the best champagne. Or they could descend to the more depressing, staid households with a grim harridan overseeing the proceedings.

Then, of course, there were the many varieties of streetwalkers, all of whom he tended to avoid, rather than risk disease. But even among his limited categories he could find infinite choice, and he had every intention of sampling the spectrum.

Starting with Violet Highstreet. He was as randy as a teenage boy, and she'd have very little to do before embarking on the sweet journey to completion.

He sank down into one of the leather chairs in his study, his long legs stretched out in front of him, and awaited her arrival.

Lady Melisande Carstairs, widow of Sir Thomas Carstairs, better known as "Charity" Carstairs to her much-disgusted social acquaintances, looked up from the tiny Louis Quinze desk with its gilt and ormolu trim, a frown crossing her face. She'd made a huge blot of ink on the letter she was writing, and it stained her fingers, which was nothing new. Since she was always petitioning the House of Lords or the House of Commons for one thing or another, and generally being ignored, her ink-stained hands were de rigueur. Wasn't that why they made gloves?

Something was wrong. She could have sworn she heard footsteps coming down the stairs, and yet no one had popped her head inside the door to talk or see what Melisande was doing. The inhabitants of Carstairs House, more familiarly referred to as the Dovecote, numbered twenty, and every one of them was a Ruined Woman, a Soiled Dove, one of the Poor Unfortunates. Every one of them had broken free of the shackles of their degrading profession and were busy training in any number of useful fields, such as housemaid, seamstress, cook, and there were even a few she had higher ambitions for, including that of amanuensis, governess or lady's companion.

Working as a seamstress or a hatmaker wouldn't necessarily provide better wages than servicing men in the alleyways, but Melisande already had funding for several cooperatives that would hire the girls, give them decent meals and a clean roof over their heads, and, with luck, prepare them for marriage.

Emma Cadbury, her second in command and capable of almost anything she turned her hand to, might eventually go on to become a governess. Perhaps to a prosperous shopkeeper's family—someone who had worked his way up in the world and wanted a genteel female to teach his awkward daughters to ape the ways of the upper class and wouldn't be too nice about her history. Though Melisande would be devastated to see her go. Emma, at thirty-two, was close to her own age, and yet so many worlds of wisdom separated the two of them. She counted on Emma for the more unpleasant facts of life, for the practicality she sometimes lacked. Melisande would have brought *any* soiled dove into her house, but Emma cautioned her against some, and she listened. She could scarcely jeopardize her work by trying to retrieve a soul already happily lost.

Such as Violet Highstreet, who was still a question mark. When Emma had closed her establishment the exquisitely beautiful Violet had come along with her, happily willing to take the easiest route. She was far from the brightest of lights, and she was entirely devoid of ambition or interest in finding an alternative way to make a living.

"The girl needs a husband," Emma had announced one evening over tea. The girls had all been tucked away in their dormitories and Emma and Melisande were discussing the myriad decisions that had to be made for their charges. "She's never worked a day in her life and I doubt she'd know how to. She's good for one thing and one thing only, and the man who wins her will be a very happy one, possibly happy enough to ignore her past and her far from intellectual leanings. Her talents are remarkable."

"Talents?" Melisande had echoed, confused. "Exactly what is so special about her occupation?"

Emma made a little face. "She's good with her mouth. The best in London."

"You mean she knows how to kiss? Or something else, like singing?"

Emma had laughed. "My poor innocent! Something else not at all like singing. She gives a man pleasure with her mouth."

"How?" Melisande asked, mystified. And Emma had explained.

From then on she could never look at Violet without feeling slightly disturbed. In the beginning the thought made her queasy, but that had disappeared long ago and left her with an odd sort of curiosity that was both shameful and unmistakable. Not that she'd ever do such a thing. She had no intention of kissing a man's mouth, much less his...

She was blushing again. She pushed back from the desk, unable to concentrate, wandering over to look out onto the London street outside Carstairs House. She'd inherited it from her husband, who would probably be rolling over in his grave if he knew to what use she'd put it. But in truth she'd ended up with too much money and too much time, and there was a world of pain and suffering out there, and she could have brought in a half dozen more if she found the space. Not that their neighbors were particularly happy about her project. But she was no more interested in her neighbors' opinions than she was in her husband's postfuneral concerns.

Right now the only thing that interested her was who had been sneaking down the stairs at a time when most of the women were having dinner and working on their reading and writing skills.

The door to her study was flung open, and Betsey stood there, positively bursting with news. The youngest of the inhabitants of the household that society, and even Melisande, referred to as the Dovecote, she was twelve years old, and she'd spent most of her life in the brothel where her mother worked, until the past two years, when she'd somehow managed to survive on the streets simply due to her impressive wits. No one had touched her, but the necessity of selling herself had been coming closer when Melisande found her, and everyone in the house looked on the child as a pet. With her bright red hair and bewitching grin she was a far cry from the women who filled Carstairs House, but she was irrepressible.

"Remember to knock, Betsey," Melisande said in a tranquil voice, trying to ignore the worry that churned in her stomach. At least it wasn't the youngest sneaking out when no one was looking. Betsey was born to mischief and as headstrong as Melisande herself, a lucky thing, or she never would have survived on the streets for so long.

"Begging your pardon, miss…er…your ladyship," Betsey said cheerfully. "But there's a note." She was holding a thick piece of vellum in her hand, and even from across the room Melisande could see the thick scrawl of handwriting. A man's, of course.

"For me?"

"No, miss. It was sent to Violet. I can't read well enough yet to tell what it says, but she took one look and just about ran for the door. No one knows where she's gone."

Violet. Of course it was Violet. Melisande crossed the room to take the note from the child's hand. She should have told her to bring it to her, but she was too worried to waste time on a lesson. "Normally we wouldn't read other people's mail," she said, scanning the words with a worried air. "But this is an emergency."

"Coo," said Betsey, impressed.

And emergency it was. Violet had been bidden to attend Viscount Rohan at his town house on Bury Street, immediately. This was no request; it was a royal summons. Melisande cursed beneath her breath, further impressing Betsey. "Get me my bonnet and pelisse, Betsey," she instructed, crumpling the note in one hand. "I'm going out."

3

La Violette was as beautiful as always, Benedick thought as he strolled into the smaller salon on the first floor. While he fully intended to put every single room in this house to use for sexual purposes he wasn't yet ready to breach the sanctity of his library. Perhaps that would be the final bastion to fall. This was a house where he had never shagged anyone. He'd always had a tendency to conduct his affaires away from home, probably because of some stray remnant of courtesy for his disastrous second marriage. He had every intention of remedying that situation forthwith.

She was waiting for him, and while his brain took in her oddly subdued clothing, his cock knew nothing but her mouth, which curved in a bright smile of promises to come. He knew his own grim mouth curved in response as he shut the doors and advanced on her.

"Your lordship," she said in that breathy voice that

was actually quite irritating. Fortunately he didn't have to listen to much of it. "I've missed you."

He put his hand beneath her chin, tilting that lovely face upward. "If I believed that, my sweet Violet, I would be very much a fool. You and I have always been honest with each other. What's this sudden sentimentality?"

Her own eyes crinkled. "It's the truth, God knows," she said with a gusty sigh. "You're a sight prettier than most of the men I've had to deal with, and you know how to show your appreciation, and not just with coin. You're generous, and kind, and a girl learns to value that in a man."

He felt a small tug of amusement. There were few in this world who would consider him either generous or kind, and the fact that it was a whore who saw that in him normally would have been pause for reflection. Right then reflection was the furthest thing from his mind.

"I'm flattered. Now if you wouldn't mind…"

She grinned at him saucily. "My pleasure, my lord," she said, and sank to her knees in front of him, reaching for the fastening to his breeches.

He closed his eyes, letting his head drop back in preparation for the supreme pleasure La Violette was more than capable of delivering, when the door to the salon slammed open, Violet let out a little shriek of dismay, and he turned his head to observe a virago standing in the entry.

Fortunately he was still properly covered, and he took a small step back, while the woman on her knees in front of him didn't move, clearly thunder-struck.

"Get up, Violet!" the newcomer said in stern tones. "You have no need to perform such demeaning acts anymore. Haven't you learned that yet?"

"But your ladyship," Violet wailed. "I like it!"

For a moment the woman was startled into silence, giving Benedick a moment to survey her. He didn't believe she was a lady for one moment—Violet was prone to calling everyone "your lordship" or "your ladyship" in hopes of creating goodwill that would lead to financial generosity. This woman was past her first youth, though still young, wearing a bonnet that hid most of her hair and a great deal of her face. She was dressed in clothes of excellent quality but little style, and her voice was that of the upper classes or someone who'd had an excellent governess. She could almost carry it off.

Finally, she spoke. "Get up," she said again. "I don't know what kind of threats this man made, but you've nothing to be afraid of. He can't hurt you—I won't let him."

Benedick decided it was time for him to interfere. "If you'd stop to listen to the girl, you'd realize that she's here on her own volition."

The woman turned toward him, and he could see blazing blue eyes beneath the brim of her hat. "She simply picked a likely door and walked in to offer her services, did she?"

"I sent her a note requesting her presence, but it

was up to her whether she wished to accept my invitation."

"Hardly an invitation." She dropped a crumpled piece of paper on the floor with a contemptuous gesture. "It read more like a royal command than an invitation."

"You read other people's private correspondence?" He didn't like this irksome woman one bit. "Perhaps you prefer I address my future requests to you."

"To me?" she said, startled.

"You certainly don't look like any abbess I've ever known, nor do you dress your girls particularly well, but times have changed since I was last in the city and I'm willing to be accommodating."

The woman ground her teeth, but she ignored him, her eyes focusing on the woman still kneeling in front of him. "Violet, do you wish to stay here or come back to the house? You cannot do both."

Violet looked up into Benedick's eyes, a woeful expression on her face, and she slowly rose to her feet. "I'm sorry, my lord," she said. And without another word she scuttled out of the room.

The *procuress* didn't move, looking at him with cool dislike. "Do not interfere with my girls again," she said in a dangerous voice.

"Your accent is really quite extraordinary," he said lazily. "One would almost assume you were a lady and not the keeper of a house of ill repute. I presume you don't allow your girls to make visits—so be it. I will take my custom elsewhere. In the meantime, however, I wondered if you might be good enough to finish what Violet has started." He reached for the fastening of his breeches, just to see what she might do.

She was gone in a flash, her simple gown flying out behind her, and he laughed as he sank into a chair. Annoying as she was, her ridiculous outrage was fascinating, much more so than Violet's cheerful enthusiasm, even if she probably didn't possess the same skills. Nevertheless, he could only assume she'd learned her trade well. If she didn't bar him from the door he would have to see if she might be persuaded to dispense her own favors. Her anger with him had burned fiery hot, and it was most... enticing.

There was a soft knock on the door, and Richmond appeared, a worried expression on his face. "I'm sorry, my lord. Young Murphy opened the door and he didn't know how to stop her. Is there any way I can be of assistance?"

"Not unless you can tell me the name and direction of the woman who just left this house," he said, not expecting success.

Richmond's disapproval was evident. "I believe your lordship is well acquainted with Miss Violet Highstreet."

"Indeed, I am, Richmond. But who is the woman who came charging in here to interrupt us? I'm surprised you didn't stop her."

If anything Richmond looked even stiffer. "You are referring to Lady Carstairs, I believe."

Benedick let out a snort of laughter. "Believe me,

Richmond, the woman who stormed in here was a far cry from a lady. She was an abbess."

"Much as I regret to disagree with you, my lord, that was Melisande, Lady Carstairs, relict of Sir Thomas Carstairs, who operates a haven for fallen women in her home in King Street. I rather believe Carstairs House is referred to as 'the Dovecote' for obvious reasons, and the lady herself is called 'Charity' Carstairs in reference to her good works."

Benedick looked at him in mingled horror and disbelief. "I believe you're making a joke, Richmond."

"I assure you, my lord, I have absolutely no sense of humor whatsoever."

Bloody hell, he thought, sinking into a chair. He could thank his darling baby brother for this one, damn him. Brandon would have known perfectly well that Violet had been attempting to retire from the business, and that sending for her would open up all sorts of difficulties. Odd—it wasn't like Brandon to play such a malicious trick on him.

"Would you be wanting anything else, my lord? Perhaps you'd like to send one of the footmen out with a note for a different establishment?"

"Stop looking at me like that, Richmond. I don't care if you've known me since I was an infant—it's not your place."

"Of course not, my lord."

And now he'd hurt the old man. His day was going from bad to worse. "Never mind, Richmond. I find

I'm no longer in the mood. Tell Cook I'll be eating at my club tonight."

"Yes, my lord."

"And Richmond."

"Yes, my lord?"

"It's good to see you again."

The old man unbent, just slightly. "And you, my lord."

By ten o'clock that evening he'd discovered all that he would ever want to know about Melisande Carstairs, from her marriage to the ailing Sir Thomas Carstairs, a son of a bitch if ever there was one, to her widowhood and her unceasing good work that most people found tedious. She had come from decent if not impressive stock—an old Yorkshire family whose money had long ago disappeared. She'd made her bow more than a decade ago, putting her around thirty, married the aging and choleric Sir Thomas and devoted herself to his last, unpleasant years. She'd returned to London a wealthy widow and instead of doing the sensible thing, throwing herself into the frivolity long denied her and embarking on a series of affaires, she'd simply continued her self-sacrificing ways, eschewing parties and public gatherings to concentrate on good works.

She'd started her current crusade almost by accident, his old friend Harry Merton had told him over two bottles of claret. A soiled dove had been hit by her carriage, and ever since that momentous occasion she'd been collecting them like so many china figurines, and taken to installing them in her town house and teaching them a respectable trade, for God's sake. Of course she was totally ruined socially, given her associating with whores, but that didn't seem to bother her in the slightest. The only time she ever came close to mingling with her own class was at the opera or the theater—even a saint couldn't abjure everything, and Lady Carstairs appeared to love music. Even if she didn't care much for men.

"But then," Harry had added, "old Sir Thomas was enough to put even the most enthusiastic female off men for the rest of her life." He'd drained his wineglass and signaled for a third bottle to be brought to them. "Imagine running afoul of her on your first day back. It could almost be a sign."

Harry was a good fellow but not possessed of a great deal of brain, and he was superstitious to a fault. "Simply a sign I've been absent too long." Benedick was too far gone to summon up the choler he should have.

"Didn't have much choice in the matter, did you? You do have the damnedest luck when it comes to women."

"It's not women I'm worrying about," he said, accepting more wine from the steward. "It's Brandon."

"What's that scamp gotten up to now?" Lord Petersham roused himself from the wine-laced reverie he'd drifted into. "Always liked your little brother, Rohan. More heart than sense, but a pluck lad, game to the backbone. Dreadful what that war did to him."

"Dreadful what war does to any man," Benedick said, pure heresy in these days of expanding empire. "But Brandon was always impulsive, rushing into things without thinking them through first." In fact, that was how Brandon had been so grievously wounded. His battalion had been under attack, and he'd gone in to pull the bodies of comrades from the fray, and nearly been killed doing so.

"I don't think you need to worry about Brandon," Harry said, his voice still jovial despite being slightly slurred. "He'll be just fine. Best not to interfere or ask too many questions."

Benedick raised an eyebrow, but Harry was too drunk to notice. Then again, there was little he could do until Brandon was willing to talk to him, to let him into the private hell that had been his dwelling place for the past six months, ever since he'd returned from the Afghan battlefield.

"So tell me, where's the best establishment for seeking female companionship?" he said, changing the subject, unwilling to have his troubled brother the topic of conversation among a group of drunken aristocrats. "I gather Emma Cadbury has closed her doors."

"And moved in with Lady Carstairs," Lord Petersham said mournfully. "And The White Pearl has been abandoned. In fact, several of the most beautiful of highflyers in town have abandoned their profession and either left London or become depressingly respectable. It's damnable."

"Are you telling me I can't find a decent whore in this city? I don't believe you."

"Wouldn't you rather have an indecent whore?" Harry said, then subsided into giggles. Benedick ignored him.

"Oh, there are still a number of reasonable establishments where a gentleman might go for a glass of wine, a hand of cards and female companionship. The night is young!"

For a moment Benedick hesitated, and the fact that he did shocked him. He'd returned to London to assuage his appetites, to feast until he was gorged on sensual pleasures, and yet for a moment he could see those blazing blue eyes, looking at him with utter contempt. Lord, there was nothing more tedious than a zealot.

"Indeed, it is," he said, rising to his feet, pleased to note that he was almost entirely sober. Sober enough to enjoy himself. A slow, wicked smile lit his face. He looked down at Harry, but his old friend was drifting, and he'd never been one for the ladies. Or the whores, for that matter.

"I do believe I'll accompany you, Petersham," he said.

"Capital!" Petersham beamed. "I can promise you clean and willing companionship, with this one little darling who has the most amazing trick of the…"

4

Melisande Carstairs couldn't sleep. It was happening more and more often nowadays, and there didn't seem to be much she could do about it. Usually she kept herself so busy she would tumble into bed in a state of exhaustion more nights than not.

But that had changed recently, and she wasn't sure why. She would lie abed and try to think peaceful thoughts, but the worries would leach through, and she would fuss over Violet, or Hetty, or young Betsey.

And when she did sleep it was worse. She would wake up, her body damp with sweat, her skin tingling, her entire body reaching for something indefinable and doubtless unpleasant.

That was what had happened tonight. After leaving Viscount Rohan in his disgusting state of arousal she'd come back home and thrown herself into a frenzy of activity, scooping up a handful of girls and leading them down into the kitchens to conduct an impromptu baking session, much to Cook's dismay. The plump and placid Mollie Biscuits had once been one of the great whores of London, but age and girth and lassitude had drawn her into the kitchen, and once there, she'd never left. She had no problem with other women of doubtful reputation joining her there, she just didn't like having someone else in charge. If Melisande had any sense, she would have ceded her place and gone back upstairs to look over her accounts.

But she needed the distraction as well as the cinnamon bread and lemon curd biscuits and apricot custard pots de crème. And eventually Cook unbent enough to join in the merriment, with flour and sugar dusting her plump cheeks and apricot preserves staining her apron.

And of course Melisande had eaten too much, she thought, her stomach in an uproar. It had always been a weakness, her passion for sweets, and she turned to them in times of great trial. Though why she should be so overwrought today made no sense. She'd come face-to-face with the slightly infamous Viscount Rohan, and he'd mistaken her for a madam, of all things! Normally that would have amused her, and she would have replied with enough hauteur to depress the pretensions of even the king himself. She was surprised she'd let such a silly thing disturb her.

And it hadn't been the first time she'd seen him. Twelve years ago, during her first season, he'd been engaged to Annis Duncan and hadn't eyes for anyone else, including the not very distinguished Melisande

Cooper. She'd watch him prowl the dance floor like a great jungle cat, always circling, always one eye on his betrothed. He'd never even noticed her, which was just as well. She had never been the sort to attract the attention of men like him; she knew it, and accepted it without grief. She had no fortune, no title, no lands to inherit. She was ordinary looking, with hair that was neither brown nor blond but a boring kind of in-between shade, and her blue eyes had a tendency to see things a bit too clearly. Gentlemen had never liked that, particularly combined with her alarming habit of speaking her mind. She was also curvy rather than willowy, bustling rather than languid, practical rather than dreamy, and those depressing characteristics had made her one of the leftovers. Those gentlemen still in search of a wife had no choice but to turn to her. And so she had attracted the attention of Sir Thomas Carstairs, and hadn't had much choice when there were no other offers and her aunt, her only surviving relative, had made it clear that one season was all she was willing to countenance.

She'd married him, perfectly aware that he wasn't going to last long. He had a wasting disease, he was already coughing blood and his uncertain temper had promised to carry him off quite quickly. He was irritable, critical, much older than she was and the most impatient person she'd ever known.

And she'd loved him.

Indeed, with her care he'd lasted years longer than his doctor had predicted. He'd railed at her, dismissed her, criticized her and loved her in return. And when he died she'd mourned him deeply, much to the surprise of those who knew her.

The odd thing was that she hadn't realized how wealthy he, and now she, was. He had no issue and no entailments, so her widowhood had made her an instant target of fortune hunters. After her year of mourning she'd returned to London and immediately fallen in love. How was she to know he had pockets to let and a marked preference for willowy beauties. She'd even gone so far as to allow him to seduce her, curious if a young man would be any different than Sir Thomas's occasional, ineffectual efforts.

It had been both boring and disgusting. Wilfred Hunnicut hadn't been particularly handsome. He had a weak chin that he tried to disguise with side whiskers, a slightly bowed posture and just the faintest hint of a belly. She had closed her eyes and instead of envisioning calm landscapes, as her aunt had suggested, she instead envisioned someone else pressing her down into the bedclothes, someone who'd looked remarkably like Benedick Rohan. Even that didn't help, as Wilfred's hunching and sweating over her proved distracting as he quickly finished his business. She might have been trapped with him if she hadn't had the good fortune to catch him pressing kisses on a chambermaid.

She'd dismissed her fiancé, retained the chambermaid and decided then and there that she had no need of a man in her life. She would fill it with good works and convivial souls, which, from her years of observation, would doubtless consist of women.

Women were practical, fair-minded, inventive and far less likely to fuss over things. When they did there was usually an underlying reason, and within a few short years she'd had any number of good female friends.

She'd even managed to retain the best of them, despite her peculiar habit of rescuing soiled doves and bringing them home with her, along with their siblings and offspring.

She drew the line at their lovers or pimps. When an unfortunate joined the women of the Dovecote, they relinquished their old ways of earning a living in return for learning a decent trade.

For some reason she couldn't ever picture Violet Highstreet hunched over a needle in a decent milliner's shop. Though she had an eye for fashion—she'd doubtless be excellent at designing hats. If she was patient enough to learn her craft, which she most certainly wasn't.

But I like it, she'd wailed, and Melisande couldn't get that picture out of her mind. Any more than she could forget Benedick Rohan's dark eyes sweeping over her in thinly veiled contempt.

Of course, he'd thought she was a madam. But she suspected he would have shown more respect for an abbess than a do-gooder. Charity Carstairs, they called her behind her back.

Well, so be it. There were worse names to be called, and the only people who'd ever flattered her had been seeking her money. But with her belated wisdom she could simply ignore the handsomest fortune hunter and rejoice in the fact that she didn't have to go through the indignity of *that* again. What reasonable woman would want to?

Warm milk and biscuits would help things, she decided, wrapping a shawl around her nightgown and sticking her feet in soft, fur-lined slippers. She headed out into the hall, moving as quietly as she could so as not to wake the others.

The ground floor of Carstairs House held the training rooms nowadays, plus her small office and library. The first floor held her formal salon and bedrooms for herself and her staff. Emma Cadbury had the adjoining room, with several of the older women sharing rooms toward the back of the house. She'd put Violet in one of them, simply because she was older than most of the girls on the second- and third-floor bedrooms. It might have been a mistake.

There wasn't a sound as she crept down the hall. She had no idea whether Violet had slipped out the moment she had a chance, to go running back to Viscount Rohan. It was hard to convince a beautiful young woman that she was better off laboring under difficult terms for pence rather than pounds for lying on her back, though Melisande couldn't figure out why. Surely any reasonable woman would willingly take a cut in her income simply for the chance not to have to let a man do those things to her. She shivered slightly, thinking of Rohan's dark eyes as he'd watched her. Finish what Violet started, indeed!

She was sitting at the scarred wooden table in the center of the kitchen, waiting for the tea to steep, when she heard a sound from the hallway. It was too early for even the sprightliest kitchen wench— the bread wouldn't need to be started for another hour—and Melisande froze in sudden fear. Only to see Emma stick her head in the room, her worried expression brightening when she saw Melisande.

"I heard you go out," she said, coming into the room and grabbing a thick white mug from the shelf. "I assumed you were Violet, but she's sound asleep in bed, looking like the perfect angel." She snorted.

"Probably not for long," Melisande said, pushing the plate of biscuits toward her.

"No, probably not. You can't save them all. Not if they don't want to be saved."

For a moment Melisande busied herself with the teapot, pouring mugs of hot tea as Emma took the seat opposite her. "I don't understand it. Why wouldn't they be happy to get away from all that degradation? When there's a decent way to live without having some man pawing you all the time, why wouldn't you jump at the chance?"

A small smile curved Emma's mouth. She was a beautiful woman, Melisande thought dispassionately. It would make a lot of sense if their names were switched. Melisande should be a raven-haired beauty; Emma should be the brown wren.

"There's a surprising amount of pleasure to be had in bed." She took a sip of her tea.

Melisande made a sound of disdain. "I find that

hard to believe. It's not as if I hadn't…as if I were still… I have experience, you know."

"Of course you have." Emma's voice was soothing. "But you will admit, not quite as much as I do."

"We're the same age," Melisande said, knowing she sounded childish.

"You're a century younger. Be glad of it, my dear."

"But you just said there was surprising pleasure to be had in bed."

"And you'll find it. With the right man."

Melisande shook her head. "I don't think so. And you've eschewed the company of men to live here, as well. Don't you miss this purported 'pleasure'?"

"What brought this up?"

"Nothing. Just something Violet said when I found her at Viscount Rohan's."

"And that was?"

For a moment Melisande hesitated, and then she spoke. "She said she *liked it*. Now I could see that if one was to enjoy the act with anyone then Viscount Rohan would be the man…" The words were already out of her mouth before she realized how damning they were.

"He's a very handsome man," Emma agreed gravely, but there was still a twinkle in her eye. "All the Rohans are beautiful and wicked and irresistible. It's only natural you would have a *tendre* for him."

"Not likely," Melisande said, reaching for another biscuit. "As you said, he's a handsome man— I'd have to be dead not to notice, and I'm not dead. That doesn't mean I want to go anywhere near him."

"But the question is, are you tempted?"

Melisande hid her instinctive reaction. "Of course not! And I'm not the kind of woman Viscount Rohan gets involved with. Thank heavens!"

"Thank heavens, why?" Emma pursued. "If you're not tempted then why would it matter whether he was interested or not?"

The very thought of Benedick Rohan turning those dark eyes on her with anything less than the annoyance or, at best, indifference, was enough to make her blood run cold. And hot. "When did you become such a matchmaker?" she demanded.

Emma smiled. "Seven years running a house of ill repute gives me a great deal of experience. I can tell when someone's interested, and I can tell when it would be a good match."

"Well, I'm not interested."

"Of course you aren't." Emma's eyes were alight with merriment.

"You'll see. Sooner or later I expect I'll run into him again, and I'll have a chance to prove I don't care. Though I'm not going after Violet again. This is her last chance."

Emma shook her head. "She won't stay."

"No. And Viscount Rohan is welcome to her." Melisande rose, yawning. "I don't know whether I should go back to bed or give it up and dress for the day."

"You'll dress for the day," Emma returned. "You're the most active creature I know—you're bound to have a hundred things you could accomplish before noon."

"Am I that predictable?"

"Yes."

Emma remained at the table long after Melisande had left, staring into her teacup. She wished she could read the leaves. She knew her past—it would be lovely to have the assurance that the future would be a calmer, safer one.

There were a thousand excuses for what she'd become, she thought coolly. A hysterical mother who'd thrown herself off the third-story roof of their ramshackle house in Plymouth. A cold, withdrawn father, obsessed with sin and salvation, whose attention took the form of beatings and ritual scrubbings. And a grandfather who touched her, who wanted to be touched, who whispered that it was her fault—she was the wicked one to lure him so, that she would burn in the flames of hell, and at the age of eleven she had believed him.

He'd died soon thereafter, and that had been her fault, as well. She'd prayed for his death. Evil creature that she was, she'd prayed that he would die and she wouldn't have to let him put his gnarled, painful hands on her. And so he had died, because she had asked for it, and her sins had been compounded.

She had run away when she was fifteen, after her father had dragged her into her Spartan bedchamber by her hair, stripped off her clothes to expose her wicked, temptress's body, and washed her. Washed every part of her, roughly, and then slowly, and the shame had paralyzed her, shame and fear, and she knew she had brought even her holy father to sin by her wanton form, and she'd run, before she could tempt him further.

She'd had enough money to get her as far as London, and old Mother Howard had been there to meet the stagecoach, as she so often was. A sweet, elderly figure with a comforting smile and soft hands, she'd offered her a safe place to stay while she found work in the teeming city, and Emma, who'd never known a woman's kindness but was at least certain that her looks would elicit no demon's temptation, had gone with her, grateful and expectant.

She always wondered at what price the old hag had sold her virginity. She only knew the bitch had chortled as someone had held her down and administered enough of the drug to keep her compliant but still awake, that the sum outstripped anything she had received in the past.

At the end of that hideous night she'd been returned to the room full of sullen girls, and she'd lay in her cot, weeping, wanting to die. Until someone sat down beside her and spoke in a matter-of-fact voice.

"Crying won't do you no good, my girl," Mollie Biscuits had said. "I'd tell you that the worst of it is over, but that might not be true. Old Mother Howard has some clients who like to hurt a girl in order to get it up, but the good news is that even more of them like to be hurt themselves. You'll end up with the chance to whip some of the men who want to hurt you, and there's revenge to be had with that."

Emma didn't lift her head, but her tears had stopped, and she listened.

"Many of them will only want you to pleasure them with your mouth, and that won't take long. Some will want you for the night, but if you know a few tricks you'll find you can tire them in less than an hour and then spend the rest of the night sleeping in a better bed than this one. Some want strange, unnatural things, and you go along with it, because you have no choice.

"But, lass, she's old and sick. I've heard her coughing, late at night, and she'll be dead before Whitsuntide. I won't say you'll be free then—her bully boys will try to keep you on. And for most of us, we have no place to go. We'll stay here, and do what we know how to do, because otherwise it's the streets, and that's a short ride to an ugly death.

"But you can go home again. Mother Howard will make certain there are no babies, and you can return to whatever country town you came from and forget any of this ever happened."

Emma had lifted her head then, and her tears had stopped. The woman sitting opposite her was large and comfortable-looking, older than the women who watched her with wary sympathy. "I can't go home…. That would be worse."

Mollie Biscuits had nodded. "Then you'll make the best of it here. We'll help you, won't we, girls? There are tricks of the trade, so to speak. And Mother

Howard's sister isn't as hard a soul as the auld bitch. If she takes over we've got half a chance to make things better in this place."

Emma had sat up then, looking around her. The attic dormitory was cold and dirty, the narrow beds lined up against the two walls. The food she'd had so far was foul, there was no way to wash and the privy was disgusting. Worse, she thought she could feel bugs crawling on her skin.

"No choice, my girl," another woman, a young redhead with an Irish accent had said. "May as well make the best of it."

And something had hardened inside Emma right then, a core of steel she'd never known she'd had. They were right—there was no choice. Her father had always told her she was born to tempt men; her grandfather had told her she would be a whore when she grew up. It was her fault, she'd been born that way and there was no escape.

But she could make things better. She didn't have to live in hunger and filth. "Yes." Her cool, elegant voice had hit a note of determination. "We can make the best of it."

Mollie Biscuits had chuckled comfortably. "Well, listen to 'er ladyship talk! You're a right proper one, aren't you? Must be some toff's bastard to end up like this, but we don't worry about where any of us come from. From now on, we're your family. I'm Mollie Biscuits, this is Agnes and Long Jane, Jenny and Agnes and Thin Polly. I'll introduce you to the others when they wake up. We look after each other, we do. Warn each other of the bad ones. Some of the girls like some tricks better than others, and if we're careful we can trade off. Mother Hubbard doesn't mind, as long as the gentlemen are satisfied, and her sister will be easier to get around. And once you're used to it, it's not hard work." She let out a wheezing laugh. "At least you're not on your feet all day."

Mollie Biscuits hadn't looked like she was born to tempt men. She was plump and plain and cheery. The other women didn't look like evil sirens either, just tired young women, most of them pretty enough. Clearly they weren't the cause of their downfall, only the victims.

But Emma had known she was different. She knew in her heart she was evil, and she belonged in this life.

But she could make it better. For herself, and for the others. And she had.

Mollie Biscuits had been right—Mother Hubbard had died soon after Easter, and her sister had taken over. It had been easy enough to start helping out. For one thing, it got her out of having to provide for as many of the gentlemen who showed up at the White Pearl. For another, as Emma had slowly gotten Mrs. Timmins, who'd never been married, to clean up the place and serve better meals, she'd been able to charge more for her stable of girls. Emma had convinced her to put the extra money into sprucing up the building, bringing in a better class of customer and correspondingly higher fees, and it had gone from there. By the time Mrs. Timmins had died Emma was nineteen years old and more than ready to take over the reins of the business. She'd dismissed all the bully boys but one, and she'd kept him on to keep the girls safe from unruly customers. She'd instituted baths and good food and most of the money going toward the girls.

She'd sold their bodies, even though they were willing and grateful for her care, and she had to pay penance, for that and for the sins her body had forced from her family. She had no doubt it was that sinfulness that had caused her mother to kill herself. She'd known what a demon she'd given birth to.

And so she'd taken to going to St. Martin's Hospital every few days, to help out, and Mollie Biscuits would go with her. No other women ever went to the public hospital—only whores were considered suitable for such work. She'd done what she could for the sick and the dying, the soldiers home from the Afghan wars with arms and legs missing, with eyes clouded with madness from the horror they'd lived through. Most of them died, and she found she couldn't be sorry. It was the only relief they could look forward to.

She'd done what she could to help keep the rooms clean; she helped change dressings, ignoring the foul stench of putrefaction. She'd helped when the doctors had taken off limbs, sitting on the chest of a screaming patient while others held him down. She'd cradled the dying in her arms, singing old Welsh lullabies in their ears as she'd rocked them. She'd washed the dead and she'd fed the living.

And she'd met Brandon Rohan one stormy winter day, and life hadn't been the same.

5

Brandon Rohan leaned heavily on his cane as he moved down the narrow corridors of the caves riddling the countryside at Kerlsey Manor in Kent. He was dressed in a monk's robe, though he found that particular conceit quite ridiculous. Everyone would know him by his limp, even if his head and face were covered with a cowl. But the Grand Master had decreed that they would no longer show their faces when they met, and he had no choice but to obey, and part of him approved. The meetings of the Heavenly Host were for darkness and privacy. He had no wish to face his fellow celebrants later at his mother's house, and, given the people who had belonged to the Host's notorious roster, it was always a distinct possibility.

No, discretion was wise. Nowadays he didn't even know who led the Host, nor did anyone else he bothered to ask. It didn't matter. The Grand Master was one of them, and that was what counted. He made the rules, set the dates and locations of the gatherings, and with his guidance their membership had swelled.

They'd been meeting in Kent ever since Brandon had first been able to get around by himself. Kersley Hall had been largely destroyed by a fire, and then abandoned by its indigent owner. Enough remained of the structure that they could meet, and the series of chalk caves beneath it proved most utile. There were an infinite number of rooms leading off those twisting caves, and one could do anything one pleased within those walls.

And the screams never carried to the surface.

He knew a moment's doubt, but he quickly pushed it away. He wasn't particularly interested in the unwilling partners some favored, the ones who were well paid for the honor. He preferred women who didn't fight him. Witnessing it had been horrifying enough.

But he wasn't going to think about that. If the others preferred their whores to simulate resistance, then who was he to judge? They were well paid, and if, by any chance, some of that resistance was real, it was hardly his concern. "Do what thou wilt" was their motto, and none of the members passed judgment upon each other.

He wondered what Benedick would think of it. Their own father had been involved in the Heavenly Host when he was young, and his father before him. Benedick would probably disapprove, but Brandon was only following in the family footsteps. If his dour older brother disliked it, he could go back to Somerset.

He could hear the low rumble of voices from a distance. They had already started, with their silly attempts to raise the devil. Brandon didn't believe in the devil, believe in hell. He'd already looked into the face of it in the Afghan.

He needed to get off his bad leg. He needed someone to distract him from the pain. He needed opium to dull the worst of it. He would find those things at the end of the corridor.

He heard a woman scream, and for a moment he froze, as the sound was quickly cut off. They were well paid for it, he reminded himself coldly.

And he limped onward, toward the dimly lit cavern.

Benedick would have happily forgotten all about the annoying Lady Carstairs had he not run smack into her in St. James Park, shepherding her little flock of soiled doves. He might not have even noticed their presence had it not been for the sudden outraged expression on his future fiancée, the very proper Miss Pennington, and he turned to follow her gaze.

"It's that woman," his intended said in a tight voice. "How dare she parade those…those creatures here among the gentry? Has she no sense of decorum, no sense of what is right and proper? Someone needs to take her in hand and explain a few things."

He looked over at the group lazily. Lady Carstairs was dressed in the same boring clothes she wore before, of cloth and execrable fashion, with that bonnet covering her hair and face. The women following her looked for all the world like overgrown schoolgirls rather than the poor unfortunate, and he gazed at them idly, wondering how many of them he'd bedded before Charity Carstairs had lured them into unfortunate rectitude.

La Violette wasn't present, and he wondered whether she was being punished. Locked in a dungeon on bread and water, perhaps. It was no wonder she'd jumped at his offer.

"They're simply enjoying a public park on a fine day," he said mildly enough.

"If they're so desirous of the salubrious effect of fresh air, they should take themselves to Hyde Park, rather than these more cultured confines." Miss Pennington's eyes narrowed. She had rather small eyes, he noticed for the first time. Hard and unforgiving. "I wish you might go and give the woman a hint."

"That would hardly be appropriate, Miss Pennington. I believe Lady Carstairs's home is nearby—it only makes sense that she bring the women here."

"Sir Thomas must be rolling over in his grave. She's turned that house into nothing more than a…a brothel."

"Hardly. I believe the point of the matter is that the women have foresworn their previous…activities."

"And you see, that's what kind of trouble she brings among us," Miss Pennington said, much incensed. "I shouldn't be discussing this with a gentleman. I shouldn't even know such women exist, and yet what choice have I, when she constantly thrusts them in our faces."

He thought for a moment that he might like one of Lady Carstairs's soiled doves to be thrust into his face. He looked down at Miss Pennington, mentally crossing her off his list of potential brides. Not only did he not want to wake up in the morning and meet those small, disapproving eyes, but he didn't want his future children subjected to them. And suddenly he wanted to get away.

"If you wish, I could go speak with Lady Carstairs," he said. "But I would be loath to leave you here without an escort."

Miss Pennington's trill of laughter was clearly supposed to remind him what a good sport she was. "Don't be silly, Lord Rohan. I have my maid and a footman with me. I often have been bold enough to walk on my own with only their company. After all, I'm no longer a green girl. Go on and tell Lady Carstairs that she's not wanted here. I'll make my way back home on my own."

No longer a green girl, he thought, but a bitter old woman, and only twenty-three to boot. He gave her an angelic smile, brought her gloved hand to his mouth and then realized his unruly passion would offend her. "As you wish, Miss Pennington," he said, bowing as she walked away, and he mentally consigned her to the devil.

He turned, and looked at Lady Carstairs. She was a bit above average height, and he liked that in a woman. It made her a worthy opponent. She was quite deliciously rounded, and for a brief moment he wished his first supposition had been right. He would have enjoyed venting some of his suppressed sexual energy on that soft, sweet body, having those long legs wrapped around his hips as he moved deep within her.

He cursed softly at the sweet picture he'd conjured up and his predictable physical reaction. As an antidote he thought of Miss Pennington's mean little eyes, and with relief he felt his arousal subsiding.

He considered strolling back home. He had no intention of warning "Charity" Carstairs off— Miss Pennington's demands notwithstanding. If a gaggle of soiled doves were going to parade around St. James Park he was going to enjoy it.

But at that moment he also had the perfect opportunity to confront Lady Carstairs, and with a grim smile on his face he started toward her.

Melisande was doing an admirable job keeping her girls from flirting with all and sundry as they walked down the length of the ornamental canal. She was a firm believer in the efficacy of fresh air and exercise, though Miss Mackenzie, her former governess and now head of the teaching staff at Carstairs House was usually the one responsible for their exercise. But apparently the girls had been causing too much of a stir, and Melisande knew that there were a great deal too many men with too much time on their hands lounging around Green Park, and she'd decided St. James might be the wiser direction.

She'd been wrong. The young women were somehow managing to make their sober clothes seem like the frivolous wardrobes of the demimondaines they had once been, further convincing Melisande of the truth that seductiveness was a matter of attitude, not dress or even natural beauty. Fortunately she was as devoid of seductiveness as she was of everything else, so she'd never had the chance to test her theory.

But the girls were sashaying along, swinging their hips, and while they loved Melisande, obeying her was the least of their worries. And to top it off, Viscount Rohan had chosen today of all days to take a stroll in the park.

Emma had spent the last few days passing on much too much gossip about the man, and all Melisande's protests couldn't seem to silence her. She'd learned about his two dead wives, the fiancée who'd shot herself, and his current quest for a conformable wife, with the Honorable Dorothea Pennington in the lead for the position. She'd learned about his decadent family, a dynasty of rakes and libertines, his estate in Somerset and a bit too much about his purported prowess in bed. Not that Emma had ever sampled him, she assured Melisande. But the girls under her care had talked, and it was seldom that the gentlemen came in for praise. Benedick Rohan was held in awe.

Which was none of her business. She didn't want to listen to Emma's disclosures, she didn't want to think about the man and his dark eyes looking at her with such cool contempt. Indeed, for the last two days Emma seemed to have forgotten all about him, and Melisande had been happy to dismiss him, as well. It was with deep regret that she recognized the tall, lean figure bent assiduously over Dorothea Pennington's skinny body.

She had hoped he'd be so busy with his flirtation that he wouldn't notice her presence. The girls had seen him immediately, with those instincts that could find a wealthy, attractive man in a crowd in under a minute, but Melisande had simply hurried them on, her face averted, praying he would leave the park before they were back from their forced march along the canal.

"Lady Carstairs," one of the girls said in a cross between a whine and a wheeze. "Could you go a little slower, if you please? I'm fair winded."

"Nonsense," she said, and quickened her pace. "We're here for exercise and fresh air, not for social purposes."

"Couldn't we do both?" asked Raffaela, and Melisande knew a moment's guilt. Raffaela was the daughter of an Italian sailor and an Irish doxy, and she walked with a limp, thanks to the badly broken leg that had never set right, due to a backhanded slap from her pimp that had sent her tumbling in front of Melisande's carriage. However, she had seen Raffaela race up the long flights of stairs at Carstairs House without a moment's hesitation when there was something she wanted, and she only slowed her pace marginally.

"We have no need of male companionship." Melisande's announcement held a practiced cheerful tone.

"Speak for yourself," one girl muttered from the back of the line, but Melisande ignored her.

"We'll have tea and cakes when we get back," she said, hoping to bribe them into behaving.

"Now there's a bit of crumpet I wouldn't mind 'aving," another girl said, looking past her, and Melisande knew a sudden, lowering presentiment. Please let him have taken off with the saintly Dorothea, she thought desperately. Don't let him be waiting here.

But she knew exactly who had come up behind her, his shadow on the pavement looming over hers. With a quick intake of breath she turned, plastering her most disarming smile on her face.

"Lord Rohan," she said cheerfully.

"Lady Carstairs." Yes, his voice was as deep as she remembered it. Really, if all men had voices like Rohan did then her job would be a great deal more difficult, she reflected. She could practically hear the sighs from her bevy of charges, but she stiffened her spine. After all, these women had already shown themselves to be susceptible to male lures, and he had what some women would doubtless consider a seductive voice to go along with his austere, handsome face and tall, elegant body.

It was a good thing she was immune, and always

had been. The women behind her were no better than moonstruck girls—she could practically hear their gusty sighs. The sooner she got them safely back to the confines of Carstairs House the better. They had been doing an admirable job of adjusting to their new lives, but Viscount Rohan could tempt a saint.

However, he was the one who'd approached her, and she wasn't going to give him the satisfaction of prolonging the conversation. He knew who she was, which was interesting. He must have asked about her.

She wasn't quite sure how she felt about that, but she knew better than to be flattered. He'd assuredly wanted to know who that annoying woman was, who'd spoiled his afternoon debauch.

Finally he spoke, and his voice sent silver shivers down her spine. "I believe I owe you an abject apology, Lady Carstairs. I was under a misapprehension about your identity and treated you…impolitely. I crave pardon."

"You treated me abominably. However, since I've never been mistaken for an abbess before, the novelty of it almost made up for the insult. I presume the gossiping tongues have filled you in on my mission."

His smile was faintly mocking. "Your mission? Indeed. You wish to deprive the men of London of their most cherished pastime."

This time she did hear an actual sigh from one of the girls. She ignored it. "I thought you all preferred horses and gaming to sexual congress?" Most men were shocked by her plain speech, but his cool, handsome face was still composed of polite lines.

"It depends on the girl."

"And the horse," she shot back.

An expression flickered in his eyes for a moment, one of surprise and something else. Respect? Amusement? She was looking for things that were not there. "And the horse," he agreed. "As for mistaking you for an abbess, I do believe I mentioned that you were an extremely unlikely one." His dark eyes slid down her deliberately dowdy dress.

Ungallant bastard, she thought calmly, wishing she dared say it out loud. But there was a limit as to how far she would go, and she had no wish to tweak the tiger's tail. She had the suspicion that Benedick Rohan would be most unsettling if roused. "Indeed," she said briefly. "Was there anything else? Because if not, I accept your apology and bid you good-day."

"So quickly, Lady Carstairs? I thought I might take the air with you. At least see you safely out of the park."

"Aha!"

"'Aha'?"

"I can see Miss Pennington has been busy. You're her errand boy, are you not? She sent you to warn us out of the sacred confines of St. James Park so we won't sully her so very proper eyes with our presence."

Really, the woman was the most tiresome prude. If a noted rake like Viscount Rohan thought he'd be happy married to such a dried-up stick, then he deserved the wretched woman.

"I don't believe it's you she objects to. And I'm

hardly her errand boy. I find the presence of your…
charges to be quite delightfully distracting." He
glanced back at them, and was rewarded with smoth-
ered giggles. "They're like a gaggle of lovely geese."

"They're equally silly!" Melisande said in disgust.
"Wave a handsome man in front of them and they
turn into blithering idiots."

"*Merci du compliment,* Lady Carstairs," he said,
and she could have kicked herself. "Perhaps they've
regretted their choice in leaving the perfumed confines of Mrs. Cadbury's establishment."

"Shall we ask them?" she said coolly, and before
he could demur she whirled around, focusing on the
dozen or so women in her company. "Ladies?" She
raised her voice. "The Viscount Rohan is interested
in our social experiment. He believes you regret the
choice you made and would prefer your previous
employment, be it in Emma Cadbury's house or elsewhere. What say you? Would you rather be back
where I found you? Raffaella?"

"No, your ladyship," Raffaella said promptly.

The rest of them answered, as well, and she turned
back to Rohan, cool and cheerful. "Of course, they
may be lying because they're so terrified by my brutish nature, but I expect they mean it. The life of a
prostitute isn't a kind one, my lord. It's a world of disease and despair, being forced to lie supine beneath
men they don't know and allow them their brutish
lusts. They age quickly and end up on the streets,
and most of them are dead by forty, of disease or accident or murder."

There was a glint in his eye. "In fact, Lady Carstairs, in most brothels the women are rarely on the bottom."

She eyed him steadily. "No, I imagine not. My assistant and friend has been very thorough in detailing the lives of these poor women, and I doubt being astride has much to recommend it."

"I gathered you've been married. Don't you know?"

"I hardly think that's your business."

"I'm merely curious that a widow who enjoyed the marriage bed is unaware of all the infinite varieties of making love. Or didn't Sir Thomas manage to perform his husbandly duty? I collect the match was uneven—your youth for his fortune. In fact, that would put you on the same par with some of your charming gaggle. Sexual congress in return for financial remuneration."

He was trying to goad her, and managing to succeed, when she considered herself relatively even tempered. She repressed a well-deserved growl. "Are you asking me if all women are whores due to the strictures of society? I won't disagree with you. And while it is none of your business, Sir Thomas certainly fulfilled his marital obligations, but only in the most proper and respectful fashion. Which would hardly include…variations." Why in the world was she discussing such intimacies with him, she wondered.

"Pity."

He was trying to annoy her. Or at least provoke

an unmannerly reaction from her, and succeeding to an alarming degree. "I beg pardon," she said, aiming for sweetness and falling short of the mark. "This is hardly an appropriate topic of conversation. At times my passion for my project can cause me to speak intemperately. Perhaps we should leave. You may assure your betrothed that we will do our best not to sully her eyes with our presence. We will walk in the mornings rather than the afternoons."

Oh, holy hell, she thought at the gleam in his eye. Now he knew she'd been asking about him, as well. She braced herself for his mockery, but he let the opportunity go, deliberately, she suspected. And not permanently.

"Miss Pennington is not my betrothed," he said mildly enough. "And I would prefer you walk in the afternoon. Depending on my...debauches of the night before I may be abed until late morning, and I would hate to miss such a decorative addition to the park."

He was talking about the girls, of course, but he was looking at her, and for the first time in her life Melisande understood why a woman might take off her clothes and lie down for someone. With his deep, caressing voice, intense eyes and handsome face he was a prime example of a rake, the scion of a family of hellions. She was playing with fire. He could talk a nun into an orgy.

She mentally slapped herself. She wasn't a nun, and he wasn't referring to her. "The answer to that, my lord, is to avoid debauchery in the first place. Rising early is good for both the body and the soul."

There was a very definite stir behind her, one of profound disagreement, and she expected Rohan to remark on that. Instead he stayed focused on her, and she felt like a butterfly pinned to a wall with that gaze. No, a moth, she reminded herself, brutally honest.

"Staying in bed can be very good for the body and quite possibly the soul, as well," he said, his voice low and almost irresistible. "You should try it."

"I may remind you I'm a widow, Lord Rohan."

"So you are, my lady. A very wealthy one, I gather. You should beware of men who seek to marry you for that wealth."

"You're in no need of a fortune."

He raised his eyebrows. "Did you think I was referring to myself? I don't believe I've shown any particular partiality toward you, have I? At least, not yet."

At that point she wanted nothing more than a huge hole to appear in the manicured lawns of St. James Park and swallow either her or, even better, the Viscount Rohan.

Did he know about Wilfred? God, she hoped not. That brief time of idiocy had been kept secret, thank heavens. Her one stupid fall from grace had only solidified her determination. But no, there was no reason to think he might know anything about it.

"Though Wilfred Hunnicut is, of course, another matter." And with that bland statement he drove a stake through her fond assumption. "It is a great deal too bad no one warned you about him."

Before she could gather her wits to respond he bowed. "Since you have no need of my accompanying you, I will bid you farewell, Lady Carstairs. I'm certain we shall meet again, and soon."

"Not if you stay away from my girls," she said, completely truthful.

His smile curved his mouth. "But what, dear lady, if I can't stay away from you?"

6

In all, Benedick had been perversely pleased with his day's work. He'd paid back the interfering Lady Carstairs in full. The expression on her face was such unflattering horror that he'd almost laughed out loud, and she'd taken her bevy of reclaimed doves out of the park at something close to a run. Sir Thomas Carstairs must have been even more of an ogre than was generally suspected, to give her such a disgust of men.

He wondered if she forced the girls to sit through endless sermons, poor things. She'd marry again, despite her disdain for his sex. She was too plump and luscious not to, and sooner or later someone, probably another fortune hunter, would overcome her scruples and pay dearly for it. She'd probably make him pray before he bedded her, lights out, nightgown lifted primly to her waist in the darkness.

Though chances were, the Honorable Miss Pennington might not have been much better. At least

Lady Carstairs had compassion for her gaggle, if not for the male half of the world's population.

Clearly he needed to set his sights on someone younger, more amenable than Miss Dorothea Pennington. He ran the risk of being cuckolded, he supposed, though with no false modesty he counted that unlikely. Women had an unfortunate tendency to love him. Unfortunate, as they tended to die.

Even Barbara had loved him in her way. At least someone like Dorothea Pennington wouldn't mourn him overmuch—she was much too practical.

But that glimpse into her ice-cold soul in the park that day had been more than sufficient, and in the following weeks he had cast his eye around the ton, sorting through the eligible maidens and discarding each one, though he found any number that would have done for Brandon. Not that Brandon ever made an appearance at any of the functions created to parade nubile and marriageable flesh in front of jaded male eyes. In truth, his stray comment, meant to enflame, had struck close to the truth. The marriage mart wasn't much better than a brothel, he mused, staring into the fire one rainy afternoon. Lady Carstairs ought to direct her energy there, preserving the virgins from a life of sexual indebtedness. There might be more freedom in being a whore.

He watched the flames, abstracted. So far, each of the contenders for the role of Viscountess Rohan had failed for one issue or another. One was too pretty, another too plain. One was too lively, another too drab. One had a shrill laugh, another had a vitriolic temper, yet another embraced too much religiosity. None of them would do.

He was having an equally difficult time with the more congenial form of feminine companionship. Despite Lady Carstairs's best efforts there were still any number of available females eager for his attention, but so far the few who had managed to engage his interest for even a short amount of time were rare, indeed. Even Brandon might have noticed, had he ever been home. He was hollow-eyed, so thin a wind might blow him away, bad-tempered and mocking. His sweet, enthusiastic little brother was now an even greater cynic than he was, though in truth Brandon had more reason. He had seen death on a staggering scale; his body had been ripped to pieces in a foolish war, though Benedick was of the unpopular opinion that all wars were foolish. It was little wonder that Brandon appeared to be burning the candle at both ends, though God knew where he was doing so. Certainly not anywhere Benedick was aware of.

He'd come to the uneasy conclusion that he was not his brother's keeper, and forced himself to stop worrying. It was no longer in his nature to fuss about his siblings. His brother Charles was so well settled into such a boring life in Cornwall that he had seemed to disappear, and as for his wild and brave sister, Miranda, she had married a man of such unforgivable treachery that his mind still reeled. He kept waiting for her call for help, and he was more than prepared to jump in a carriage and rescue her from the monster she'd married. Instead she kept popping out children and being blissfully happy, which annoyed him no end.

Not that he wanted her to suffer. He just wanted her away from the Scorpion.

Ah, but he wasn't his sister's keeper, either. He needed to concentrate on his own concerns, and he was having a devil of a time fulfilling either of his two objectives. The women were accommodating, the virgins were lovely, and he had no taste for either.

Indeed, perhaps he ought to go back to Somerset, where at least...

He heard the commotion at the front door, and he dropped his feet to the floor. Richmond and the footmen should be more than capable of dealing with any disturbance, particularly after their previous failure in letting Lady Carstairs storm into the house, but he was bored and in the mood for a fight. Perhaps he ought to see what was disturbing a gentleman's peace.

He didn't have to go anywhere. The door to his library was flung open, and the virago stood there, breathing heavily, her bonnet askew, her eyes blazing, and for a moment he wondered if she had had a brawl with his servants. A moment later an un-ruffled Richmond appeared behind her, announced in quite unnecessary accents, "Lady Carstairs," and then closed the door behind her, sealing her in the room with him.

He rose—his mother *had* raised him to be a gentleman—and raised an eyebrow. It had been more than three weeks since he'd seen her in the park, and he had sincerely hoped she was plainer than he remembered. Unfortunately, the opposite was true. Melisande, Lady Carstairs, was a surprisingly pretty creature despite the dowdy clothes and shadowing bonnet. "What a charming surprise!" he murmured, the correct social lie. "To what do I owe this pleasure, Lady Carstairs?"

For a moment she looked nonplussed. Clearly she'd been expecting a battle, and instead found him on his best behavior. How delightful that being polite was even more upsetting to her than his customary rudeness.

But she was a worthy opponent, and her eyes narrowed, surveying him. "I've come to ask for your help," she said abruptly. She was nervous, he noticed, which surprised him. She hadn't struck him as the kind of woman to be afraid of anything or anyone.

"I would be delighted to be of service, Lady Carstairs, but if you think I would be of any assistance in persuading women to forego the pleasures of the flesh then I must tell you that you've chosen the wrong—"

She let out an exasperated sigh. "Aren't you going to invite me to sit? I practically ran from Carstairs House."

He frowned then. "You should have taken a carriage. There are some less than savory areas in between King Street and Bury Street. And I presume your abigail or your footman is waiting outside?"

"I seldom bother with the absurd trappings of convention, Lord Rohan, and I employ neither of them.

Besides, I was in too much of a hurry." She didn't wait for his invitation, stripping off her bonnet and sinking down on the chair by the fire, fixing her fierce blue gaze on him.

He was, for a moment, startled. Lady Carstairs was prettier than he'd realized, with soft wings of tawny hair framing an oval face, a wide, mobile mouth, straight nose and those piercing eyes. Combined with her luscious body, the total of her assets caused him to mentally reevaluate his timeline. She'd be wed by the end of the season. Some wise man simply wouldn't take no for an answer.

He realized he was staring at her, and he quickly pulled himself together. "The trappings of convention are there for a reason. If we are shut up alone together for any length of time people might surmise that I compromised you."

"Stuff and nonsense," she said. "I'm hardly the sort of woman who catches your eye. They're more likely to think I compromised *you,* and I assure you, you're safe from any claims on my part."

"And I assure you, Lady Carstairs, that there are very few women who don't catch my eye, and you underestimate your charms."

She blushed. Charity Carstairs, the Virago of King Street, actually blushed, and for a moment he was enchanted. And then she recovered, fixing him with a stern gaze. "Don't waste your time, Rohan," she said, using the familiar form of his name simply to put him in his place. It didn't work, he thought with amusement. "I'm beyond such flummery. And no,

I'm not an idiot. I don't want you anywhere near my girls—you're far too great a distraction as it is. I have a far greater problem, and you have reason to share in the blame, given your family's history."

"I have no intention of taking responsibility for my father or grandfather. They were two of the finest rakes England has ever known, and I could never hope to equal their feats. They were like gods, I, merely a godling. I only take responsibility for my own debaucheries, which are many." Though not as many as he could have wished, he thought dejectedly.

But she was undeterred. "And you're proud of this?"

He was spared having to respond by the appearance of Richmond carrying a tea tray, lavishly outfitted with cakes and trifles as well as the best china, the set his mother had picked out for him and which seldom saw the light of day. Richmond must approve of Lady Carstairs, for some as yet unfathomable reason. He would hardly approve of her visiting a gentleman's house, and Richmond had very severe standards. There must be something else to make him overlook such a shocking breach of etiquette and signal his approval.

She poured, of course, the ritual almost unconscious, and he was pleased to see she hadn't forgotten that much in her devotion to good works. He took his with lemon only, and he sat back, holding his cup, as she filled hers with enough sugar and milk to destroy the taste completely. So Lady Carstairs had a fondness for sweets? Clearly she hadn't given up all pleasures of the flesh.

She took a cake, nibbled it, then devoured it, her movements quick and nervous. He waited, entirely at his ease. This was the most interesting thing that had happened in weeks. In fact, since he'd run into her in the park. It was a shame Brandon hadn't returned last night. Then again, there was no telling how the new Brandon would act.

The old Brandon would have been amused and polite, and probably defend her once she left. The new Brandon simply wouldn't care.

No, it was just as well he wasn't here.

Lady Carstairs took a second cake, not that he could blame her. He retained a most excellent kitchen staff, though he seldom paid attention to sweets. Apparently Lady Carstairs made up for his abstinence.

She must have realized he was watching her, for she finished the cake, sat back and took a deep breath. "It concerns the Heavenly Host."

7

Benedick looked at her for a long moment, marshalling his thoughts. "I would ask how you even know of the existence of that organization, but I assume you learned of it from your protégés. As far as I know the Heavenly Host has been disbanded for almost ten years. And even if they did still exist they're hardly any of your concern, unless you now wish to rescue bored aristocrats from their sexual indulgences."

She was unfazed. "They've reconvened. Apparently there was some outrageous contretemps ten years ago that caused most of them to lose interest, but in the last three years they've re-formed and are far worse than they ever were before."

Most women of the ton had no knowledge of what went on with the Heavenly Host, not unless they were part of it. A surprisingly large number of outrageous sisters and wives of the original participants had joined in, lessening the need for paid companionship. He himself had attended a gathering of the Host when he was in his early twenties, more out of curiosity than anything else, and found their play-acting tedious.

"Perhaps you'd care to elaborate. How are they *specifically* different from the past?" He was hoping to make her blush again. The last one had stained her smooth cheeks. He wanted to see if it could travel down the neckline of her tasteless dress.

But he'd underestimated her. "According to my resources, the Heavenly Host has always had a history of consensuality. Everyone must be agreeable to whatever depraved acts are committed."

"What sort of depraved acts?" he asked in his sweetest voice.

"The sort of act you were about to perform with Violet Highstreet," she said, unruffled.

"In truth, she was the one who was going to perform it. I was simply the happy recipient...."

She'd done a good job of keeping her color down until that point; he gave her credit, but her cheeks flamed once more. He decided to press his point. "So *fellatio,* which is the technical term for it, is one of the acts performed at gatherings of the Heavenly Host? I regret to inform you, Lady Carstairs, but that same act is performed in almost every bedroom in this city."

"And street corner and alleyway."

"Yes, well we know your opinion of that, and I'm not about to argue with you. So is your mission to stamp out oral pleasuring, or something else? Because I can assure you that convincing people to refrain from it is unlikely…."

"Would you stop!" she cried, her sangfroid finally showing cracks. "I didn't come here to talk about… about…"

"Fellatio," he supplied helpfully.

"*That*. It's the Heavenly Host that needs to be stopped. Their new mandate is total depravity, the kind that knows no limits."

"Such as?"

"Such as binding people so that they have no recourse. They are forced to receive the attentions of someone and are unable to move, and occasionally even to speak, but must simply endure."

He laughed. "You'll find that in any whore's bag of tricks, Lady Carstairs, and even in the best bedrooms, as well. You misunderstand the game. Trust me—it can be quite…stimulating."

"They rape women."

His amusement faded. "Don't be absurd. The women who attend the gatherings are there willingly and always have been. The ones who participate in rough play agree to it and are well compensated."

"Rough play?" she echoed. "Is that what you call it when a woman is whipped until she bleeds, whose face is scarred so badly she won't go out in public? Is that what you call it when young girls are brought in to satisfy the base urges of the foulest men on the face of the earth?"

"*No,*" he snapped. She was no longer such a charming diversion. "The Heavenly Host has always

had an edict against using children, and that wouldn't
have changed. People have always believed horror
stories about them, when in fact they harm no one.
They're just a group of spoiled aristocrats enjoying
being wicked. Their gatherings are not about innocence."

"True enough. They're about innocence despoiled."

He waved her piety away. "As for the woman who
was scarred, I'm certain that was an accident and
deeply regretted. And I expect that the woman was
well compensated for the fact that her future earning
power is greatly diminished. That has always been
the way of the Host, and I can't believe things have
changed that much."

"The girl was raped, whipped and slashed with
a knife. When she escaped she tried to report it to
the police, but they simply handed her back to her
tormenters. She hasn't been seen since."

His eyes narrowed. "And how do you know all
this?"

"Her sister has joined us."

"And you're trying to convince me that someone
has done away with the woman? I don't believe it,"
he said flatly.

"It doesn't matter what you believe. It happens to
be true. Aileen would never have abandoned Betsey
on the streets if she had any choice. And now they're
working toward their most horrifying act of all."

Bloody Christ, he thought irritably. The world
had always had ridiculous theories about the essentially harmless activities of the Heavenly Host, and

it was no wonder someone like Charity Carstairs believed them.

"Pray do not tell me they're planning an orgy." He did his best to sound bored. "That's de rigueur for the Host. I've even participated in them when I was a guest at their gatherings. Quite entertaining the first time or two, but it pales after a while. You never know whose bum you're stroking, a high-priced courtesan or your father's best friend." He shuddered delicately.

"I'm delighted you find this is amusing," she said. "And, indeed, why shouldn't you? No one will ever miss the girls they take, and as long as you're not a part of it then no blame falls on you. But in fact if you do nothing you're just as much to blame as the men who stand around and let them."

"Let them do what, exactly, Lady Carstairs?"

She took a deep breath. "They intend to summon the devil on the night of the full moon."

He laughed, unimpressed. "They've tried that before. His Wickedness always fails to respond to the invitation, no matter how politely phrased."

"This time they're planning to sacrifice a virgin to ensure success."

For a moment there was silence in the room. He noticed that in her nervousness she'd eaten all the cakes, and he would have ordered more if he didn't feel slightly ill. "Absurd! They wouldn't."

"They would. A number of young girls have gone missing over the last few weeks, though it's unlikely any of them were still unmolested."

"I hate to disillusion you, Lady Carstairs, but there are any number of ravenous creatures out there who would have taken those girls. Depravity is not the sole possession of the Heavenly Host. These young women may have even left on their own."

"You may make all the excuses you want, Lord Rohan. One of those girls is destined for horror, and we have no idea where they're keeping her. The full moon is only six days away, and we're running out of time."

"And just how does that involve me?" he inquired coldly. The woman was clearly deranged. There was no way that members of society would descend to such heinous acts. "If you think I'm going to accuse my childhood friends of such depravity then you've miscalculated. It's none of my concern."

"And what if I can convince the police to raid their gathering and arrest those childhood friends?"

"I doubt you'll be able to. But in case they're unwise enough to listen to your ridiculous accusations, then I would say that those childhood friends deserve what's coming to them. I am not, nor have I ever been, my brother's keeper."

"Even if one of the organizers is, in fact, your own brother?"

He'd been about to ring for Richmond to see her out, having tired of all this. But something stayed his hand, and his gaze sharpened. "What are you raving about now, Lady Carstairs?"

But she wasn't raving. She was sounding much too logical and calm, despite the absurdity of her charges. "Your brother, Lord Brandon Rohan, lately Lieutenant of her majesty's arm and newly returned from the Afghan wars, has been instrumental in the rebirth of the Heavenly Host. No one knows exactly who is in charge, who sets the evil path they've embarked upon, but your brother participates, quite willingly. Sooner or later this will all blow up in their faces, at least if I have anything to say about it, and I warn you right now, I'm a very stubborn woman. I don't give up. I would think your brother has suffered enough."

He looked at her blankly, his mind awhirl. As appalling as the idea was, it made sense. Brandon had seldom been home, and his actions had been secretive in the extreme. He was thin and hollow-eyed, and instead of healing, his limp was becoming more pronounced as he burned the candle at both ends. It was possible.

"How did you come by this information?" he snapped suddenly.

"I told you. One of the girls escaped and joined us. She was the one who told us what was going on, and since then we've all been finding out anything we can. They wear masks and hoods, she said, but for obvious reasons your brother stands out. The demi-mask fails to cover the scarred side of his face, and he has a lame leg. She's recognized a few others, but not the leader of the organization, the one who orders everything. And now she's disappeared, leaving her little sister behind, and I very much fear she's dead."

He'd been dismissing everything she'd said earlier

as arrant nonsense, but now he was concentrating, allowing for the possibility that she wasn't a deranged zealot after all. Indeed, she didn't look like one. With her fierce blue eyes and determined chin, her soft, rose-colored lips set in a hard line, she looked angry and sensible, a modern-day Boadicea ready to take on the decadent Romans. She was a Viking, a warrior, everything abhorrent in the weaker sex.

Except that he'd never been fool enough to consider women to be the weaker sex. He'd been surrounded by strong women all his life, his mother and sister included, and he knew when to duck and run.

Now wasn't the time. "All right," he said. "What is it you want me to do?"

8

Melisande blinked. She'd come expecting the battle, expecting abject failure in the end, but she'd come anyway. She'd run out of options. "Next?" she said blankly then cleared her throat. "We need to come up with a plan."

Viscount Rohan was looking at her with half-closed lids that hid the expression in his eyes. Just as well, she thought. He was much too handsome a man, but all those damned Rohans were gorgeous. Even the youngest, Brandon Rohan, had a savage beauty only emphasized by the sad ruin of half his face.

Not that she'd ever been distracted by a handsome face. Her husband had been fifty-three years older than she was, and dying when she'd married him. Her one foolish mistake of a lover had possessed only ordinary attractiveness, nothing like the bone-melting grace of Benedick Rohan's stern profile. If she were still a green girl she could dream about a man like him. But she wasn't. She was a grown woman, with no use for men ever again, and totally impervious to his male beauty.

"I would have thought you'd have a plan already in place," he said, his low voice sending a momentary shiver down her spine.

She was about to reach for a cake, realized she'd eaten them all and had to make do with another cup of tepid tea. "If I had a plan I could have implemented it myself," she said, keeping a caustic note in her voice. "I assumed this was a fool's errand, but I always was one to fight for lost causes."

"Tilting at windmills, Lady Carstairs? And you expect me to be your Sancho Panza. I'm not sure I care for a reenactment of *Don Quixote*. It ends badly."

"*Life* ends badly. And you never struck me as particularly optimistic."

"Never struck you as particularly optimistic?" he echoed. "Do we have an acquaintance that I've forgotten?"

"You would hardly remember every chit making her curtsey each year. I made my debut the year you were married. I remember your wife. She was very beautiful."

"Which one?"

She'd forgotten he'd been widowed twice. And there was some ancient scandal concerning another woman, but no one would tell her the details. Not that she'd asked, of course. At least, not more than a couple of times.

Before she could answer he went on. "Never mind. It hardly matters. So you've come here to dump this incipient disaster in my lap, with no plan, no idea how to forestall it. My brother is my main concern. I could simply have him forcibly removed to one of the remote family estates so he wouldn't be able to participate. That solves my problem even if it doesn't address yours."

"Then you believe me?" She was still astonished by that fact.

"At least partially. It's just the sort of thing my brother would get involved with, and he's been particularly secretive. I expect some of your concerns are simply fiction. I know a great deal about the history of the Heavenly Host—after all it was formed by my great-grandfather's cousin, and kept alive through the offices of my grandfather and father."

"Why am I not surprised?" Melisande muttered.

"But the Heavenly Host are far from the nightmare creatures you're talking about. They started out as a group of bored intellectuals, curious about the relationship between God and the devil, and curious to taste all the forbidden fruit of human desire. But there were rules. No children. No unwilling innocents, though I gather they paid highly for the participation of willing virgins. And no coercion. Their motto is 'do what thou wilt,' and agreement is part of that. Not 'do what is forced upon you.'"

"I appreciate the history lesson. Things have changed."

He was already regretting his agreement to help

her; she could see that. She went on. "If you could see what they did to poor Aileen…"

But she'd underestimated him. "There's no need. I believe you. Since you haven't got a plan I expect we'd best come up with one." As if by magic the stiff but charming majordomo appeared with a fresh pot of tea and another plate of cakes. "If you wouldn't mind pouring me a fresh cup I'll consider what we need."

She was already in the midst of doing so, for herself, as well. "We need to identify the other members of the organization, including the leader."

She half expected him to sneer, but he merely nodded. "Finding other members should be relatively easy. There are certain likely ones, including Lord and Lady Elsmere. We find one…we can follow them to the others."

"What about your brother? Wouldn't he tell you about it?"

"My brother is the least likely person to answer my questions."

"You don't get on? But you're so charming—I would have thought everyone loved you."

"Sarcasm is not a becoming trait, Lady Carstairs."

"I'm not interested in what is becoming or not."

"Clearly," he said dryly. "I expect Winston Elsmere would be our best line of attack. And by the greatest good luck they're holding a party tonight. The guest list is supposed to be small—a mere thirty or so. I declined their invitation, but they should be more than happy to welcome us anyway. Supper is optional, and the dancing starts at ten. I'll pick you up at half past nine."

She stared at him in disbelief. "I'm not going to their party! For one thing, I wasn't invited."

"That hardly matters. If you come as my guest you'll be welcomed. There's an excellent chance that at least two or three members of the Host will be in attendance. Once we identify them we can go from there."

"I don't want to attend a party!" she protested. "I keep out of society."

"You don't have a choice. Not if you want to stop the Host."

"I want more than that," she said, trying to keep her passion in check. "I want to smash their entire wicked organization. I want to expose them to such shame they don't dare meet ever again."

"Then we're agreed," he said, ignoring the fact that she hadn't agreed to anything.

She reached for another cake. "Some women might like masterful males. Personally I find them tedious in the extreme."

But he didn't rise to the bait. "Then you'll simply have to be bored. Do you have anything more—" he waved an elegant hand "—more festive? That gown looks like it belongs to a Quaker."

She didn't blush. "I might have something older. From my season, perhaps."

"Lovely," he said wearily. "I have a choice between a hopeless dowd and someone ten years out of date. I'm not sure my consequence will survive such a blow."

"You'll manage." She reached for another cake. "So first step is to identify the members. What next?"

"Let's see how far we get with step one," he said and passed the plate to her.

She eyed it suspiciously for a moment, then took it with an air of defiance. He raised an eyebrow, though she wasn't sure if it was for her defiance or the fact that she took another cake, but she didn't care. He was the one who ordered extra cakes.

A moment later the majordomo reappeared. "Richmond, have my carriage brought out. Lady Carstairs needs to be returned to her house."

"I can walk," she protested, swallowing the last bit of cake.

"From my house? Alone? I do realize you don't care about your reputation, but I have mine to think of. Either take my carriage or I'll walk you home, but since there's a cold rain I prefer the carriage."

She had little choice. And besides, it did look awful outside, the rain running down the windows in icy sheets. "There's no need for you to accompany me," she said haughtily.

"I had no intention of doing so, though my mother would be appalled. Since I now have to change my previous, far more convivial plans for tonight, I shall have to come up with an alternative." He gave her a slow, assessing look. "I'll simply have to look elsewhere for feminine companionship."

She wanted to arch a brow and say, not with me, just to prove how little she cared, but he'd already given her a major set-down, and she didn't want to give him another chance. "I'm certain you'll manage," she said. "If we accomplish our goal early in the evening, then you can take me home and go on to whatever institution has replaced the White Pearl to slake your…your…"

"My thirst?" he offered in an innocent tone. "I'm afraid their cellar is of indifferent quality. Or were you perhaps talking about some other desire I need taken care of?"

Two could play at that game. She smiled back at him, her gaze limpid. "I'm certain you'll manage to take care of whatever needs you might have. You are, after all, a wealthy man." She rose. "As delightful as this has been, I'd best return home and see if we can find something presentable for me to wear."

He rose as well, punctilious as ever. "I am in a positive terror of anticipation." His eyes slid over her, slowly, assessingly, and she had the odd notion that it felt like a physical touch. She wanted to shake it off. "One more thing, Lady Carstairs," he said, and his voice had lost that taunting edge. "You are not to come here unaccompanied again. In fact, you are not to come here at all. I refuse to be trapped into compromising you—I have far more convivial plans for my future."

"As do I, Lord Rohan," she said in an even voice. "Point well taken. I'll be ready by half past nine."

"If you're punctual you'll be the first woman in my acquaintance to manage it."

"That's simply because women put off having to be with you for as long as possible," she said in her sweetest voice. "Good afternoon, my lord."

"My lady." She left, but, before the butler could close the door behind her, she heard his soft chuckle. Benedick sank back down in his chair, rubbing his chin thoughtfully. He must be very bored, indeed, if he found he was looking forward to an evening in Charity Carstairs's company. He didn't believe the *faradiddle* she was coming up with, not for a moment, but it was clear she thought it was gospel truth. And he hadn't anything better to do tonight. The Elsmeres were bores, but he knew others among his friends would be there, and if his recent visitor wanted to play at being a detective then he had no problem encouraging her. She tried so very hard to be calm and matter-of-fact, and it was so very easy to trip her up. He would take her to the Elsmeres, make the proper inquiries and see how wicked he could be before she cried off. Her concerns about the Heavenly Host and its nefarious activities were just one more fairy tale. The group had disbanded shortly after a horrendous gathering at the edge of the Lake District, where his sodding son of a bitch brother-in-law had dared to bring his sister. The repercussions had been so scandalous that no one had even dared to suggest resurrecting the group of tiresome little sybarites.

At least, he was relatively sure he would have

heard if they did. Except that he hadn't been in town for years, not since Barbara had taken to bedding every one of his acquaintance, and not, of course, for the following year of mourning. And if they had re-formed, wouldn't Brandon be more than likely to have been one of them?

No, he refused to consider the possibility. But in the meantime, Charity Carstairs, with her sweetly curved body, her soft mouth, her stern blue eyes would provide quite a delightful diversion.

He heard Richmond clear his throat, and he glanced up at him. "Did you put the box of cakes in the carriage?"

"I did, my lord. Shall I ask Cook to bake more?"

He considered it for a moment. He'd never had much of a sweet tooth. Except when it came to a certain crusading female. "It might be wise to keep a supply on hand, Richmond. We'll be seeing more of Lady Carstairs, I suspect."

"Very good, my lord," Richmond murmured.

And oddly enough, Benedick was quite sure he meant it.

Rohan's coach was the epitome of elegance, and Melisande sat back against the leather squabs with a sigh. She could more than afford such an equipage, but luxury always seemed a bit obscene when contrasted with the life the gaggle had led. Still, that didn't mean she couldn't enjoy it when it was forced upon her.

He really was the most annoying man.

She'd tried to come up with any other alternative—going to one of the Wicked Rohans was the last thing she'd wanted to do. In fact, she'd set out this afternoon without the proper companions because she was afraid she'd lose her nerve. She hadn't really expected him to agree, but she could think of nothing else and she simply couldn't give up.

The ride to King Street was short, and she didn't notice the box on the seat opposite her until they'd almost arrived. She reached out for it, looking at the card on the top. Written in a heavy scrawl, it was addressed to her. No note, no signature, but she knew it was from Rohan. She untied the string and opened it, and an unbidden laugh came from the back of her throat.

It was a box of the tiny cakes she'd eaten as she'd drank his tea. Curse his black soul, he'd noticed her inability to resist them, and if she had any sense, she'd leave them in the carriage as a message.

That was the last thing she was going to do. There were gestures and there were gestures, and Mollie Biscuits, while an excellent cook, had yet to achieve the perfection of these little masterpieces. She was going to take the box inside and she was going to eat every single one and be damned to the consequences.

Emma was waiting for her, a troubled expression on her face. "Melisande, where were you?"

Melisande handed her the box, pulled off her bonnet and gloves and tossed them on the table. The girls who were learning to be housemaids were newcomers and not adept at showing up promptly when someone arrived, though Betsey, the youngest, was the most eager to please. The last batch had already secured positions and were well on their way to new lives, and sooner or later the new batch would prove ready, but right then Melisande had more important things to worry about. "At Rohan's," she said. "He'll help."

Emma said nothing for a moment, and Melisande paused to look at her more carefully, a sudden, dreadful suspicion coming to her. "You didn't want me to go... Was there a reason?"

"I just think the Rohans are not the best choice to help disband the Heavenly Host," Emma said carefully. "Particularly since rumor has it that they helped found it."

"And I think that makes Viscount Rohan a particularly good choice. He knows the workings of the organization, knows most of the members, even if he himself is not a current participant." She brushed an errant crumb off her dull gray skirt.

"And how do you know that?"

"Because he told me so. Shouldn't I have believed him?"

"I've seldom known you to trust a man's word," Emma said carefully.

Melisande looked at her. Emma was a lovely woman, though a far cry from the painted and perfumed abbess that Melisande had first met two years ago outside her London establishment. Her speech and her manners were not mere affectation, though she seldom spoke of her past, and Melisande was wise enough not to ask. Emma would tell her if she needed to. In the end it hardly mattered.

"I know as well as you how trustworthy men are," she replied. "But in this case I believe him. He was genuinely shocked when I told him what they intended." She thought about it for a moment. "Well, perhaps not shocked. Perhaps grimly surprised might be a better description. And he wasn't going to do anything about it, even so, until I told him his younger brother was part of their foul organization."

"He believed you?"

"He has doubts. But he's willing to help. Which means I have an engagement this evening."

Emma's eyebrows rose. "With Viscount Rohan?"

"Among others. He's taking me to a party held by Lord and Lady Elsmere. He says if anyone is involved in the organization, they are, and it's as good a starting place as any. Maybe they'll let something drop about their plans for the solstice. Maybe we'll discover other members of their foul group. At least it's a start."

"I see." Emma took a step back, surveying her. "So you're going into society on Rohan's arm tonight. What will you wear?"

"I hadn't thought about it," she lied, pushing her loose hair away from her face. "I must have something left from my season."

"Jesus God," Emma muttered. "We've got our work cut out for us." And suddenly she raised her voice. "Girls! We have a project!"

The gaggle appeared, as if they'd been eavesdropping just out of sight, which Melisande suspected they had been. That was another thing she could blame on Benedick Rohan. The term "gaggle" had been so accurate for her recalcitrant, squabbling brood that no matter how she tried she couldn't think of them in any other terms. Not that a gaggle should live in a dovecote—she knew perfectly well her house had received that sobriquet, just as she was called Charity Carstairs behind her back. She had no idea where geese tended to reside, but she hoped Rohan didn't share his fitting term for her soiled doves. She had trouble enough being taken seriously.

The next few hours passed in a whirlwind of activity. She found herself drawn into the small salon where the girls practiced deportment, surrounded by a bevy of chattering females. Trunks appeared from storage, gowns tossed here and there.

"No, that yellow is atrocious." Emma dismissed one outmoded ball gown that Violet held up. "It would make her too sallow. She needs something of a soft rose."

"Rose wasn't in fashion the year I made my debut," Melisande protested, but she was ignored as Emma took charge.

"Betsey, order a bath for Lady Carstairs. She'll need a good soak, an application of Cowper's Milk to try to make her skin more fashionably pale. You should have known better than to have gone out in the bright sunlight without a parasol. Even the best bonnet cannot shield one entirely from the sun."

"I'm sorry," Melisande said meekly.

"Never mind. We'll work with what we have."

"I'm good at arranging hair," Agnes, a bright red-head by way of Ireland and the streets of White-chapel, offered. "She'll need something better than that awful lace cap she wears."

"I'm a widow!" Melisande protested.

"She will, indeed," Emma overrode her. "You're on, Agnes. Jane, I know you're good at using paint. Not the usual stuff you used to shovel on your own face, but something more subtle. Just enough to brighten her eyes and give her a becoming blush."

"I don't blush!" Which was immediately proven a lie, as eager hands began pulling off her unfash-ionable gown, and nothing she did could keep them from stripping her down to her undergarments.

"Lady Carstairs, you have a figure!" Sukey, former mistress to a Catholic bishop, breathed. "One would never know with those clothes you wear. Quite a nice bosom."

Melisande slammed her arms over her chest, only to have a swathe of silk tossed over her head. She had no choice but to put her arms through the sleeves, looking down at the pale green gown she'd never worn, her aunt insisting it was too risqué.

"The neckline's too high," Emma said judiciously. "And we'll need to lace her in tighter. Take off the train—they're dreadfully out of style right now, and perhaps some lace tucked in the bodice."

"I've got some lace," Thin Polly called out.

"That chemise has got to go," Violet announced. "Who's got something skimpier?"

The room was filled with laughter. Hetty spoke up. "Who doesn't? We'll see who's the closest fit. And don't you worry none, your ladyship. They've all been properly washed—you made us wash everything, including ourselves, when we got here. Besides, the chemises were simply for show. They came off in a matter of moments."

"I can't wear something like that!" Melisande protested, scandalized.

"You can and you will. It will give you courage, and make you feel deliciously naughty." Emma pulled at the dress. "Good God, did you have everything made three sizes too large for you?"

"My aunt was convinced that if I kept eating sweets I was going to be enormous and she wanted to ensure that the clothes would continue to fit me," Melisande admitted with some shame.

Emma eyed her sternly. "Nonsense! Have you continued to eat sweets?"

"I'm afraid so."

"And you've got a lovely little figure. Just the right side of plump, and men adore curves."

"You could have made right good money, Lady Carstairs," Violet announced ingenuously. "The skinny girls were always the last to be chosen."

Melisande choked.

"Time for her bath," Emma announced, pulling the gown back over her head and waving her away. "Violet, I'm putting you and Agnes in charge. You know what to do."

"Right you are, Mrs. Cadbury! Me and Agnes will get her trussed up good enough for a royal duke."

"I'm not going to be doing what…what you would have been doing," Melisande said faintly.

"And get her a glass of claret," Emma said, dismissing her. "We've got work to do!"

9

Melisande glanced at herself in the mirror, doing her best to keep the blush from rising over the vast expanse of exposed chest. She'd hoped the call for lace had been to preserve her modesty in the already low-cut gown, but in fact the girls training to be dressmakers had adjusted the neckline down even farther, to a truly scandalous level, and the scrap of lace was a sop to fashion, not modesty.

Oh, God. Viscount Rohan due in half an hour, and she was already exhausted.

She'd been poked and prodded, her skin pinched and bleached and smoothed, her hip-length hair twisted into a painful series of arrangements until fifteen women agreed upon the right one. She'd been practically wrestled into a chemise of such fine weave that it was completely transparent, a tiny corset that was nevertheless lethal in its efficiency, and layers upon layers of petticoats, many of which were definitely not hers. Most of them were far more expensive than the plain but sensible stuff she tended to have made, and she knew the girls had kept their clothing as one of the few valuables they owned.

The gold embroidered dancing slippers had belonged to Thin Polly, the clocked stockings were in Hetty's hope chest and the silver shawl was Emma's own. Even the lace-trimmed drawers were from a long-ago delivery of fancy underthings that she'd had tossed in a closet and forgotten. She'd ordered them when she'd embarked on her ill-fated affaire, and been too thrifty to toss them when she'd discovered Wilfred was a snake.

"No one is going to see my drawers!" she'd hissed, scandalized, when Emma had insisted she wear them. "Certainly not Lord Rohan."

"You never know," Violet said judiciously. "He could talk you right out of them."

"Not likely!" Long Jane said with a crack of laughter. "Her ladyship's got more sense than that. She's not going to spread her legs for someone like him, no matter how pretty he is."

"And he is pretty," Violet said with a gusty sigh.

The rest of the women were vociferous in their agreement, and Melisande turned scandalized eyes on them. "Good God, did he sleep with you all?"

Sukey grinned. "And after the first time he could have had us for free, your ladyship."

"Girl, girls, girls—I don't think we need to discuss that," Emma said sternly. "You look gorgeous, my dear. I only wish we had the proper jewelry for you."

"We do," said Hetty quietly, coming in from the hallway with a velvet bag in her hand. "This was me retirement money, but I don't mind lending 'em to you, your ladyship. The Earl of Selfridge gave 'em to me. Said they were family heirlooms, since his pockets were to let and he knew he had to come up with something."

Emma had taken the bag and opened it, letting out an uncharacteristic whistle. "Perfect, Hetty. You'll get them back, I promise."

The emeralds were exquisite. They brought out the green of the totally revamped dress. They even gave a green tint to her dark blue eyes. The matching earbobs swung just below the artful tousle of curls that Agnes had arranged, and the touch of carbon on her eyelashes, the dusting of rice powder on her skin, made her reflection seem to glow.

"I can't do this!" she said in sudden panic, turning from the mirror.

A chorus of protests greeted that pronouncement. "You can." Emma was firm. "It's for the greater good."

And for a moment Melisande was ashamed of herself. These women had had to sell their bodies, lie beneath strangers simply to survive. She could certainly manage the night in an effort to help them.

"Go along now, girls!" Emma shooed them away. "I'll keep Lady Carstairs company until the viscount arrives."

The girls vanished, leaving them alone. The clock

stuck half past the hour, and Melisande felt her stomach knot.

"I will give you a little hint," Emma said with a wry smile. "A whore's trick, but a good one. It's a part that you're playing, like a grand actress on the stage. It isn't you. It has nothing to do with you. You're simply using your body in service to something necessary. You can smile and flirt and dance and pretend you're someone entirely different, and it won't matter. You, the real you, will still be safe inside."

"You make me ashamed of myself."

"Nonsense. Nothing to be ashamed of. We've all got different roles to play in this world. Was there ever someone you wished you were? Someone in society who seemed impossibly beautiful, impossibly graceful, who had everything and was everything you thought you wanted to be?"

"Yes." Her voice was hollow.

"Then pretend to be her. Do what she would do, laugh as she would laugh. Be as happy as she would be."

"She's dead," Melisande said.

Emma shook her head. "Try not to be so gloomy. Be as she was, then. When you feel uncertain, tell yourself you are...what was her name?"

"Annis."

Emma only hesitated a moment, as if the name sounded familiar but she couldn't quite place it. "Then tell yourself you are Annis, out for an evening of gaiety, and you have no intention of letting anyone make you sad. Will that do?"

Melisande tried to smile.

"Wider, my dear. Have it reach your eyes."

She tried it again.

"Very good. And I do believe I hear Viscount Rohan below. You're more than a match for him. Don't let him intimidate you."

"Hardly," she said with a shaky laugh, pulling the light shawl around her bare shoulders.

But she wasn't a match for him, not in any way. Any more than she could ever think of herself as Annis, the gay and beautiful woman who'd married Benedick Rohan ten long years ago and then died in childbirth.

But she could use him. For the greater good, she reminded herself. And sailed toward the stairs, her head held high.

He'd been regretting his impulsive decision for the past five hours, and by the time Benedick Rohan arrived at Carstairs House, he was in a thoroughly bad mood. He'd been a fool to believe her wild tales of the Heavenly Host and their evil doings. For as long as that group of profligates had existed the stories had been far wilder than the actual doings. There'd been talk of blood rituals, satanic rites, rape and murder from the very beginning, and he knew how absurd those rumors were. His grandfather had been a notorious hellion, and even now he still heard stories of his father's years as a dedicated rake, but neither of them would have ever been involved with something as unsavory as Lady Carstairs was suggesting.

Melisande, Lady Carstairs. He probably wouldn't have listened to her if he didn't find her quite such a taking creature. If only she were one of the poor unfortunates she wished to help and not their savior, he could enjoy himself quite happily. He'd been determined not to take a mistress for the season, his craving for variety overriding the convenience of having a prearranged partner. But if Melisande had been a highflyer he might have considered changing his mind. He was entranced by the promise of her hidden curves in those abominably ugly clothes. He wanted to see what she looked like when he kissed her.

When he took her to bed. When he was inside her.

He shrugged, taking the steps to Carstairs House two at a time. The heavy rain had slowed to a drizzle, but it wasn't the weather that was making him hurry. If he didn't he might end up crying off entirely, and he had never been a coward.

In the best of houses a servant was always watching the door, opening it before one even had to knock. This wasn't the best of houses. He rapped on the heavy door with his walking stick, hoping against hope that she'd developed a sudden dire illness, one that would require her to absent herself to the country for the next few months, so he could continue his determined debauch in happy peace, safe from crusading viragos and the unexpected temptation they offered.

The woman—no, girl—who opened the door looked about twelve, far too young to be one of Lady Carstairs's reformed doves. At least, he hoped so. She looked him over for a moment, with a far too assessing look in her eyes, then remembered the lessons she'd been taught, ushering him inside and offering to take his hat and cloak.

"Her ladyship will be down in a minute," she said, still looking at him as if he might be the devil incarnate. She really was too young to have been selling herself, he thought absently, and gave her a reassuring smile. He wasn't an ogre and he had no interest in terrifying children. Lady Carstairs was a different matter.

"Lord Rohan." Her voice came from the stairs and he looked up to see a complete stranger coming toward him, graceful, elegant. He stared at the woman for a moment, trying to recognize her. And then he realized that she wasn't a well-known mistress or Cyprian; she was Melisande Carstairs, her tawny hair arranged in an artful tousle of curls, her skin dusted with powder, her eyelashes darkened with charcoal. He knew all the tricks, having watched his mistresses over the years, and for a moment he was angry. The dress was far from the dowdy, outmoded creation he'd been expecting. It was de rigueur, the lines of the skirt the very latest in fashion, the bodice exposing her neck and shoulders and the tops of her luscious breasts. She wore a lovely emerald necklace and earbobs, and she looked so exquisite he wanted to take her hand, drag her into the nearest room and pull that distracting bodice down to her waist. He wanted his mouth on her, everywhere, and he glowered at her. She was already enough of a distraction—he didn't need this new, glossy version of the slightly frumpy Lady Carstairs to drive him mad.

"Lord Rohan?" she said again, a note of inquiry in her voice.

"I see you've been taking lessons from your whores," he said, a harsh note in his voice, and then he was ashamed of himself. He was being ridiculous.

She smiled at him, her gorgeous mouth curving in a wicked grin. "Indeed, I have. I think they've done an excellent job, don't you? Unless you think it's too much? I have to admit I'm no judge of such things, but Mrs. Cadbury assures me that I simply look like a fashionable lady, not a demirep. But if you think I should change…"

"Mrs. Cadbury? Is she staying here, as well?"

"Of course. Though why it should be any concern of yours escapes me."

"The most notorious madam in all of London is now your acquaintance?"

"No, my lord Rohan. She's my dear friend."

For a moment he thought she was being sarcastic, and then he realized she was simply being truthful. "Charity" Carstairs, destroying her reputation one fallen woman at a time.

He decided dropping the subject was the better part of valor. Besides, what could he say? It was none of his business—he had no interest in Melisande

Carstairs except to determine the truth of her allegations and how involved his brother might be.

That, and enjoying the random indecent fantasies about her ripe body, which was even more delightfully distracting in the pale green dress. He was a fool to worry about anything more. She could send her reputation to hell in whatever manner she wished to—it was scarcely any of his business.

"The dress is perfect, and your face paint is only recognizable to a connoisseur." He was leaving her to draw her own conclusions. "Shall we go? Or have you changed your mind?"

"Of course I haven't changed my mind," she said caustically. "We have a mission."

"God help me…" he muttered. And held out his arm.

He never before thought his coach was too small. Granted, it was the landau, meant for city driving, not the large, heavy traveling coach he used for greater distances. She sat opposite him in the confined space, and the faint scent she had used drifted to his nostrils, reaching into his bones. It was elusive, evocative, erotic. Had the Fates combined forces to kill him?

It was a cool spring evening, and even after nine o'clock there was still enough light remaining that he could see her a little too well. The shawl she'd brought was very pretty but not extremely warm, and he imagined she'd have gooseflesh by the end of the night.

She looked calm, self-possessed, as she always

did, but he knew that wasn't the case. He sat back in the shadows so she couldn't see his face, his eyes as they lingered over the tops of her breasts. He could see the beating of her heart through her translucent skin, and despite her determined calm she was nervous. He wondered why.

"I suggest we give the appearance of old friends," she said suddenly. "Otherwise my arrival would seem a bit odd."

"No one will believe it. They will think we are lovers," he said lazily.

She blushed, the color very pretty on her pale skin. "No one who knows me would make any such mistake."

"Ah, but no one knows you. You've eschewed society in favor of your oppressively good works."

"Wouldn't that make it clear that I'm not the sort for a dalliance?"

"True enough. A dalliance, as you call it, would be easy enough to avoid. A full-out, heart-stopping, body-pulsing physical affaire is more difficult to resist. And they know me. They will assume you're infatuated with me and that you've tumbled off your pedestal and into my bed, at least for a time."

He could practically feel her horrified intake of breath. "I trust you will do your best to disabuse them of the notion."

He laughed, enjoying himself once more. "I'll do what I can, but I suspect my protests would be for naught. If you promise not to hang on me and gaze at me with adoration we may be able to convince people that we've simply made an arrangement to assuage our physical needs. Even saints must have physical needs, I suspect."

"I'm not a saint." Her voice was low in the darkened carriage, and he remembered the stories about Wilfred Hunnicut and her brief fall from grace.

"No, you're not," he said softly, watching the rapid rise and fall of her beautiful breasts, the tight line of her mouth, the dark pools of her eyes in the shadowed carriage. He could feel it, he thought with surprise. It wasn't his imagination. He could feel the deep strand of longing that was wrapping around both of them. "Charity" Carstairs wanted him, probably about as much she disliked him. Which was a considerable amount. She most likely hated herself for being attracted to him, probably even refused to consider the possibility. It was part of the reason she was skittish tonight.

He smiled in the darkness. He was going to enjoy himself after all. "I suggest we not worry about what people imagine concerning our relationship. They'll think what they want. We need to discover who among them are involved in the current incarnation of the Heavenly Host, if the absurd worries you've brought to me have any validity, and if so, where and when they're meeting next."

"Don't we need to discover if your brother is truly part of them? Or do you believe me on that one?"

"If the organization is as you've described then I have no doubt that my brother is involved. He's…he's troubled. The Afghan war was very difficult for him, and he was grievously wounded. It's taking a long time for him to pull himself together, and I'm certain anything nihilistic would appeal to him. Apart from that, he's been quite secretive recently, and I've had reason to worry." He was telling her more than he wished to, and he wondered why. She had a calm demeanor that was oddly soothing. Soothing, when he wasn't consumed by lust.

Which he could ignore, he reminded himself. He'd come to London to assuage that lust, and so far he'd had very little success. It was only natural he would look at Melisande Carstairs and her magnificent breasts and think wicked thoughts.

Though to be truthful, he'd had those same thoughts when she'd been decently covered and looking like a nun.

"I'll tackle Lord Elsmere. You approach his wife," he said.

She frowned. "And when did we decide you were in charge of this investigation?"

"When you asked for my help. This is my world, Lady Carstairs, the world you've walked away from. I know it, and its inhabitants, quite well, and you'd be a fool not to listen to me. And you're many things but not, I think, a fool."

She glowered at him, then her expression smoothed out. She didn't want to let him know how much he annoyed her, a mistake on her part, he thought. The more she withstood the more determined he was to ruffle her.

"No, I'm not a fool," she said. And she wasn't.

Except, he hoped, where he was concerned. He was finding her more and more tempting, and he wasn't in the mood to fight it too strenuously.

The coach had drawn to a stop, and one of his footmen had already jumped down, and the sound of the steps being dropped was like a death knell, he thought with lazy amusement. He was being fanciful, but he couldn't rid himself of the notion that this was the point of no return.

Abandon hope, all ye who enter here, Dante's welcome to hell read. *Do what thou wilt,* read the entrance to Rabelais's fictional Abbey of Theleme.

The door opened, and he looked up at the Elsmere town house, then back at the woman with him. And he wondered which greeting was more accurate.

10

"Benedick, old man!" Harry Merton *would* have to be the first person they ran into, Benedick thought with resignation. Melisande had her back turned as she was handing her shawl to the maidservant when Harry came in the vestibule, a broad grin on his slightly foolish face. "Just the fellow I was wanting to see, don't you know. I've found just the right piece of crumpet for you—a girl with the most amazing flexibility. You wouldn't believe what she could do with her…"

"Good evening, Harry," Benedick said hastily, though he wasn't quite sure why.

Harry blinked. A gentleman never showed his liquor, and it was only the slight owlishness of his eyes that gave any hint that Harry had already been drinking steadily. "Good evening," he managed to reply. "Any luck with Charity? Now there's a field I might like to plow, assuming I could pry those legs apart…"

Melisande turned, her vivid blue eyes sparkling with something dangerous, and Harry blinked again, clearly embarrassed. "Beg your pardon, old man," he mumbled. "I didn't realize there was a lady present. Been an ass. Excuse me." He sketched an unsteady bow. "Your servant, ma'am."

Melisande Carstairs surveyed his old friend for a long moment, and he half expected her to attack. Instead she managed a seraphic smile and held out one gloved hand, which Harry bowed over, kissing the back of it a little clumsily.

"May I make my old friend Harry Merton known to you?" Benedick asked formally. "As he said, he's an ass, but a good-hearted one. Harry, I believe you might know Lady Carstairs."

"Of course," Harry said automatically, starting to rise when Benedick's words sank in, and he stumbled, a horrified expression on his face. "I mean, I know of…that is…" He finally managed to pull himself together, but it was a Herculean effort. "I knew your husband, Lady Carstairs. Sir Thomas was a good man."

"Not really," she said, and her frankness did little to calm Harry's amour propre.

Benedick decided to deliver the coup de grâce. He pulled Melisande's arm through his, drawing her close to his side in a proprietary gesture. "You'll excuse us, won't you, Harry? Melisande is famished and I promised I would feed her." He could feel her sudden start, and he simply pulled her closer, smiling down at her with only a touch of malice. She really was the most delicious creature. "Shall we go join the others, my sweet?"

Oh, she didn't like that, he thought with satisfaction. And there was nothing she could do about it. She couldn't pull away; she could only let him draw her up the wide marble stairs, feel his body heat leaching into hers, his hand on hers as he led her across the crowded floor of Lady Elsmere's formal salon. It was a Pyrrhic victory—the feel of her against his body was playing havoc with his own hard-won sense of self-control. He was as unsettled as he was hoping to make her, and he wanted to curse, but he simply smiled down at her, noting the confused, slightly nervous expression in her eyes.

"Don't look so anxious." His voice was barely audible. "I'm not going to throw you down on the floor and molest you."

"I didn't think you were," she said, managing to sound both dignified and vulnerable at the same time. "You would never be so clumsy as to have to use force."

He smiled at her. "You're learning, my love."

"Please don't call me that."

"I'm afraid I must. I have a reputation to uphold, and if people suspect I have another reason for bringing you here we'll be scuttled before we even leave land."

"I get seasick."

"I'm a very experienced sailor. Put yourself in my hands and I promise you a smooth sail." He let his fingers stroke the back of her hand, so gently that she probably didn't notice it, any more than she understood his double entendres. But he'd underestimated her.

"Save it for when people can hear us."

"I'm getting in practice," he said, his upper arm pressing against the side of her breast. It was most disturbing—the longer he was in her company the more aroused he became. Right now even the thought of Violet Highstreet couldn't distract him. For some reason the thought of Charity Carstairs kept distracting him.

He should have done something to assuage the state of arousal that burned inside his body, but the uncomfortable truth was that right now he wasn't interested in any of the demimondaines available to him. There were no new and nubile widows and wives among the ton eager for a bit of sport, at least, none that tempted him. His determined debauch had been a sad failure so far, and it was all Melisande Carstairs's fault. Every time he thought to lose himself in some Cyprian's ripe flesh the thought of her determined blue eyes distracted him, and he ended up feeling vaguely empty and unsatisfied.

He glanced down at her. A dark, wicked thought had come to mind, and try as he might to dismiss it, it remained stubborn. Lord and Lady Elsmere were at one end of the large room, greeting their guests, and as he waited for the butler to announce them he leaned down and whispered in Melisande's ear, "I'm afraid I might have to seduce you, my precious," he whispered, feeling her sudden start.

But a moment later they were announced and all eyes were upon them as the cream of the ton looked up and wondered what in the world Charity Carstairs, the saint of King Street, was doing with one of the wicked Rohans.

Lady Elsmere was an ancient, heavily painted dowager with a taste for young men, and she greeted them with her usual assessing gaze. "Good God, Rohan. What are you doing robbing a nunnery?"

He put his face close to Melisande's, pressing his forehead against hers in a manner that looked romantic to an outsider but had the felicitous effect of keeping her stormy gaze downcast. "Hardly a nunnery, Lady Elsmere," he whispered in a low, sensual voice.

Again that start of reaction through Melisande's body. Really, she was too easy. If he wanted he could waltz her into a different room and have her skirts over her head with no effort at all. Which was a totally lovely idea, his heartbeat informed him. He planted a light kiss on Melisande's nose and drew back, assured she was flustered enough not to let anyone see her usually direct gaze.

"We're delighted you could join us tonight, my dear," Lady Elsmere was saying. "I see Rohan has managed to persuade you to reenter society. You must be careful of him—he could persuade a saint to bed down with Satan. Or has that, perhaps, already happened?"

"I haven't..." she began, but Benedick gave her arm a slight, hard pinch, and she let out a little squeak. She glared at him swiftly from beneath her eyelids and then smiled at Lady Elsmere. "That is, I haven't decided as to just how social I wish to be, but tonight Lord Rohan wouldn't take no for an answer."

"No, I imagine he wouldn't," Lady Elsmere said with a bray of laughter. "Don't say I didn't warn you, Lady Carstairs. He's a very dangerous man."

"Don't be ridiculous, Lady Elsmere," Rohan said coolly, "I'm a woolly lamb."

Again that noisy laugh. "Come sit by me later, my dear, and I'll tell you all about him. In the meantime, why don't you two dance? That will at least keep his hands decently occupied."

He pulled her away, keeping a tight grip on her. "Did you have to pinch me so hard?" she demanded in an angry whisper.

"You looked as if you were about to start in on a lecture about the rights of women or something equally tedious. You're supposed to be here as my lover."

"As your friend," she corrected.

"And why would my 'friend' join a party of notorious hellions for the evening? Curiosity?"

"Perhaps. Maybe I wanted to make converts to my cause."

"Then you chose the wrong group."

Music was coming from one of the adjoining rooms, and he began to steer her in that direction. "You'll dance with me," he said. "Lady Elsmere's orders."

"What a charming request. No, I won't!"

He sighed. "If every step is going to be a battle we won't discover what the Heavenly Host is planning until next Christmas," he said in an undertone. "May I have the honor of this dance?"

He could see her hesitate, and she would have liked to say no. But he didn't make the mistake of underestimating her intelligence—she knew perfectly well that if she didn't make an effort they'd get nowhere.

"It's a waltz," she said in a wary voice.

"Exactly," he said. And before she could say no he pulled her into his arms and whirled her into the next room and onto the dance floor.

She stumbled at first, as if she weren't used to dancing, and he slowed his pace, letting her grow accustomed to the sound of the music, the feel of his hands on her, the closeness of their bodies. She was as stiff as a board, awkward, and he tried to quiet his impatience. He danced well, particularly for such a tall man, and he usually tried to avoid clumsy partners.

"Relax," he said in her ear, her curls tickling his nose.

"I can't relax, I'm trying to dance."

"You're failing." He spun her, just a bit, in an effort to throw her off guard. She was trying too hard, and the only way they were going to get through the dance without his reputation in shreds would be to startle her into relaxing. "It's like sex, my darling," he murmured in her ear. "Just stop fighting and let me lead."

11

Melisande stopped abruptly, astonished and out-raged, and he almost knocked into her. And then before she realized what he was doing he'd pulled her back into the dance, and she was so disturbed that she didn't stop to worry about following him, about her steps, about anything, as he moved her across the dance floor. "I beg your pardon," she said, her magnificent blue eyes glaring up at him.

"Fighting so soon, Rohan?" Harry Merton said with a grin as he waltzed by with a scantily dressed young lady in his arms.

Melisande immediately controlled her reac-tion. She didn't like Harry Merton, she didn't like Lady Elsmere and right now she positively detested Benedick Rohan. He hadn't meant a word of it, of course, he just wanted to throw her off balance, and he'd succeeded. If she had any choice at all, she would have kicked him in the shins and walked out of the party without a backward glance. But the memory of Aileen's scarred face was enough to stop her. Who was she to complain about putting up with the manners of social ninnies when there were lives at stake?

"Lady Carstairs has a passionate nature," Rohan said calmly as they circled around Merton. "She enjoys fighting."

"Enjoys making up even more, I'll warrant," Merton said with a loose grin. "You're a lucky man, Rohan."

"Indeed," he said, glancing down at her, and she stared up, momentarily disconcerted. His eyes were a dark, dark green, not black after all, and his dark eyelashes ringed them, framing them. It was no wonder he was reputed to be such a rake, she thought dizzily. Who could resist someone who could look at you with such vivid stillness, drawing you into their gaze? She could feel herself falling, falling…

And then the music stopped, and he was no longer holding her. His hand dropped from her waist and for a moment she felt dizzy, almost bereft. "You can dance after all," he said in a low voice. "As long as you're too angry to think about what you're doing."

"I wasn't angry," she said in a deliberately sweet voice. "Merely astonished at your good taste."

He laughed at that, and several people turned to observe them. "You really are delicious, Lady Carstairs. Perhaps I'll decide to seduce you in earnest, not just to shock you into dancing well."

She did it before she even stopped to think, stomping on his foot beneath the curtain of her skirts, hard.

He jumped back with a muffled curse, and she froze, unable to help herself, shocked at herself, wondering how he was going to retaliate.

But to her astonishment he laughed again, the sound rich and full. "You'll pay for that," he said softly, his amusement too evident for her to be worried.

She made a dismissive noise, moving away from him. Lady Elsmere was ensconced on a gilt settee on the edge of the room, and her duty was clear. She moved across the floor, ignoring Harry Merton as he tried to gain her attention, reaching her hostess's side a moment later and taking the seat beside her, fanning herself vigorously with one hand. "I'm exhausted," she said in faint tones. "Lord Rohan is such an energetic dancer I wonder he doesn't trample everyone in his way."

She made certain her voice carried to her companion, but Rohan simply gave her a seraphic smile, that promise of revenge still clear in his dark eyes.

"I hope he's as energetic when he's off his feet," Lady Elsmere said with a smirk. "I do like a man with stamina."

"Quite exhausting." Melisande refused to think about Lady Elsmere's meaning. "Indeed, there are occasions when I wish it were possible to…er…share the brunt of his attentions."

Lady Elsmere raised her skimpy gray eyebrows. "Really, my dear? I had the impression you were a devoted crusader, part saint, part nun. And instead you exhibit this totally unexpected degenerate streak. I find it unexpectedly delightful."

Melisande had been worried at the start of this speech, but by the end she was reassured. She glanced across the room. Rohan was deep in conversation with Lord Elsmere and two other men she couldn't identify, and he must have felt her eyes on him. He raised his head and met her gaze for an infinitesimal moment, then turned back to concentrate on his quarry.

At least, she hoped he was his quarry and not his partner in crime. It was always possible that Rohan had simply been humoring her when she'd asked for his assistance. After all, if he were a member of the organization himself, wouldn't he be likely to try to distract her from her mission? What better way than to pretend to help her.

She turned back to Lady Elsmere. "My personal interests have nothing to do with my social conscience, Lady Elsmere. And I must say Lord Rohan has introduced a whole new world of experience into my life, one I find immensely pleasurable." Holy God, but the words burned in her throat, and she wished she could wash away the taste of them. On top of everything else she had rapidly come to the conclusion that he was right, and posing as lovers was the only possible choice given their circumstances. No one would believe she was simply his friend, particularly given the way he'd manhandled her. But he'd had reason—if he hadn't kept his hands on her, she might have bolted. Or Harry Merton might have demonstrated his interest in "plowing her field" or whatever that revolting man had said.

In truth, Merton was an attractive man in his early thirties, with bright eyes and clear skin and a sunny smile. He had also appeared to be on the edge of inebriation, but for some reason Melisande wasn't quite sure if she believed it. There was a sharpness to his gaze, above the foolish smile, that suggested there was more to Harry Merton than the fop he appeared to be.

Lady Elsmere's chuckle was…there was no other word for it…lascivious. "I envy you, my child. I'd love a chance to taste Lord Rohan's energy."

She couldn't push, tempted though she was. The Heavenly Host was the epitome of a secret organization—there was no way they'd invite her in, given her reputation, until they were really sure of her. Besides, the idea of Lady Elsmere touching Rohan was revolting. The thought of any woman touching Rohan filled her with a sharp stab of anger that was totally inexplicable. She had always prided herself on her equable frame of mind, but somehow Benedick Rohan had a genius for upsetting her.

She wasn't going to examine that too closely. She returned the old woman's smile. "For now he's all mine."

"Indeed, I am, my heart." A voice came from behind her, and she felt the heat flood her face. His hands slid down over her bare shoulders, and in a few more inches he would have been cupping her breasts.

She let out a squeak and jumped up, half-afraid he wouldn't let her go. But he continued with his cool, slightly teasing smile, and she wondered if she could get away with slamming her elbow into his ribs. His feet had certainly survived her previous attempt.

Her urge toward violence shocked her again, and she took a deep breath, determined to regain her equilibrium. But then he moved beside her, sliding his arm around her waist in a shockingly intimate gesture, and his hand was dangerously close to the underside of her breast. She tried to disguise her sudden intake of breath as he leaned down and breathed in her ear with a gesture that would have looked more like a nuzzle than the warning it was. "Remember we are lovers, Charity. At least try to act the part, or I'll be forced to give them more graphic evidence."

She moved her foot, but he sidestepped her quite neatly this time. "Come along, my pet. Lord Elsmere wants to dance with you. I warned him that it would be a challenge, but he's more than willing to undertake it. Just make certain his hands stay above your waist, not below it. And don't let him dance you off into a corner."

"But I don't want…"

"Lord Elsmere! Lady Carstairs was just telling me how much she'd adore a dance. But be gentle with her—she hasn't had much chance to practice."

He really was the most annoying man, she thought, giving him a tight smile as the wizened old man took her into his arms. She should have had the gaggle help her with her dancing. If this absurd partnership lasted for more than this night she'd have to practice. Which didn't mean she wouldn't still attempt to stomp on his feet given half the chance. Any violence she could deliver on his person was earned well in advance.

She danced perfectly well with the old man, who did have a tendency to let his hands roam southward. She kept him busy talking, but he said little that could be helpful, apart from extolling the beauty of the Kent countryside and a place called Kersley Hall. After Lord Elsmere she danced with a hearty gentleman name Robert Johnson, a quadrille with Harry Merton, and by the time she finished with another waltz she was feeling quite comfortable. She'd never had much of an opportunity to dance when she was younger—her hand had not been sought during her season and Sir Thomas had been too frail to attend dances. But she'd had the requisite lessons, and by the time supper was announced her nervousness had vanished and she was quite enjoying herself.

Lord Elsmere claimed the right to take her into supper, and she went happily enough until Rohan brushed by her with the whispered admonition to watch her intake of cakes. She glared at him, but he'd already turned away, bending his attention toward the scantily clad young lady who'd been dancing with Harry Merton. Which didn't please Melisande particularly. The girl looked as if she didn't have a brain in her head, her dress was falling off her ample curves and she had a laugh almost as annoying as

Lady Elsmere's raucous one. It was enough to make a woman need that extra serving of cake.

It took a number, because she needed to make certain that Rohan caught her eating them, and he was barely paying her any attention. By the time he noticed even she had had more than her fill, and she put down her fork, resisting the impulse to stick out her tongue at him.

"You and Rohan should join us some weekend," Lord Elsmere said, dropping his hand onto her knee in a friendly gesture. She wanted to squirm away from him, but she forced herself to sit still. If she seemed prudish they would hardly be likely to invite her to an orgy. "A few friends of ours get together and…"

"My dear, I'm certain Lady Carstairs has better things to do than waste her time with our harmless little gatherings," Lady Elsmere broke in with a laugh in her arch tones, and Lord Elsmere withdrew his hand and grumbled something inaudible. "You know how young people are nowadays. They have their own friends, their own house parties. I can hardly believe they would want to tarry with our stodgy crowd." She put her hand on Melisande's arm, drawing her away. "Come and sit with me, dear. I know my husband, and his supper conversation is always dismal. You and I can share a comfortable coze and you can tell me more about Viscount Rohan's prowess."

Melisande threw a glance in Rohan's direction. He was talking with the bluff man, no longer paying attention to the sultry young woman who was busy displaying her décolletage to the old roué on her other side, but he caught her gaze as she was forcibly borne away, and his eyes narrowed thoughtfully.

By the time the music started again Melisande was almost desperate to get away from Lady Elsmere, who seemed determined to drone on and on about the most stultifying of topics, not the off-color tales she'd been hoping for. She looked up with unfeigned pleasure when Rohan appeared before her, jumping up before he even requested a dance, and a moment later they were back on the dance floor once more.

"I need to talk to you," she said in a whisper. If Rohan could manage to corner Lord Elsmere before they left they might leave with an invitation to their gathering, where the old lady could have a taste of Rohan's…energy. It would serve him right. He could pleasure the old hag while Melisande could find a way to stop them.

"Later," he murmured under his breath, swirling her gracefully around the room. "You've just gotten to the point where I don't have to manhandle you to move you."

"Now," she shot back. "There's a room over there. Dance me into it." Curtains draped the doorway on the far side of the room, and the door stood ajar, the other side dark and beckoning.

He glanced at it, then back at her, and an odd expression danced in his dark green eyes. "That's probably not a good idea…are you certain?"

"Absolutely," she said, starting to lose patience with him.

"As you wish, my lady." And a moment later he twirled her into the room, and the door closed behind them, locking them into the darkness.

12

Maybe not a good idea after all, Melisande thought, as Rohan's grip tightened, and she felt her body being drawn closer to his lean, hard chest. "What are you doing?" She tried to keep the nervousness out of her voice, but it trembled anyway, and she put her hands between them, trying to push away from him. He was much stronger than she would have guessed, and his arms were around her now, holding her.

"This, my sweet, is one of the rooms the Elsmeres keep for dalliance. Once someone disappears in here they don't emerge for an hour or more."

"What in the world do they do for an hour?"

There was silence in the darkness. Then he spoke. "You're a widow, Lady Carstairs, and you've had at least one lover. Surely even you can guess."

She'd forgotten he somehow knew about Wilfred Hunnicut, damn him. She was the one who'd made the wretched mistake of giving in to Wilfred's blandishments; she needed to pay the price. "But what do they do for an hour?" she persisted. "What do they do after the first ten minutes?"

There was a soft explosion of laughter from the man in the darkness, an almost enticing sound. She had no reason to feel uneasy, she reminded herself. He wasn't hurting her, wasn't coercing her. He was simply holding her, and in the inky black of the room she couldn't see him. He could be anyone. He could be someone she actually wanted to be with, someone who attracted her, aroused her. If such a man existed.

"Please, my angel," he said softly, "tell me your lovers lasted longer than ten minutes."

They shouldn't be talking about this. But somehow, in the dark, it no longer seemed forbidden. "Do you count the time it takes to rearrange your clothing?"

"No. It takes more than ten minutes to strip a woman completely, though I'm adept enough to do it in a little less."

"Strip?" She was horrified. "Naked?"

"Precious, don't you talk to your gaggle at all?"

It was just as well he couldn't see her. Her face felt hot, and she knew it was flooded with color. "Occasionally… If I'm confused about something. It's not as if I'm without experience in these matters."

"It seems to me you're confused about a great many things. Someone needs to take your education in hand." His hands were on her arms, and they tightened just slightly as she felt her body being pulled closer to his.

"I don't see any reason for it." Her voice had a

slight waver in it, and she cleared her throat. "I don't intend to marry again, and I fail to see any value in having a lover. If one has to put up with being pawed one might as well be married, I suppose, and I can do very well without either."

"You don't like being pawed?" His voice was low and sinuous, and she could feel a strange heat curling at the base of her spine.

"Not particularly. In fact, you might release me."

"I might. But I'm not about to," he said softly. "What about kisses? Are they equally heinous?"

This was getting to be dangerous, and she had the sudden fear that she wasn't going to escape this room without being kissed. Though why in the world an accomplished rake like Benedick Rohan would want to kiss her was beyond her imagining.

"Chaste kisses are perfectly all right, if there's strong affection between partners," she said with what she considered great fairness.

"And how do you define chaste kisses?" There was still that damned amusement in his voice. She considered trying to pull free, but she knew that loose hold on her arms could tighten instantly.

She refused to let him embarrass her. "A kiss that lasts less than five seconds is usually sufficient to express affection."

"Five seconds? You timed it? Oh, my darling Charity!" He was laughing at her, and she moved to stomp on his foot again, but clearly he was more comfortable in the dark than she was, because he moved deftly out of her way. "Have you ever had a kiss that lasted more than five seconds?"

"I know what you're talking about," she replied. "Emma told me about that kind of kiss, which, I must inform you, sounds utterly disgusting. Why in the world would you kiss someone with your tongue?"

"Allow me to demonstrate." And before she knew what he was going to do his mouth came down on hers, unerringly in the dark, and she froze.

One arm was around her waist, holding her against him. He caught her chin with the other hand, and her arms were free to bat at him, push him away, and she tried, she absolutely tried, but the feel of his mouth against hers was really quite delightful, and it lasted longer than five seconds.

"Open your mouth, vixen," he whispered, his breath warm against her lips. "You can't spend your entire life in ignorance."

"Why not? I think…" Her mistake. Opening her mouth to speak gave him enough opportunity, and his open mouth closed over hers, moving it apart, and oh my God, she could feel his tongue touch her lips.

She struggled, momentarily panicked, and he lifted his head. "Don't be such a Sabine about it, my precious. It's only a kiss." And he slanted his mouth over hers, his tongue pushing inside her mouth and touching her own, and she could hear her own horrified moan.

It was strange, it was vile, it was awful. It was… odd. Unfamiliar feelings were fluttering through her, and the darkness of the room felt like a cocoon wrapped around her, cradling her, and suddenly it was something she wanted. She wanted him to kiss her like that, full and deep, holding nothing back. She wanted to be kissed like she was loved, needed, like she was the most desirable woman in the world. The hands that were pushing against his shoulders stopped, then moved upward to clutch him, and when his tongue curled against hers she found herself kissing him back, moving her own small tongue in response to his.

He lifted his mouth, trailing damp kisses along the side of her jaw, and she drew a deep breath, not realizing she'd been holding it. Her body was softening, flowing against his, and he was moving her, slowly, carefully, until her back came up against a wall and she let her head sink back, closing her eyes.

"You really are indescribably luscious, my sweet Charity," he said, his voice almost a growl against the side of her neck. His mouth caught her ear, his teeth nipping lightly just above the emerald earbob, and she let out a moan, shocking herself. She could feel his hips pressing against her, holding her against the door, and she could feel the ridge of his erection.

It astonished her. It was like nothing she'd ever experienced—Wilfred's response to her had been slow to build and…and small compared to what she felt now. He couldn't be putting that part of his body to the same use that Wilfred or Thomas had—it was too big.

She lifted on her toes, pressing against him experimentally, rubbing against him like a curious cat. She heard a strangled moan from him, and she felt a spark of satisfaction that she could make him feel the same kind of reaction he was busy getting from her.

"Bloody hell, Charity," he whispered against her skin. And he kissed her again, as she felt his large, deft hands slide down her skirts, tugging them slowly, inexorably upward.

It was the touch of his long fingers on the bare flesh of her knee that froze her, shocked her out of the sensual web he'd managed to spin around her. She moved her hands to his chest and shoved hard. "No!" she cried, and he fell back a step, no longer touching her.

He was only a few inches away, she knew it, even in the inky darkness of the little room. He was breathing heavily, and her own heart was thudding so hard in her chest that it felt as if it might break through. She was trembling, her legs felt weak and she wanted to slap him.

"What in heaven's name do you think you're doing?" she managed to say. She would have loved to have sounded unaffected, but right now that was beyond her.

He let out a sigh, and she could almost picture him, those dark green eyes narrowed and assessing, his mouth curved in a slight smile. His mouth, the one that had kissed her more thoroughly than she'd ever been kissed before. His mouth, his kiss, that had felt more intimate than lying with her husband with her chemise pulled chastely up to her waist and her face turned away. She felt despoiled. She felt invaded. She felt…claimed.

He moved closer, and his forehead pressed against hers as he sighed. "That's the point, my sweet Lady Carstairs. You don't recognize a full-bore seduction when it's aimed at you. You simply can't continue to be such an innocent and live the life you do. It's too dangerous. Some big bad wolf is going to snatch you up and devour you."

She caught her breath. "So *you* being this big bad wolf—this is a charitable act on your part?"

There was a moment's silence, but he didn't move away. "What if I told you it was? Are you so innocent that you'd really believe it?"

She curled her hands into fists, trying to will strength back into her limbs. "I have no idea, Lord Rohan. I have no experience being debauched."

She didn't know if that muffled sound was laughter or exasperation. "It was your idea to come in here, my love. I thought you were ready to experience the delights of the flesh."

"I experience any number of physical delights. Such as spring breezes blowing through my hair, or the taste of sugar cakes, or playing with a kitten, or holding a child's hand."

"You don't have to tell me you like sugar cakes," he said. "You like kisses, too."

"I do not."

"Do you want me to prove it again?"

"No!"

He moved away then, backing into the darkness, and she suddenly felt bereft. She could see him now, a shadow in a room of shadows, no longer in danger of touching her, thank God. She released her breath, trying to decipher the sudden pang of…regret? Disappointment? Freedom.

"I want to go back," she said sternly, ignoring it.

"Well, my darling girl, you can't," he said frankly. "I told you, my reputation as a lover is at stake. You're not leaving until there's been enough time to shag you properly. Which I'm guessing is another forty-five minutes. So you might as well sit down and tell me whatever it was that made you drag me into here in the first place. Not that I mind. If the Elsmeres and their ilk think I've managed to so thoroughly debauch the Saint of King Street that she can't spend a few hours without having me between her legs, then my credit will only rise. When we leave you'll need to be languid, mussed and dreamy."

"Must you be so crass?"

"Oh, my sweet Charity."

"Stop calling me that!" Her usual good humor seemed to have eroded completely.

"Oh, my sweet Lady Carstairs? It doesn't have quite the same ring. And Melisande sounds like a medieval martyr doomed to perish. Hasn't anyone ever called you by a pet name?"

"No. And if they had I'd hardly give you the use of it," she said and pushed away from the wall. He'd pulled back from that dangerous seduction that had filled the tiny room, and he was simply Lord Rohan, the man who promised to help her. Her legs still felt weak, and she crossed the room to sit on the surface near him, wondering what it was. Wondering why he had held her, kissed her and then just as suddenly stopped.

Not that she wasn't grateful. She didn't want his hands on her, his mouth on hers. She still wasn't sure why he'd done it in the first place. To teach her a lesson? To prove to her just how naive she was. What a child, what an innocent, what a ridiculous creature she was.

It was a good thing they were in the dark. She suddenly felt quite confused and miserable. She had responded to his touch, his mouth, and it shocked her. Perhaps he hadn't noticed, but Benedick Rohan was a man who noticed everything. Why had she liked it? Something that she had simply borne as the least of unpleasant intimacies was suddenly unbelievably enticing.

It wasn't as if Sir Thomas hadn't cared for her. And she had loved him, deeply, and been very happy when she'd been able to provide him with that physical outlet, the few times he'd felt up to it.

She'd been infatuated with Wilfred, as much as the memory now embarrassed her. She'd wanted his kisses. His chaste kisses. That hadn't moved her nearly as much as Benedick Rohan's shocking embrace.

"What did you want to tell me?" he said in his deep voice, and she felt it slide down her backbone like a caress.

She had to stop thinking about that. "Lord Elsmere was about to invite us to a party in Kent. At a place called Kersley Hall, I believe. I presume that is one of their estates? Lady Elsmere stopped him, but I thought if you talked with him you might get him to proffer an invitation. It would be a way in to the workings of the Heavenly Host."

"Kersley Hall?" he echoed, and she heard the surprise in his voice. "That belonged to the Earl of Cranston, but I'm certain it burned down last winter. Why in the world would anyone want to go there?"

"Are there outbuildings? Some place for the Heavenly Host to gather?"

"I have no idea," he said, and she could tell by the sound of his voice that he'd practically forgotten her existence. "But I intend to find out."

He leaned back, and she could hear his sudden exhalation. And then his large hand caught hers, though how he could find it in the darkness she couldn't begin to guess. He held it lightly, his long fingers tracing each of hers, gently caressing her palm. She wanted to yank it away from him, but for some reason she let it rest there, as the strange pleasure of his touch on her skin danced through her body. "It's only a few hours' ride—it should be simple enough for me to go out and investigate. If the Host meet there, then there's bound to be signs. None of the possible members would ever tolerate anything less than comfort on a sybaritic scale. Trust me, shagging someone on hard ground is no fun."

"And you would know." Her voice was caustic.

"And I would know," he agreed pleasantly. "To-morrow promises to be a pleasant day. I'll go then and report back to you."

"No."

His hand stopped its almost unconscious stroking. "You are calling a halt to our investigation? Very wise."

"I mean I'm going with you. Two pairs of eyes are better than one, and I have nothing planned for the morrow." She didn't stop to think why she was throwing herself in his company again. He was dangerous, and what she needed was distance, not proximity.

But she didn't trust him. He was necessary—he knew more about the current workings of society than she did, and she couldn't do it without him. She would survive being around him.

He was stroking her hand again, clearly an absent gesture, and she felt the surface beneath her shift as he leaned back, her hand still clasped in his. "I'll have my cook prepare a picnic lunch," he said lazily. "What would you like besides sugar cakes?"

She gave full rein to her annoyance in the darkness, sticking her tongue out at him like a fractious child. She heard a low rumble of laughter, and she had the sudden thought that he'd seen her. Impossible.

"Stick out your tongue at me, my sweet," he said in a low, charming voice, "and you might find…"

"Stop it!" she said, her temper finally frayed. Anger filled her. But she was made of sterner stuff than that. "I'm tired of your innuendos, Lord Rohan," she said in a steadier voice.

"And you might find I treat you like the infant you're emulating," he continued over her protest. She had no idea whether that was what he'd originally meant to say, and she didn't care. For the moment, just for the moment, she gave up the fight. He was too good at this. He could dance rings around her, in more ways than one. He had an answer for everything, annoying creature that he was, and she was feeling demoralized. If he hadn't kissed her, put his hands on her, she wouldn't be in such a mess.

But he had.

He moved suddenly, and she braced herself, but he had released her hand, and his voice was all efficiency. "Just to further your sexual education, Lady Carstairs, there is such a thing as a quick shag. Usually done up against a wall, it's more along the lines of your experience, simply adding actual pleasure into the mix. The guests can assume that's what we've done if you wish to return to the party."

"I do."

"But I'll need a piece of your clothing," he said, his voice languid. "I'm assuming you won't relinquish your drawers, but I imagine one of your garters might do."

"I beg your pardon?"

"Granted. It's customary in the Elsmeres' set to provide a trophy. Lord Elsmere probably fondles whatever gets left behind in the privacy of his rooms, where I doubt Lady Elsmere ever ventures. Your garter."

"You can't have one of my garters!" she protested, scandalized. "My stocking will fall down."

"Even better. I'll take one of your stockings."

"No!" she said, but he managed to catch her ankle and pull it into his lap. She kicked at him with the other one, but he clamped his own foot down on it, immobilizing her.

"I'm getting quite tired of being kicked, Melisande," he said in a low voice, pulling off her soft dance slipper, his hands sliding up her silk-covered leg.

But she fought back, shoving at him, and a moment later she found herself lying down, his body covering her completely, holding her there.

They had been sitting on a bed, she realized belatedly. And now she was lying on it, with a very large, very annoyed, very aroused man on top of her. She kept hitting at him, but he simply caught her wrists in one hand and hauled them over her head, while his hips pinned her, the hard ridge of desire full against her as he pushed between her legs.

"Stop fighting me," he said, and there was amusement in his voice. "I'm not about to rape you. And you can just ignore my cock. Anytime I wrestle with a beautiful woman I get an erection—it's simply nature taking its course."

She froze, his matter-of-fact language shocking her. He was lying with that part of his body, his cock, pressed against her, and she could feel a strange, heated response. Heat, and dampness, and it shocked her. Simply nature taking its course, he said. It had nothing to do with her.

"I can do this by force, or you can behave yourself," he continued. "Either way, it's going to happen." And for a moment she thought he meant sex. Sexual congress between them, his cock pushing inside her. And then she realized he was talking about her stocking.

His hand had slid up, under her skirt. Her garters were beautiful ones, made of pale green ribbon with pastel-colored rosettes, and she felt his hand untie one, his long fingers way too close to parts that needed to be ignored. And then he moved his hand beneath the silk stocking, pulling it down her leg, the removal of it almost a caress, and she held her breath, closing her eyes in the darkness as his hand brushed against her skin.

What was she doing? Was she totally shameless, enjoying the touch of this man, this scion of degenerates, as he stroked her leg, all the way down to her ankle, cradling her foot as he slipped the stocking off?

He was so close. So hot, so hard, and she could feel the beat of his heart against her. Her breasts felt strange, tight, tingling, and she wondered what would happen if she arched against him, as her body was telling her to do, if she raised her hips up and pushed against that hard part of him. What would he do?

He released her wrists, but she didn't hit him. An

odd stillness had crept over her limbs, and it seemed to be affecting him, as well. She could see the glitter of his eyes in the darkness, but she couldn't see his expression.

"Lady Carstairs," he said in a soft voice after a long moment, "I'm beginning to believe you might be a very dangerous woman."

She swallowed, uncertain what to say. She wondered what would happen if she slid her arms around his shoulders. If she pulled him down to kiss her. What would he do?

He rolled off her, standing up in one fluid movement, and for a moment she lay still, trying to sort out her feelings. He'd put her slipper back on her one bare foot, and a moment later he'd pulled her to her feet, holding her arms for a moment until she steadied.

"Remember. Languid. Dazed." His voice was low in her ear as a sliver of light entered the room.

"I shouldn't have any trouble with that," she muttered.

13

It was a good thing he needed very little sleep, Benedick Rohan thought the next morning, or he would be in very deep trouble. The previous night had been hellacious. First, he'd had to trot Sweet Charity out among the Elsmeres' guests like a shy mare successfully covered by a prize stallion, her silk stocking draped across the door handle leading to their little rendezvous. The garter he'd pocketed himself, though he had no idea why. He also had no intention of looking into the matter too closely. He had her pretty little garter with him, and he'd be damned if he'd give it back.

They'd left as soon as they could, giving a reasonable simulation of a couple who couldn't wait to get back in bed. At least, he did. She'd been unnaturally quiet, simply letting him lead her around. She'd been silent in the carriage as well, and he hoped she'd forgotten about her plans to join him on his ride to Kersley Hall, but as he'd accompanied her to her door, his hand hovering near her elbow, ready to touch her if he had half an excuse, she'd turned and said, "And what time shall we meet, Lord Rohan?" in a creditable approximation of her normal voice.

He hadn't been able to sleep. All he'd done was kiss her, most thoroughly and most enjoyably, but in the end it was simply a kiss. True, he'd lain on top of her, feeling the softness of her curves, the tenderness of her breasts, the sweetness of her parted thighs. He'd felt the smooth skin of her leg, the crook of her knee, and it would have been so easy to pull that knee up, around his hips. She was no virgin, after all.

But he hadn't. And she was still as rattled as if he'd done exactly what he'd been thinking about doing in the past few hours. The past few days. He lusted after the sober little crusader—the saint of King Street, the savior of soiled doves—impossible as it seemed. He wanted her naked beneath him, he wanted to wipe that cool, distant smile off her face and have her hot and sweaty, weeping with her release. He wanted to take her, and take her hard. And there were so many reasons why he shouldn't. Mostly because, despite her widowed state, she wasn't the kind of woman to bed and then discard. She was someone who played the game seriously. If she thought it a game at all.

He'd finally dragged himself out of bed when he heard the clock chiming three, taking himself in search of a brandy and something to read, when he heard a crashing in the hallway below.

He caught his robe in one hand and strode out onto

the landing, about to demand who the hell was there, when his angry voice died away, and he looked at his brother trying to make his way up the stairs with the help of Richmond.

He had blood on his head. He was singing softly, a ditty of such obscenity that even Benedick was impressed. He was very drunk, but he was more than drunk. His eyes glittered, the pupils tiny pinpricks in the shadow as he looked up and saw Benedick.

"M'brother," Brandon announced to Richmond. "Not a bad fellow, but completely conventional. Wouldn't approve."

Benedick had already started down the stairs, reaching them midway and taking his brother's other arm. There was a sweet smell clinging to him, mixing with the unmistakable smell of alcohol, and he wondered what the hell his baby brother had gotten into. "Wouldn't approve of what, old boy?" he asked easily, looking at the blood. It was dried, and there was no head wound, which was a relief. And then he looked down at Brandon's hand, the one which had seen war and despair, that had meted out death with grim certainty. There was a deep gash in his palm, still oozing blood.

Brandon followed his gaze, oddly alert despite the whiskey he could smell on him. "Don't look so worried," he said in an irritable voice. "Did it myself."

"Why?"

"None of your damned business, that's why," Brandon replied. He paused, looking around him, his eyes going out of focus. "I need my room," he said abruptly.

"Are you going to be unwell, sir?" Richmond inquired anxiously. "I could bring you a basin."

"No Rohan would cast up his accounts—we come from a long line of degenerates—" And then he'd proceeded to get violently ill all over Benedick.

Which was enough to put anyone off the idea of sleeping. They'd managed to get Brandon's nearly unconscious form into his bedroom, and he'd left him in Richmond 's care, not bothering with instructions to clean him up and bandage the hand. Richmond had taken care of him very well over the years—he didn't need his master telling him his business.

Fortunately the noise had already roused a number of the staff, and it didn't take long to get a hot bath to wash off Brandon's excesses. By the time he'd finished it was already growing light outside, and he gave up the thought of sleep entirely.

It was just as well. Lack of sleep sharpened his intellect and destroyed any semblance of courtesy. He'd doubtless be such a bear that sweet Charity would develop a total disgust of him, and look elsewhere for a confederate. He would be better off investigating Brandon's possible connection to the Heavenly Host on his own, without having to worry about anyone else.

Not that it was in his nature to worry about anyone, with the possible exception of his siblings. And Brandon had managed to get himself into a totally disreputable state while he was nowhere near the

Elsmeres or any of the other possible members he'd talked with the night before, which made the connection less likely.

Today should put an end to any speculation. He would give Lady Carstairs such a disgust of him that she would refuse to even speak to him in the future, which would be better for both of them. Because she'd kissed him back. Inexpertly, to be sure, but she'd responded, and the sweetness of her momentary, unexpected response had been…distracting. And he'd already been distracted enough from his main goal.

No, today would put an end to it. Thank God.

It was a good thing she managed very well on only a few hours of sleep, Melisande thought over her second cup of strong tea. Because last night had been distressing, indeed.

It had started with Viscount Rohan, of course. Try as she might, she couldn't stop thinking about the feel of his body pressed against hers, between her legs, the same and yet so different from the two other men who had once lain there. Of course last night they'd both been fully clothed, so she'd been able to notice things without being in a high state of anxiety over the indignities that were about to follow. She could feel the hardness of his chest against her breasts, the heavy rhythm of his heart. The hand that had held her wrists over her head, the other hand sliding up her leg, unfastening her garter with the practiced ease of a rake.

She hadn't wanted him to stop. That was the miserable, unacceptable truth, but she'd always prided herself on facing it, no matter how unpleasant. If they'd been somewhere else, if he'd been someone else, she would have succumbed faster than a leaf falls from a tree in autumn. His kiss, his vile, tonguing kiss, had been revelatory. Because she'd liked it. She could have gone on kissing him all night.

Not that he would have kissed her all night. She knew perfectly well that men kissed simply in order to inflict more indignities upon a woman, and that once they were done the best one could hope for was an affectionate pat on the cheek before the sod would roll over and fall asleep, dismissing her and her feelings from his consciousness....

She stopped herself, taking a deep breath. If she liked his kisses, more than she'd ever liked kisses before, did that mean she would also like what normally followed? She had the horrid suspicion that she might.

Which led her to an obvious conclusion. Celibacy might not be the best answer for every woman.

Oh, to be sure, someone like Benedick Rohan was the worst kind of choice a woman could make. Fortunately he was totally beyond her touch if she had any illusions in that direction. Her background was respectable but undistinguished, he was the scion of an old, if notorious, family. He would be a marquess eventually, and he would choose a very young virgin to be his marchioness, not a widow who was long in the tooth and most likely barren. Viscount

Rohan was busy looking among the most beautiful of this year's crop of marriageable ladies, and he didn't have to consider fortune among his requirements. He could simply take the prettiest, most amenable one with a snap of the fingers, and she, and her parents, would come willingly. If she hadn't distracted him with her charges' problems, he probably would have already announced his engagement.

But she was hardly going to settle for a fortune hunter like Wilfred, if she did decide to marry again. Nor an old man like Thomas, no matter how dearly he'd loved her. No, she would want someone strong and young and yes, handsome. Someone to adore her, to devote himself to bringing her pleasure with the same kind of dedication Rohan brought to kissing. Was it too much to ask for?

Of course, men, even charming men, could turn into brutes. But surely not all of them? She needed to keep an open mind. She might have been hasty in dismissing the entire male gender. Perhaps there might be children in her future after all.

Emma Cadbury appeared in the door, worry creasing her beautiful face. She poured herself a cup of tea and sat down opposite Melisande, managing a distracted smile. "That's a very pretty riding habit," she observed.

"It's seven years out-of-date," Melisande said, kicking at the long skirt. "Which is one reason why it's a little too…a little too…"

"Attractive? Flattering?" Emma supplied dryly. "I don't understand why you refuse to wear clothes that show your figure. The habit looks lovely on you—it brings out the blue in your eyes. There's no reason why you can't enjoy pretty clothes, Melisande."

"I don't want to attract unwanted male attention."

"What about wanted male attention?"

Melisande flushed, hoping Emma couldn't read her recent thoughts. "Is there such a thing?"

"Yes," Emma said firmly. "And I suspect you're beginning to realize it. You still haven't told me how last evening went."

She would have given anything to have poured out what had happened in that little closet off the Elsmeres' ballroom, but something stopped her. She wasn't sure whether it was embarrassment or something else, but she wasn't ready to share.

"I'm more interested in how Maudie is." She'd just managed to drift off to sleep when Maudie had showed up, covered in blood, with bruises on her throat, wrists and ankles, another victim of the Heavenly Host's brutal games. She hadn't spoken much since they'd managed to clean her up and bandage her, but her blackened eyes were filled with suffering, a suffering that should only have increased Melisande's disgust for all mankind. Unfortunately it only increased her disgust with the base aristocrats responsible and the worthless examples of humankind who found pleasure in hurting the helpless.

And Benedick, Viscount Rohan, was her ally in stopping them. She had no choice—she couldn't do it on her own. At least she was secure in the knowledge that without good reason he would have no interest in touching her. And when she survived without sleep she became, as Emma had frankly informed her, a captious shrew. She would give Viscount Rohan such a disgust of her that he wouldn't want to venture any closer than strictly necessary.

"Maudie's sleeping," Emma said. "She's lost a bit of blood, but she doesn't seem to have suffered any permanent injury."

"With any luck this might work out for the best." Melisande roused herself. "She's come and gone from here three times already, each time drifting back into the life of a whore. This time she may have finally had enough."

"Perhaps," Emma said doubtfully. "But there are some who never learn. And God knows, it's easier work than hauling coal to an upstairs bedroom and working in a dressmaker's shop. You're off your feet and it's all over and done with quick enough."

Melisande frowned. "That reminds me. Lord Rohan said that…that physical encounters can take an hour or longer. I presume he was lying, but…"

"What were you doing discussing lovemaking with Viscount Rohan?"

Melisande picked up the newspaper, endeavoring to look matter-of-fact. "It was an intellectual discussion."

"Hmmph," said Emma, clearly not convinced. "If you want to have intellectual discussions about lovemaking then you should come to us. If you put all our years of experience together our wealth of knowledge rivals that contained in the British Museum."

"Does the British Museum contain knowledge of lovemaking?" she asked. "I'll have to go in search of it instead of wasting my time learning from the gaggle."

"Don't try to distract me. You know I worry about you."

"Yes, ma'am," she said in a meek voice. "Then is it true? Does it take longer than five or ten minutes?"

Emma surveyed her judiciously. "It all depends. With experienced lovers it can last the entire night. When money changes hands it's usually over quickly. The provider of the service wishes to end it quickly, and, being a professional skilled in her craft, she can do any number of things to speed the process along. The purchaser usually wants it over quickly as well, since he's more than likely ashamed of needing to pay money for it in the first place or concerned that he might be discovered by a wife or friend.

"Among lovers it's a different matter. In that case the longer it takes the more exquisite the pleasure. There are any number of tricks for prolonging things, bringing someone to the very edge of climax and then falling back, only to approach it again."

"Climax?"

Emma's smile was rueful. "Clearly we haven't been nearly instructive enough. I'm talking about that moment of exquisite bliss that occasionally blesses women. For men it's simple enough—a matter of biology, and almost any aperture will do for them. For a woman it requires care and skill from the man, and usually deep feeling from the woman, or so I've been told."

Melisande stared at her, momentarily confused. "So you've been told?" she repeated. "But you were the most notorious madam in the city, as well as the youngest. How could you not know…?"

"Prolonging a man's pleasure is a fairly simple matter. Prolonging a female's release is, for my part, merely theoretical. There are very few men who specialize in providing pleasure for females, and I have never been troubled by tender feelings about anyone. Most of the men who worked for me were there for other men to enjoy. Yes, I know, you don't want to hear about it, and you don't need to, though I assure you most of those young men are in as great a need as the women who live here. But as it is, even professionally speaking, a woman's pleasure is of little value. Occasionally a really good lover can make it last for his partner, but I gather either such men are very rare or, once discovered by wife or partner, they're never given the chance to stray. So Lord Rohan estimates that his usual lovemaking takes an hour?"

"Including the removal of all clothing."

A slow smile curved Emma's gorgeous mouth. "No wonder the whores fought over him. If I'd known I would have investigated myself, just to see if it were true."

Melisande frowned. "You didn't, did you?"

"Sleep with Lord Rohan? No, I did not. Does it matter?"

"Why should it matter?" Melisande said, picking up her newspaper and then setting it down again, distracted. "Besides, I already knew that Violet and others had…er…serviced him on a number of occasions."

Emma's expression was far too calculating, if only in the nicest way. "If I were you I wouldn't think about who had taken care of Viscount Rohan and concentrate more on the man himself."

"Why?"

There was a small, secret smile around Emma's mouth. "Why don't we wait and see what happens?"

"Nothing's going to happen. You know how fractious and unpleasant I can be if I don't have enough sleep, and I barely managed an hour last night. After a few hours in my company he won't want to be anywhere near me."

Before Emma could reply young Betsey barreled into the room. "There's a cove what's outside, waiting for you. Sez to hurry up or he'll leave without you. Right pretty, he is," she added judiciously. "I'd hurry if I were you."

It took all of Melisande's strength of character not to jump to her feet. She rose slowly, glancing at Emma. "I'll leave Betsey up to you," she said. "Apparently my presence is demanded."

She heard Emma's words trail after her. "Give him hell, Melisande." And Melisande grinned sourly.

She intended to do just that.

14

It was a ride of close to two hours from the Dovecote on King Street to the ruins of Kersley Hall in Kent, and it was a ride conducted in silence. He waited, just waited, for her to come up with something inflammatory to set his barely banked temper into a roaring blaze, but she barely said a word, damn her.

And he couldn't summon the energy to engage her. After the first few minutes he settled back into an exhausted semistupor. He should have cried off, but one didn't stand up a lady, even as big a hoyden as Charity Carstairs, and besides, he despised giving in to weakness. He should have been able to sleep, at least until Brandon had come home, and instead he'd lain awake reliving those disturbing moments in the Elsmeres' closet.

He was still uncomfortable thinking about it, physically so, and he shifted in the saddle, glancing at his companion. Her eyes were shuttered, her face expressionless, so he let his gaze roam down the rest of her. The habit was deplorably out-of-date, but it fit her better than most of her clothes, with the exception of that wicked gown of hers last night, and the color made her skin luminous. She rode well, which surprised him, and her mare was a beautiful piece of horseflesh, well trained and responding to her slightest gesture.

"Where did you learn to ride?" he asked abruptly, making it sound more like a demand than polite conversation.

"Why? Do you think I lack skill?" she said in a voice bordering on annoyed.

That was what he was looking for, he thought. A fight, to keep him awake, and to remind him of how totally inappropriate she was on every level. "You're adequate," he drawled, giving her an insolent look. "I'm afraid I remember very little of your past, apart from your marriage to Sir Thomas Carstairs. You come from an old Lincolnshire family, do you not?"

"If you're asking me if my parents were wealthy enough to provide a horse for their only child then the answer is no. My father was a baronet addicted to gaming, my mother was devoted to her ill health, and they had neither the inclination nor the money to spend on their ill-favored daughter. I didn't learn to ride until after I was married."

He didn't respond to her "ill-favored" remark—it was simply fishing for compliments and he wasn't about to react. "If they were so poor and uncaring how did they manage to provide you with a season in London? Or were they that desperate to get rid of you?"

She flashed a dangerous smile at him. "They died. My father from a drunken fall, my mother from a fever. My aunt offered to give me one season to come up to scratch, and after that... In fact, I have no idea what my future would have been if Sir Thomas hadn't offered for me. I'd probably be a governess somewhere."

"Terrorizing small children," he murmured. "Was yours a happy marriage?"

She slowed her mount, turning to look at him. "And which of your marriages did you prefer, Lord Rohan? Were they both equally satisfying to your carnal appetites?"

"And why should you care about my carnal appetites?"

A slight flush tinted her cheekbones. Rather nice ones, he thought absently, and they set off her intense blue eyes. "I don't. My point was that your questions were discourteously intimate."

"I've never been known for my courtesy," he said with simple truth. "My first wife, Annis, was the love of my life. She was strong-minded but passionate, and if she hadn't died in childbirth I imagine we'd still be very happy. My second wife, Lady Barbara, also died in childbirth, though in that case I doubt the child was mine. She was headstrong and sexually voracious, and she fed those appetites with rare conviction. I'd rather not be tied to marriage again—I find it smothering, but I suppose I must

Anne Stuart

eventually come up with an heir. Which is why, for a change, I'm looking for a docile young wife with no interest in anything other than pleasing me."

Melisande snorted inelegantly. "I'm certain you'll have your pick of them, my lord. I hope you don't grow tired of your eventual choice. Docility can be very wearing after a while."

"I'm surprised you even know the meaning of the word. Clearly it's something you've eschewed. And as for being bored, I will, of course, look elsewhere for stimulation."

He could almost hear her grind her teeth, and his mood lightened. Astonishing how entertaining it was to annoy his unwanted confederate.

"That's hardly surprising. Most men have mistresses. Unfortunately that means you're in search of two women, not one, and with your exacting standards that might be rather difficult. Particularly since I've removed a fair number of candidates for the second position."

"The sad truth about whores and Cyprians and demimondaines," Rohan began, "is that there are always more where they came from."

She kicked her horse, surging ahead, and he let her go for a moment. By the time he caught up with her she'd managed to get her temper under control, unfortunately. She looked at him.

"Lord Rohan," she said, her voice tight, "I am not in a good mood. I'm tired and bad-tempered and I don't feel like dealing with what passes for conversation with you. We'll make it through the day more successfully if we simply do not converse."

He managed to put a contrite expression on his face. "I beg your pardon, Lady Carstairs. I had no idea I'd managed to upset you."

"You haven't *managed to upset me,*" she snapped. She took a deep breath then. "Are we almost there?"

He pulled his horse to a stop, glancing around. They'd been following a rutted and overgrown road, the trees overhead forming a tunnel of leaves. There was a forlorn, neglected air to the place, and he knew they couldn't be far. "I think over the next rise," he said, no longer interested in baiting her. "I'm not certain—it's been twenty years since I've been here, but I have a fairly decent sense of direction. It certainly doesn't appear to have had recent visitors. Are you certain Elsmere said Kersley Hall?"

"Certain," she said, her voice clipped. The road took a sharp turn, heading up over a hill, and she reached the summit before he did. She stopped and waited for him, an odd expression on her face.

Kersley Hall, or what was left of it, lay spread out before them. It had burned most thoroughly, blackened spires reaching toward the sky, the stones scorched, the windows long gone. There was no roof left, and only the outbuildings remained, though they looked abandoned, as well.

"If the Heavenly Host were planning to disport themselves here then they're a hardier bunch than I imagine," Rohan said pensively.

"It looks so sad." His companion was no longer

paying attention to him. "It must have been here for centuries, and now everything's gone."

"Built at the end of the Tudors, I believe." Rohan nudged his horse forward. "I don't even remember who ended up inheriting the place. The family died out, and some poor relation ended up with it, but I recall now that it burned before he could take possession. Then he died as well, and God knows who owns it now. Clearly we've wasted our time."

"I don't know that." She was staring at it meditatively. "It would be a prime location for a secret society bent on evil deeds."

"Most of the members of the Heavenly Host have their own estates and all the privacy they might command. Why choose a ruined, abandoned estate where anyone might see them?" he countered.

"I don't imagine this place has many casual visitors. I would think the Heavenly Host could expect a great deal of privacy which they might not get at their own homes. There's not much to see here. It also has a convenient proximity to London, which would recommend itself to the members."

He didn't want to consider it but she made sense. "I suppose it's possible. According to my father they used to meet at house parties out in the countryside, though those sounded much more comfortable. If I had my choice between slogging out here on a day trip, reveling in massive debauchery, and then riding home, compared with a leisurely trip to someone's country estate and a comfortable room to recover from my excesses, I would most definitely choose the latter."

"How convenient that you come from a family of degenerates," his companion murmured. "But I still hold that the Heavenly Host has changed from a silly group of playacting gentry to an organization of dangerous deviants, and what was true in the past is no longer the case. In the past their crimes were simply against the laws of decency. Now they are breaking the law of the land. They would need to be far more circumspect."

"I bow to your superior knowledge of degeneracy," he said, stifling a yawn. They had started closer, and he could smell the scent of burned timbers on the air. The ruins had a sad, eerie air to them—at night it would appear almost haunted. The sun had come out at one point during the morning ride, but even with it bright overhead the place still depressed him. He pulled his horse to a stop, reaching out to catch the bridle of his companion's horse.

She was most definitely an excellent horsewoman. Her temper at having her mount controlled by another was understandable, and he'd done it to annoy her, but she didn't jerk her horse's head or do anything to break his hold and upset her mount. "If you want to stop you need only say something," she said, managing to be polite at what he suspected was great cost.

"I want to stop." He released her horse, then slid off his own, tossing the reins over a low-slung branch of an overhanging oak tree. "Why don't we have lunch before we explore the place? I find I'm in need of sustenance."

He moved to help her down, but she'd already managed to dismount on her own, no mean trick given that her mare was a good fifteen hands or more. He looked forward to helping her remount, and then he wanted to kick himself. He was like a school-boy looking for excuses to touch the object of his adolescent desire. If he wanted to touch Melisande Carstairs he'd damned well do so.

He slung the picnic hamper off his saddle, plus the woven coverlet Cook had provided as ground cover, and shoved them into her hand. "Here," he said un-necessarily. "I'm going for a short stroll."

She glared up at him. "And you expect me to ar-range things?"

"Your fault for not bringing a servant as chaper-one," he replied.

"If you felt your chaste reputation was in danger you should have said so at the outset of our journey."

"Would you have brought someone?"

"Of course not. But I would have enjoyed your discomfiture more."

He had to hide a smile. She was so deliciously argumentative. He had no choice but to accept the truth of her earlier observation. A docile wife was going to be a dead bore. Fortunately he planned to spend as little time with his as-yet-unknown bride as possible.

"I'll be back shortly," he said, strolling toward the ruins.

"Don't you dare start exploring without me!" she called after him.

He simply waved a dismissive hand and moved on.

It wasn't that he wished to annoy her. At least, that wasn't his main ambition. The wreckage of Kersley Hall might very well be dangerous, and he didn't fancy having to rescue her from some potential cave-in. A brief reconnoiter was called for, even if she'd most likely be furious with him for doing so. Which was more than acceptable for him.

By the time he strolled back toward their make-shift picnic spot he was feeling both annoyed and relieved. He had seen no sign of any presence in the area, neither nefarious nor innocent, and they'd obviously made the trip for naught. He had every intention of taunting her, but when he crested the hill he saw the picnic blanket stretched out on the lawn and a veritable feast laid out on it. Charity Carstairs lay sound asleep amid the food, the sun dancing through the leaves overhead and leaving a charming, shifting pattern on her body.

He froze, looking at her for a long, contemplative moment, unsure what he was feeling. He'd brushed those curves the night before, but hadn't had much time to explore. Her breasts were plump and pretty, and he wondered what they'd look like uncovered. Would her nipples be dark or pale? Would the hair between her legs be the same tawny gold? What kind of sounds would she make when she climaxed? Would she come silently, or would she scream?

He moved then, coming closer, and a wave of exhaustion rolled over him. Curse Brandon and his excesses. If it hadn't been for him, he would have had a decent night's sleep. If it hadn't been for him, he would never have gotten involved with Lady Carstairs.

Which, he thought after a moment, would have been a damned shame.

He sat down on the coverlet beside her, expecting her to wake and break the languorous spell that had covered him, but she slept on, her eyes closed, her breathing deep and regular. A wicked smile crossed his face, and on impulse he lay down beside her, almost touching her, turned on his side to watch her as she slept. He let his eyes run over her, feasting on her, devising a thousand plans to get her into his bed, all of which he regretfully abandoned. She might think herself a woman of the world but she was most definitely an innocent compared to the likes of him, and everything he'd done to her shocked her. Seducing her would be the first step on the road to perdition.

She smelled like roses. The sun painted soft freckles on her nose, and he wanted to touch them, see if they brushed off. She hadn't had them at the start of the day. Her maidservant was going to scold her quite fiercely. Assuming she even had such a thing.

He moved closer, brushing his face against her arm, breathing in her scent. Sun-warmed skin married with the roses and something indefinably female that stirred his senses. Danger, he reminded himself, his instincts well-honed. This was a very dangerous woman.

And then he fell asleep.

15

She dreamed she was in Thomas's arms once more, but instead of the gentle, almost tentative hold of his frail arms, this time his grip was stronger, more possessive, and the body he cradled her against was young and strong, freed of the weakness of age and illness. She burrowed closer with a happy sigh, reveling in the feel of him, the scent of him, like sunshine and raspberries. He caught her hand and moved it across his chest, down his flat stomach to that most essentially male part, and it was a hard ridge of flesh, surprising her. She tried to pull her hand away, but he simply caught it and brought it back again, and she let her fingers dance along that mysterious bulge, discovering it, listening to his sleepy groan in her ear.

She edged closer. She was warm, but she wanted to move closer still, to lie against him, have him wrap his arms around her. He smelled like spring and soft green grass, which was silly. Thomas hated the outdoors—it aggravated his gout. But this was Thomas transformed, young and strong and wonderful, and she buried her face against the sun-warmed wool of his jacket, closed her eyes, and drifted deeper into sleep.

He was there. He was the man she would have chosen, young and healthy, slightly bad tempered and strong-minded and protective. They would live forever, the two of them, and there would be babies and battles and laughter and tears. It wasn't too late after all. Thomas had defied time and fate and come back to her.

She felt the wetness of her tears on her cheeks, and his fingers brushed them away before sliding behind her neck and tilting her face up to meet his. She knew him by his kiss, soft and sweet and persuasive, but Thomas didn't like to kiss. Everything had changed, though, and she was dreaming, happy, feeling more alive than she'd ever felt before as she burrowed against him, his arms holding her close, and she slept, she slept.

She was cold. She was alone again. Thomas had left her, and the bed was hard beneath her, too hard, and someone was shaking her, hard. Her eyes flew open, she looked up into Viscount Rohan's cold face, cold eyes, and she knew.

"Wake up," he said in a rough voice. "You were dreaming."

She managed to scramble away from him, her brain still fogged from sleep. And then she realized it hadn't been Thomas at all, it had been Rohan who'd slept beside her. Rohan, not Thomas—who was dead, who wasn't coming back—and to her complete shame a harsh sob broke from her throat, followed by another.

It was nothing compared to the horror in his face at her tears. "For God's sake, Charity, it wasn't my fault," he snapped. "I was asleep, as well. You were the one who curled up beside me. I didn't know what I was doing." Another sob came from her chest, and he looked even more harassed. "I hardly meant to kiss you, but in truth you were climbing all over me, and I was three-quarters asleep myself."

Her stomach hurt, her chest ached, and she wrapped her arms around her body, trying to force the overwhelming sorrow back into the secret place where she kept it locked, but it was too strong. She swallowed, but looking at him made it even worse, because he wasn't Thomas, and because she wanted to kiss him, not Thomas, which was the final betrayal.

She'd almost managed to get it under control by biting down on her lower lip, when he ruined it all by saying, "It was nothing. It was just a kiss."

And the dam broke, and she howled, throwing her hands over her face, weeping into them helplessly as Thomas's elderly, dear, choleric face faded from her memory. She knew she should stop, calm herself, but the release of tears was a blessing. She couldn't remember how long it had been since she cried, but letting go felt good, and too bad if Rohan felt uncomfortable. She needed this.

She drew her knees up and pressed her face

against them, sobbing and gasping, unable to calm herself. And then she looked up at Rohan's horrified face, and managed what was no doubt a ghastly smile. "It's...not you," she managed to choke out between sobs and struggles for breath. "It's Thomas."

"Your husband?" he said, clearly confused. "Why are you crying about him?"

"I miss him!" she wailed.

He stayed perfectly still, and she stopped thinking about him, concentrating on her own misery. Through her blinding tears she could see the quizzical expression on his face, but she simply turned away, trying to burrow into her grief.

His hands startled her, but she was past fighting. He pulled her into his arms, but there was nothing lascivious about it. He simply folded her against him, his strong arms wrapped around her, protecting her as she had dreamed, and his heart beat strongly against hers as he tucked her head against his shoulder and pulled her onto his lap.

She should have struggled. Her tears should have dried up in outrage and she should have managed to break free from him, at least a small shred of her dignity intact. But she was lost, sobbing in his arms, sobbing for her husband, her dear friend who had unexpectedly become everything to her and then left her.

Rohan didn't say a word. No soothing noises, no "there theres." Just voiceless comfort as she finally released the last of the sorrow she'd kept bound up for so long.

He seemed to sense when she was ready to move away. All she had to do was tense her muscles and his arms loosened, and she knew he would release her as soon as she made a move to climb off his lap. Which she certainly should do, but instead she lifted her tearstained face to look at him.

There was no triumph in his eyes, no air of superiority. He simply looked at her, still and silent, and she suddenly remembered the kiss in her dream, a kiss that had come from him after all, not Thomas. The feel of male arousal against her hand. Again, from him.

But she'd been asleep. There was no need to acknowledge it. As far as he knew she didn't remember, and she intended to keep it that way. And try not to remember the hard shape of him beneath his breeches.

"You tell anyone that I cried, and I'll cut your liver out."

"Do you even know where a human liver resides?" His voice was light, distant, the usual tone he used with her. Thank God.

"Yes," she said, and punched him in it.

She slid off his lap as he groaned, clutching his side. "You should have seen that coming," she said, much cheered. "Are you ready for lunch?"

He scowled at her. "I may have just lost my appetite."

"You'll regain it. It appears you have a very fine chef. Though if you're as tired as I was I might suggest you avoid the wine."

"I'm quite well rested. You looked so peaceful lying there on the blanket that I gave in to temptation and napped myself, even though you kept encroaching on my side of the blanket. Has anyone ever told you that you're quite a restless sleeper?"

"I've never slept with anyone." She could have bit her tongue when the words were out, and she quickly reached for a sandwich.

"You surprise me. Then again, you had no siblings to share a bed with. I may assume you and Sir Thomas had separate beds?"

"This is hardly any of your business."

"And that your pathetic excuse for a lover didn't spend the night when you succumbed to his blandishments?"

She looked at him. She was feeling reckless, emotional, out of sorts, and she was tired of his constant hints. "I found the experience so unpleasant with Wilfred that I kicked him out lest he want to repeat the whole thing." She shuddered. "I was expecting someone younger and healthier than Sir Thomas would convince me that lovemaking was worth the trouble. It isn't. It's nasty and ugly and dirty."

He stared at her for a long moment. And then he spoke. "Dear girl," he said softly, "don't you know that any reasonable man would take that as a challenge?"

She jerked her head up to look at him, into those very dark green eyes. "Don't be absurd. Why would anyone bother when there are so many willing females around? I'm too much trouble. And besides, I don't consider you a reasonable man."

His smile was fleeting. "I'm an eminently reasonable man." And before she realized what he was doing she was back in his arms and he was kissing her, openmouthed and hot and wet, no teasing approach, just raw, sexual demand that should have filled her with disgust and dismay.

Instead her stomach tightened, her heart raced, and the place between her legs grew hot and tingling. For some reason she put her arms around him, and she'd automatically closed her eyes, reveling in the unwanted sensation of his kiss, the hard pressure of his mouth against hers.

At her compliance the kiss changed, no longer a fierce demand, now a teasing caress, a slow, languorous series of kisses as he caught her lower lip between his teeth, using his tongue, his lips, everything to bring her closer and closer to complete surrender. She was out of breath, her heart pounding so hard it was almost painful, and when he lifted his head she reached up and pulled him back to her, returning his kiss with all her inexpert passion.

He was teaching her, she realized dizzily. Demonstrating what to do with his tongue, leading her, showing her what pressure, what gentleness, could do. He lured her tongue into a sweet dance, until she could no more resist him than she could have flown. When he finally set her away from him she almost cried out and reached for him again, but something gave her the strength to put her hands in her lap, clenching them. She'd liked it. No, she'd more than liked it. She wanted more, and yet his kiss was like poison to her. It could lead to things, to feelings that could destroy her utterly.

"So I can respond to a kiss, Rohan," she said, using his name in a deliberately informal manner. "I'm human, you know. And you kiss very, very well. Not that I'm a connoisseur, of course, but I expect you're one of the best kissers around. I should take a survey from my girls, see what they think." Her voice was cool, dismissive.

His eyes crinkled as he smiled. "Now you've put me in my place. Sweet Charity. You don't need to discuss me with your gaggle. I'll tell you anything you want."

"Doves don't come in gaggles."

"Yours do. And I think you're a very dangerous woman, Lady Carstairs." He reached for a sandwich himself, and she had to admire his tanned, graceful hand against the white of the bread.

"You do? How lovely!" She beamed at him. "What else can I do to terrify you?"

"You don't really expect me to tell you, do you?" He glanced at the ruins. "I've already taken a quick look around the house. There's no sign that anyone's been there, and I don't think the footing is safe. I expect I've seen enough. We should probably go back once we finish eating."

"Don't be absurd. We came this far for a purpose, one I intend to fulfill. You can't fob me off with stories about uneven footing. You'll find I'm hardier than most women of your acquaintance."

"I expect you are…" he murmured. "Very well. But stay behind me and walk only where I walk."

"Of course," she said.

"You're lying, aren't you?"

"Of course," she said again. "You may follow me."

He ran a hand through his hair. It was dark, long and curling slightly, and she wondered what it felt like. It looked soft, like the fur on a wolf cub. "You really are driving me mad," he said.

She smiled sweetly, getting to her feet. "Then I've succeeded in my goal. Why don't you clean up the mess while I go look around the ruins? It's only fair since I set the food out in the first place."

He jumped to his feet, going after her. "The mess will wait." He took her arm in what might have seemed a polite social gesture, if it weren't for the hard, possessive grip of his hand. And they started toward the towering spikes of the ruined building.

He should have been in a foul mood, Benedick thought, trying to hide his smile. After all, she'd insulted him, lured him, challenged him and even threatened him. She'd wept all over him, and he despised tears. He considered them a feminine weakness used to manipulate men into doing what the female in question wanted.

He couldn't really blame Melisande, though. She seemed to want nothing but her bad-tempered husband back again, astonishing as that notion seemed.

She also seemed to believe she really wasn't interested in the sins of the flesh, even if her body rose to his every time he touched her.

He had no problem with allowing her to keep her delusions. She was safer believing she had an intrinsically cold nature, even if she burned hot against him. As long as she was convinced that celibacy was, to paraphrase the Shakespeare his mother was so addicted to, "a non-consummation devoutly to be wish'd," then he had a much greater chance of being able to keep his hands off her. He had absolutely no idea why he found her so tempting, but the unfortunate truth was that he did. And he needed to get her back to London and to her gaggle of soiled doves so he wouldn't be able to give in.

She'd already started off, without her bonnet, which she'd discarded at some point, and the sun had kissed her cheeks with a soft blush. He scrambled to his feet and followed after her. Damnable woman.

Whether she liked it or not he took her arm when he caught up with her, but to his surprise she didn't yank away. It was rough going over the scattered rubble, and they picked their way carefully.

There wasn't enough left of Kersley Hall to provide shelter for a family of mice. The fire had torn through the old place, devouring everything not made of stone, leaving only the outer walls and chimneys in place. She stopped in the cavernous front doorway, staring into the rubble beyond, and shook her head. "I don't think anyone has been in here since the fire," she said.

"I agree. Now can we…"

"What is that building?" She pointed to a neat cottage set off away from the house. The roof was partly burned, but most of it was in solid shape, and curtains were drawn across the deep-set windows.

"I have no idea. These outlying cottages can be used for any number of things. It might house a gatekeeper, or the head gardener, possibly the gamekeeper. It's possible it might serve as a dairy or a laundry, though I would think there would be more chimneys. Perhaps it was simply a home for the housekeeper, though most often they prefer to live in the main house. If you're thinking the Heavenly Host meets in such humble surroundings, you're mistaken. For one thing, there would scarcely be enough room for a full-blown orgy in such a small place. For another, the Host only likes to pretend to endure privation. In truth they like warm bedchambers, plenty of the best wine and comfort above all else. They would hardly sink to the level of a housekeeper's cottage."

"Indulge me," she said and started toward it.

He muttered a curse under his breath and started after her. "Wait." An odd feeling was coming over him. She had already reached for the doorknob of the derelict building, and he caught up with her, catching her arm roughly. "Let me go first."

No sooner were the words out of his mouth when the ground beneath them gave way. He saw Melisande sink, and he flung out his arms to grab her, going down with her, deep, deep into the darkness, her body held tightly against his.

16

Benedick managed to turn them as they tumbled, so that he landed beneath her, his body protecting hers from the brunt of the fall. He let out an inelegant "oof" as he landed, the combination of the fall and her body bouncing on top of his knocking the wind out of him. He struggled for a moment, still holding her, and then it came back with a whoosh of relief, and he could breathe again. She didn't appear to be in any hurry to let go of him. She wasn't moving, clinging tightly, and he had the sudden fear that she might be hurt. He moved his hands, touching her carefully, looking for broken bones, when she rolled off him, slapping his hands away.

He sat up, wincing slightly. "Melisande, are you all right?" he asked urgently.

There was dust and dirt in the air, and she coughed. "I seem to be," she said finally. "What happened?"

He looked around him, slowly, taking it all in.

"I believe we may have found where the Heavenly Host meets."

"In a cellar?"

"Look around you. We're not in a cellar. We're in the middle of a tunnel, with torches and crude drawings on the walls. Not the kind of thing they use for mines. The combination of the fire and the elements must have weakened the ground overhead, enough so that our combined weight collapsed it." He began to brush the dirt and dust from his abused coat, then realized it was a lost cause. Richmond would kill him.

He saw her shiver. "I don't actually like enclosed places," she said in a small voice.

He'd gotten to his feet, shaking himself slightly, but he paused, looking down at her. He'd known people to became half-mad with fear when forced to be in a confined area, and the memory wasn't a happy one. "Exactly how much do you dislike enclosed places?" he inquired politely. "Do they make you uncomfortable, or do you curl up in a ball and start screaming?"

She looked at him indignantly, and he breathed an inner sigh of relief. "Do I strike you as the type who would scream?"

I could make you scream, my girl, he thought. *I could make you scream and weep with pleasure.*

"No, I suppose not," he drawled imperturbably. "Then you'll simply have to bear it until we find our way out of here." He held out a hand to her. There was a streak of dirt across her cheekbone, her tawny hair was halfway down her shoulders and there was a delicious rent in the side of her riding habit. Apart from that she appeared relatively unscathed, thank God.

She considered him for a moment, considered his proffered hand, and then, reluctantly, put her hand in his and let him pull her to her feet.

Wherein she immediately let out a shriek of pain and began to buckle, but he caught her before she could fall, holding her against him, too close, and they were frozen for a moment.

She was looking up at him, all magnificent blue eyes and soft mouth trying to hide the pain she was clearly feeling, and he had the sudden absurd urge to shelter her from any danger or discomfort, to fight dragons for her. He ignored it and went for deliberately provocative. "Apparently you do scream."

She was white with pain and dust from the chalk caves. "My ankle," she said with a tight voice. "I must have twisted it when we fell."

He glanced upward. The light was unlikely to be much better anywhere in the tunnels—at least here they had the filtered sunlight beaming in from overhead. He levered her back down on the hard ground, knelt at her feet and flipped up the hem of her riding habit.

She flipped it back, kicking at him with what must be the undamaged foot. "What do you think you're doing?"

"Checking for damage. I assure you I'm quite capable. I had to patch up my brothers and sister any number of times before our parents discovered what kind of trouble we were getting ourselves into. We had a tendency to climb cliffs and play pirate. I can at least ascertain if your ankle is broken."

"And what good would that do? If it's broken it's broken."

"If it's broken the sooner you get it bound and splinted the less likely you are to have permanent damage. How would you feel if you could never dance again?"

A moment's consternation showed on her face, then quickly disappeared. "There are certainly worse catastrophes in a woman's life," she said stiffly. "I've never been much for dancing.

"I remember. You did learn quite quickly, though, once you relaxed."

"It hardly matters when you think about the women I care for…"

So tiresome. "How would you feel if you couldn't storm around saving your wounded doves? A crippled ankle could effectively damage your charitable activities."

And it was that easy. "All right. *That* makes a certain amount of sense."

"If it's broken, I'll get you to the nearest doctor. There has to be one in the nearest town, and your ankle can be properly dealt with. If it's simply a sprain we can ride back and you can summon your own doctor. Surely that sounds reasonable?"

"It does." She looked at him from beneath her furrowed brow. "But I don't trust you."

"Very wise," he said. While they spoke he'd managed to get his hands beneath her skirt and clasped around her riding boot. At that moment he yanked, hard, and it came off, and she let out another shriek of pain, this one louder than the first.

He hadn't wanted to hurt her, a fact he viewed with surprise. In matters like these, one usually did what one had to do and didn't stop to consider how much it hurt. Charity Carstairs had an unfortunate effect on him.

She'd fallen back on her elbows, pale and sweating. "You could have warned me!"

"That would have made it worse."

"Impossible." Her foot jerked as he put his hands on it, gently, his fingers probing for damage. It was a nice foot, narrow, with surprisingly pretty toes. He'd never found feet particularly enticing, but hers were another matter. Then again, he was coming to the unfortunate conclusion that he found almost everything about her enticing.

"All right," he said, keeping his voice impersonal, "this is going to hurt."

She managed well enough as he poked and prodded, only muffled groans letting him know when he'd reached a particularly tender spot. He began to slide his hands up her shapely calf, and she jerked, glaring at him. "You don't need to go any higher."

He ignored her protest. "The pain might come from your knee, sweet Charity. I need to rule that out."

It was a lovely knee. He could just imagine pulling them around his hips. And he needed to stop thinking about bedding her and concentrate on the dilemma at hand, no matter how preferable the former was. Her ankle was already beginning to swell, and there was no way he'd be able to replace her boot. Which meant he'd have to carry her, which he didn't mind but she would doubtless find maddening. He smiled.

"Not broken," he said. "I can't be completely sure, but I expect it's nothing more than a sprain. You need to get it elevated, and iced, if possible."

"I can do neither at the moment," she said reasonably, sitting up. "Hand me my boot so I can put it back on."

He shook his head. "I'm afraid not, my lady. *Regardez là*."

She glanced down at her swelling ankle and cursed most impressively beneath her breath. So she'd learned at least one useful thing from her gaggle. "How am I supposed to walk with only one boot?" she said with some asperity.

"You aren't." He rose, bent down and scooped her up effortlessly. She was fairly light, and he was strong, used to controlling difficult horses. He could handle her with ease.

"I don't like this," she said in a warning voice, her usual serenity deserting her. A good thing, that. Her usual calm infuriated him, when he wanted to see her as rattled as she made him feel.

"I know you don't," he said with great good cheer. "One of the few blessings of this afternoon."

He expected that would make her ire rise even higher, but to his astonishment she laughed. "You," she began, "are a very bad man. Though I don't know why that should surprise me—you're one of the wicked House of Rohan, are you not? I imagine your family's perfidy predates even the Heavenly Host."

"Most assuredly. We're devotedly incorrigible. Which direction would you prefer—right or left?"

She put her arms around his neck. It was a simple gesture—clearly this enterprise would go a lot better if she held on. For some reason, though, it touched him. It was a gesture of trust, of acceptance, whether she knew it or not. She glanced in both directions. "Let's head to the right," she said at last.

"Left it is," he replied. And started off.

She should be a great deal more upset, Melisande thought as she clung to Viscount Rohan's strong neck. Her ankle throbbed like the very devil, she'd lost her boot somewhere and she was being carted around by her arch-enemy as if she were nothing more than a sack of potatoes.

They were in the middle of nowhere, stuck inside a tunnel with no discernible way out, and he'd called her "Melisande." He probably didn't even realize that he had. It had come out spur of the moment, when they'd tumbled down into this subterranean passageway, which made it all the more interesting. When he wasn't taunting and teasing her, he thought of her as Melisande?

He'd started down one corridor, where they'd swiftly been enveloped in first shadows and then darkness as he'd turned a corner. There was no artificial light down there at the moment, though she could see unlit torches set into the walls as they passed, and scorch marks on the white cave walls. He carried her easily enough, as if she weighed no more than a feather, which she knew was a far cry from the truth. She was, admittedly, curvaceous, even bordering on plump. Carting her around would be a strain on a lesser man. Rohan wasn't even breathing heavily.

It was getting darker. She wanted to cling more tightly to Rohan's strong body, but she resisted the need. Really, she had no choice but to let him carry her, given the condition of her ankle, but there was no excuse for cuddling. "Are you certain we're going in the right direction?"

He let out an irritated growl. "I'm not certain of anything. I was going on instinct."

"Instinct being that you do the opposite of what I suggest?"

It was too dark to see his expression, but she knew he would be amused. "Indeed. I wonder…" His voice trailed off as he came to an abrupt halt.

"You wonder?" she prompted, only to be dropped from his arms summarily, though he still supported her, and a hand came over her mouth, silencing her.

And then she heard it. Voices arguing, and a growing pool of light heading in their direction.

He moved, fast, as the light came around a bend in the tunnels, and she felt herself being pushed into a dark hole, onto a padded surface, with his hard, heavy body on top of hers, his hand still covering her mouth. "Don't say a word," he breathed in her ear.

She nodded, or tried to, though his imprisoning hand made it difficult, and he moved it away, keeping perfectly still in the darkness.

She could see light in the tunnel beyond, and the voices were clearer now. "Did you see someone?" The voice sounded vaguely familiar. A man, in his middle years, clearly of the ton.

"Don't be ridiculous." The next voice was younger, slightly petulant, and that of a stranger. "We didn't see any sign of horses near the ruins, did we? Who else would be down here? We came in the only entrance and it was locked when we got here."

"I thought I saw someone moving. Over by one of the training rooms." The voice and the light came closer, and Rohan pushed her back into the corner of the alcove with his body, pressing her face against his shoulder. He stayed very still, but Melisande could sense the light beyond him, and panic swelled inside her. They'd been discovered.

Apparently not. "It's black as pitch in there," the older man said. "Nothing but bedding and rags."

"You could always walk in and look," the younger voice taunted him. "I promise not to lock you in."

The light moved away, and Melisande felt relief flood her body. "Do you seriously think I'd be fool enough to trust you, Pennington? Your sense of humor has always been a bit outré."

"Coward."

"I could call you out for that."

"You could. But we have better ways of settling our differences, do we not?" The man called Pennington had a smooth voice, but there was a chill to it.

The other man chuckled, though. "True enough. There are few things more enjoyable than watching two whores trying to cripple each other."

Melisande jerked, sickened, but Rohan simply pressed harder, keeping her still, his hand over her mouth to silence her. She closed her eyes, forcing her body to relax. Much as she wanted to leap up and start beating at the degenerates in the room beyond, she wouldn't get very far with a sprained ankle and no stout stick to bash them with. She would have to find other ways to stop them.

She could feel him pressing against her, their bodies almost plastered together. Her breasts felt strange up against his chest. Sensitive, almost abraded, and tingling. His legs were between hers, she realized, holding her down, and his hips were cradled against her.

He was getting hard, she realized. She thought about it, concentrating on the sensation, and realized he was becoming noticeably more aroused, the longer he stayed pressed against her. And yet he couldn't very well move, not without drawing attention to their hiding place.

So she couldn't shove him away, or slap him, or do any of the dozen or so things she could think of to halt the direction in which his body and her mind were going. Because her mind was most definitely going there, whether she wanted it to or not.

He was lean and strong, delightfully so. She'd never thought whether there was one particular physical form she preferred—she'd done her best to concentrate on the person rather than their appearance. But in truth she liked being around tall men, and she liked strength, and she liked long, lean, elegant bodies. She liked the way Benedick Rohan looked, and felt, and, yes, tasted, and she could feel a slow heat begin to build between her legs.

It was all wrong. They were in danger, and those two men, members of the foul Heavenly Host, could walk in on them at any moment. She should be concentrating on anger and escape. Not on the feel of him, the hardness between his legs pressed against the softness between hers.

And then, to her shock, he bumped against her. Just a tiny little bounce almost, and her body tightened with surprise.

He did it again, and she realized it was deliberate. She was pressed up tight against him, and he was holding her head against his shoulder, her face hidden, and his other arm was tight around her waist, imprisoning her there. She knew she should try to get her hands up between them, to push him away, but there was simply no room.

He bumped again, and she could feel her nipples

harden almost painfully. She wanted him closer still, she realized, moving her legs so he could settle more fully against her. With the next jerk against her she pressed her face harder against his shoulder, to stifle her instinctive cry.

She was burning up. Her breasts, her heart, between her legs, everything was on fire, and she waited for the pulse of him against her welcoming heat once more.

But Rohan didn't move. The voices had drifted away, though she could still hear them, and the light was faintly visible when she lifted her head from his shoulder. He moved his head, just a bit, and she tried to look up into his face. She could just see his eyes, and they gleamed as they looked down into hers.

She shifted beneath him, restless, longing, half hoping he'd move away from her, half hoping… She couldn't think clearly. She didn't know what she wanted.

And yet Rohan asked her the one thing she couldn't answer. "What do you want, sweet Charity?" It was just a taunting breath of sound, and no one outside of their tiny cave would hear it.

She turned her face away from him, staring at the wall, trying to control her wayward body, envisioning it packed in ice, frozen. But the ice melted against him, and her body was soft and welcoming.

"What do you want?" he persisted, his breath hot against her ear, and his teeth closed lightly over the lobe, and she wanted to moan in pleasure. "What… do…you…want?"

She gave in. She had reached the end of her ability to fight him. "More," she whispered.

She knew he smiled in triumph. She knew she didn't care. He pushed up against her, slowly this time, grinding against her, and she lost her breath as sensation danced through her. It was as if they were having sex, she thought dizzily, except that instead of inside her he was outside, rubbing against her with the hard ridge of his erection, a pressure that was making her tremble and dampen in the place where he pressed, and she felt a soft little explosion course through her, leaving her shocked, astonished, as she fell back on the cushioned ground beneath her.

She tried to speak, to say something airy and dismissing, but for the moment she was unable to make a sound. She felt strange, unsettled, anxious, and she knew she should be angry at what he'd done to her, except that she'd asked for more, hadn't she?

She tried to relax, but her legs were restless, entwined with his. The voices had faded, though there was still just the faintest light emanating from the tunnel outside their pillowed cave. "We…uh…we should go," she finally managed to say. She could pretend that unexpected response had never happened. After all, how was he to know?

"Not yet." His voice was against her ear, tickling her, arousing her. Arousing her? Had she gone mad? "You're not finished."

"Not finished? What…?" Just as her voice rose slightly, he clamped his hand over her mouth again. He'd moved, his body lying partly across hers, pinning her there, and she felt his hand on her skirt. Pulling it upward, slowly, his warm, hard hand beneath it, and for a moment she was too shocked to protest.

Then she tried to push at him, but he simply caught her hands in his arms and held them. "Don't make a sound," he whispered. "Not if you want to rescue your doves. This won't take long."

"What won't?" she whispered, but then she felt his hand on her thigh, long fingers stroking, caressing, moving upward beneath her loose cotton drawers till he reached the damp, most secret part of her. Vagina, she told herself sternly, remembering Emma's lessons. Vulva. Clitor...

She slammed her face against his shoulder to muffle her reaction when he touched her, his fingertips sure and practiced. And then his hand cupped her, holding her still by that simple expedient, and he released her wrists. A moment later she felt something thrust in her hands, a soft cloth. "Stuff my handkerchief in your mouth," he suggested, a note of laughter in his voice. "That will drown out any noise you might make."

"I don't want this," she whispered.

One of his fingers had begun to move, lightly stroking, and that anxious, aching feeling was back, tenfold. "Are you certain?" He was somehow able to speak with only the breath of a sound coming out. His hand slid down farther, and she felt one of his fingers slide inside her, and her hips jerked at the sudden invasion. He moved his mouth to hers, running his tongue along her trembling lower lip. "Do you really want me to stop?"

Of course she did. This was madness; this was pleasure that was oddly painful. She needed him to leave her, she needed…

Her body arched up, almost of its own volition, and without thinking she shoved the cloth into her mouth, smothering her instinctive cry. She felt his laughter against her cheek. "That's right, my precious. Charity begins at home." And he slid two fingers inside her, and the slippery dampness would have embarrassed her but she was well past that point.

She could no longer think about how he was causing such sensations to rocket through her body. His fingers thrust inside her, his thumb rubbed against that most sensitive part of her, and she wanted to yank the cloth out of her mouth, to beg him to stop. It was too much, too powerful, she couldn't stand it, she wanted…

And then all conscious thought vanished in a white haze as her body arched, rigid, as thousands upon thousands of tiny pinpricks shot through her, and she lost herself, the pleasure-pain exploding into a rich darkness she never wanted to leave. It was glorious. It was heaven.

It was disaster.

She came down slowly, brought back to safety with his gentling strokes, and she realized that despite the cloth she'd used she'd managed to bite her lip. She pulled the cloth from her mouth and hid her face from him, pressing it against his shoulder even though it was too dark to see. He was going to say something horrible, she just knew it. He was going to mock her pathetic reaction to his practiced touch, he was going to make her feel…

"Lovely," he whispered against her ear, smoothing her tangled hair. "Perfectly lovely."

And she wanted to weep.

17

She lay in his arms, trembling like a virgin, and he tried to stifle his guilt. In truth, she hadn't said no. She'd even asked for more, and there was no way he was going to stop with just that small climax. Because he was fairly certain that in some ways Melisande Carstairs was a virgin. It seemed she'd never felt any pleasure at all in bed, much less the most exquisite pleasure of what the French called *le petit mort*. The little death.

Right now he would have surrendered himself to that little death quite happily, but there was a time and place for everything, and this wasn't the place. He smoothed her skirts back down as he held her, breathing in the sweet scent of her, flowers and feminine arousal, and he wondered how his life had gotten so complicated. He'd come to London to find a wife and to have sex, and so far he'd failed at the first and not done terribly well at the second. No one seemed to interest him. Except for the enigma that was Charity Carstairs.

Just as well he'd changed his mind about Miss Pennington. That had been her brother out there in the corridor, talking with Lord Petersham, and he already had one brother entangled in the Heavenly Host. He didn't want to rescue two.

Slowly, slowly, her trembling had stopped. Her face was still pressed against his shoulder, hiding from him, hiding from herself, but her hands had released their bruising hold on his arms and fallen back. He wondered if she'd marked him. He expected her hands would ache later on. She'd realize why and she'd remember, and she'd presumably feel angry and shamed and ridiculous. But her body would remember and warm at the thought.

Jesus, he needed to start thinking of other things—and right now—or he was going to flip her skirts back up and take her there and then. He had no doubt he could persuade her. She was still in that slightly dazed, postorgasmic trance, but before long strength would return to her limbs and she'd be ready to slap him again. He was already going to have a difficult time dealing with her after this delicious moment of intimacy. If he actually tupped her she'd probably come after him and shoot him.

He slowly released her, setting her back against the corner of the little cave. He knew what it was for, and he hoped she wouldn't notice the restraints that lay about the place. He wanted her to think of the room fondly.

"I'll make certain they're gone," he whispered against her ear.

She nodded, and closed her eyes, and he wanted to kiss her eyelids. But she was already withdrawing, and if he tried she'd probably clout him.

There was no sign of the two men, though they'd left torches burning, so presumably they were coming back. He wondered if they'd found the cave-in yet. Would they come running back here once they found it, or would they stay to investigate? Did he have time to get Melisande out of this place before they returned?

What was the worst that could happen? He could always pretend someone had told him how to get here, and he'd been enjoying Lady Carstairs. What would they do, report him for trespassing?

But it would destroy any advantage they'd gained. He'd considered trying to persuade them to let him join, but he had no idea whom to approach, and he suspected he'd be blackballed. He'd never had much of a reputation for unbridled lechery—he found he preferred one partner at a time, and that should be a willing female. Not what the Heavenly Host seemed interested in nowadays.

No, his best bet was to get Melisande out of there before they were found out, and the longer he hesitated the less likely he was to succeed.

He ducked back into the cave. She was sitting up, and she'd made an effort to tidy her hair. "Time to go," he said, and scooped her up.

"I can…"

"No, you can't," he interrupted her ruthlessly. "If you try to walk it will take us that much longer. Trust me."

Her mirthless snort was answer enough.

The men left torches burning the way they'd come, and he followed the light, coming out into a large underground room that led off to an absolute rabbit's warren of tunnels. Fortunately light only came from one, and he followed it, moving swiftly.

The sight of the steps leading upward was the best thing he'd seen in weeks. He took them two at a time, careful not to jar the woman in his arms, and then they were out in the late-afternoon sunshine again, at the far end of the ruins.

He cast a surreptitious glance down at her. Her eyes were closed, her face calm and slightly averted. So she was going to ignore what happened in the so-called "training room." So be it. He wasn't going to bring it up—it was up to her if she wanted to discuss it, and if she didn't, so much the better. Women had a tendency to put too much importance on sex, and this had hardly been sex. Just a little treat for his partner in crime, to prove that she wasn't the cold creature she thought she was. Harmless enough.

It took him a while to reach their tethered horses. The picnic was still spread out on the coverlet, and he simply wrapped it all up and dumped it in the basket, ignoring Melisande's squeak of protest from the rock where he'd set her. Her ankle was swollen to twice its normal size, and he wondered if he'd been wrong and she'd actually broken it. It would be hard to tell beneath all the swelling—he needed to get her home so she could elevate it.

"You'll ride in front of me and we'll bring your horse behind us," he said, coming for her.

"I most certainly will not. I'm perfectly capable of riding." She didn't meet his gaze, and it both amused and annoyed him. Then again, he didn't want to discuss it, either, did he?

"I doubt it. It's your right foot. How are you going to guide your horse?"

"I can manage. If you'll help me mount."

He sighed, reaching for her and carrying her across the clearing. He picked her up and placed her in the saddle, then vaulted onto his own horse, taking the reins in his hand. "Let's go," he said in a bland voice, and waited, letting her go first down the overgrown road that had first brought them there.

She made it about ten feet, then shrieked with pain as she tried to use her foot. He moved to catch up with her, all smug complacency.

There were tears in her eyes and pure irritation in her mouth. "You're right," she said briefly.

"I always am," he said in a silky voice. He reached out for her, waiting to see if she'd cross the distance and come into his arms.

Clearly she thought about it for a minute. And then she held out her arms and he caught her, pulling her off her mount's broad back and onto his. He settled her back against him, her skirt covering her legs with as much decency as he could muster.

"Don't talk," she said tersely. "Just ride."

You mean you don't want to discuss the pleasure I just gave you in the Heavenly Host's depraved caverns? You don't want to acknowledge that there's a bone-shaking attraction between us, and sooner or later we're going to do something about it, even if neither you nor I want it?

But he could give her her wish. He rode at a steady pace, trying to avoid jarring her ankle too much. She had it modestly tucked under the hem of her habit, but that was doubtless making it even more painful, and he wished there was something he could do. Teasing her would take her mind off the pain, but he suspected she'd rather have the pain.

She tried to sit in front of him without touching him, but he knew the effort must be costing her dearly, and there was a limit to how much he'd allow her to hurt herself. He hauled her back against him, clasping one arm around her waist in an unbreakable hold. "Relax," he said in a cool voice. "I'm hardly going to molest you on the King's highway, and you're going to fall apart if you keep clenching your muscles like that. As soon as we come to a tavern we'll stop and I'll send for a carriage."

"No," she said. "Just take me home."

He didn't bother to point out that they were most likely already an on-dit, having been seen together on at least two occasions. If they arrived back in town with her unceremoniously cradled in his lap the gossips were going to go wild with conjecture. He considered whether it might hurt her silly charities. If so he'd insist they stop—he wasn't going to be responsible for taking her raison d'être away from her, even if he thought it was a lost cause.

But people were more likely to see Charity Carstairs as human, with all humanity's frailties, and they would be more sympathetic to her efforts. At least, he hoped so. Because truth be told, he liked riding with her bum up against him, his arms under her luscious breasts. He liked the fact that the gossips were going to link her with him, inextricably, so that she couldn't look elsewhere.

Of course, that would affect him, as well. If the ton was certain he was having an affaire with Sweet Charity then he might have difficulty forging an alliance with an eligible young female. But society was a great deal more liberal when it came to men's foibles, and he didn't think a mistaken rumor would interfere with his plans.

Even if the rumor ended up being true.

He wanted her in bed. Quite badly. It could be as simple as proximity, and the erotic atmosphere of the caves. Indeed, as a man he tended to find caves automatically sexual, and it was no wonder he'd reacted, particularly when he'd been rubbing up against her in the tiny room.

Once he was free of her, back in his own house, he could turn his attention to more congenial company. Despite Melisande's best efforts there were still a great many beautiful and willing Cyprians available, and he would have no trouble filling his bed tonight.

But he didn't need to think about that with Lady

Carstairs cradled against his cock. She'd already become too closely acquainted, first, in her sleep, when she'd unknowingly caressed him, and then later when they were hiding in the cave and he couldn't help his response.

But he was going to think about cold rain and war and piglets and anything else that could get his mind off sex.

He took a circuitous route back to her house on King Street. The likelihood of avoiding being seen by at least one nosy person was not good, but at least they wouldn't have to make conversation with anyone. By the time they arrived at the Dovecote it was late, and clearly her gaggle had been watching for her. To his horror, they all came flooding out her front door, some twenty strong.

He slid down from the saddle, then reached up for Melisande. "Someone take the damned horses," he said, and carried her up the stairs, hoping one of the women knew enough about horseflesh to deal with them. The door was still open and the woman he had once known as Emma Cadbury, owner of one of the finest brothels in town, came rushing toward them, her face free of paint, her hair and clothes plain, her beautiful face creased with worry.

"What happened?" she demanded breathlessly.

"I fell," Melisande spoke up for the first time.

"Where's her bedroom?"

"You're not taking me to my bedroom!"

"Yes, I am. And have someone call for a doctor. I don't think she's broken her ankle but I could be

wrong. She'll definitely need it elevated and ban-
daged," he said, overriding her objection.

"I can elevate it downstairs!" she shot back.

Mrs. Cadbury wasn't the kind of woman who was
easily intimidated, but he was a man who knew how
to get his own way. He looked at Emma Cadbury.

"Her bedroom is on the second floor," she said
after a moment. "First doorway on the right. I'll send
someone for a doctor."

"Traitor," Melisande said bitterly as Benedick
started up the stairs.

He ignored her. A couple of the younger girls
met him at the top of the stairs, rushing ahead to
open the door for him. Melisande was fuming now,
rigid and silent and outraged, and he wondered what
kind of tongue-lashing she was dying to deliver. And
whether she'd let loose if her doves were around.

He glanced around the room in surprise. It was
utilitarian but a far cry from the kind of place a
wealthy widow like Lady Carstairs should live in.
No chaise, so he set her down on the plain bed, letting his hand caress her bum as he withdrew it, his
face blandly innocent. He took a pillow from the top
of the bed, lifted her leg and placed it on the pillow
with as much care as he could manage. Even that
much of a touch left her white with pain.

"Has someone gone for that damned doctor?" he
snarled over his shoulder.

"Of course, your lordship," Emma Cadbury said
in a cool voice, coming into the room. "I expect he'll
be here shortly. You needn't trouble yourself further."

He glanced at her. "Mrs. Cadbury, it's very difficult to get rid of me when I'm not ready to go. I don't take hints very well. I intend to stay until the doctor has seen her. After all, Lady Carstairs was in my company when she was injured and I count it as simply my responsibility to ensure she's all right."

"I *absolve* you of your responsibility," Melisande snapped, her temper finally shattered. *"Go away, please."*

He turned back to her. "Don't waste your breath, sweetheart. I'm not leaving." And in order to demonstrate, he took a seat on the bed beside her.

"Your lordship!" Mrs. Cadbury sounded scandalized. And faintly amused, which surprised him.

"Don't bother. You've seen a great deal more shocking things than my sitting on Melisande's bed. Go and get her a glass of brandy—it might help with the pain."

Mrs. Cadbury looked at the two of them for a long, speculative moment. And then, to his astonishment, she swept from the room, taking the other members of the gaggle with her. Leaving him alone with a very angry Charity Carstairs.

"I'm going to kill her," she said beneath her breath.

Benedick stretched out on the bed beside her. "Save your energies, Charity. You can't budge me until I'm ready to go. Just close your eyes and breathe."

"I'm not closing my eyes anywhere around you. I don't trust you."

He reached out to touch her face, and she jerked it

away, her eyes troubled. "I'm not going to hurt you," he said quietly, suddenly serious. She turned back to look at him, and there was one of those odd, eerie moments of understanding between them. The kind of moment that shook him, disturbed him more than he cared to admit.

"You already have," she said.

18

Brandon Rohan opened his eyes, staring lazily up into the hooded figure that loomed over him. The opium dream was at its zenith, and he didn't want anyone to draw him out of it. What was the Master doing in here, anyway? He'd never seen him here before. This small, dark place that was akin to his childhood closet didn't hold more than half a dozen men, and he was familiar with most of them. It was an exclusive meeting place for those with a taste for the poppy, and while none of them spent time socializing, he'd grown used to them. He couldn't believe any of them could be the mysterious Master of the Heavenly Host.

"Go 'way," he said thickly to the man. "You don't belong here."

Not that he knew for certain. No one knew who currently led the Heavenly Host. The new rules were clear enough that even he could remember them in his current state. The leadership of the Heavenly

Host rotated, and no one ever knew who the current one was. That way there would be no repercussions.

"Your brother's been causing problems, Rohan," the Master said, his voice that breathy whisper of sound from beneath the enveloping hood. "We warned you when you took your place among us that we couldn't afford to have family members interfering."

"Not my fault," he managed to protest. Damn Benedick. If he was kicked out of the Heavenly Host he would kill him. "Can't…control him."

"You'll need to. Or we'll control him for you."

Brandon's eyes were drifting closed. Even the dim light of the opium den hurt his eyes, and he disliked having anyone interfere with his desperately needed dream state. This was the only way he could shut out the voices, shut out the sounds and the smells of war and blood and death. Of hacked bodies and screams of pain and death all around him. "Don't care," he said sullenly.

The hooded figure straightened, though in the dimness of the room he probably wouldn't have been able to see him even if he were bareheaded. "So be it," the man murmured, his faint lisp clear.

And then he vanished, like the opium dream he had to have been. And Brandon closed his eyes once more and drifted into oblivion.

Melisande fell asleep. She couldn't quite believe it. One moment she was lying in her bed, her ankle propped up, the dastardly Viscount Rohan stretched out beside her, for all appearances like the knight and his lady on a medieval grave, and the next she was asleep, dreaming. It took the arrival of the doctor to awaken her, and by that time her nemesis was across the room, shoulders leaning against the mantel, watching her with an unreadable gaze.

"If the gentleman would leave us," Doctor Smithfield said and Melisande could have kissed him. There was no reasonable way Benedick could refuse.

But why had she ever thought him to be reasonable? "I don't believe so," Rohan proclaimed. "I've already examined the lady's ankle—I won't see anything that would shock me. Go ahead."

"I really must insist…" The doctor's voice trailed off as Benedick rose to his full height.

"And I would insist you don't attempt to insist upon anything. This lady is my responsibility, and I'm not leaving her in the hands of a sawbones I've never seen before."

"Are you impugning my qualifications, my lord?" Dr. Smithfield was a dear man, and he volunteered his services toward the doves for free, but he was possessed of a certain amount of pride.

"I'm impugning nothing. Stop arguing with me and attend to Lady Carstairs."

Smithfield opened his mouth to argue but Melisande quickly intervened. "Ignore him, Doctor," she said amiably. "He enjoys being difficult. Do you think my ankle is broken?"

After one last grumble he turned back to Melisande. There followed a few extremely uncomfortable minutes before he stepped back. "It's my belief you've merely suffered a strain, your ladyship. I'll bandage the afflicted appendage and prescribe some laudanum. If you remain off it for the next fortnight then I expect you'll have no repercussions." He glared at Lord Rohan, who serenely glared back.

"I'll make sure of it," Benedick said smoothly. "You may send your bill to me, of course."

"Don't be absurd. I'm responsible for my own bills," she snapped, but Rohan simply ignored her, ushering Dr. Smithfield out the door.

When he turned back around, she fixed Rohan with a stern expression. "All right, you can go now. The doctor has seen me, pronounced his verdict and prescribed treatment. Now go away."

He didn't seem in any particular hurry to leave. "So, are you going to stay off your feet for two weeks?"

"What do you think? The full moon is in five days. I can either stay in bed and coddle myself and let innocent women be tortured and perhaps killed, or I can deal with it."

"By dealing with it you mean getting out of bed and risking crippling yourself?" He sounded no more than casual. "I don't think so. Our partnership is over, Lady Carstairs. You'll have to trust me to deal with the Heavenly Host."

She glared at him. "I don't. Not for one moment."

"You don't have any choice in the matter."

"Then I have no choice but to follow my investigations on my own." She would have climbed out of bed, just to prove to both herself and him that she could do it, but Dr. Smithfield had already given her a generous dose of tonic and she was having trouble lifting her head from her pillow. No trouble glaring, however.

He moved swiftly, so fast that she had no warning, and he was on the bed, his hands braced on either side of her as he leaned over her, and all pretense of manners had gone. "You will not," he said in a dark, angry voice, "do anything more to endanger yourself. Do you hear me?"

She stared up at him, her mouth set in a stubborn line. For a long moment he didn't move, and then his hands gripped her arms and yanked her up, and he kissed her.

Oh, God, she thought, as sensation washed over her, pure, bloody wonderful sensation. How many times had he kissed her? she thought. More than any other man. She knew his mouth by now, the touch and taste of him, the rich thrust of his tongue, the hard edge of his teeth, the sweet smoky flavor of him. Night had already closed in around the room, and the only candles were beside the bed, left there to assist the doctor's examination. It was only a blur of light, and she closed her eyes against the shimmering brightness, lifted her arms and slid them around his neck, pulling him closer, wanting to feel him against her body, heat and hardness and living flesh. He shifted, and she knew he'd moved onto the bed, covering her, and she didn't even think of making a protest. This was going to be the last time she would see him, she thought dazedly. He was going to refuse to help her after this, and she was going to have to proceed on her own. He would never come near her again, and she had every right to take what she wanted right now, and what she wanted was him. To indulge in the forbidden delight that was Benedick Rohan.

The doctor had tucked her beneath the covers. He pulled them away, so that their bodies were touching. She opened her eyes for a brief moment, wanting to see his face, see whether there was any affection, any tenderness, but he reached out and pinched the light from the bedside candle, plunging them into darkness, and it was as if there were no more restraints. No one could see them, therefore there were no rules. He rolled to his side, bringing her with him, and she ran her hand down his chest, inside his open coat to the loose white shirt he wore. His skin was hot beneath it, and she tugged at the fabric, wanting it out of the way. He reached down and yanked at it himself, and she slid her hands beneath, reveling in the silken feel of his skin.

She moved then, putting her mouth against his throat, and he tasted salty and sweet, wonderful. A faint thought danced through her brain—why had she never felt this for someone reasonable? Someone she could have? With dear Thomas it had been an uncomfortable burden. With Wilfred a disappointing experiment gone wrong.

But Benedick Rohan was richness and delight, setting every inch of her skin alive with feeling, and she wanted to lie beneath him, to have him take her, thrust inside her, cover her. She wanted…

She was dimly aware that he had frozen, and his hands covered hers, stilling their feverish exploration. She made a muffled sound of protest, but he moved away from her, releasing her, and she was very cold.

"I may be a bastard," he said in a soft voice, "but I do draw the line at taking advantage of drugged women. You and I both know this is a very bad idea, and it's just as well we're forced to end our association."

His words weren't making sense, but she blamed the laudanum. Damn Dr. Smithfield and his silly concoctions. She hadn't been in more pain than she could bear, and she should have been able to argue Benedick out of his absurd idea that they should sever their connection. And if she weren't shatter-brained from that vile stuff he wouldn't have stopped what he was doing. She wanted him to touch her the way he had in the darkened room in the tunnels. She wanted to feel that astonishing surge of feeling that was almost painful in its intensity. She wanted…

But he was already gone. She heard the click of the door as he closed it behind him, and she wanted to cry. But the laudanum robbed her of even that much. All she could do was fall asleep.

Benedick Rohan was in a toweringly foul mood, and he had no wish to pass the gauntlet of staring women and girls, all scrubbed and fresh-faced and a far cry from their earlier profession. He particularly didn't want to have Violet Highstreet staring at him with disapproval, nor did he want Emma Cadbury to stop his headlong pace toward the front door, putting her trim little body in between him and safety.

"Your lordship, we need to talk," Mrs. Cadbury said in the pure, well-bred tones that were clearly natural to her.

"You tell 'im, Mrs. C.!"

"This is none of your business, Violet. You may join the other girls while I speak with the Viscount."

"Don't let 'im get around you," she said, and he stopped his annoyance to look at her in surprise. The last he'd seen her she'd been fighting for the chance to service him—now it seemed as if he'd become persona non grata.

"What in the world is the matter with you?" he said, and then was astonished at himself. The opinion of whores had never mattered. Then again, those of Charity's gaggle were no longer whores. They were women and girls, human beings. Not faceless bodies for his pleasure.

Damn the woman, he thought absently.

"Just because I fancy you doesn't mean I'll stand by and let you hurt the mistress," Violet announced in strident tones. A chorus of bellicose assent echoed from the women who lined the stairwell, looking down on them.

"*That's enough*, girls," Mrs. Cadbury said, sounding more like a schoolmarm than a notorious madam. Then again, she looked more like a schoolmarm, albeit a badly dressed but still exquisitely beautiful one. If she were planning to live a life of celibacy it was a damned shame, he thought absently.

At another time he might have considered changing her mind. At another time he would have signaled Violet and he knew, despite her disapprobation, that she would follow him home and do anything he required her to do, and do it with great pleasure and enthusiasm. He preferred his women, even the ones he paid for, to honestly enjoy themselves in his bed, and Violet had a natural ability for pleasure.

Unlike the frowning Mrs. Cadbury.

"I'm afraid I don't have time to speak with you, madam," he said with thinly veiled impatience.

"If you do not speak with me then I will be forced to call on you, and to keep calling on you in your house in Bury Street until you're willing to meet with me. You may as well get it over and done with."

He looked at her with real dislike. A year ago, six months ago, six days ago, he would have given a great deal to have this woman in his bed. Now he wouldn't touch her if he were the one paid to do so. He glanced up at the staircase at the faces leaning over, watching them, and he realized he didn't want any of them, or their painted sisters who still populated the elegant houses he knew so well.

There was only one woman he wanted, and he needed to get far away from her. One didn't seduce a gentlewoman merely for sport, even if widows were considered fair game. Melisande, for all her calm good cheer was closer to a virgin than a woman who understood her own body and needs, and it would get very messy indeed if he didn't put a stop to it now.

In fact, he could consider himself fairly noble. He'd given her just enough pleasure to let her understand what could exist between a man and a woman. She would find someone suitable and marry him, living a rich, full life, all thanks to him.

Yes, he was a hell of a fine fellow, he thought mockingly. Always willing to do what was necessary for the good of womankind.

Mrs. Cadbury gestured toward an open door that clearly led into a salon, and short of manhandling her there was no way past her. "Five minutes," he said tersely. "After you."

She blinked in surprise. "I beg your pardon?"

"I said, 'after you.' Don't worry, I'm not going to make a dash for the door the moment your back is turned. I'll come in with you."

She stared at him for a long moment. "I'm not used to gentlemen having me precede them… We're usually bidden to follow meekly behind."

"I believe I have manners," he said, his sharp tone belying his words.

"Manners usually don't extend to whores," she replied.

He was tired, he was frustrated and he was angry. He wanted to reach out and strangle her. "Consider it one of my quirks. I believe in treating everyone equally."

"You mean you treat everyone this abominably?" Mrs. Cadbury murmured.

"No, madam. This is how I treat my friends," he said icily.

"We're friends? How delightful," she said, sweeping ahead of him into the room. He considered making a run for it, after all, and then stopped himself. Just how craven was he?

He strolled into the room after her, all insouciance, to see her already seated behind a massive mahogany desk, and his image of her as a stern schoolmarm increased enough to force him to smother a laugh with a false cough.

"Please sit down, your lordship," she said in that same stern voice that was no request but a clear command.

It wasn't too late—he could still run.

He took the nearest comfortable chair, sat back and crossed his legs, the picture of insolent grace. "What can I do for you, Mrs. Cadbury?"

"You can stop trying to seduce Lady Carstairs."

19

The sixth Viscount Rohan, son of the Marquess of Haverstoke, scion of the ancient and thoroughly wicked house of Rohan, was not likely to listen to orders from a retired abbess. He stared at her haughtily, not changing his indolent position.

"You will have to explain to me why I would have any wish to discuss my private life with you, Mrs. Cadbury."

"It's not your private life I'm interested in, your lordship. It's Melisande's. You don't mean well by her—any fool can see that, and I won't see her heart broken."

This time he didn't bother to hide his amusement. "I don't have any particular interest in Lady Carstairs's heart."

Emma Cadbury shot him an angry, contemptuous look, and he noticed for a moment that she really was magnificent. Not to his particular taste, but then, those tastes seemed to be getting more and more narrow. "Do you think I don't know that, your lord-ship? It's not her heart that you desire. I have been in the business of men's particular interests for many years, and I understand them quite well. Melisande's innocence intrigues you, and like most men you find it a challenge. You don't like that she's chosen to eschew the selfish desires of your gender, and you fool yourself into thinking it would be a kindly act on your part to awaken her to the so-called pleasures of the flesh."

He stifled an uncomfortable response, raising an eyebrow, as if he hadn't been thinking that very thing. "So-called, madam? Am I to infer that during your short but impressive career you never experi-enced those 'so-called pleasures of the flesh'?"

If he'd hoped to disconcert her he'd failed. "That, my lord, is none of your business. We are discussing my benefactress, not my personal life."

"We're discussing *my* personal life—yours should be equally open for perusal. Though in truth I don't really care about your dubious past, and I do assume it's in your past. Unless of course you have managed to convert Lady Carstairs to the joys of Sapphic en-counters and I have misunderstood the nature of this house. Pray enlighten me."

"You're disgusting."

"Not at all. I have no opinion of that particular variation, save when it affects women who interest me. Does it?"

Mrs. Cadbury straightened her already straight back, recovering. "Your prurient interest does you no credit. But I will be more than happy to satisfy it. It is not unknown among some of Lady Carstairs's rescues. Some have been grievously treated by men, some simply have that inclination, and it matters not to us. But no, my concern for Lady Carstairs's well-being is that of a grateful, loving friend and nothing more. And if she were of a Sapphic inclination I would hardly be worried about your effect on her."

His effect on her. She wasn't taking into account Lady Carstairs's deleterious effect on him, he thought resentfully. "I find this conversation boring, Mrs. Cadbury." He was genuinely tired, and he didn't bother to stifle his rude yawn. "Say what you wish to say and allow me to retire."

"I want you to leave Melisande alone. She needs a good man, a gentle man, not someone with your reputation. Some women do very well with a cold-hearted rake. Melisande would not be one of them, even assuming you mean marriage, which I am assured you do not. You wish to bed her and then discard her for another diversion, do you not?"

He knew a moment's discomfort, but he regarded her blandly. "Pray, continue."

"I hope with all my heart that Melisande can find a kind man to marry her, someone who will understand her work and help her with it, someone who treats her with respect and cherishes her. I doubt you've ever cherished anyone in your entire life."

He didn't let even a flicker of reaction cross his face as he thought of his beloved Annis, dying in childbirth and taking his son with her. "I've done my best not to," he drawled.

"Then leave Lady Carstairs alone!"

He could stand this no longer. He rose, half expecting her to rap a ruler on the desk and order him to sit again. But of course she did no such thing. He looked down at her, once more admiring her beauty in a distant, appreciative manner. "You may set your mind at rest, Mrs. Cadbury. This uncomfortable conversation was entirely unnecessary. My only connection with Lady Carstairs has been in service of discovering exactly what the Heavenly Host are up to. With her injury she will no longer be able to go into society, at least for the all-important days leading up to their next gathering, and I will have to persevere on my own. I will, of course, keep her apprised of my success or failure, though I imagine a note will suffice. But any danger I might offer to her chastity would have only been caused by proximity, and that will no longer be an issue."

Did he imagine he saw disappointment on that coldly beautiful face? It couldn't be, since he was doing precisely as she demanded. She was right—Melisande offered a delicious temptation, but it was the kind best avoided. He already knew she wasn't an adventurous widow looking to alleviate her banked frustrations, despite her one foray into an affaire. She was a woman to marry, and she was a far cry from anyone he'd want to spend the rest of his life with. She wouldn't be ignored, left in the countryside while he pursued his own pleasures and interests. He was looking for boredom and placidity in a wife, two characteristics Lady Carstairs was sorely lacking. She was also, most likely, barren, and his only reason to marry was to provide an heir.

No, he had no lasting interest in Melisande Carstairs, no matter how incredibly tempting he found her, no matter how the sound of her strangled cry when he brought her to climax kept reverberating in his brain and stirring in his loins.

Mrs. Cadbury was still watching him, her expression dubious. It was no surprise that she didn't believe him—he was having a difficult time believing it himself. But he was a man with his own twisted honor, and he had no desire to make someone else's life a misery simply to assuage an itch.

The strained ankle had been a blessing in disguise. He had come perilously close to shagging her a number of times today, and the longer he was around her the more overpowering that urge was.

Suddenly he could bear the schoolroom-like parlor no longer and set his words in a cool voice. "Good evening, Mrs. Cadbury. Look after her." And he was gone, cursing himself as he went.

It wasn't until he was on the street that he realized how absurd his grand exit was. He hadn't bothered to have his mount retrieved, and he had two choices— go back into the house sheepishly and demand his horse, or go wandering behind to the mews and find where their rides had been stabled.

Or the third choice, which was the one he took. He could send a servant for Bucephalus. In the meantime he desperately needed to clear his head, and a cool spring night was the way to do it.

He didn't like mysteries, any more than he liked emotions, weaknesses or unsatisfied lust. And he had absolutely no idea why he reacted so strongly to Melisande Carstairs. After all, she was no great beauty. She dressed badly, her hair was usually scraped back away from her face, and she had the most disconcerting habit of looking one directly in the eyes, rather than lowering her own in either a shy or provocative glance. He could think of a dozen women far more beautiful than she was, without her unsettling, straightforward demeanor.

And it wasn't as if she reminded him of the women in his life. Genevieve, his poor, mad fiancée who had eventually killed herself in a horrific public scene, was an exquisite, unstable beauty with coal-black hair and brilliant eyes, and he'd been young and totally besotted, until her madness had come to the fore. He seldom thought about her anymore, the memory too painful. If he had been wise enough to keep her in his memory, his own sister might not be married to Genevieve's brother, the wretched Scorpion, a man he considered to be a villain and a monster. His sister might not be lost to him now.

Annis had been sweet but strong-minded, totally devoted to him. Barbara had been the opposite, a force of nature with the appetites of a sailor and the sweetness of a rutting boar. What he'd thought had been passion for him had instead been passion for anything between her legs.

But Melisande was nothing like the women he had loved, all of them diamonds of the first water. She was pleasant-looking but not much more, though the night he had taken her to the Elsmeres' rout she had been astonishingly lovely. Much as he wished, he couldn't dismiss her opinions as ill-informed, mad or wrongheaded, and he had no intention of spending the rest of his life having to consider someone else's point of view.

Because that was what he would have to do. Mrs. Cadbury was right; Melisande was a woman to marry. And marriage to her would be one more disaster among a lifetime of disasters. Two out of three times he'd chosen poorly, and he had no intention of making another mistake.

No, the association was at an end, thankfully so. He would keep her apprised of his progress, and once the situation with the Heavenly Host was dealt with he would allow himself one brief visit, chaperoned by the lovely Mrs. Cadbury, to deal with any extraneous bits of business. Then and only then could he concentrate on finding a proper wife.

Though it was a good thing he'd decided against Miss Pennington, who would probably freeze him to death in bed. He wondered if she knew what her ramshackle brother was up to. The Heavenly Host was an expensive indulgence, and the Penningtons' fortune had all but vanished, hence her willingness to consider the suit of a member of the notorious Rohan family.

The sooner he contracted a marriage the safer he'd

be. The sooner he managed to find the sexual relief he'd been longing for the safer he'd be. Though *safe* was a strange word to use when it came to Melisande Carstairs. She was hardly a threat, except, perhaps, to the cut of his breeches. Blasted woman.

He walked briskly, the cool night air a balm. He almost hoped he'd be set upon by footpads. Beating someone to a bloody pulp would go a great deal toward assuaging his boiling frustration.

He'd come to fisticuffs with his brother Charles often enough, though his baby brother, Brandon, had always been one to be protected rather than confronted. But all that had changed—Brandon was thirty now, a soldier. He could go beat the truth out of him.

But Brandon was a shell of a man, still recovering from his grievous injuries, and the fight would hardly be fair. Confronting Brandon would get him nowhere, but he could at least try. Assuming he could catch his brother at home anytime in the next few days. Surely the once-sunny boy would respond to him, if he approached it properly. His main concern was keeping his brother out of the debacle that was the Heavenly Host—unlike Charity Carstairs he had no illusions that he could save everyone.

But he could save Brandon. He had to. His parents relied on him; his sense of duty insisted. His exasperated love for the siblings who would never do as he thought they should drove him mad, but he couldn't afford to lose another.

He strode up the front stairs, handing his hat and

gloves to Richmond, who was waiting patiently, and ordered a hot bath. It had been a long day. Tomorrow was soon enough to deal with Brandon. If necessary, he could simply truss him up and keep him prisoner until the full moon was done. It wouldn't solve Lady Melisande's problem, but she could find herself another knight errant, one better suited to her, and together they could fight injustice and cruelty, and he wished them happy.

"Would your lordship like some supper?" Richmond inquired politely, trailing after him.

He hadn't eaten since the picnic on the blanket, staring at Melisande's luscious mouth as she devoured everything in sight. Food might improve his choleric mood, but right then he felt like indulging himself. "No food, Richmond. A bottle of brandy will suffice." And he continued up to his rooms, prepared to get completely and totally drunk.

Emma Cadbury sat back in her chair, putting her fingertips together, her brow creased with worry. She'd hoped she'd been wrong. Benedick Rohan had been an occasional visitor at the establishment she had once run, and the girls had always been generous with their praise of him. She knew Melisande was totally besotted, and she'd hoped against hope that there might be a corresponding affection.

She should have known better. Women did love a rake, and Melisande, for all that she pretended she was above such feminine weakness, was as vulnerable as the greenest girl. She'd taken one look at

Benedick Rohan's dark, haughty visage and fallen like a stone into a well, drowning in his cynical charm.

One could hardly blame her. No woman had ever been able to resist a Rohan, and Melisande was alarmingly innocent, despite her attempts to become more worldly. Wilfred Hunnicut should be drawn and quartered, and instead he was enjoying the fruits of his labors, a comfortable marriage with the daughter of a cit.

If Benedick Rohan had given any sign, any hint that he cherished tender feelings toward Melisande, then Emma would have done what she could to support the match. She snorted, an elegant little sound. As if a man such as Benedick Rohan were capable of tender feelings! No, Melisande needed someone to watch over her, keep her from charging headlong into dangerous situations, protect her from her own good heart. Benedick Rohan was not that someone.

Even if Melisande desperately wished otherwise.

Not that she'd admit it, even to herself. But Emma was wise in the ways of men and women, and she could see Melisande's longing. And she was hardly going to stand by and watch her heart be broken.

Viscount Rohan was a little more difficult to read. He'd denied any particular interest in Melisande, but given the amount of time he'd spent with her recently she wasn't certain she could believe him.

At least she'd effectively warned him off. If he had ever thought of seducing Melisande, he had now been shown the error of his ways. She would be mournful; she would miss the excitement and danger of his company. Emma knew far too well how enticing that danger was.

But in the end she'd be ready to find the right sort of man, one who would cherish her. And Viscount Rohan could go to hell with the rest of his kind.

20

Lady Melisande Carstairs had erotic dreams that night. For the first time in her life she woke up as her body convulsed with a little shiver of pleasure, and so she sat up, horrified. There was the faint light of dawn filtering through her curtains, and she could see the bottle of laudanum on her bedside table beside a half-filled glass of water.

No more laudanum for her, she thought grimly. She hadn't wanted it in the first place. Rohan had tricked her, the slimy snake, and right now he was probably off celebrating his escape from her.

Except he was probably asleep at that hour, she decided fairly, closing her eyes again. Which was a good thing, because he hadn't escaped at all. If he thought she was staying off her strained ankle and leaving everything up to him then he was far too trusting, and Rohan didn't strike her as the trusting sort. She would be up and about once the vile drug was out of her system. It was Tuesday, and thanks to her presence at the Elsmeres' rout, she had received invitations on her own to attend a ball given by the rather notorious Duke and Duchess of Worthingham, and if Rohan refused to accompany her she would go alone. There was some reason why women should not attend social gatherings on their own, but she couldn't remember. Perhaps most of them had companions to accompany them.

Of course she had more than her share of companions. Miss Mackenzie, her aging governess who oversaw the reading lessons, would occasionally fill in as a duenna, but she didn't approve of Viscount Rohan, and she might very well refuse, leaving her with the choice of Emma or Violet, either of whom would throw the assembled multitude into a state of disbelieving horror. It was tempting, but she couldn't afford to risk losing one of her last opportunities to make progress. The night of the full moon was fast approaching.

It was past ten when she hobbled downstairs, accompanied by the strictures of half the gaggle. "I'm perfectly fine," she said by the time she made it to the first floor. In truth, her ankle hurt like blue blazes, but she was still able to walk, and she was hardly going to let a little discomfort get in her way. "Stop fussing!"

Emma had appeared at the bottom of the stairs, watching her halting progress with a stern look in her eye. "You shouldn't..." she began, but Melisande forestalled her.

"There's nothing to worry about. I'll rest when

this is over. It's not as if the damned thing is broken. I can stand a little pain."

"You are the most stubborn creature," Emma said in her calm voice. "Why wouldn't you listen to good sense?"

"Because I don't see it as good sense. Is Lord Rohan's horse still here?"

Emma shook her head. "He sent someone over to collect it last night. He…er…also took your horse, as well. He said you shan't be using it for the next few weeks and he had need of it."

Melisande stared at her, incredulity and anger warring for control. "And you just let him?"

Emma's smile was wry. "Do you really think I could stop a peer of the realm from doing exactly what he wanted? Did you expect me to throw myself in front of the horses?"

"Stealing a horse is a capital offense," Melisande said darkly.

"Stealing a teaspoon is a capital offense," Emma replied. "I think it would be a waste of time to try to charge him with the crime. Surely you're not thinking of leaving the house? The doctor ordered bed rest."

"The doctor is an old woman."

"Am I going to have to have one of the girls sit on you to keep you from racing around?"

"It won't do any good. Truly, Emma, I'm fine!" she insisted. "Just a little bit of pain in the ankle, but I can certainly handle that. I need to go see Lord Rohan. We have things to discuss." Things like the moments in the darkened room in the caverns, or the way he'd kissed her.

"You know as well as I do that young women do not pay visits to the establishments belonging to gentlemen. If you wish to see him you send him a note asking him to call on you. How many times do I have to remind you of this? And how many times have you ignored me?"

"You know as well as I do that we can't afford to wait. He's just as likely to wait until next winter to respond. No, if I want Viscount Rohan's attention I'm going to have to track him down to his lair and force him to listen to me. I need a carriage."

Emma looked at her, fully as stubborn as she accused Melisande of being. "And what if I refuse?"

"Then I'll simply ask someone else. Don't be difficult, Emma. If you thought about it you'd admit I'm right. If you're worried about my reputation you may accompany me, but I've already ridden through London sitting in Rohan's lap, so I would think any reputation I had left is completely shattered," she said cheerfully. "Which is just as well. Reputations are tiresome things. I'll do much better without one."

"If you think my presence would do you any good then your intellect has shattered, as well. Being accompanied by a notorious madam is no way to ensure respectability."

"Well, I live with a notorious madam and twenty former prostitutes, Cyprians, courtesans and streetwalkers. I would think that would pretty much put paid to any hope I have of being considered proper.

Give it up, Emma. It's a waste of time. You know I'm quite devoid of sensibility. I may as well be practical."

Emma's mouth set in an attempt at a stern line. "You're tiresome, you know that," she said in a repressive voice.

Melisande limped toward the settee, settling gracefully, not allowing even a grimace to cross her brow, prepared to wait her out. "I know. In the meantime, why don't you show me how the girls are progressing."

It had ended up a peaceful afternoon, watching Emma put the younger girls through their paces. Betsey had done her irrepressible best, an impish grin on her face, and it was all Melisande could do not to laugh. The child was darling, and the thought of the life she'd been headed for made her blood run cold. It was children like Betsey, women like Rafaella with the scars and the limp, women like Emma, who was just learning to smile again, who reminded Melisande that she didn't dare lessen her efforts.

She tried to remind herself that she could wait a day before confronting Rohan, but she couldn't sit still. She'd been restless, edgy, her skin prickly, her body in an odd state of nerves. Her breasts tightened uncomfortably in the soft cotton shift, and between her legs she felt a strange tightening and dampness when she least expected it. She'd taken a warm bath that morning, hoping it would ease some of the tension that ratcheted through her, but it had only made things worse.

She blamed the laudanum. People said it gave you strange dreams, and while she couldn't remember any of them they had to be responsible for the uproar her body was in. The thought of staying home that night had become unbearable, and in the end she looked Emma Cadbury in the face and lied.

"I did promise Rohan I would meet him at the Worthingham's ball tonight," she said blithely. "I know you'd prefer I stay home, and I understand your reservations about visiting Bury Street, but even you must agree that this is unexceptional. I'll bring Miss Mackenzie with me until he arrives, just to make sure everything is proper."

Emma looked at her suspiciously. "It's hardly proper for you to be there with only Rohan as your escort."

"Of course it is. I'm not a green girl. I'm a widow, and the rules are different." At least, she was relatively certain they were. "He'll bring me home—you know how ridiculously protective he is."

Emma's eyelids had lowered. "And I wonder why that is."

"Oh, because he's madly in love with me," Melisande said airily. "He can't bear to be away from me, and he…"

"Is that wishful thinking on your part?"

"God, no! I was simply being facetious. He's the most controlling creature I've ever met. And do you think there's a chance in this world that he'd be faithful?"

"No."

The monosyllable stopped her cold for a moment, and then she continued gamely. "He just wants to make certain nothing happens to me while I'm around him. He doesn't want to be held responsible if I bring the whole of society crashing down, which he seems to think I will." Melisande pushed her hair away from her face. "Don't worry, Emma. He'll keep an eye out to make sure no evil rake takes advantage of me and he'll see me home safely."

"Are you sure that's what you want?"

"Of course," she said. Believing it. Until she remembered the weight of him, on top of her, between her legs, and the prickling of her skin increased, and the tightness between her legs.

"You know, I find I don't believe you," Emma said after a moment. "I believe you're far too interested in Lord Rohan for reasons that have absolutely nothing to do with the Heavenly Host, and I have to warn you that that can be extremely dangerous."

"Dangerous? Why? Do you think he'll try to murder me?"

"I'm sure he's tempted," Emma said wryly. "Women love rakes. You haven't been in society enough to realize it, but a rake is almost irresistible, and I believe you're on the point of succumbing."

Melisande looked at her across the tea table for a long moment, then gave in. "Well, in truth," she said carefully, "I was thinking it might be a good idea to have an affair with the Viscount Rohan."

Emma had been pouring, and at that she dropped the teapot with a clatter, splashing hot tea all over the place and breaking one of the delicate china cups. "Hell and damnation," she said, desperately mopping up tea and milk. And then she looked up. "What did you say?"

"You heard me." Melisande reached out and took one of the tea-soaked biscuits. "I thought I might have an affair with Rohan."

"Are you out of your mind?"

"Don't be so narrow-minded, Emma. You've always insisted that there are real pleasures to be had with a man, and I thought it was past time I discovered what those are. According to the gaggle, Rohan is a particularly gifted man in that department, ensuring even his hired companions enjoy themselves. He seems the logical choice." She congratulated herself on her practical tone.

Emma stared at her in amazement. "I see… And what made you come up with this idea all of a sudden? Last I had heard you'd sworn off men for the rest of your life."

Melisande took two more biscuits before they become hopelessly soggy. "Well, I had. But I thought it would make an interesting scientific experiment. I've had…relations with my elderly husband, who I adored, and with a young man I thought I loved, and I failed to find any of the messy business enjoyable.

Now I'll try an expert, and if he can't make it palatable then I expect I'm better off doing without."

"Is that the only reason?"

Melisande thought of Rohan's mouth, hot and wet against her, of his hands beneath her skirts, touching her, rousing her, shocking her with that intimate pleasure. She shook her head, as if to shake the thoughts out of her brain. "That's it."

"That's it," Emma echoed flatly. "I'm not against the idea of you having an affaire, even marrying again. Assuming you found a good man. Viscount Rohan is most definitely not a good man."

"Well, I didn't intend to marry him. I just thought I might…shag him."

"Oh, lord, where did you hear that word?"

"From you. And it seems like a good enough word. I could use tup, I suppose, or even f—"

"Don't!"

Melisande grinned. "Well, I'm certainly not going to call it making love, since love will have absolutely nothing to do with it."

"And you think his lordship will be amenable to this? I got the impression he wanted to keep you at arm's length."

Sudden doubt squeezed at Melisande's heart. "Do you think he wouldn't want me?"

Emma looked at her for a long, contemplative moment. "He wants you," she said at last. "Trust me, I'm an expert at seeing what men want, and Rohan most definitely wants you. I'm just not convinced that he'd be any good for you. Why don't you choose someone a little easier? Surely there are other men whom you find charming."

"I don't find Rohan charming," she said with great truthfulness. She didn't want to consider what she found him.

"He's not. He is, however, very enticing. Even I can tell that much," Emma said. "Isn't there someone a little less…dangerous?"

Melisande thought about it, trying to picture the men at the Elsmeres' party, the men she'd seen in the park. "Well, there's Harry Merton. He's pretty enough, but he has a tendency to giggle…"

"No!" Emma's reply was so quick and sharp that Melisande stared at her.

"Why not? He seems perfectly pleasant."

"I'm sure he is. Nevertheless, I'd like you to keep as far away from Mr. Merton as you can. Rohan is a lamb compared to Harry Merton."

"I don't think we're talking about the same man," Melisande said doubtfully. "Mr. Merton is charming and rather foolish, and I'm certain he wouldn't hurt a fly."

"Perhaps I'm mistaken." Emma's smile was forced. "But humor me on this one. If you must have an affaire then take Viscount Rohan. Just be certain not to fall in love with him."

Melisande hooted with laughter. "That," she said, "would be completely idiotic."

"Yes, it would. But women have an unfortunate tendency to think that they have to be in love in order to enjoy sex. I don't want you to fall into the same trap. He doesn't love you, is incapable of caring for you or any woman, I expect. I don't want your heart broken."

"Pish. My heart is made of sterner stuff than that. If I don't like it, then I'll walk away. Besides, I don't expect to enjoy it much anyway, and then it will be over before he has time to dismiss me. That's what men do with their mistresses, isn't it? Dismiss them?"

"You could always dismiss him."

"And I will. I'll use him and discard him," she said grandly, almost believing it. "Starting tonight." She rose, trying not to wince as pain shot through her ankle. "I'm going to need to find something to wear, I suppose. I don't suppose the gaggle…"

As if on cue they filed in. Rafaella had a diaphanous gown over one arm, and the rest of them were laden with hair ornaments and face paint.

"I presume you were all listening in," Emma said in a tone of acceptance.

"Of course we were," Violet piped up, and Sukey shot her a quelling glance.

"We've decided to have a discussion with you, Lady Carstairs," Sukey said. She was a natural leader, her years with the bishop notwithstanding, and the others nodded.

Melisande resisted the temptation to roll her eyes. "I suppose you're going to tell me that Viscount Rohan is up to no good."

"Of course he's up to no good," Violet broke in with a saucy smile. "That's half the fun."

"Violet," Emma said in a reproving voice.

"Leave this up to us, Mrs. Cadbury," Sukey said. "You've had your say. It's time for ours. Now that you've decided to sleep with my lord Rohan you're going to need a bit of advice."

"I really don't think it's necessary."

"Well, that's where you're wrong," the girl replied. "You're going to be flat on your back with your heels in the air before you even realize what's happened, and that can be a dangerous position to be in."

Melisande envisioned that position and felt her face grow crimson, her tongue too strangled to speak.

"We're not talking whores' tricks," Hetty offered. "Well, in fact, we are, but we're not talking about games and such. We're talking about babies."

"You don't want to get pregnant," Sukey said earnestly. "And there are ways to avoid it. Where are you in your monthly courses?"

Melisande could feel her face flaming. "I may not even go through with this. Lord Rohan might not want me. Or I might decide it's a bad idea."

"It *is* a bad idea," Emma broke in resignedly, "but you're going to do it anyway. Trust us, we've all seen it often enough. Answer Sukey's question."

"Perhaps two weeks since my last."

Sukey shook her head. "Bad timing. If you could put off shaking the sheets with the gentleman for another week, it would be safer, but I know that's hard when the blood is up. We'd best tell you what to do."

"I like a sponge and vinegar," Agnes announced.

"I prefer a copper penny," Hetty said.

"It's not an issue if you simply use your mouth," Violet offered, but was quickly shouted down.

"She's not going to start with that, you idiot," Sukey said sharply.

Melisande was embarrassed, horrified, and unwillingly curious. "What in the world do you do with a copper penny? Offer a prayer to some saint."

Agnes, the only practicing papist in the group, laughed. "You do the same thing you did with the sponge and vinegar, my lady. You insert it into your—"

"Stop!" Melisande cried, her curiosity more than satisfied. "I promise you I have no need of such stratagems. I'm barren."

"What makes you think that?" Emma said. "Just because you didn't conceive with an old man or a singular occasion with a younger one doesn't mean someone with Lord Rohan's...vigor...wouldn't do the job."

Enough was enough. The last thing Melisande wanted to be thinking about was Benedick Rohan's vigor, or inserting peculiar things into the most private part of her body, or letting Rohan put anything of his into that same place.

"Or there's coitus interruptus," Sukey said. "He can just pull out and spill his seed on the sheets, or on you. It's not foolproof, and not as much fun for the gentlemen, but I imagine Lord Rohan's not interested in fathering bastards. He may even have a French letter."

"What's a French letter got to do with anything?" Melisande inquired, more mystified than ever. "If you're expecting me to put a piece of paper in my..."

"Such an innocent!" Sukey said, shaking her head. "It's a wonder we allow her out at night. A French letter, Lady Carstairs, is something the gentleman wears over his rod. He spills his seed inside it, not inside you."

Rod, she thought, momentarily distracted. It seemed like rather a nice word. Evocative. "I think Rohan will be prepared," Emma said. She looked at Melisande for a long, thoughtful moment. "Is there any way I can make you change your mind?"

Melisande shook her head, half determined, half terrified.

"Then ladies, we need to make her irresistible," Emma announced. "Hetty, where are your emeralds?"

21

Emma sat alone in the library after Melisande and the strongly disapproving but very proper Miss Mackenzie had left. There'd been no talking Melisande out of her sudden decision, and in truth Emma hadn't been that surprised. She'd seen the signs for days. She knew when the heat rose in the blood; she'd seen it often enough. It should have been no surprise that even Melisande would succumb when faced with the delectable temptation that was Rohan. Even she had been tempted, for the first time in her life, just a few short months ago.

Her work at the hospital, her effort at penitence, had been grueling, not for the faint of heart. She held the patients' hands when they died, but she seldom looked into their faces. Until that night.

The boy—for he looked like a boy, his hair tumbled over his pale, sweating face—he should never have been there in the hospital. People of his class were taken care of at home, the doctors being summoned, the care provided by upper-class maids and butlers. But when Lord Brandon Rohan arrived back on the ship he'd been delirious with fever and somehow his papers had gotten lost. No one knew who he was, or even that he was an officer. He'd been shunted off like so many of the wounded men, to the stink of a hospital, there to live or die as may be.

He still had all his limbs, though one leg was cruelly wounded, and he would never walk without a limp. That was, assuming he even lived long enough to go home. The scars that covered so much of what must have once been a strong young body bore testament to the horror he had been through, and his pretty face was a travesty. He had been brought in at the end of a long day, and Emma had taken one look at him and known he would die. Not from any mortal wound—each of his terrible injuries had been tended to, and given a strong constitution he would normally recover. But he had opened his bright, fever-glazed eyes, and she'd known he'd given up.

It was a Catholic hospital, run by stern nuns, and Emma had chosen it, knowing the very thought would have offended her antipapist family, had they known. Mother Mary Clement had assigned her the young man, and Emma had known better than to protest. She pulled the curtains around his little cubicle and prepared to make him comfortable enough to die in peace.

She had changed his dressings, not flinching from the mangled flesh. There was no smell of putrefaction, and whatever fever he had contracted hadn't come from any of his wounds, which were all a healthy pink. He lay perfectly still on the bed as she bathed him in cool water, trying to bring his fever down, knowing it was a wasted effort.

She talked to him as she worked, her low voice keeping up a steady stream of inconsequential pleasantries. The dying often retreated so far that they never heard a human voice or felt the touch of their caretakers, but on rare occasions that voice or touch could call someone back. She covered him again, then sat back in the spindly chair beside his bed, rubbing the small of her back absently. "Are you going to die, young man?" she said softly, thinking that he was older than she was, feeling like his grandmother. "There's no need. You can fight this—you're young and strong. You're far better off than half the men in this hospital—you have all your limbs, and even if half of your pretty face is ruined you still have the other half to charm the girls with. If you can cultivate the right brooding, Gothic air, the young women will find you vastly heroic and romantic, and you'll have to beat them off with a stick."

He didn't move, and she could almost feel the life force draining from his body. "You don't have to die," she said again with some asperity. "But if you're determined to then I'm damned if I'll waste my time with you when there are other men who are fighting to stay alive."

Not even a twitch suggested there was anyone left inside the spare frame of the young soldier, and she decided to try one last time. "Have you got a sweetheart, perhaps a wife somewhere? A mother who's worried about you? You can't just give up, child. Fight, damn you!"

Nothing. She rose slowly, her shoulders bowed in weariness and defeat, and she was turning to go when a small movement caught her attention. She turned back to see that his eyes were open, bright blue staring up at her. "Is that supposed to convince me to live?" he asked, his voice a weak croak. "Aren't you supposed to hold my hand?"

"I already tried that," she said matter-of-factly, hiding her burgeoning hope. "It didn't seem to work."

He might almost have smiled. It was difficult to tell with the scarring, but suddenly she released her pent-up breath. It was as if there'd been a third entity in the cubicle with them. Death had been there, waiting.

And now it was gone.

She sat back down, taking his thin, clawlike hand in hers. "What is your name? You were brought in without papers, and if you'd been selfish enough to die we would have had to bury you in an unmarked grave."

He looked at her steadily. "I don't remember," he said finally, and she knew it for a lie. Even with the weak, thready quality of his voice she could tell he was a far cry for an ordinary soldier.

"You're being difficult," she said lightly. "But I'll have the truth from you sooner or later. Mother Mary Clement gives me the difficult cases. Of which you are one. But at least you've decided to live."

"Why do you say that?" he whispered, looking at her.

She smiled, squeezing his thin hand lightly. "I just know." She rose, releasing him. "I'll be back tomorrow. Don't give the night sister too hard a time, all right? And don't die while I'm gone—I'll be very cross with you."

It was definitely a smile. "I'll endeavor not to. What's your name?"

She shook her head. "I'll tell you when you're ready to give me a present of yours. At least tell me your rank, so I can address you as lieutenant or something."

"Call me Janus," he said.

She didn't miss the allusion; Janus was the god of two faces in Roman mythology. "Don't be tiresome, child," she said in her best governess-y tones. "You're way too pretty as it is—too much loveliness for one face. You needed to do something to tone down that handsome profile."

He laughed then, a choking sound that nevertheless made her feel warm inside. "And I think I'll call you Harpy, if we're going with classical allusions. I'll endeavor to survive until tomorrow, if only to spite you."

"Do that," she said, pushing the curtain aside and preparing to depart.

"Oh, and Miss Harpy," he called after her.

She glanced back, eyebrows raised in question.

"I'm most definitely not a child."

He hadn't told her his name. In the week he stayed

at the hospital under Mother Mary Clement's watchful eye he stubbornly insisted his memory was gone, even as his body grew stronger. When she came in she would go straight to him, to reassure herself that he was getting better, and then she would do her rounds, leaving him for last. He was her reward for the onerous work she did. He looked at her as if she were a mixture of the Madonna and the harpy he'd likened her to, and she chivvied him like he was her younger brother. No, that wasn't true, because she'd been uncomfortably aware of the niggling pinch of longing he brought out in her.

All would have been well if he hadn't developed another fever, this one stronger and more virulent than the first. She'd seen it happen in other patients, seemingly strong and recovering. The hospital was a dangerous place, full of illness and disease, and the patients were already in a weakened condition from whatever had brought them there in the first place. It came over him swiftly, and by nightfall, when she was scheduled to leave, he was delirious.

Mother Mary Clement had looked in, clucking beneath her breath. "It's a sad case, Emma," the old woman said. "I had hoped he would make it."

Emma hadn't looked away from him. "I'll stay here for a bit if you don't mind," she said in a quiet voice. "Do what I can for him."

"Wake him up if possible. I assign the dying to you, simply so they can see what's worth living for. Remind him of why he wants to be alive."

She did look up at her then. The nun knew everything she needed to know about Emma's history, and she didn't judge her. Mother Mary Clement nodded briskly. "I'll leave him to you. Call me if you need anything. Otherwise there's naught we can do. Either he'll make it through or he won't."

And she'd left them there, together in the gathering darkness, the moans of the sick and dying around them, her young soldier still and silent in his narrow bed.

It was around midnight when she crawled onto the cot with him. He'd begun to shiver, and she put her arms around him, cradling him against her breast like the baby she knew she would never have. He clung to her like a drowning man, and she closed her eyes and slept, knowing that when she awoke he'd be dead, but that at least he would die in her arms, loved, when she never thought she would love any man.

And indeed he was gone the next morning. But not to his heavenly reward, Mother Mary Clement informed her. His family had been putting out inquiries, and they'd finally managed to track him down. They'd only just removed him to his family home while she'd slept on, blissfully unaware. She'd been so exhausted she hadn't even felt him being taken from her arms, and Mother Mary Clement had let her sleep on.

There was always the chance that he was the scion of an industrialist, or perhaps a highborn bastard. Someone not completely beyond her touch, who looked at her and understood what she had been and hadn't cared.

But no, life couldn't be that generous. He was Captain Brandon Rohan. Lord Brandon Rohan, no less, brother to a viscount, son to a marquess. Someone so far out of reach that it would have been better for her if he'd died that night. Then, at least, he would have stayed hers.

And now the vagaries of fate had brought this family back into her life. Her darling boy was no longer a wounded soldier, but from what Melisande had discovered it appeared that his sickness had gone far deeper, burrowing into his soul. It broke her heart, when she thought she was invulnerable.

22

Benedick couldn't rid himself of a strange feeling of melancholy as he dressed that evening for the Worthingham's ball, one he ascribed simply to the unsettling effect of having such a whirlwind as Melisande Carstairs thrust herself into his life. He was rid of her now, well rid of her, and her twisted ankle had been a blessing. He had been growing closer and closer to seducing her, and that would have been a very bad idea, indeed, for both of them.

He pondered that as Richmond helped him into his perfectly tailored coat. A widow was considered fair game, and sooner or later someone would break through the wall of cheerful unconcern she'd built around herself. He'd done a great deal to shatter the foundations of that fortress—all it needed was an enterprising man to breach it.

He frowned. Not, for God's sake, a useless fribble like Wilfred Hunnicut. She ought to have better taste than that. He cast his mind through his acquaintances, trying to envision the perfect man for her. She was someone who needed marriage, and a firm hand to control her more extravagant starts. Someone who understood and sympathized with her charitable work, not someone who'd take advantage of the more willing members of the gaggle behind her back.

"Your lordship?" Richmond's voice was anxious. "Is there something wrong?"

Benedick stepped away from him, picking up his neckcloth. "Why should something be wrong?" he said irritably, turning toward the mirror to tie it. And then he caught sight of his face. He looked positively thunderous.

He could remember his father looking just that way, when confronted with some injustice or wrong. He'd looked that way when they'd all travelled to the Lake District to see Miranda's firstborn and to prove they could tolerate the villain she'd fallen in love with and chosen to marry.

He was feeling the same way toward any of the men he pictured marrying Charity Carstairs, which was absurd. She could hardly match his sister's wretched choice in the Scorpion. Lucien de Malheur wasn't your ordinary scoundrel, and there was no one imaginable who could reach his depths of depravity.

Except, of course, the mysterious members of the Heavenly Host, and whoever among them was guiding them into such treacherous waters.

He composed his face into his usual saturnine calm, tying his neckcloth deftly. At least the interfering, disturbing Lady Carstairs was out of the way for the next fortnight, and he could concentrate on the Host without worrying about her. Without being forced to endure her proximity. Without being tempted.

Worthingham House took up a good half a block on Grosvenor Square, a massive edifice built at the end of the last century to demonstrate the Worthinghams' consequence in society and political power, a consequence that was still in order. He doubted the duke or duchess had anything to do with the Host, but the guest list for their annual ball was massive, and no one dared ignore it, lest they be considered disrespectful and find themselves on a decidedly lower rung of the social order as punishment. Which meant most or all members of the Host would be in attendance, and perhaps growing giddy, and reckless with the night of the full moon fast approaching. He'd even done a bit of research that afternoon in the massive library his parents had acquired. In the Old Religion they were nearing the festival of Imbolc, festival of the maiden, though he was relatively certain his pagan ancestors hadn't performed rape and blood sacrifice as part of their celebration. He knew from his years at Oxford that men could twist anything to their own meaning, and he'd even remembered a class studying myth and folklore, including the Old Religion. There'd been several of his acquaintance taking that class, though for the life of him he couldn't remember which ones. It had been more than twenty years ago and while it had fascinated him at the time, he hadn't thought of it since. Was the leader of the Heavenly Host one of his erstwhile classmates?

Maybe seeing his schoolmates tonight would jog his memory. Though in fact that same class would have been held other years, and younger students, older students would have learned of the same ritual, been able to take and pervert them to their own use.

He glanced at Richmond. "You can send the other servants to bed, Richmond, and retire yourself. I won't be back till late, and I can certainly put myself to bed."

"And what of Lord Brandon, my lord?"

He thought back to their short but vicious fight early that day. "He won't be returning."

"Very well, my lord." Richmond's perfect expression showed nothing of what he was feeling. Only his old eyes reflected the same pain and resignation that filled Benedick.

He'd been in his library, waiting for Brandon to drag himself out of bed. He had no idea whether last night's debauch was singular or not, and he didn't care. He could turn a blind eye to his brother's self-destruction no longer, and he'd been determined to have it out.

In the end he'd almost missed him. Brandon was never the most furtive of people, his long, loose-limbed body casual and noisy. Now, with the limp, he made more noise than ever, and Benedick had been sure he would hear him. But Brandon knew him just as well, and he'd waited until Benedick had been deeply involved in his books, almost making it past the door before he looked up.

"I want to talk to you." He'd sounded like his

good-natured father when he was on a tear, he thought ruefully. He softened his voice. "Brandon, please."

"Sorry, old boy," Brandon mumbled, not meeting his gaze. "I've got an appointment. Can't stand up my friends."

"It won't take but a minute. Come in, please."

Brandon's haunted face was torn, and Benedick suspected that if he hadn't had a bad leg he would have simply gone on. But in the end he moved, coming into the room and taking a seat, staring at his older brother defiantly.

He looked like bloody hell, Benedick thought distantly. While his ravaged face was slowly healing, the unmarred side looked pale and deathly. The hollows beneath his cheekbones were unmistakable, his mouth was thin and hard, and there was a faint tremor in his hand. His eyes were the worst of all, Benedick thought. They were the eyes of a man already dead.

What had happened to the obstreperous boy who'd bounded through life like an overgrown puppy? But he knew what had happened. The full-blown horrors of war, the ceaseless pain of cruel injuries, and the search for oblivion that had followed. The old Brandon was probably gone forever. He still wasn't ready to give up on the new one.

"I suppose you want me to apologize for casting up my accounts all over you," Brandon said. "No, I don't remember, but Richmond chided me quite thoroughly. It's amazing how that old man can make me feel worse than you and our father combined. Only Mama can make me squirm as badly."

"Unfortunately she's in Egypt with Father, or else you might stop this horrific behavior."

Brandon's mouth turned in an ugly smile. "Brother mine, you have no idea of the meaning of horrific, and I see no point in educating you. And in fact I have no regrets about spewing all over you. You doubtless deserved it."

"I appreciate the token of your esteem," Benedick said dryly. "Are you involved in the Heavenly Host?" The question came out more abruptly than he'd wanted.

Brandon didn't even blink. "If you're interested in joining, I would advise against it. You're far too judgmental."

He almost laughed at that, having spent years being chided for not being judgmental enough. But that was the least of his concerns. "Then you are a member?"

Brandon shrugged negligently. "I gather the Heavenly Host goes by a strict rule of anonymity, which I think is rather wise. You don't want to play cards with someone you've seen servicing another man the night before. Not that I have, of course."

"Played cards or serviced men?"

Brandon smiled unpleasantly. "I prefer not to answer."

"Are you saying you're not a member?"

"I'm saying mind your own damned business."

He'd controlled his temper with an effort. "I can't

sit back and watch you destroy your life. Not to mention our family name, disgraced as it already is. I had hoped there might be room for improvement, but given your behavior I think it unlikely. The Heavenly Host is going too far, and it's all going to explode in your face. Do you want to bring that kind of shame on your family?"

"Oh, I think Father would survive. After all, he spent time among their unhallowed ranks himself. As for Mother, I know everyone will keep the truth from her." His voice was offhand.

"And how will you look her in the eye, knowing the company you've kept, the crimes you've committed?"

"Dear brother, I have no intention of surviving long enough to worry about it." He rose, oddly graceful despite the limp. "And I will now take myself out of your presence. I've already arranged for my bags to be sent on to lodgings, and you won't have to...how did you put it...sit by and watch me destroy myself. I'll do it quietly and discreetly."

"Not if you're a member of the Heavenly Host."

"You underestimate me. Goodbye, Neddie." It was the old childhood name, and for a moment it stabbed Benedick to the heart.

He was gone before Benedick could react, too late for him to have the footmen restrain him, disappearing into the gloomy afternoon. And Benedick knew that if Brandon had his way, that goodbye would be final.

Richmond appeared in the open door. "I gather Master Brandon won't be here for dinner."

Benedick sighed. "No." He looked at Richmond's impassive face and sorrowful eyes, and he felt the same pain in his own heart. "Don't worry," he said softly. "I won't let him go forever."

"Yes, my lord." There were tears swimming in Richmond's old eyes. "I have faith."

Benedick wasn't much in the mood for dancing, but staying home and brooding would be even worse, he thought as he strolled into the brightly lit vestibule of Worthingham House, surrendering his greatcoat to a waiting servant. Another crush, another night of heat and noise and boredom. He glanced around at the other late arrivals, nodding at one couple, exchanging a few words with another as he mounted the massive staircase. He could hear the music drifting down, and he grimaced. The Duchess of Worthington preferred the music of her youth, all from the past century, requiring stiff, practiced moves and very little pleasure. He had every intention of going straight for the card room when Lady Marbury, a plump young matron he'd once shared a few pleasurable nights with, came sidling up to him, a sly expression on her face.

"There you are, Rohan," she said. "We wondered what was keeping you! You'd best be careful, or Harry Merton will steal a march on you."

He kept his confusion from his face, smiling blandly. "I doubt it. Harry's tried to best me a number of times and always failed. What, pray, is he attempting now?"

"Why, Lady Carstairs, of course! She said you had sent her on ahead, but really, Lord Rohan, you shouldn't keep a lady waiting quite so long."

His expression was so well schooled that the avid Lady Marbury didn't notice that his face froze as every curse he'd ever known danced through his brain. He smiled at her. "Then I'd best protect my field," he said. "Direct me to them and I will explain to Harry that trespassing is never a wise idea. Particularly when there's a Rohan involved."

"He's over by the embrasure on the left," she said. "Just right for them to slip into, if Lady Carstairs were a little more mobile. Alas, she has that sprained ankle, but I imagine she could hop if the urge hits her."

He knew he should say something pleasant, flirtatious, even kiss her hand. Without a word he turned and stalked across the ballroom floor, barely acknowledging any of the greetings. He couldn't see her, but he could see the men ranged around her, and he wasn't sure whose neck he wanted to ring, Merton's or Melisande's.

He slowed his pace as he approached them. He could see her now, sitting in state on a divan that must have been brought in for her use, surrounded by laughing, flirting men, and he ground his teeth. What the hell was she doing being the center of attention? And where had she gotten that totally indecent dress? It showed most of her exquisite breasts, and he felt a sudden surge of fury. He hadn't seen her breasts, touched her breasts, and yet here they were, on display for every lascivious idiot in London.

He pushed through the crowd, and they parted easily enough until he loomed over Melisande, who looked up at him with a limpid smile. "Rohan!" she greeted him with feigned delight. "I was afraid you might stand me up."

Merton was sitting next to her, holding her gloved hand in his, and Benedick simply looked at him, a possessive glare in his eyes, his smile a dangerous warning.

Merton dropped her hand and stumbled to his feet, but he giggled anyway. "Heavens, Rohan, you terrify me. I was merely keeping your lovely lady company while you were dreadfully late. Really, I would think you'd know better how to treat a lady. If you send her on ahead, you risk having other men poach on your lands."

"I'm not a fallow deer," Melisande said brightly.

Merton giggled again, looking down at her. "No, my dear lady, you're a plump little partridge, just ripe enough to be irresistible. But I have no interest in being called out so I will cede my place." He gestured toward his abandoned gilt chair with a flourish, and Benedick took it, keeping his gaze averted from Melisande's.

"Clearly I owe you a debt of gratitude, Harry," he said. "I should have known I could count on you to keep my property safe."

"I beg your pardon?" Melisande began in a dangerous voice, but one look from his blazing eyes and she subsided, though he suspected that wouldn't be the last of it.

"Always, old fellow. Might I bring you and the lady something to drink? It looks as if you headed straight for us once you arrived."

"Of course I did. And all Lady Melisande and I need at the moment is a little privacy. We have, after all, been parted for hours."

Merton smiled. "Ah, the flush of young love!" And he sauntered off.

By then the other suitors had faded away, like young cubs bowing before an alpha wolf, he thought, remembering another class on animal nature. It was just as well. He felt like tearing out the throat of anyone who got close to her.

Melisande spoke first, though not to him. "Miss Mackenzie, you can leave now that the viscount has arrived. He'll look after me."

He followed her gaze to the tall, thin, disapproving woman in the shadows.

"Harrumph," the woman said, or something like it, expressing strong disapproval of her, of himself, of everyone there and life in general.

"Don't tell me she was a courtesan, I beg you," he said. "I won't believe you."

"She was my governess," she said, smiling up at him, and for a moment he was dazzled. And then he remembered he was furious.

His laugh was mirthless. "It's no wonder you have a twisted view of life!"

"Don't pick a fight with me, Lord Rohan," she said sweetly. "You should have known I wasn't going to stay immured in my bedroom. Indeed, I've already made a great deal of progress."

"With Harry Merton. He was almost drooling down the front of that indecent dress."

"Hardly indecent when compared to some of the others," she pointed out. "And when did you become such a prude?"

He pulled himself together. "Hardly a prude, Lady Carstairs. And if you wish to distract yourself with Harry, then you have my blessing. He's a useless fribble but essentially harmless."

"I have your blessing, do I?" she purred. "I didn't realize that I needed it."

He knew enough of women to realize he was on dangerous ground. Still, there wasn't much she could do in public. "I beg pardon, madam," he said immediately. "Of course you may sleep with whomever you like." He could see Lord Elsmere approaching him, probably wanting a game of cards, and from a distance he could spy Dorothea Pennington's dissolute older brother. "I asked you to leave this to me," he added in a lowered voice.

"And I told you I wouldn't. Besides, I've come to a decision and it seemed only proper that I share it with you."

Elsmere was trying to get his attention, and he was only half paying attention to her. "What?" he said absently.

"I've decided to become your mistress."

23

Benedick froze in sheer astonishment, staring at her as if she'd suddenly grown two heads. She was looking entirely rational, smiling up at him from her divan like a queen receiving visitors, and for a moment he couldn't move.

"You're out of your mind," he said finally. "You're the last woman in the world I'd take as a mistress."

There was a flicker in her dark blue eyes, one he couldn't read, but her calm was unimpaired. "That's hardly flattering."

"I wasn't intending to flatter you. Merely to tell you the truth. I have no interest in having any mistress, least of all you."

"I'm hardly an innocent, Lord Rohan. I know men's bodies, and I recognize desire. You can hardly convince me that you don't want me." There was only the slightest note of strain in her voice, and he suddenly realized what that flicker was. Beneath her self-assurance was a very real doubt, and he knew that, strong as she was, he could crush her. Ensure that she never dared offer herself to any man ever again.

It should have been tempting. He'd come to the unhappy conclusion that he didn't want her bedding anyone else, and he knew better than to sleep with her himself. But he couldn't be that cruel.

"I do not want a mistress," he said again in a steadier voice. "And if I did, I would be a very bad choice for you. I'm not particularly kind or thoughtful, and we annoy each other, even if you try to pretend we don't."

"We don't..." she began, but he interrupted her.

"Well, you annoy me. You're a wealthy, beautiful widow, and you could take your pick of half the men here. Look at the way they swarmed around your indecent dress tonight," he said in a tight voice. "If you wish to have an affaire, choose one of them." *And I'll break his legs,* he thought savagely.

He didn't believe her offer of an affaire for one moment. She'd said over and over again that she had no interest in men, and while he had no false modesty about his own charms, a furtive climax was not likely to change her mind. She was probably simply looking for a way to get back in the hunt, and he was damned if he'd give in, no matter what delicious bait she dangled in front of him.

Her flicker of fear was gone. "I don't want anyone else. I don't trust them."

His amazement was real. "And you trust me?" He stared at her. "Don't be ridiculous. You can't possibly."

"Well, perhaps saying I trust you is going a little too far. But I trust you to know what you're doing in the bedroom. I've had an old, infirm man and a clumsy, selfish young one. The gaggle assure me that you're a remarkable lover, and it seemed only reasonable to start with you. I've decided that I might not be cut out for celibacy after all, and if I wish to embark on a series of affaires I want to make certain I'll find them enjoyable." She looked up at him, her voice and face as calm as if she were ordering her menus for the week, and continued ingenuously, "I like your kisses. And you're remarkably good at touching. So I choose you."

"No. Never in this lifetime."

She stared at him. "Why not?"

"Because I…because I…it's not a good idea," he said, knowing his excuse was lame. Indeed, he wasn't quite sure why he was resisting so fiercely. Bedding her would at least distract her and he could still finish his investigation on his own. And he wanted her so damned badly his hands shook with it.

And the longer he stayed the more tempted he was. "No," he said again, his voice flat and implacable. "You're a lovely, tempting woman, but you're not the kind of woman I want."

Without another word he left her, afraid to look back.

She couldn't very well burst into tears in the middle of a ball, Melisande thought calmly. She'd been an idiot to spring her plan on him when they were surrounded by people. When they were alone he tended to touch her, whether he said he wanted to or not. She should have waited until he came to see her.

Except he wouldn't come. He considered himself well rid of her, and there was no way she was going to leave the Heavenly Host up to him. He'd extricate his brother and consider the job done.

But it didn't seem right. The gaggle had once more come up with a stunning gown for her to wear, cobbled together from three of her old ones. It was a rush job, and a good thing she couldn't dance, because the seams would never have held, but for reclining gracefully it would do very well, indeed. And she'd waited for Rohan to make his appearance.

He was so late she was almost afraid he wouldn't come at all, destroying her plan and her hard-won confidence. Men had surrounded her, Harry Merton had flirted delightfully, and she told herself she should forget about Rohan entirely, when suddenly he had appeared, tall and forbidding, with his dark cat's eyes and high cheekbones. He was furious with her, she realized as he stalked toward her. That was as good a start as any.

She probably should have calmed him down first before springing her plan on him. She knew very well he didn't wish to get involved with her, though she couldn't discern why. It wasn't as if anyone would think he'd compromised her.

She glanced over at him speculatively. He was talking with Harry Merton now, his saturnine face amused, and despite Emma's warning she mentally compared the two men. Mr. Merton was by far the more traditionally handsome. A bit shorter than Rohan, he had a square, muscular build that was possibly more pleasing than Rohan's lean, elegant length. His riotous curls, his sunny smile, his flattering eyes matched his charming, shallow nature. He was at such odds with Rohan's intense gaze and cynical visage that it made him the obvious choice for her first official affaire. And yet he faded into obscurity standing next to Benedick.

Benedick. It should have felt strange to think of him by his Christian name. Instead it felt oddly right.

A servant was hovering close at hand, and she signaled to him. If she were the kind of woman who let setbacks affect her, then she would have curled up in a ball years ago and shut out the world. So Viscount Rohan insisted she was the last woman in the world he'd have an affaire with?

It was time to show him otherwise.

24

Benedick was determined not to look back. He could feel her dark blue gaze on him, almost like a brand. Damn the woman! As if things weren't bad enough.

"She's a pretty bit of pastry, ain't she?" Harry said appreciatively. "I never realized how tempting Charity might be."

"Not tempting for you, my lad," Benedick replied. "She needs a good man, and I know from old acquaintance that you are most definitely not he."

"I beg your pardon!" Harry protested. "I'm an absolute lamb!" He giggled. "Not that she's the mistress type. She's the sort to get leg-shackled or I miss my guess. Not out for bit of hide-the-sausage."

Benedick controlled his urge to glare at him. "Exactly. Which is why I'm keeping my distance, as well."

"It didn't appear that way a few days ago… Elsmere's closet seemed put to good use."

How could he have forgotten that little tidbit? The woman was scrambling his brains. He still had the garter he'd taken from her. For some odd reason he carried it with him. Perhaps to remind him of how much trouble she was. "It was enjoyable enough," he acknowledged. "But you're right, she needs a husband whether she realizes it or not, and you might have a difficult time escaping."

It had been exactly the right thing to say. Harry shuddered. "Heavens! That's the last thing I want."

In for a penny, in for a pound, Rohan thought. "And I doubt she'd be to your liking between the sheets. Despite my best efforts she lay there stiff as a board, and if you think you could get her to do anything more than lie on her back you'd be sadly mistaken. She thinks mouths were meant for closed kisses and nothing more."

Fortunately Harry was too much of a shatter-brain to notice that tonight was the first time in their decades-long acquaintance that Rohan had ever participated in gutter talk. "Good God," Harry breathed. "I'd best steer clear of her. Next thing I know she'll start putting out her lures toward me, especially if you've dropped her. In fact, I believe she already has tonight. I count this a fortunate escape. Thank you, old man. I appreciate the warning."

Rohan bared his teeth in what should have been a smile. "It's the least a friend could do."

He finally allowed himself to turn then, to glance back at her, but there were too many people in the way, obscuring her divan. Probably surrounded by more fawning young men, he thought sourly. He couldn't very well scare them all off—he'd have to count on her unstoppable energy to terrify the rest of them.

"Merton!" A voice came from behind him, light and affected, and he turned around to find himself looking down into Arthur Pennington's bloodshot eyes. Pennington glanced at him and an expression of uneasiness came into his eyes, and Rohan wondered why. Did Pennington suspect they'd been in the tunnels at Kersley Hall? But how was that even possible?

"Rohan," he said in a high-pitched voice. "Didn't know it was you."

"Your servant, Pennington," he said politely. "Have you been keeping yourself busy?" It was a loaded question, but he could hardly hope Pennington was about to confess to all his debauched pastimes.

He was surprised. Pennington's tight grin was positively salacious. "Indeed, I have. Not that it's for public knowledge, but a few of us have been having quite a grand time…"

"Lord Elsmere's attempting to gain your attention," Harry said suddenly, then giggled. "Excuse me, Pennington, didn't mean to interrupt."

But Benedick was not about to let Pennington go if he felt inclined to be informative. "Harry, would you do me the great favor of seeing if Elsmere is interested in a game of cards?"

A look of unexpected frustration crossed Harry's

face, but then he smiled again. "Of course. I need hardly worry that you'd believe any of Pennington's fairy tales."

Pennington failed to look offended, probably because he hadn't heard Harry's deprecating comment. "In fact I need to talk to you," Pennington said, his speech slightly slurred. "It's important."

Harry's affability had vanished, a singular occurrence. Benedick didn't remember when he'd seen Harry less than amused by life.

"'Bout my plague-y sister," Pennington continued.

Did he imagine the lessening of tension surrounding him? But why would Harry be tense? He couldn't imagine anyone less likely to be involved with the Heavenly Host. As far as he knew, Harry, for all his talk, didn't particularly like women, and he was far too good-humored to be involved in such a furtive, ugly affair.

Normally he'd fob Pennington off with some excuse. The last thing he wanted to do was be pressured into making an offer for Dorothea. For someone who had seemed so promising a month ago she'd devolved into his idea of hell on earth. He'd take Melisande first.

No, he wouldn't, he reminded himself. At least Dorothea would leave him alone. Melisande would cling to whomever she ended up with. She would hover and suggest and scream bloody murder if he strayed. She would love him, and the very thought filled him with complete horror.

He gave his version of an affable smile, and Pennington missed the cold glint in his eye. "What may I do for you, Pennington?"

"It's m'sister, don't you know," Pennington said, straining to be affable. "She wanted me to chat you up, give you a little hint. She asked me to invite you to our country place this weekend, and I told her I was busy but she wouldn't hear of it."

"And are you busy, Mr. Pennington?"

If anything he looked even more strained. Pennington might not be very nice, but he was far from bright, either. "I am, Lord Rohan. So you see, I can't possibly invite you. But Dorothea wouldn't hear of it. She's not getting any younger, of course, and she's got the personality of a viper." He suddenly realized how that might sound to a prospective suitor, and immediately attempted to regain lost ground. "A pet viper," he said hastily. "A very nice tame one. And only to her brother, of course. Sisters are the very devil."

Benedick thought back to his own younger sister, married to the monster. If Miranda insisted on staying with someone so completely unsuitable she might at least have had the grace to be miserable about it, instead of ridiculously, breathlessly happy.

No, he didn't want his sister miserable. He just didn't want her with the Scorpion. But that was the least of his worries right now. "They are, indeed," he said politely.

"But you'll come the following week, won't you? You're the closest she's come to an offer in years. Men seem just about ready to come up to scratch when she frightens them off. You don't strike me as a man who frightens easily."

If he offered for Dorothea this would be another idiot he'd have to rescue from the machinations of the Host, he thought, annoyed. And possibly his old friend Harry, as well. Three of them, as well as Melisande's virginal trollop. He may as well do his best to bring down the entire organization—it would be easier than picking and choosing.

"I'm afraid your sister has read too much into my attentions," he said quite formally. "While I hold her in great esteem I was not, in fact, contemplating making her an offer."

Pennington bowed, taking his refusal politely. "I told her that," he drawled. "Told her you were too smart not to see through her."

"But I'm interested in this weekend, Pennington," he went on smoothly. "I haven't heard of any particular social event being held. Have I somehow been deemed unworthy of an invitation? I confess I'm not sure how I could have offended." An arrant lie. He very often offended people, and while he regretted it, he wasn't sure there was much he could do about it. One thing he could say for Melisande Carstairs—she was remarkably difficult to offend.

"Oh, no, nothing of the sort," Pennington said, assessing him. "It's…well, you know, these things are all hush-hush, secret society mumbo jumbo and all that. A bunch of us have revived a…er…fraternal organization, and we're holding a little gathering this weekend. You're welcome to join us." The invitation was automatic, and then memory darkened Pennington's countenance. "Except, of course, that it is a secret society, and we don't let anyone in who hasn't been thoroughly vetted."

Benedick gave him his slow, cynical smile. "Are you telling me I wouldn't pass the standards of this secret organization? I believe my family has been the making of it."

For a moment Pennington lost his cool composure. "I could ask, of course. Can't see the harm in it myself, but you never can tell. Some of the members are downright ridiculous. But then, it's supposed to be a special gathering. Some dashed pagan holiday or suchlike. Can't pay attention to that sort of thing. Best wait till the next time. I can bring up your name at the meeting and see if anyone has any objections."

He could just imagine what his brother would say. "Indeed. Enjoy yourself then, Pennington. And give my regards to your sister."

"Won't do that… She'll simply berate me again. Told her she should concentrate on old Skeffington. He's got just as much blunt as you do, but he hasn't got a title, and he's sixty if he's a day. Stands to reason she'd prefer you. Though I have to say the thought of my sister in bed with anyone is enough to send shivers down my back."

"Pray, don't think of it," Benedick pleaded, a little horrified himself. "I look forward to hearing of her engagement."

If Harry had seemed slightly odd earlier in the evening, he was all affability and silly stories during their card game with Elsmere and several others. He lost a great deal, but then, Harry had always had a tendency to play too deep and lose too much. At the end of the night Benedick had yet to wrest an invitation to the weekend's festivities, no matter how many broad and subtle hints he dropped, no matter how decadent he tried to appear. There was no choice for it; he was simply going to have to show up. He wondered if he could still find the old monk's robes that hung in his parents' wardrobe. He never knew quite why, and when he'd asked his mother she'd blushed, a singular occurrence, and his father had changed the subject. He'd decided he'd rather not know.

Melisande had left by the time he emerged from the card room, and he felt a moment's guilt, coupled with disappointment. He should have at least made certain she had an escort home. Clearly she'd taken care of it herself, and he should be relieved. He wasn't. He'd been looking forward to sparring with her. To telling her he wasn't going to touch her. Right before he did.

It was after two when he let himself into his house. The servants were all in bed. For once even Richmond wasn't hovering. He took a candle and started up the stairs, his mind in turmoil. By the time he reached his rooms on the second floor he was yawning. His bedroom door was ajar, with faint light spilling out, and he closed it behind him, setting the candle down to unfasten his neckcloth.

And then froze as he realized he wasn't alone.

She was sitting in the middle of his bed, waiting

for him, and he stared at her in disbelief. She was wearing a nightdress, a warm, old-fashioned one, buttoned all the way to her neck, voluminous and practical. Her long, tawny hair was in two braids, and her face was scrubbed and clean. She looked like a schoolgirl ready for bed—all she needed was a stuffed doll to complete the picture.

"I'd almost given up on you," she said.

"What are you doing here?" His voice was cold, clipped. He'd been trying so damned hard to do the right thing, and she was stopping him at every turn. He looked at her, and he was furious.

"I would think that would be obvious." Clearly he'd done his job too well in assuring her she was desirable; there was only the faintest note of uncertainty in her voice.

"Do you really think appearing in a man's bedroom in the middle of the night is a good idea? Men tend to be the ones who initiate these things."

"Why?"

"Men have stronger appetites." He watched her through slitted eyes.

"That's ridiculous," she announced. "You've already teased me on more than one occasion about my fondness for sweets."

As if he'd needed any further proof of her innocence. "Not that kind of appetite, you little idiot. I'm talking sexual appetite."

The word *sexual* made her blink, and he allowed himself an evil half smile. She wasn't nearly as bold as she was trying to convince herself she was.

"But if women have weak…sexual appetites then how do you ever manage to have affaires? It seems terribly mismatched."

"Those with strong appetites tend to drift together, just as couples with little interest in bedsport do, as well."

"Which are you?" she inquired in a dulcet voice.

It was a weak attempt to rile him, and he didn't allow himself to react. "I think you know perfectly well the extent of my sexual appetites, Lady Carstairs."

"You called me Melisande before."

"And clearly you mistook it for a carte blanche. How can I make this any clearer? Bribery won't work. I'm not going to let you get involved in this mess any longer, and all the offers won't have any effect on me. I don't want you. I don't desire you. You have nothing I look for in a mistress—you're inexperienced and clumsy, and your choice of a life of continuing celibacy was probably a very wise decision. Now put your clothes on while I go summon my coach."

He was almost at the door when he heard the sound. It was just a small noise, something choked back, and he paused. He who hesitates is lost, he thought. And turned.

He'd expected her to rage at him. He expected fiery eyes and flashing words and high dudgeon. Instead she looked as if he'd shot her puppy. Despite the silly high-necked nightgown, she looked stripped bare, whipped and broken, and he cursed his nasty, vicious tongue that he'd never been able to control.

She struggled, bravely, beautifully, giving him a ghost of her insouciant smile as she pushed back the covers. "You know, I think I've changed my mind." She swung her legs over to the side of the bed, and he could see the strapping on one foot.

It was her toes that did it. He'd forgotten about her lovely, straight, pink toes. Absurd, because he never noticed women's feet—there were always too many more interesting parts to observe somewhere to the north. It was the fragility of them. The humanity of them. He'd been sparring with her for days, thinking of her as an annoyance, entertainment, the enemy, and yes, a sexual toy.

Now she simply looked human, and shattered by his deliberately cruel words. They'd done what he'd intended. She would never come near him again, never look at another man.

And he couldn't bear it.

He leaned back against the door, closing it again, and he reached behind his back and locked it, pulling out the key. "Too bad," he said. "Because I've changed my mind, as well."

25

She'd been a complete and utter idiot, Melisande thought, staring at the cool, cynical beauty that was Benedick Rohan. She was doing her best to hide her misery, but he was looking at her from hooded eyes, and she knew he saw through it. He saw her a little too well, past all the careful defenses she'd built up. He'd known her cool self-assurance was mostly a lie; he'd known she looked at him and something inside of her melted, every time, despite his caustic tongue.

Foolish creature that she was, she'd thought she could handle him without getting burned. Of course he would be willing to bed her, she'd thought, never considering that he might outright refuse. After all, she was a widow, not a virgin. He had no reason to demur unless he simply didn't want her.

He was watching her, reading her every emotion. She tried to summon up her cheerful smile but for once it deserted her. "Changed your mind?" she echoed. "I'm afraid the offer is withdrawn."

He held out the key. "Convince me."

Anger flared, hot and hard, and she slid onto the floor, her toes flinching at the cold of the floorboards. The fire had burned down and the room was chilly. Perhaps Benedick Rohan preferred to sleep in a chilly room. She would never know.

She'd imagined lying in his arms, against his strong, warm body, safe and protected. She'd glossed over the whole unfortunate business that involved naked body parts and wetness and grunting, concentrating on the absurd glory of the way he'd touched her, wanting that again, willing to let him do his worst in order to have it.

But surely someone else could provide the same thing. Granted, Benedick Rohan was an accomplished lover, even the professionals that made up the gaggle knew that. But with their intimate knowledge of half the men in London they could doubtless point her to someone else just as talented and far less...threatening.

And if she found him threatening, why in God's name had she come here?

Her clothes were in his dressing room, but she couldn't see disappearing in there and putting them on again. Her cloak lay across the chair by the fire, as well as her thin evening shoes. She could leave in those.

She held on to the bed as she tried her bad ankle. It was tightly taped, with a rod of wood to give her further support, and she managed relatively well once she got her balance. She let go of the bed and limped toward the chair and her discarded cloak.

He was frowning at her. "You'll catch your death." In a few quick strides he'd crossed the room. Before she realized what he intended he scooped her up in his arms and deposited her back on the bed, pulling the covers up around her before she had time to react. "Stay there while I build up the fire," he ordered.

She started to push the covers away again, but he simply caught her shoulders and shoved her back onto the bed. "The next time you try to get out of the bed you'll most likely regret it," he said in a lowered voice. "At least, at first."

The threat in his voice was sexual—she wasn't so untried that she didn't recognize it. Then again, everything about Benedick Rohan seemed that way. His words were cold and clipped, the expression in his dark green eyes was threatening, but the fingers on her shoulders were absently caressing, the thumbs rubbing against the tight muscles, unconsciously soothing her.

And then he released her, turning his back, and headed toward the fire. She watched with astonishment as he built it up with the expertise of a man accustomed to such menial tasks when most men would be helpless to accomplish anything so practical. The heat began to pour from the coal fire, and she realized she'd been shivering, holding her body tightly against the cool night air and her own fears.

Her fears hadn't abated, but the room was filling with warmth, and he sat back on his heels, watching the flames with satisfaction. They threw his face into strange shadows, making him look half-satanic in the flickering firelight. He looked up at her then, a meditative expression on his face. "What in heaven's name made you choose that nightdress for your first attempt at seduction?" he inquired lazily. "And your hair..."

"What's wrong with my hair?" she said, offended. "This is what I wear to bed. This is how my maid does my hair so that it doesn't get tangled when I sleep. I do realize that demimondaines wear filmy clothing, but I don't really have any, and this is how most women dress for bed."

"It is not, however, the way a woman dresses for her lover. If that's what you wore with Wilfred then it's little wonder he was a sad disappointment."

She flinched. Of course she'd considered that possibility—that her lack of real beauty and feminine wiles had been responsible for the failure that was Wilfred. While she hadn't communicated her uncertainties to Emma and the gaggle, they had made it quite clear that all a man really needed to enjoy himself was a naked, willing female, and she'd definitely been that. Well, not particularly naked, but most definitely willing, and she'd let him do what he wanted.

Which was disgusting. For some reason the same base acts didn't seem nearly as foul when she thought of Rohan practicing them. And that had been her downfall. For the first time she'd considered sexual congress with a man and not felt ill, and she'd decided to act on that relative enthusiasm. Only to be summarily rejected.

"I'm certain the unpleasant nature of my time with Wilfred was entirely my fault," she said in a cool voice as she drew the shattered bits of her self-esteem back around her like the cloak she longed for. "And you've made it very clear that you have no interest in me, but I've been too besotted to listen." *Damn, where did that word come from?* She quickly went on, hoping he wouldn't notice her slip. "You have made me see the error of my ways, and I promise I won't suggest anything so untoward again. Now if you'd hand me my cloak I will cease to bother you."

He rose, with that casual, lazy grace that caught her eyes every time, and he drew his neckcloth out and tossed it on the foot of the bed. "I am afraid, my pet, that you are doomed to bother me. And you're going to have to convince me that you've changed your mind before I let you go."

It should have frightened her. Outraged her, terrified her, disgusted her. Instead, as he started toward her with his lazy, sinuous grace, she felt that sudden clenching in her stomach, the tingling in her skin, and she knew if he touched her she'd be lost.

She wanted to be lost, didn't she? At least, that's what she'd thought several hours ago when she'd come up with this absurd scheme. Now, of course, she wasn't so sure.

"I don't think…" she began, when he picked up the end of one of her plaits and untied the ribbon, slowly pulling her hair free. She looked down at it, mesmerized, the tawny gold against his strong hand, the way he let if drift through his fingers. Hair had no feeling, and yet she could feel the caress in every inch of her body. He spread it out against her shoulder and then took the other braid, repeating the act, running the strands through this thumb and forefinger like fine silk.

"You really do have the most glorious hair," he murmured in that cool, detached voice. "It's a crime to hide it in those dreadful bonnets."

She couldn't move. She wanted to lift her hands, to push him away, but she was frozen, if heat could freeze, staring up at him. He sat on the bed, and the mattress sank a little beneath his weight, and she started to roll toward him. She put her hands down to hold herself still, and he laughed softly. He leaned down and feathered his lips against hers, and unwillingly she responded, her body rising into the touch of his mouth, and she wanted to cry. She closed her eyes, so he wouldn't be able to see the hurt and longing in her gaze. *Let it be over soon,* she thought dazedly. *Let me just get through the next half hour and it will teach me that I wasn't made for this sort of thing. I can survive anything.*

He kissed her closed eyelids, so gently, then her trembling upper lips, the arch of her brow, finally the lobe of her ear. And then he sank his teeth into it, biting her hard, and an electric shock went through her body as her eyes flew open in outrage and something else that she didn't want to examine.

He sat back, an expression of bemused satisfaction

on his face. "Besotted, are you? That should make my job a great deal easier." He rose, and she felt a momentary panic. He was going to let her go. He'd made his point—she was really terrified of doing this no matter what she said. Now he would send her away and she would go, defeated and humbled, and she'd never be fool enough to...

He had shrugged out of his jacket, no mean feat given the perfect fit of the garment. He unfastened the shirt studs and set them on the table beside him, slowly exposing his sun-darkened skin to the candlelight, and she took a swift breath. Wilfred had been very pale and thin, almost scrawny. Thomas had been covered with grizzled gray hair.

She'd thought Rohan was thin as well, but she'd been wrong. He was all sleek muscle and tanned skin as he stripped his shirt off, and she stared at him, conflicting emotions roiling through her.

She cleared her throat, searching for some kind of normalcy in the charged air. "Well, it's no wonder I'm drawn to you," she said in what she hoped was a pragmatic tone. "You're ridiculously beautiful, and you know it."

He was amused. "Do I?"

"Of course you do." Now she could be acerbic with no effort. "You carry yourself that way, like a man who knows his own worth and recognizes his value. You stroll and swagger and move like a pirate surveying his prey."

He let out a hoot of laughter as the snowy white shirt fell onto the floor. "And just how many pirates are numbered among your acquaintance?" he asked politely.

She wanted to come up with a clever response, but the sight of all that bare flesh momentarily silenced her. Until he reached for the fastenings of his breeches, and she let out a strangled cry. "Don't!"

A look of irritation crossed his face. "Sweet Charity, if I wait much longer to shuck my breeches I'll have a damned hard time getting them off. It's not as if you're a virgin. You've seen a man naked before."

"No, I haven't."

He paused, then shook his head in disbelief. "It's little wonder you have no idea what you want. Your initiation has been criminally botched."

"My husband was elderly," she said, trying for dignity. "And ill, besides."

"Then why did you marry him?"

"He was my only choice."

He looked even more incredulous. "I don't believe you," he said flatly. "The men of London aren't all such blind idiots."

He couldn't have said anything more certain to soothe her ravaged pride. "I don't think my aunt would have lied to me. I didn't have any money, I was far too serious and I didn't take. I was lucky to get Sir Thomas."

"Sir Thomas had thirty thousand pounds a year, and he would have made a generous settlement on your cousin as well as yourself. If anyone less plump in the purse came along I expect she would have sent them about their business."

"She wouldn't have!" Melisande gasped.

Benedick sat in a chair by the fire and proceeded to pull off his shoes and stockings. "You are still astonishingly naive," he said, leaning back in the chair. "Next thing you'll be insisting that I don't want you."

That was enough to bring her head up. "I am fully aware that you feel a certain physical response to my proximity," she began. "But I also know that anyone can arouse that reaction in a male—it means nothing."

His smile was grim. "I'm not that easy, my precious. I prefer my bed partners adventurous and experienced. You're going to be hard work and nothing but trouble."

"Then why don't you unlock the door?" she snapped.

"Because you'll be worth it." His voice was soft then, and he rose, pinched out the candle by the chair and approached the bed.

"I don't…"

"Stop talking, Melisande," he said, sliding his hands behind her neck and cupping her chin with his thumbs. "We've already wasted too much time." He put his mouth against hers, and this was no sweet salute, no soft seduction. With the pressure of his thumbs he pushed her mouth open beneath his, and she felt his tongue against her, tasted him, dark and hot and sweet.

She should argue. She should fight. She did neither. She lifted her arms and slid them around his neck, dancing into his kiss. He pulled her down on the bed, covering her, and the feel of his hot skin against her hands was a shocking intimacy. His fingers brushed her throat, and the collar of her night robe began to part. He moved his mouth away from her, down the line of her jaw to the hollow of her throat, heated breath warming her as he slowly unfastened the row of tiny buttons that usually took her so long to fasten, his mouth lazily following the exposed flesh.

She still had the covers around her, and he pulled them away, pushing them off her. The heat from the fire had begun to fill the room, and she closed her eyes, feeling his mouth on her skin. His hands moved up and covered her breasts, and she jumped, momentarily startled, then subsided as he stroked her, slowly, into a kind of dazed submission.

She was doing this, she was really going to do this, she thought. Her nipples hardened against his fingers, and the sharp intensity of the pleasure was almost painful. He was watching her, rubbing his thumbs back and forth across her breasts, and the feeling burned straight down to that place between her legs.

"Don't," she gasped, afraid of the sensation.

"Don't be absurd, my pet. This is simply pleasure. You need to learn to get used to it."

She sucked in her breath, wanting to squirm. "It's…uncomfortable."

He laughed. "Sex isn't about comfort. At least, not what lies between you and me. It's hot and hard and aching, and it won't feel better until we're finished."

"Then why do it?" she whispered dizzily.

He smiled. "Because it feels so good." And he set his mouth against her breast, sucking at her, and she let out a strangled cry.

It was too much. And it was not enough. He'd pushed the nightgown open to expose her breasts, and the sight of his head down against her, drawing her into his mouth made that ache grow stronger still. He put his hand on her other breast, his fingers dark against the pure white of her skin, plucking at her, and she let out a long, low wail as the burning grew hotter, harder.

He lifted his head to look at her. "Touch me," he whispered. "Put your hands on me."

She realized she'd been lying there like a virgin bride, clutching the sheets in her fists. She released them, slowly lifting her hands to touch his shoulders. They were rock hard with tension, and there was no shirt to cling to, only warm, smooth flesh. He seemed satisfied, though, and lowered his mouth again, this time to her other nipple, and she wanted to cry out, to beg him. She didn't, because she had no idea what she'd beg him for.

He pulled his mouth back, and ran his tongue across the distended peak, causing her to gasp in reaction. And then he blew on the dampness, cool in the heated air, and her fingers dug into his shoulders as she squirmed on the mattress in mindless need.

"Let's get this over and done with," he muttered, climbing off the bed to reach for the fastening of his breeches.

She didn't plan to look. She knew she should be curious, but both Thomas and Wilfred had been so secretive about their...rods that she suspected there was something shameful about them. But Benedick had already stripped, and it was too late to look away. She simply stared in awe.

He was magnificent. His torso and legs were long and lean, muscled and strong. He didn't have the thick mat of hair that had covered seemingly every inch of her husband's body. His chest was smooth, with just a bit of hair in the middle, moving in a line down below his waist, setting off the jutting erection he somehow thought was going to fit inside her.

"No," she said, shaking her head. "You're too big."

He laughed then. "There's something to be said for having such an ingenuous lover. *Merci du compliment.* It will fit."

She opened her mouth to protest but he simply silenced her with his tongue, climbing onto the bed beside her, and started pushing off the rest of the nightgown.

"You really want me naked?" she whispered, still uncertain.

"I really want you naked," he said, moving his mouth to the sensitive skin between her neck and shoulder, biting her gently as his hands divested her of the voluminous nightgown. And now they were both naked in the bed, and she knew there really was no going back.

It should have frightened her. Instead it empowered her, and she reached up to touch his long, thick hair, as she'd wanted to do countless times before, letting her fingers sift through the silk strands, wishing she could bring it to her mouth, to taste it.

His mouth was moving down, kissing her, licking her, biting her, and she arched up in delight, wanting something, not sure what it was.

"For God's sake, would you please touch me?" he said in a strangled voice.

She blinked. "But I am touching you."

"I mean my cock."

It took her a moment to realize what he meant. He took her hand, drawing it down his chest, and she shivered in delight, entranced with the feel of his hot skin. And then he placed it around him, the hard, silken part of him, and she tried to pull her hand away in sudden shyness.

He held her there, wrapping his fingers around hers, so that she had no choice. She cupped him, and he drew their hands up and down the rigid length of him, and she heard him groan in pleasure.

"How do you feel?" he whispered in her ear, his voice rough.

She was so caught up in the feel of him that it took her a moment. "Afraid," she said finally. "A little bit."

"And…?"

"And restless. Needy. Wanting," she said, shocked at herself.

He kissed her. "That's good. Anything else?" He kept moving their hands in unison.

"And…and wet," she said, knowing she was

blushing. The one candle that still burned offered little illumination, just enough to embarrass her.

He smiled then, and kissed her again, full and openmouthed. "Good… You've had me hard for days. It's only fair that I should make you wet."

"But…but…"

His hand released hers, but she didn't let go. Instead her grip loosened and her fingertips touched him, glanced across the hot skin, the rigid, protruding veins, the flared head. It still seemed mysterious, but as she let her fingers learn him she felt reaction shudder through his strong body.

He moved then, pulling away from her, lying on his side next to her, watching her out of hooded eyes. She had the sudden fear that she'd hurt him, offended him, but the intent look on his face made her skin heat.

"Relax, sweet Charity," he said softly. "I'm just going to make sure you're ready." His hand covered her stomach, warm and strong, and she shivered in response, as he moved it down, between her legs, his fingers slipping through the curls, into the wetness, and he closed his eyes, smiling. "Oh, my precious, you most definitely are ready. I had so many other things in mind, but I'm afraid I'm simply going to have to take you now. I'll have to lick you another time."

"But you did. My breasts."

"Not there," he said, brushing against her hard nipples. "Here." And his fingers slid inside her.

She arched up in shock, crying out. He stroked

her, slowly, spreading the wetness around, and then he moved between her legs, and she tensed, knowing what was coming, knowing it was going to be miserable.

The touch of him against her silenced her, stilled her. She was trembling, trying to hide it, but lying naked beneath a man made subterfuge almost impossible. "I'll stop if it hurts you," he said, pushing against her. "We'll go slow. Just tell me how it feels."

She trusted him. She'd forgotten that salient point—she trusted him. She nodded, unable to speak, bracing herself, and his smile was so sweet it almost shattered her. "No, my love. This isn't a torture chamber. Relax."

"I c-c-can't," she stammered, shivering despite the warm of the air.

"I'll help." And leaning forward, he bit the top of her breast, just hard enough to shock her into loosening her muscles. At that he pushed into her, so hard, so big, and she should tell him to stop, tell him that it hurt.

And it did hurt. Just a little bit. So little that the pain was almost a kind of pleasure, and she shifted, lifting her hips, needing more of him.

"Am I hurting you?" His mouth was against her ear.

"More," she said, her voice ragged. "Please. More."

He held himself still for a moment, and then he pushed, slid deep, filling her, and she cried out, arching against him, taking him.

He began to thrust, slowly at first, watching her,

and she knew he was afraid of hurting her. She wanted to scream at him, to demand, to beg. Did she want him to leave her body? Did she want him to slam into her? She needed something, so desperately, and she didn't know how to reach it.

His hands cupped her hips, angling them. He continued to thrust, ignoring her efforts to speed him, slow and hard and deep, each push one more claim on her body, and she felt the darkness began to bubble beneath her skin, felt the need blossom and grow and spread through her body, reaching every inch of her skin, tiny pinpricks of reaction. It wasn't too late, she thought desperately. She could make him stop. She didn't have to go to this terrifying place he was taking her, where nothing existed but the man inside her, their bodies joined, sweating, slapping together. There was no escape, she didn't want to escape, but she kept fighting, pushing it away.

"Stop it, Melisande," he growled in her ear. "Take it. Claim it."

"No," she sobbed.

"Take it," he said again, hard inside her, slamming into her so that the bed shook and her body trembled and she knew she would break apart, and she couldn't stop, couldn't stop shaking, couldn't stop crying, couldn't stop…

She froze, as an endless, keening delight stiffened her body and tore away the last of her defenses. She felt him cry out, spill inside her, and she welcomed it all, the wet heat of his seed, the shaking of his body, the crazy-mad delight that caught her in its grip, so tightly she thought she would never unravel.

And then it loosened its hold, and she fell back on the bed, panting, weeping, taken and destroyed. He collapsed on top of her, his chest heaving, and she could still feel him inside her; she still shivered around him in her fading response.

He released her then, rolling to his side, and she was suddenly so cold. Covered in ice, she thought dizzily, knowing she had to get away. She'd been wrong, he'd been right. This was a terrible idea. Because she'd needed him too much, and the having, and the letting go, were too painful.

She wondered if her legs would support her if she tried to get out of bed. Men fell asleep afterward, didn't they? How long could she safely wait?

And then, to her surprise, he pulled her into his arms, tucking her close against him. "You're not going anywhere," he said sleepily. "We've only just begun."

She didn't question him. She would stay there as long as he'd have her. Lie in his arms to the break of day and beyond. Anything he wanted.

And while she waited for him to fall asleep, she drifted off herself, lost in exhausted oblivion.

26

Benedick lay on his back in the slowly gathering dawn. His body felt so richly sated that any move on his part would require superhuman effort, and he had no intention of attempting it. He felt…he could think of no adequate word for it. *Confused* was inadequate, *shattered* too emotional when he was a man who eschewed emotions. He lay in his own bed, the bed he'd never shared with anyone, and listened to her breathe, deep in sleep. He'd worn her out, as he'd planned to. He'd taken her to places she had no idea existed, again and again. He'd taken her hard, he'd taken her fast. He'd made love to her with heartbreaking tenderness. She was the one who was supposed to be shattered.

Instead she slept, and he lay beside her, his mind in turmoil.

Damn her. He should have simply shagged her the first chance he had, and those occasions had been numerous. He'd recognized the sensuous nature beneath her practical exterior, and it would have taken very little effort to have her and then dismiss her. He had no interest in a long-term mistress, and there was no reason why he should be hard again after last night, wanting her, unaccountably furious with her for sleeping so soundly.

He forced himself to move, slipping from the bed and heading into his dressing room. The dim light from the early dawn gave just enough light for him to see her discarded clothes on the slipper chair, and he gathered them up once he'd pulled on his thick wool banyan. He came back into the now-chilly bedroom and looked down at her.

She looked like a child, an innocent, sweetly sleeping, though he knew for a fact that she had to be at least thirty years of age. Even if he were insane enough to consider marrying she would be the last person he would choose. She was too old to be of prime childbearing age, and since she'd spent ten years of married life without conceiving she was most likely barren. His only reason for considering marriage was to provide an heir, and Melisande Carstairs wasn't the way to do it.

He was better off with her as far away as possible. There was no earthly reason for the sex to have been as disturbing as it was. She had no skills, no experience; he'd had to coax her and please her when he was used to being the one who needed to be pleased. She was simply wrong; he'd always known it, and the impossible hours they'd just passed simply proved it.

And the longer he stared down at her, the harder he became.

He dumped the clothes on top of her, and she awoke with a start, momentarily disoriented. She sat up, realized she was naked and quickly pulled her discarded clothes against her body, covering herself. Her eyes narrowed as she saw him, and a rich color rose to her cheeks, suffusing them, and he could see her mouth, soft, tremulous, uncertain.

"I would suggest you dress and return home before it's full light," he said, his voice clipped and distant.

"Why?"

Damn the woman! Didn't she know a dismissal when she heard one? He needed her dressed and out of there, before he changed his mind and threw away everything he'd planned so carefully.

"I wouldn't want the gaggle to jump to any conclusions."

"What kind of conclusions might they jump to?"

He wanted to strangle her. He wanted to wrap his hands around her neck and hold her still while he kissed her. "That this was anything more than a momentary lapse on your part and a mistake on mine. I've done my duty, aided in your education, and now you're free to apply that knowledge in a more suitable direction."

She was very still. No expression crossed her face, but then, she was good at hiding her reactions. He wondered if that was pain in her dark blue eyes. If so, that was a good thing. It would make the lesson stick.

"Indeed," she said finally. "Have you already taught me everything you know?"

It was a worthy comeback, and he fought his admiration. "All that you're capable of assimilating. I believe I made myself clear. If there was a chance in hell I'd ever find myself harboring any kind of feelings for you I wouldn't have succumbed to the very ripe temptation you offered. Awkwardness and enthusiasm is an interesting change now and then, and I won't deny I enjoyed myself, but in general I prefer a more sophisticated pleasure. Go find some earnest young man who'll share your charitable activities and leave me alone."

She blinked. Such a small reaction to his deliberately brutal words, and he wanted more. He wanted to lash out at her, to cause her the same consternation that she'd caused him. But she simply looked at him for a long moment, and he had the odd feeling that she was taking his cruel words and translating them in her brain, as if from a foreign language.

"I see," she said after a moment. "Perhaps you would be so good as to summon your carriage to drive me home? Or would you prefer I take a hackney?"

He refused to flush. "My carriage will be at your disposal, madam."

"And would you also allow me to dress in private? I find I have no interest in displaying my body in front of you."

"Trust me, it would have no effect on me," he said, ignoring his damned erection. In truth, he wasn't sure he'd be able to continue with this if he saw her naked once more. The curve of her pale breasts; the soft, perfumed skin; the tawny curls between her legs…the very thought made him break out in a cold sweat.

"And what about the Heavenly Host?"

He had already turned toward the door. "You may trust me to take care of the situation."

"But I don't," she said softly. "I don't trust you."

He remembered her words from the night before. She'd told him she'd chosen him because she trusted him. He'd managed to do an effective job of smashing that trust. "Very wise. But I give you my word—there will be no murders on the night of the full moon."

She didn't respond. She merely looked at him, seemingly calm and unmoved, and yet he remembered her body clenching his, remembered the shuddering climax that had shaken them both. He could see the mark his mouth had made at the top of one breast, and knew there would be others on her sensitive skin. He remembered when she had sunk her teeth into his shoulder rather than cry out, and the spur that tiny bit of pain had forced.

"Goodbye, my lord."

Even then he wanted to change his mind. Wanted to cross the room in two swift strides, pull her back into his arms and kiss her senseless. Wanted to bury his aching cock in her sweet, welcoming body, drinking in the richness of her response.

He gave her a nod, and left the room, before he made an even bigger disaster of his life than he already had.

She pushed the covers back, looking down at her body. She was damp and sticky between her legs— the last time he'd been too tired to do anything more than collapse on top of her, and they'd slept. Or so she thought. He'd washed her the other times, gently ministering to her, and she'd let him. Foolish, foolish woman.

The room was cold, the fire out, and she looked down to see her nipples puckered against the icy air. There was a red mark on her breast, another on her thigh, and she closed her eyes for a moment, remembering.

She was made of sterner stuff than that, she reminded herself, opening them again. This was all working out for the best. She'd chosen Benedick Rohan for one reason and one reason alone. He was purportedly a brilliant lover. If the previous night was any judge of his skills, he'd been sadly underestimated. He was *astonishing*. So good that even with his cruel words echoing in her ears she'd still lie down for him if he wanted her.

So now she knew. The pleasures of the flesh were, in fact, desirable, and how much more delightful they'd be with someone she loved. She could now search out a good, decent man to marry and, perhaps with a miracle, bear children. She wanted to be a mother. She now had enough information to ensure that the next man she fell in love with would be able to bring her pleasure, as well. She needed to get home swiftly, to make notes as to what had been most pleasurable so she wouldn't forget, and then she would instruct her future husband….

There was a strange, choking noise in the room, and she looked around her, appalled, then realized the sound came from her own throat. She swallowed, convulsively, shoving the pain back. She was being ridiculous.

She washed swiftly with the now-icy bowl of water before dressing. She was shaking from the cold, and perhaps something else, but she wasn't going to consider that possibility. When she finally rose to her feet, her ankle almost gave way beneath her, and she welcomed the pain, a distraction from what she refused to consider.

Her cloak lay across the chair by the dead coals, and she wrapped it around her shoulders, pulling the hood up over her face. She found the walking stick she used to help her perambulate, then opened the door, half afraid she'd see him again. She wasn't quite sure she'd manage to keep her icy calm much longer if she had to look at him again. Into his dark green eyes, cool and assessing, at his beautiful, distant face.

Someone was waiting for her, and she almost jumped when she recognized Rohan's majordomo. "Your ladyship," he said, his voice soft and inexpressibly kind. "Your carriage is waiting. I've had it brought to the side portico—there's less of a distance for you to walk on your bad ankle."

"That's very kind of you." She struggled for a moment, then remembered his name. "Richmond," she added, and was rewarded with his smile.

"It's my honor, your ladyship. May I offer you my arm?"

She took it. She didn't want to lean on him, didn't want his kindness, but she really had no choice. They made their way down the flights of stairs with stately grace, and the pain was a welcome distraction from that stronger, bleaker pain inside her. By the time he handed her into Rohan's town carriage she was biting her lip to keep from crying out, a film of sweat covering her forehead. She'd been an idiot, as always. If she'd simply stayed home, as Rohan had instructed her, this never would have happened. She would be in happy ignorance of the wonders of the flesh, and she could continue to think of Rohan as an annoyingly attractive thorn in her side.

She sat very still on the seat as she was conveyed the short distance to King Street, and she directed the coachman to take her around the back, to the garden entrance, rather than up the twelve steep marble steps to the front door. She was handed down with great care, far more care than Rohan had ever shown toward her, and she limped up onto the terrace, pushing open the French doors that led to what had once been a salon and now served as a sewing room. The house was still and quiet, the gaggle still asleep in their chaste beds, while she had been carousing.

She couldn't think of them as the gaggle any longer. That had been his term for them, and he was no longer any part of her life. She moved into the deserted hallway, glancing up at the interminable flights of stairs.

She couldn't face them. She went into the front room, where she and Emma both had desks, and sank down on the chaise, leaning back and closing her eyes. The morning was still and quiet and beautiful, and she had a new life to begin. What a glorious morning, how delighted she was with her little experiment, and how good it was that Rohan had retained his boredom with her while proffering her exquisite, sublime pleasure.

Indeed, life couldn't be much better.

"Are you crying, miss?" A small, anxious voice came from the general vicinity of the banked fire, and Melisande made a damp, choking noise as a bundle of rags emerged from the shadows. It took a moment for her vision to clear through her streaming tears, and she saw Betsey's bright young face, creased in uncharacteristic worry as she looked up at her.

For a moment Melisande's voice refused to obey her. She struggled, then managed to come out with something faintly akin to a conversational tone. "My ankle is paining me, Betsey."

"Yes, miss."

Betsey was still proving remarkably stubborn

when it came to proper forms of address, and Melisande knew she should instruct her in the proper form. *Your ladyship* for a titled female, *miss* for an untitled one. On no account was she a miss, and yet Betsey persisted, possibly because the only comfort and safety she'd known had been provided by a miss long ago.

Melisande swiftly wiped the dampness away from her cheeks. "What are you doing up so early, Betsey?"

Betsey moved into the light, and Melisande could see that the child had been crying as well, and her own heart turned over. "I couldn't sleep, miss. I curl up down here when I can't. That way, when Aileen comes back, she'll be able to find me right away."

It took all Melisande's self-control not to wail. Aileen wasn't coming back; of that one thing she was absolutely certain. Whether the Heavenly Host had murdered her, or Aileen had simply run off to a place where she didn't have to work quite so hard, Melisande didn't know. She only knew she wouldn't be back.

"You need your bed, child."

"You do, as well, your ladyship."

Melisande smiled briefly. For once Betsey had got it right. "I'll tell you what. You and I will both go up to our beds. I'll leave word with Mrs. Cadbury that you're to be allowed to sleep late today, and by the time we're both up and dressed we'll both be feeling much better. Does that sound like a good idea?"

Betsey looked at her doubtfully. "I don't think I'll

be feeling better until Aileen comes back. I don't know what I can do if she doesn't come home." She yawned unselfconsciously, and for the first time that morning Melisande felt like smiling.

"You can stay here for as long as you want to," she said, and paused. "If Aileen doesn't come back, you still have more than twenty women who'll be your older sisters."

"Not Cook," Betsey said judiciously. "She says I get in the way. She's more like a mum. But she says I might not be a total disaster in the kitchen."

Melisande did smile then. "That's good news. If you learn to cook you'll always have a job."

"Violet says working's harder than lying on your back. I think she's wrong, though."

"She is wrong. If you don't feel like sleeping, you could go down to the kitchens. Cook is usually awake by now, starting the bread. She could use the help."

"Yes, miss." *Your ladyship* had been forgotten once again, but Melisande simply nodded. If Mollie Biscuits was taking Betsey under her wing then the child would be well looked after and well trained. One less soul she had to worry about.

She waited until Betsey had vanished, then struggled to her feet. She needed her bed; she needed a bath to wash away the taste and the touch and scent of him on her skin. It was time to put that part of her life behind her. She had no choice but to trust his word. He would stop the Heavenly Host.

In the meantime, she had to move ahead with her own life. The wicked temptation of Benedick Rohan belonged in the past. The future lay bright and bold in front of her. All she had to do was get through the next twenty-four hours and she'd be fine, perfectly fine.

She locked her bedroom door. She cried as she washed herself, cried as she took her clothes and shoved them into a hamper. Cried as she took a clean shift and drawers, new stockings and garters and then climbed into her narrow bed. It wasn't until she closed her eyes that she remembered he'd lain with her in that bed, his body covering hers as his deft fingers pinched out the candlelight, leaving them alone in the darkness.

And it was then that the foolish tears finally stopped, as the pain wrapped around inside her, crushing her into silence. She rolled over on her stomach, burying her face in the soft feather pillow, wondering if it was humanly possible to smother oneself.

It didn't matter. It was over. Time to move on.

There was still laudanum in the bottle beside the bed. This time she didn't hesitate. She took her dose, swallowed it and closed her eyes, waiting for oblivion to come, for the waves of pain in her ankle to cease.

It took far too long. In the distance she could hear Emma's voice, calling someone, but it wasn't her. And it didn't matter. They could wait. Just for this one day she wasn't going to take care of anyone but herself.

Just this one day.

27

Benedick was a man who could hold his liquor. At times in his life he'd been a three-bottle man and still been able to hold an intelligent conversation and make his way home without stumbling. The ability to drink and not show it was almost more important to being a gentleman than paying one's gambling debts, and when he was seventeen years old his father, a reformed rake and ne'er-do-well, had taught him those salient social graces, much to his mother's annoyance. Then again, Charlotte Rohan had always been alarmingly strong-minded. She'd had to be, to deal with his charming father's ways, and Adrian Rohan had ended up being that most original of creatures, a devoted husband, much to his secret embarrassment.

Like father like son. It didn't matter that the world considered the Rohans to be profligates and degenerates—the moment they found their soul mates they became, if not the epitome of righteous behavior, at least excellent husbands. Even his distant cousin

Alistair, one of the founding members of the Heavenly Host, had retired to Ireland with his English bride and lived out an exemplary life breeding horses and children and worshipping his wife.

His own grandfather, Francis Rohan, had been the stuff of legend, which had been difficult to imagine when he thought of the charming and devoted old man he'd adored. He'd been unable to keep his eyes or his hands off his plump grandmother, much to his father's embarrassment, but in truth, his father was just the same.

Benedick had had every intention of following in the family tradition. He'd sown his wild oats, even attended a few of the waning gatherings of the Heavenly Host before falling in love with Annis Duncan. They should have lived happily ever after, with that same comfortable devotion that had been a shining example.

But apparently his generation was cursed. His darling Annis had died, and he could no longer remember what she looked like. His second attempt had been disastrous, confirming the suspicion that the luck of the wicked Rohans had run out. His brother Charles had married a prig, his brother Brandon was courting ruin and an early death, and his sister Miranda had married her kidnapper, a master of thieves, for God's sake! And had the effrontery to be happy about it.

Benedick leaned back in his chair, eyeing the brandy bottle with a jaundiced eye. He'd been drinking steadily, pacing himself, in order to blot out these very thoughts that were plaguing him. Better to think about his family than that other, horrific memory that was eating at his stomach and heart and soul. Assuming he even had a heart and soul—he took leave to doubt it. He reached for the brandy bottle, missing, and then clasped it. He spilled more than he managed to get in the glass, and he decided it might be wise to forgo the glass altogether for the next round. Less trouble for the servants.

Why he should care about the servants was beyond his comprehension, but that was his mother's influence again. Why couldn't he have had some distant mother who never saw her children and left their upbringing to capable nannies? Then he wouldn't be plagued with such ridiculous concerns like fair treatment for the servants, responsibility for his siblings, general decency.

And he wouldn't be doing his best to blot out the memory of his evil, vicious tongue. He was capable of being a nasty son of a bitch, and he knew it. He'd proved that early this morning, letting his evil inner demon free to slash and hack like a medieval warrior, leaving his victim broken and bleeding on the ground.

Except that he wasn't a medieval warrior, and his weapons had been words, not maces and broadswords. Words that were lies, slashing at the woman he'd just made love to, destroying her until there was nothing left.

He could still see her face, calm, unmoving, the utter bleakness in her dark blue eyes. He'd managed to smash Charity Carstairs's infernal amour propre, gotten through to the heart of her, the soul of her, and crushed her.

He'd drained the glass, he realized, and he could still see her. He reached for the bottle and took a deep drink, letting the fiery taste of it slide down his throat. He should see if he could get some good Scots whiskey. That would work even better than French brandy. Too bad the British weren't as adept at creating something to knock a man on his arse.

He could ask his brother the direction of the opium den he habituated if he got desperate enough. Anything to forget what he'd done. But Brandon had disappeared, and wouldn't return, at least, not until the infernal fraternity lost its hold over him. The opium would still lay claim to his soul, but Benedick would help him deal with that when the time came.

He cursed, with long, inventive, impossibly obscene phrases. He had the unbearable suspicion that he wouldn't be able to save Brandon. That no matter what he did, he couldn't stop the spiral of self-destruction that was driving him, any more than he was able to save his sister from her disastrous marriage.

He took another swallow, letting the blissful veil of confusion float down over him. There was something else he was trying not to think of, something that kept pushing through to torment him. It had something to do with Charity Carstairs. Melisande. A beautiful name for a beautiful woman. Creamy skin. Magnificent breasts. Sweet little sounds when he took her, delicious shudders when she climaxed, shock in her eyes each time she reached her peak. He'd shown her, hadn't he, he thought dismally. Taught her just what she was missing. And then made sure she'd never seek it out again, if cruelty was the price she had to pay.

Why had he done it? He was adept at ridding himself of females he'd lost interest in, all without offending them. But maybe that was the problem. He hadn't lost interest in her. He'd become so wretchedly obsessed and entangled with her, after one night of sweaty, wicked delight, that he'd panicked.

He was supposed to hold his liquor, treat women with civility and never show fear. He'd cocked that up to a fare-thee-well. His mother would be horrified. His father would thrash him. No he wouldn't. Too big to thrash. B'sides, his father always hated to punish him. His mother's disappointment would be reward enough.

Melisande's face swam in front of him, the softness of her mouth, so vulnerable, so sweet, so innocent. The Saint of King Street, and here he was, debauching her. He shouldn't feel guilty, but he was. It didn't matter. He still wanted that mouth. He wanted so much more—there'd barely been time to do more than touch the possibilities of the flesh. He wanted to do things to her that had never interested him before. He wanted to cover every inch of her creamy skin with his mouth. He wanted to see if he could make her scream in pleasure. He wanted…he wanted…

The brandy bottle slipped from his hand, hitting the Aubusson carpet and rolling toward the fire. He reached out for it, and his balance faltered. The chair went over, and his head smashed against something hard. Might knock some sense into him, he thought dazedly.

But maybe he could sleep just a little bit, since he was already lying down. The floor was as good a place as any. He hadn't taken Melisande on the floor, had he? He'd wanted to.

Bloody hell. She was still haunting him. He reached out for the brandy bottle, but it had rolled out of his reach, and there was something wet and warm on his head. He reached up a hand to touch it, then brought it down to look at it.

Blood. He didn't like blood. In fact, among his other, un-gentleman-like transgressions, he couldn't stand the sight of it.

And he finally, happily, passed out on the library floor.

28

Miranda Rohan de Malheur, Countess of Rochdale, let out a shriek of dismay, raced into the room and sank down next to the unconscious figure of her oldest brother. There was blood everywhere, and she threw her arms around him, terrified that he was dead.

He rewarded her with a loud snore, and she caught the reek of brandy. She sat back on her heels with annoyance, turning to look up at her husband. "He's dead drunk, and I think he hit his head. He's bleeding like a pig, the carpet is ruined, and I thought we were here to save Brandon, not Benedick."

Lucien de Malheur, the lady's husband, lately referred to as the Scorpion for his less than honorable habits, limped into the room, staring down at his brother-in-law. "How the mighty have fallen," he murmured softly. "My heart, you're getting blood all over that lovely frock. Leave him to me. The Rohans are blessed with very hard heads, and I don't doubt he's suffered worse. He's going to be more troubled by his hangover than a little scalp wound."

Miranda looked back at her brother, the stalwart she'd always depended on, fear and annoyance fighting for dominance. "Are you quite certain?"

"Absolutely. Go find that elderly manservant and see if he can round up a few strong footmen to remove your brother to his bed. I doubt we'll need to call a doctor—even from here the wound looks superficial, but he'll need a cleanup. Do your brothers tend to cast up their accounts when they've drunk too much?"

"They don't usually drink too much. Something must be very wrong. Benedick usually fixes things. He doesn't give up and drink himself into a stupor. Things must be very bad, indeed."

"Things are never as bad as they seem. And that's why we're here, my love. I received word that the Heavenly Host are holding a gathering in Kent this Saturday, and according to Salfield, the newly reformed organization is a far cry from the harmless activities I remember."

"Harmless?" Miranda said with a screech, her flashing green eyes promising retribution. "I seem to remember a very unpleasant evening…"

"Pray, don't!" Lucien said with a shudder. "Haven't I paid for my transgressions sufficiently?"

"No." She blew him a kiss before turning back to her brother. His color was good, his breathing even, and the blood, while horrific in appearance, seemed to have stopped flowing. Her husband was right: Benedick was foxed but perfectly fine. She rose, taking the handkerchief her husband offered and wiping the blood off her hands. "You take care of him, and I'll go in search of Brandon."

"I thought the old man said he had moved out."

"Richmond," she corrected. "And he knows more than that. He always does. You clean up this mess—" she cast a withering glance at her favorite big brother "—and I'll start working on the other."

The brandy had betrayed him completely this time, Benedick thought, in between being violently ill. Not only was Melisande Carstairs still haunting him, but now he had the infernal vision of his despised brother-in-law holding the basin for him. He could think of no worse punishment than imagining the Scorpion at hand, but at least, in his still-drunken state, he knew perfectly well that his sister and her husband almost never left the Lake District and the bastard would never dare show his scarred, ugly face at Benedick's house.

He slept, awoke to cast up his accounts once more, demanded brandy, received none, imagined his brother-in-law conversing with Richmond, the traitor, and then slept again.

When he awoke it was the full light of day, though which day was anybody's guess. His head hurt like the very devil, his stomach was tender, and he felt both raw and sticky. He sat up, slowly, to see that he was in one of the guest rooms. He vaguely remembered the footmen trying to get him upstairs, and then having a battle when he refused to be put in his own bed. The servants would have changed the sheets. But they couldn't change his memories. Nothing could, sod it. Not bottles of brandy, not smashing his head. Nothing.

He reached up and felt the matted strands of his hair above the tender lump. Served him right, he thought. And the visions were nothing more than he deserved. Seeing his mortal enemy in his drunken dreams wasn't much better than Melisande's face, but at least it engendered rage, not despair.

The door opened, and he stiffened, expecting a disapproving Richmond, come to clean him up and lecture him simply by looking at him, and then he froze. He was no longer drunk. And Lucien de Malheur was standing inside his bedroom door.

He didn't think, didn't hesitate. He launched himself across the room, flattening his brother-in-law, and began pummeling him with enthusiasm.

But the Scorpion was a strong man, despite his bad leg, and Benedick had the hangover of the century, so it was over quickly. Benedick lay curled up, breathless in pain, as the Earl rose to his feet, brushing himself off.

"You dirty bastard," Benedick gasped. "You fight like a street rat."

"Of course I do," Lucien said calmly.

Benedick said nothing, trying to catch his breath and wondering if his plan for an heir was now moot, when he was vaguely aware of someone else in the room.

"What did you do to him?" came his sister's caustic voice.

"No less than he deserved. He decided it was time to avenge your honor."

"Too late," Miranda said cheerfully, leaning down beside him. She smelled of lemon and spice, her familiar scent, and beneath all the misery, fury and pain he felt a surge of remembered affection. "You shouldn't try to hit Lucien, Benedick. He has no scruples."

Benedick coughed. "I remember." He was beginning to breathe again, and he decided ignoring Malheur was the best thing he could do. For now. "What are you doing here, Miranda? Are you well?"

She placed a hand over her swelling stomach. "Perfectly."

He stared at her. "Good God, are you increasing again? How many children is this, twenty-seven?" Another hideous thought struck him. "They aren't here, are they? Because while I adore your children this is hardly the time for a social visit, and there are things going on…"

"This will be my sixth baby, and the other five are back at home with their nanny. This isn't a social visit, darling. Lucien and I are here for a reason, and you're just going to have to swallow your outrage for the time being and put up with us."

At that moment he was incapable of moving, but he grunted unencouragingly. The moment he could get to his feet he was heading straight for the Scorpion again.

"*What* reason?" A sudden fear struck him. "Father and Mother…are they all right?"

"Perfectly fine, as far as I know, and it's a good thing they're still in Egypt and not here to watch you make such an utter cake of yourself."

"And that's why you're here?" The wheeze had almost gone out of his voice. "To make me behave?"

"Hardly. We're come to stop Brandon from destroying his life. You seem to have forgotten his very existence, but Lucien had it from good authority that the Heavenly Host has…"

"Regathered, yes I know," Benedick said, managing to sit up. "You didn't need to come all the way down here and subject me to your husband's presence in order to tell me that. I have the matter well in hand."

"Yes. It really seems like it." She sounded skeptical, as only a sister could. "And exactly where is Brandon now? Richmond said he moved out a couple of days ago and hasn't been seen since."

"I'll find him," Benedick snarled, his eyes narrowing as he saw Lucien looking at him.

"The question is, will you find him in time?" the Scorpion asked in a deliberately civil tone. "Or not until he's slaughtered some innocent female and gone beyond any hope of a future."

"Why should he slaughter an innocent female?" Benedick snapped. "I'm still presuming those rumors about a virgin sacrifice are highly embroidered, even though I've promised to check them out. I never thought you so gullible that you'd come haring down all the way from the Lake District."

"They aren't rumors, Neddie," Miranda said in a quiet voice. "Lucien knows people—his sources are unimpeachable. They're planning some hideous ritual on the night of the full moon, involving an innocent girl, and our brother has been chosen to wield the knife. And apparently he's so far lost to drink and opium that there's no common sense left to stop him."

"Why would he be chosen?" Benedick demanded.

"No one has any idea who's in charge, who chose him, or why," Lucien said. "But my sources are never wrong. If we don't find Brandon before tomorrow night, it will be too late. We haven't the faintest idea where they're planning to meet, and…"

"That's where you're wrong. I know exactly where they're meeting, and if we haven't found Brandon before then I suppose I can go and stop them myself." He got to his feet, albeit a little shakily; his hangover and the recent sucker punch still left him reeling. He glanced at Malheur, wondering if he dared go for him again, but Miranda was in the way, and he expected she'd make certain to keep between them from now on. He'd have to wait to wipe the smirk off that toad-sucking son of a bitch.

"And if we do find Brandon? Are you going to stand by and let some poor innocent be murdered?" his sister demanded, for all like the woman he'd just sent from his life. Why did they all have to be so damned emotional?

"All sorts of poor innocents get murdered every day, Miranda. I can hardly be responsible for them," he drawled.

"You can if you know about them." Her fine eye narrowed. "What's happened to you, Neddie?"

Fallen in love, he thought morosely, and then froze. Where had those words come from? At least he hadn't said them out loud; he only had himself to chastise. "I'm a practical man," he said instead. He looked away. For some reason the disappointment in Miranda's eyes was too painful.

He was becoming adept at disappointing women, he thought sourly. Perhaps he deserved a cold-blooded bitch like Dorothea Pennington after all.

"Miss Dorothea Pennington has arrived to see you," Richmond announced from the doorway, like a voice from the grave. It had to be some bloody sign.

He shoved his hair away from his face, wincing as his hand bounced against his head wound. "Tell her I'll join her directly."

"Dorothea Pennington?" Miranda said, aghast. "What in the world has that mean-hearted piece of work got to do with anything? I thought you were… were involved with Lady Carstairs."

He wanted to whirl around and snap like an angry cur, but he kept his temper in check, saying the one thing he knew would horrify her. "Your sources are nowhere near as reliable as you seem to think. I intend to marry Miss Pennington, of course."

29

By the time he managed a hasty wash and changed his ruined clothes Benedick had kept Miss Pennington waiting a goodly amount of time. Miranda had flatly refused to entertain her while he made himself halfway presentable, so he'd sent Richmond in with sugar cakes and tea while he stripped, washed, changed and took one horrified look at himself in the mirror.

The cut above his eyebrow was absurdly small to have caused so much blood, and it did little to distract from his bloodshot eyes and the circles beneath them. He needed to be shaved as well, but there was hardly enough time to manage that. Richmond usually did the honors, and if he attempted it himself, he'd probably cut his throat.

Which, in retrospect, wouldn't be a bad thing.

Well, if they were to be married, she'd be seeing him unshaven, across the sheets of the marriage bed. He shuddered, instinctively, and paused outside the door to the blue salon. He shouldn't have had Richmond put her in there. He'd spent too much time with Charity Carstairs in that room.

Though presumably he'd be sharing his bedroom, his bed with Miss Pennington. The same room and bed he'd shared with Melisande. If anything would lay her ghost it would be Dorothea's pinched face.

Straightening himself, he opened the door.

Miss Pennington was sitting by the fire, ramrod straight, her gloved hands folded perfectly in her lap, her face set in impatient lines. It was a handsome face, he realized with surprise. Good bones, clear skin, symmetrical, with wide-set eyes and a Cupid's bow of a mouth. If she were a little softer, she might have been considered a beauty. Perhaps he could soften her.

She turned to look at him, rising, and there was disapproval in those flinty eyes. "You hardly look ready to receive guests, Rohan," she observed.

"Indeed, I must ask your pardon. I decided I had kept you waiting for too long and hoped you would forgive me my dishabille."

She didn't look like she was about to forgive anything, but then she smiled, mechanically. "Of course, dear sir." She sank back down, allowing him to take the chair he so badly needed.

"And to what do I owe the extreme and unexpected honor of your visit, Miss Pennington?" He had no idea whether it was his hangover or the blow on his head, but he could fathom no reason at all why she'd be here.

"It's dreadfully forward of me, I know, but I hadn't seen you in a while, and I was concerned. I wanted to assure myself that you were quite well."

He hoped the hunted feeling didn't show on his face. She was like a prize spaniel in search of its prey. Except that he liked spaniels.

"Quite well, Miss Pennington. I beg your pardon—I've been dealing with a pressing family matter." He glanced around, desperate to change the topic. "But you haven't touched your tea. Allow me to ring for fresh…"

"No, thank you, Rohan. I have a strong dislike of sweets and consider afternoon tea to be a weakness of the constitution."

He couldn't help it. The plate was piled high with the sweet cakes that Melisande adored. Left alone with them, she probably wouldn't have left a crumb. There was something so…reassuring about a woman with an honest appetite.

He wiped the thought from his mind. Dorothea Pennington wasn't improving his headache, and the sooner she departed the better. "So true," he said vaguely, knowing he would give his right arm for a cup of even lukewarm tea. "And how may I assist you, Miss Pennington?"

Her posture was so rigidly correct that he would have said it impossible, but she seemed to draw herself up even more. "May I be frank, Lord Rohan?"

"I wish you would, my dear Miss Pennington."

"I think we should be married."

It was a good thing he wasn't drinking tea—he

would have choked. As it was he kept his expression schooled, shielding his shock. "I beg your pardon?"

"Yes, I know, it's completely forward of me, but you and I are mature people, and you have already shown a marked partiality toward me. Several people have noted it, and I am certain you would never have paid such particular attention without meaning to follow through. You are, above all things, a gentleman, and I know I can count on you to behave as you ought. You would never bring me a moment's shame, and your title, though connected to a name that is ramshackle in the extreme, is high enough that a Pennington would not blush to be connected. My family goes back to William the Conqueror, and we may look as high as we please when it comes to marriage, but I think you and I should suit extremely. I would like to get married in the fall, and it takes a great deal of time to arrange a wedding on the magnitude that would befit a Pennington, and I really cannot afford to be patient any longer. I decided it would make things a great deal simpler if I took the bull by the horns, so to speak."

He assumed he didn't look as aghast as he felt. "Very thorough. And very direct, Miss Pennington. I appreciate your forthright attitude."

"I imagined you would." A self-satisfied smile curved her small mouth. He didn't trust a woman with a small mouth. Melisande's was wide and generous. "I thought St. Paul's would be the logical choice for the ceremony. Westminster Abbey is inconveniently located—" she made it sound like a personal affront "—and we would have to wait until next spring for a proper date."

"You've already checked?" he said faintly.

"I am a thorough woman. I presume you will leave these petty details to me? I am more than capable of dealing with them."

"I am sure you are," he said. He could stand it no longer—he reached for the teapot. Cold tea was better than none, but Miss Pennington, eyeing him with disapproval, took the teapot from his hand.

"If you feel in need of a reviving beverage I will ring for fresh water. Your servants are not what I would call remarkable. The old man who brought me in here is far past the age of usefulness. He should be replaced with someone younger."

"That would quite break Richmond's heart."

She looked at him, for the first time honestly confused. "Is there any particular reason why his feelings should be considered in the matter? One needs to be practical about such things."

"Indeed," he said slowly. She didn't ring for fresh water, and he knew there was no way he was going to be able to pour himself tea without her wresting the pot from him once more. He settled back to suffer in silence.

"I am glad we're agreed upon that." A trace of smugness now tinged her small mouth. Melisande hadn't liked her, he recalled. In fact, she'd referred to the woman as "a mean-spirited piece of work." Unfortunately apt.

"While we're on the subject," the mean-spirited

piece of work continued, "we should come to an understanding on other matters. I would expect to run my household with no interference from you. I have been trained my entire life to run a gentleman's estate, and the size of yours should offer no challenge at all." Thus with a few words she dismissed his admittedly impressive estates and inheritance. "We would, of course, expect to have children, and I would scarce deny you the marriage bed, but you have a certain reputation for...lasciviousness. No gentleman would ever insult his wife by making her suffer such lewd attentions, but I wanted to make it clear from the outset that I will countenance no displays of lustfulness. We will come together in the hope of being fruitful. I rather thought three children—any more and it hints of ill manners. An heir and a spare for you, and a daughter I can raise and mold in my own image."

Christ, he thought, aghast. Two Dorothy Penningtons in this world beggared description. Two in his own family was insupportable.

"One cannot always control the sex of one's offspring," he ventured.

She frowned at him. "The word gender is more genteel. You will find I am a very forward-thinking woman, my dear Rohan. Our country is headed for a correction, a move into more circumspect times, where language will be tempered and behavior will be just as it ought. The ramshackle times of our fathers is past."

More's the pity, he thought. He schooled his expression into one of polite interest. "And did you have any other thoughts about our future together?"

"Of course." He half expected her to whip out a list, but apparently she'd memorized it. "This house is too small for a proper town residence. It does fine for a bachelor, but would scarcely do for entertaining, and I am not fond of the address. I thought a house in the vicinity of Grosvenor Square might be nice."

"Indeed," he said noncommittally. He loved his house.

"I have yet to inspect your country estates, but since we won't be spending much time in either one of them I doubt it matters. I'm a city woman, dear Rohan. I dislike the country and all form of sports. I do hope you don't hunt."

"I do occasionally," he admitted, though he had his own misgivings about the sport.

"You will cease. And another thing. I suppose I should handle this delicately, but I believe in facing things with no roundaboutation, and we may as well start out as we mean to go on."

"Indeed," he said politely.

"Your family." She concealed a delicate shudder, but just barely. "I realize we must certainly continue an association with your parents, and while your father's past is reprehensible, your mother appears to be beyond reproach, and she has provided a civilizing effect, just as I expect to do with you."

He was a far cry from the wild young lord Adrian Rohan in his heyday, but he decided that silence was best at this juncture. He simply bowed his head in seeming acquiescence.

"However, the rest of your family is another matter. While I have no quarrel with your brother Charles and his unexceptional wife, your other siblings have proven themselves to be...shall we say, undesirable...company."

Shall we say, take a damper, Benedick thought with a certain amount of savagery. He plastered a smile on his face. "Indeed?" he said in an encouraging tone.

"We both know your sister has proven herself beyond the pale more than once," she continued. "She was ruined, and yet, instead of retiring to the country and living out her life in genteel obscurity she chose to stay in London, her very presence an affront to decent women. And then, to marry that awful man who is no more than a...a criminal! At least she has the sense to keep out of London. I gather she drops babies like a peasant. We shall need to cut that connection entirely. You would hardly expect me to acknowledge her socially. I have my own reputation to consider."

"And you think it isn't strong enough to withstand association with my sister? I wonder you even considered my suit in the first place," he said evenly.

"I did think long and hard on it," Miss Pennington admitted frankly. "But I knew you abhorred your sister's choices as much as I did, and would be more than happy to cut the connection."

"And my brother Brandon?"

She made a face, as if she'd tasted something unpleasant. "Indeed, I gather he's been in town, though thankfully he's kept out of the public eye. It's a very difficult situation. I know the poor boy has suffered dreadfully for his country, but we really can't expect our guests to have to look at his disfigurements and still manage to have a pleasant evening. We can entertain him when we're in the countryside, of course, as long as we have no houseguests and our children are kept in the nursery. But you must understand my hesitation. I prefer to be surrounded by beauty."

He wondered what would happen if he took the teapot and dumped its contents on her head. "I understand you completely."

"Then we're agreed," she said, too well-bred to sound too overtly smug. "I would like a ring to signify our betrothal. Something discreet, valuable but not too flashy. I've chosen one at my jewelers—I'll give you the direction and you may pick it up tomorrow."

"You're very thorough, but I'm afraid I'll be busy tomorrow. I have to go into the country."

"Not that wretched house party that my brother is attending? I'm not sure I approve. I think in the future you should use your influence to help my brother get a post in the government. Nothing that requires real labor, more a social nicety. You can do that, can't you?"

"I can," he said. *Where I would or not is a different matter.*

"Then you may fetch the ring next week. I've had

my secretary draw up an announcement, and she will send it to the papers as soon as I return home."

Christ's blood, he thought in horror. He had to move fast or he'd find himself leg-shackled to his worst nightmare. She'd give him children. She'd leave him alone. He would never care about her. Exactly what he'd been so sure he wanted. Now he wanted to drown her in the Thames.

She was already preparing to leave. She rose, casting her gimlet gaze his way. "You may kiss me, my dear Rohan."

He'd rather kiss a charging boar. "One moment, Miss Pennington," he said politely, heading for the door, prepared to send Richmond on a hunt. It was easier than he expected. Richmond and his sister were hovering by the door, clearly eavesdropping, and the Scorpion lounged nearby on one of the love seats in the hallway.

Miranda's expression was a cross between amusement and doubt, and he felt a moment's shame. She really thought it was possible that he might repudiate her for someone like Dorothea Pennington. "Well, my dear," he said to her, "are you prepared to meet my fiancée?"

Her expression was stricken. "I gather she doesn't wish to meet me."

"Nothing good comes to those who eavesdrop. Usually." He swung open the door and ushered his sister's very pregnant form inside, leaving the door open for his brother-in-law and Richmond to observe.

Miss Pennington's face had frozen, making

her look like a startled hake. "Miss Pennington," Benedick said smoothly. "I don't believe you're acquainted with my sister, Lady Rochdale. She is quite my favorite sibling, even if I haven't always cared for her choices, and when I marry again I would want her as one of the bride's attendants. Mind you, she'll most likely be in some stage of pregnancy, given her alarming level of fecundity, but dressmakers know how to adjust for such exigencies. Her husband, of course, will be one of my attendants, though I expect my baby brother, Brandon, will stand up with me as well. We've always been very close."

Miss Pennington's mouth opened and closed without a word issuing forth, and Benedick continued on. "Of course, Brandon is currently dealing with an unpleasant addiction to opium and alcohol, but I imagine we'll be able to prop him up long enough to get through the ceremony. Your own brother has been keeping company with the Heavenly Host, so I doubt his behavior has been much better, but the two of them can keep each other company, can they not?"

He heard Miranda's gurgle of laughter from beside him, and he realized how much he had missed that sound. Missed his sister. So much that he'd stomach the Scorpion to have her back in his life.

Miss Pennington was glaring. "You insult me, sir. If you think I don't know that my brother has been disporting himself with those gentlemen then you think I'm a great deal stupider than I am. There's a difference—their activities are held in secret, among their own class, and the only ones who are hurt are whores and peasants."

"Peasants, Miss Pennington? That seems an oddly archaic term. Do you still keep serfs on your estates in Cumberland? Oh, but I forgot. Your father lost all the family estates years ago, leaving you forced to marry for money. Though why in heaven's name you thought I'd be a suitable choice astounds me."

"I assumed you were a man who shared my values and opinions," she said tightly. "Apparently I was quite deluded in my opinion."

"Quite, thank God," Miranda broke in.

Dorothea Pennington refused to even acknowledge her. "I'm afraid, sir, that the engagement is off."

"I'm afraid, my dear Miss Pennington, that the engagement was never on. You are the very last woman I would consider marrying."

He could almost imagine smoke coming out of those perfect, shell-like ears.

"No decent woman would have you," she hissed.

"Now that's where you're wrong. You may expect a happy announcement from me quite soon." He wasn't quite sure why he said it—it seemed to spring into his mouth from nowhere.

"Do not bother to send me an invitation." Her voice was frosty.

"He won't," his cursed interfering sister volunteered. "I don't believe Lady Carstairs would want you anywhere near her."

He jerked to look down at her in astonishment when Miss Pennington let out an outraged shriek.

"Lady Carstairs?" she cried. "Charity Carstairs? You're marrying her? Why, she must be thirty years old."

Damn his sister—he should drown her in the Thames as well. "I have yet to ask her," he temporized.

"But she'll say yes," Miranda jumped in. "Because they're in love. You don't know the meaning of the word, Dorothea Pennington, and you never will. Now go away, do. We have a wedding to arrange."

If the exquisitely well-behaved Dorothea Pennington had something near at hand she would have thrown it, Benedick decided, horror and amusement warring for control. He watched her stalk from the room, and he could tell from her horrified shriek when she clapped eyes on his scarred brother-in-law, lazily stretched out in the hall. They waited until they heard the front door slam, and then he turned to Miranda.

"What the hell did you mean, I'm marrying Melisande?" he demanded in a choked voice. "I most certainly am not."

Her smile broadened. "I know you better than you think, Neddie. Stop fighting it. You want her, whether it's practical or not. You should have her."

"We don't suit," he said stiffly. "Besides, she despises me."

"Well, that's always a good sign. But we can deal with your love life later, once we've found Brandon. Any idea where he might have gone?"

He gave up then. His head ached too much to

deal with all of this, and Dorothea Pennington would hardly be likely to spread rumors of her former suitor's engagement—it would reflect too badly on her. He would have a few days to sort things out.

"Brandon," he agreed, heading toward the open door. Lucien de Malheur was still there, an ironic expression on his face. He tensed when he saw Benedick, as if expecting another assault.

"I'm not going to kill you now," Benedick said. "We need to fetch Brandon."

"You're not going to kill me ever," Lucien said lazily, getting to his feet, his gold-headed cane in one strong hand. "Lead on, MacDuff."

30

It started as a soft scratching on her bedroom door, the one Melisande had locked before she'd collapsed into bed. That much she could ignore. It was morning, and she'd just gone to bed, and it simply wasn't fair to try to wake her. She put the pillow over her head as the scratching went to a soft knock.

"Open the door, Melisande." Emma's soft voice came from the other side. "I need to talk to you."

She didn't need to talk with anyone. Emma would know full well that she hadn't returned home last night, and she would know where she'd been and what she'd been doing. And that was absolutely the last thing Melisande had any intention of discussing.

The knocking grew louder, penetrating the layers of feathers and laudanum-induced fog, and Melisande rolled over, cursing. From the angle of the sun she could tell it was early morning, not much past six. She hadn't closed her curtain, but the overcast sun was still an annoyance. Why should anyone expect her to wake up at such an ungodly hour when she'd been out all night and...

And not returned home until after nine in the morning. She'd slept the day and night away, wrapped in misery and laudanum, and they were one day closer to the solstice. Bloody hell.

Emma was pounding by now, and the wood door was shaking in its frame. Melisande sat up, groaning, and climbed out of bed. She was vaguely aware that her ankle wasn't bothering her as she limped toward the door. Vaguely aware that muscles she hadn't known she had were protesting. And she wasn't going to examine that thought too closely.

By the time she opened the door, Emma was using both fists, and one look at her expression and Melisande's bruised heart sank. Something was very wrong, indeed.

She looked past Emma to the gaggle, all in various states of undress, watching them. "When did you last see Betsey?" Emma demanded breathlessly.

"This morning," Melisande replied immediately, confused.

"Oh, thank God."

"At least, I think so," she added. "What day is it? Friday?"

Emma's relief vanished. "It's Saturday. You've slept the clock around. Do you mean you haven't seen Betsey since yesterday morning? Where was she?"

"In the library. We talked for a bit. She was missing Aileen, and worried about the future. I told her she could stay here as long as she wanted, and then she went down to visit Cook. Did you ask Mollie Biscuits?"

"Of course I did!" Panic was shredding Emma's usual calm. "She said Betsey came in, helped her with the bread, then took some pasties and said she was going to eat them out in the sun. Mollie thinks she was heading for St. James Park, but we can't be certain. She might have walked farther ahead to Green Park or even all the way to Hyde Park. And she never came back. No tea, no supper, and her bed hasn't been slept in."

"She wouldn't have run away," Melisande said flatly, trying to force her brain into full working mode despite the lingering effect of the damned laudanum.

"Of course not. Which means only one thing."

The gaggle were listening avidly, but they were all women of the world, and knew the answer as well as she did. "It means she was taken."

"No!" Mollie Biscuits let out a cry, tears running down her plump cheeks. "Not that poor wee child!"

"It's the Heavenly Host," Violet piped up helpfully, causing the rest of the gaggle to start talking, so loudly that Melisande could barely think.

"Enough!" Emma cried, temporarily shutting them up while doing absolutely nothing for Melisande's headache. "If they've taken her, and there's no guarantee that they did, then Lady Carstairs can get her back. She's been working very hard this week, and Viscount Rohan has been assisting her. Cook, bring us up a pot of strong tea and some of those little cakes you've been experimenting with. Violet, you take the others and go out looking. It's always possible that Betsey simply got lost and found an alley to sleep in. She had to do it often enough when she was younger, poor thing."

"Yes, Mrs. Cadbury," Violet said importantly. "And lord knows she's at a good age. Too old for the gents who like the young ones, yet not old enough for those who like a bit of meat with their brisket." She plumped her full breast with one hand.

"What does that even mean?" Long Jane, beside her, demanded.

"It means she's got a good chance at being safe enough," Sukey said. "God willing." Sukey's tenure with the bishop had left some of his piety intact.

There were a few added "God willings" from the more religious of the gaggle, as they slowly started to disperse, and Emma took Melisande's arm, hurrying her back into her bedroom.

"I'll help you dress," she said briskly. "We haven't any time to waste." She paused enough to look at her. "I wish we had time to talk about your night with Rohan, but Betsey's been gone for far too long, and we can't afford to waste any more time."

"Nothing happened," Melisande said stoutly.

"God give me strength," Emma muttered, pulling the robe off her shoulders. "Of course it did. You just don't want to talk about it, which I assume means he either botched the job or you didn't like it. Whichever it was, we can deal with it later."

"There's nothing to be dealt with. I told you, nothing happened." She let Emma hand her into one of her narrow walking dresses, then began fastening the long row of buttons up the front.

"Then why is your body adorned with such interesting signs, may I ask you? Clearly my lord Rohan likes to mark his partners, though that must be something new. Unusual for someone who prides himself on his self-control."

Melisande touched her breast instinctively, then snatched her hand away. "I don't know what you're talking about. I fell."

"Of course you did. And the bruise just happens to be the size and shape of a mouth. I didn't see teeth marks, which is a good thing. The ones who leave teeth marks can be a little strange."

For a moment the memory, almost physical, of Benedick biting down on her earlobe as her arousal built to hit her like a blow. "Don't we have something more important to discuss? Has anyone been seen loitering around here? Half of London knows the women live here, but Betsey is the only innocent. It makes no sense that anyone would be searching for a virgin here. Unless Aileen was forced to tell them."

"I don't know," Emma said bleakly. "But I have a very bad feeling about this. Do you want me to have a note delivered to Viscount Rohan, or will you go there directly?"

As if things weren't desperate enough. She ducked her head so that Emma wouldn't see the absolute horror that suffused her face. She would go nowhere near Benedick Rohan, ever again. He had made his disdain for her perfectly clear.

Which meant she had to find Betsey on her own. "Have the girls finished with the monk's robe they were making?"

"It's in your closet. Does that mean you think the Heavenly Host really did take her?"

"They need a virgin for tomorrow…tonight. How and why they knew is beyond me." Maybe Rohan had betrayed her and told them in order to rescue his brother. Anything was possible. "I cannot risk losing her. I must go, even if I'm wrong."

"And you know where they're meeting? You and the viscount?"

"We do," she said, sticking to the absolute letter of the truth. "I'm not going to let anything happen to Betsey." She strode to the wardrobe, caught the dull brown robe in one hand and started limping toward the door.

"You can't go out with that bad ankle," Emma said belatedly. "Let me send a message…"

"No! On no account are you to correspond with Viscount Rohan." The panic was seeping into her voice, but she averted her face on the off chance Emma wouldn't notice. She was usually far too observant, but her worry over Betsey was bound to distract her. "Just leave it up to me. I wouldn't want a letter to get into the wrong hands—we certainly don't want his brother to know we're so close."

An odd expression crossed Emma's face. "Are you certain his brother is tied up with those deviants?"

"Absolutely. According to Benedick…er, Viscount Rohan, his brother is equally fond of the opium pipe and excesses of alcohol. It's little wonder—he was grievously wounded in the Afghan wars, and he's yet to recover." She looked Emma directly in the eyes, unblinking, and flat-out lied to her. "I'll go there directly and we'll decide what to do next. You may rely on me. I'll bring Betsey back." *If it kills me,* she thought. If Emma thought she was with Rohan she wouldn't worry, and it would give her more time to accomplish what she had to do.

She made her way slowly down the two flights of stairs, breathing a sigh of relief that her ankle had definitely improved. By the time she reached the ground floor a hired carriage had been brought round, the gaggle had dispersed in what Melisande knew was a fruitless search for Betsey, and Emma was watching her with a doubtful expression on her face. "I hate to send you out alone," she said. "But I can't very well accompany you, and Miss Mackenzie is too elderly to be of any assistance. If it weren't for Viscount Rohan, I would feel very grave doubts about letting you go."

Melisande plastered a totally believable smile on her face. "I'll be perfectly fine, I promise you. We've got this well in hand."

"And what if you're wrong?" Emma trailed after her. "What if Betsey turns up, none the worse for wear? How can I get in touch with you?"

"If Betsey is safe then so much the better, but it still means that some other innocent is in danger.

Even if it's a stranger I can hardly turn my back on her." She needed to get out of there, before Emma asked one too many questions and realized she had no intention of going to Rohan at all, before she looked too closely into Melisande's deliberately limpid gaze.

"Of course. But still…"

"I need to go, Emma. Remember your promise. It would do no good to be in touch with Viscount Rohan—he'll be out of town with me. I promise I'll be back as soon as I can, once I'm assured that the Heavenly Host won't be enacting any cruel rituals."

"There's something you're not telling me," Emma said sharply.

"I don't have time to tell you everything!" Melisande cried. "I'll explain it all when I get back. But right now there's no time to waste."

She finally managed to escape, limping down the front steps to the small carriage awaiting her. Emma had helped her down, giving Rohan's Bury Street address to the driver, and Melisande had no choice but to sit on the edge of the seat until he turned the corner before knocking at the small hatch.

"Yes, my lady?" The driver inquired.

"I'm afraid my friend had the wrong address. I require you to drive me out of town, to the village of Kersley Mill. It's only a few hours from London, and you'll be well compensated." Her reticule was stuffed with every bit of money the household had boasted, and it should be enough to put the coachman up for the night at the local inn if that was what he preferred.

"Yes, my lady," he said, and she sat back, breathing a sigh of relief. One hurdle, no, a great many hurdles had been leaped. The rest was up to her.

She only felt a moment's guilt at misleading Emma into thinking she'd gone to Rohan for help. He'd made it abundantly clear that his only interest in all this was in rescuing his brother. If she wanted to guarantee Betsey's safety she was on her own.

It had nothing to do with the fact that the very idea of facing Benedick Rohan ever again made her want to curl up into a ball and weep.

She was a stronger woman than that. She didn't need anyone to help her, particularly not a grudging, cynical, scum-sucking, pig-swiving sack of offal like Benedick Rohan.

The two hours it took her to get to Kersley Mill was more than enough to gird her loins. It was still early in the day, given Melisande's crack-of-dawn start, and while the driver was loath to drop her off in what seemed like the middle of nowhere, the purse she thrust on him more than made up for any misgivings. It was a warm afternoon, though the day was overcast, and she waited until the coach was out of sight before she found a copse of trees and proceeded to don the monk's robes.

Unfortunately her petticoats were too full, and she had no choice but to reach under her skirts and untie the tapes that held them. By the time she slid out of all three of them the dull monk's robe sat a little closer to her body, though she wasn't sure it would pass close inspection. The trick, then, was not to let anyone get too close.

According to Rohan's idle conversation on their last trip to Kersley Hall, the original Heavenly Host allowed for certain members to attend ceremonies merely as watchers. If they wore a monk's robe and had a white ribbon around their arm then they were allowed to pass among the assembled celebrants with a vow of silence, and no one conversed with them nor expected them to partake of the depraved activities. She hadn't bothered to ask him how he knew of this particular variation—he'd assured her it had been the case some forty years ago, and considering he hadn't been born back then she took leave to doubt the veracity of that notion, but she had no choice. She could hardly mingle as Charity Carstairs, do-gooder and semivirgin. The only way she was going to find Betsey was if she went in disguised.

She'd overestimated the improvement in her ankle. By the time the ruins of Kersley Hall came into sight she was moving very slowly indeed, and she could only hope she wouldn't be called on to run for it. She'd be in big trouble if she was.

She'd almost waited too long. It was Saturday— tomorrow was the night of the full moon, the night of virgin sacrifice that Melisande suspected had absolutely nothing to do with the old pagan religions and everything to do with the twisted mentality of the humans involved in this degenerate organization.

The gloomy ruins of Kersley Hall looked as abandoned as they had a few days ago, when she and Rohan had ridden there. Of course they'd run into two of the members that time, even though there'd been no sign of them, so there was no guarantee the place was deserted this time, either. She could see the area where the tunnels had collapsed and they'd fallen through. The collapse could have been caused by the heavy spring rains just as easily as trespassing humans, and she could only hope the members who'd already found it had attributed it to natural causes. Otherwise there was always the devastating possibility that they'd changed their location.

Pulling the cowl up around her head, she moved forward, trying to disguise her limp. She was usually acutely aware when someone was watching her, and thankfully that feeling was absent, but it didn't hurt to be as circumspect as possible. There was no way she was going to slide back down into the collapsed tunnel—her only way back into the caves was through the abandoned dairy.

She moved carefully, holding her breath as she came up behind the building and peered in the smoke-stained windows. No sign of anyone. Her heart was hammering, her palms were sweating and she wanted to turn back. But running from Benedick Rohan was one thing—that was no one's business but her own. There was no way she could run from someone in need, no matter how dangerous the situation.

She moved around the front of the building, pushed open the latch and stepped inside. Even in

the brightness of the midday sun the room was dark
and shadowed, and it took a moment for her eyes to
adjust. She started for the doors leading down to the
tunnels and then stopped.

The door was barred and locked, an ancient pad-
lock the size of a platter holding an equally heavy
chain in place. There was no way she was getting
past that.

Which meant she had no choice but to see whether
she could climb back in using the cave-in, this time
without landing on her ankle. Of course, the first
time she'd had a full-grown male end up under her,
which hadn't improved matters. And she wasn't
going to think about Benedick Rohan being underneath her anymore. That didn't help matters, either.

She had just reached the door when she heard a
noise overhead. A scuffling sound, louder than even
the largest rats could make, and she froze, her hair
standing on end. If it were any of the Heavenly Host,
they would hardly be hiding, she thought, forcing
herself to calm down.

There were stairs at the back of the room, and
before she could cry off she started up them, as quietly as she could so as not to alert anyone who might
be up there. The hallway was dark and deserted,
with a doorway on either side, both doors closed and
locked. Light was coming through the door on the
left, as if there was a window, and she tiptoed toward
it, flinching every time a floorboard creaked.

The door had a barred window in it, with no glass,
and she stood on her tiptoes, her ankle screaming

in protest. At first she could see nothing inside, just a cot, a table and chair, and a bundle of rags. But slowly that bundle of rags began to look familiar, the blue serge that all of her gaggle wore.

"Betsey?" she whispered urgently. "Is that you?"

The bundle stirred, very slowly, and then resolved itself into the familiar figure of a young girl. "Miss?" she said anxiously, her young voice raspy.

"It's me, Betsey. Are you all right?"

Betsey scrambled to her feet, running over to the door. "Oh, miss, you shouldn't be here. They've locked me in and there's no way out, and they're very bad men. You should leave."

Melisande rattled the door in frustration. "What about the windows? If I were able to find you a rope could you climb down?"

She shook her head. She was filthy—straw in her hair, dirt and what looked like a bruise across her young face. "There are bars on the windows."

Melisande cursed, and Betsey looked impressed. She looked around her, but the hallway was empty of everything, and she hadn't even thought to bring the small lady's pistol she carried with her when she traveled in the more dangerous areas of London. What an idiot she'd been! "I'm going to need to find something to break the lock, Betsey. Just be patient—I'm not walking too well. I hate to leave you locked in here even for another moment, but I'll try to hurry."

"I'll be fine, miss. I've been here one night already, and they bring me food and leave me alone. Do you have any idea of why they want me? I ain't pretty like the others, and I'm too old for those that likes the little ones."

Melisande didn't bother to ask her how she knew of such foul practices. After all, the child had lived on the streets for years, just barely managing to maintain her innocence. There would be few things she hadn't seen or heard.

But she wouldn't have heard of girls being murdered in a ritual sacrifice, and Melisande wasn't about to enlighten her. "I don't know," she said. "But it doesn't matter. I'll be back as soon as I can with help, and we'll get you away from here, safely back home."

An odd expression crossed Betsey's face. "I don't think so, miss," she said in a hollow voice.

"You don't? But why not?" she demanded, puzzled.

The sudden darkness that descended answered all her questions.

31

The house on Bury Street existed in what could best be called an armed truce. While Benedick would have liked nothing better than to kick his wretched brother-in-law to the street, that would involve losing his sister as well, and he wasn't in any particular mood to pass judgment on anyone, or to drive another female from his life.

For the time being there wasn't anything particular that he could do. His brother-in-law had connections in the London underworld, and right now their criminal minions were out and about, scouring the city for any sign of Brandon, and it stood to reason that they would have far more success than he would. Miranda had taken over his library, and was even now making long lists. He was wise enough, or cowardly enough, not to ask why. He had the dreadful suspicion she was already planning his forthcoming nuptials, and he didn't know how to tell her that Melisande Carstairs wouldn't have him if he were the last man on earth. She'd ask him why. And he certainly couldn't tell her.

Which left him with nothing to do for the next few hours but try to recover from his hangover. Soaking in a hot bath for half an hour helped, opening all the windows in his bedroom and letting the warm spring air rush in was even better. He considered seeing if another tot of brandy might finish the job, but his stomach rebelled at the very thought. Which left him, clean and shaved and dreadfully sober, to face the future.

He wasn't marrying her. Even if she'd have him, which she certainly wouldn't, he had no intention of leg-shackling himself to such a difficult woman. She'd always be racing off to save some new stray lamb, and if she even caught wind of the Scorpion's criminal associations she'd probably try to save them, as well. She was a dangerous woman, never content with the status quo, and she would drag whoever was fool enough to marry her along for the ride.

Mind you, she was quite exquisite when she wasn't on a tirade. She had the softest mouth, the creamiest skin, the loveliest breasts that beaded perfectly beneath his hungry mouth. He could still hear the sound she made when he first thrust inside her, and the other squeaks and murmurs and cries when she climaxed. He could feel the heat of her body beneath him, her arms around his neck, her legs around his hips, pulling him into her. He could close his eyes and remember the weight of her on top of him, head thrown back in mindless delight.

He needed a woman. He needed sex; it didn't matter with whom. For some reason he'd been unable to summon up even the slightest bit of interest in anyone else ever since he first ran afoul of Charity Carstairs. Now that he'd effectively driven her away for good he should be able to find a suitable bed partner quite easily.

Except…when he went over possibilities in his mind he found he dismissed each one. None of them suited; none of them aroused him in the slightest. Not even Violet Highstreet's most sophisticated talents could fill him with even the slightest trace of longing. Thinking of Melisande Carstairs's soft mouth, however…coaxing her to take him. They hadn't gotten to that particular delight. Now they never would.

His sister walked in without knocking, and he slammed a book over his loins to hide himself from her curious eyes. "People do knock, you know," he said coldly.

"I knew you were dressed. Besides, I'm not people…I'm your sister."

"More's the pity."

Miranda plopped herself down on the bed, her noticeably pregnant belly making the move cumbersome but still graceful. "How do you manage with that thing?" he demanded, fascinated.

"You get used to it," she said with a grin. "Don't you remember with Annis? With Lady Barbara?"

His momentary curiosity vanished. "I prefer not to dwell on those times in my life. Considering that both times the pregnancy led to the death of my wife I can hardly consider the memories to be cheerful ones."

If she'd showed pity he would have thrown something. Instead she was practical. "Pregnancy is always a difficult prospect. Some women aren't strong enough for it. Clearly I have the constitution of a broodmare."

"Even broodmares have a high incidence of birth-related mortality," he said gloomily. "I raise horses on the side, remember."

"All right then, think of me as a milk cow. I can drop my calves in the field and keep on munching grass. So can a great many others. Most women, in fact. Just because you had abominable luck doesn't mean you shouldn't try again."

"In case you haven't heard, I have every intention of remarrying and providing an heir. That was why I made the mistake of considering Dorothea Pennington."

"God help us all," Miranda said with a shudder.

"And that is why I would never consider Melisande Carstairs."

"Melisande?" Miranda said, diverted. "What a pretty name!"

He snarled. "She's thirty years old," he said. "She was married ten years without giving birth, so presumably she's barren."

Miranda sat on the bed, watching him out of eyes that saw too clearly, knew him too well. Finally she spoke. "Then I don't see what you're so damned terrified of. If she can't get pregnant she can't die, and you don't have to worry about losing her. It's all right to love her."

"But I..." His voice trailed off as her words sank in. Melisande wouldn't die. It didn't matter if he made the mistake of loving her—she was barren. The rigors of childbirth wouldn't rip her away. He looked into Miranda's sympathetic eyes. "You think you know me so well," he said sourly.

"I do. I've known you all my life. You try to pretend you don't care about things, but inside you're like a nice warm bowl of porridge."

He looked at her with profound dislike. "Your pregnancy won't keep me from kicking you out on the street if you continue with such asinine similes."

She didn't look worried. "Lucien will let us know the moment he gets word. I think you need to tell me about her. Why wouldn't she have you if you were the last man on earth?"

The damnable thing about erections was that it took forever for them to subside, even when faced with the most daunting of circumstances, and he couldn't very well get up and walk away without embarrassing them both. No, that was probably not true. Nothing could embarrass his wretched younger sister. "She has no particular need for men. In fact, she had decided to live a life of celibacy, devoted to good works."

Miranda shuddered. "She doesn't sound much better than Dorothea. What is this current mania of yours for joyless women?"

"She's not a joyless woman," he snarled. "She just doesn't see the need for the opposite sex. Her life was carefully arranged, her efforts going toward rescuing fallen women and soiled doves, and it gave her satisfaction and yes, joy."

"And you changed her mind?"

He looked away. "I was a damnable fool. Though I must say in my defense that it wasn't strictly my fault. She wanted my assistance in stopping the Heavenly Host, and she knew that Brandon was a part of them."

"Then I like her already. So what happened next?"

"We made discoveries. We found they were meeting at Kersley Hall, and we discovered several of the current membership, though we still have no idea who their mysterious leader is. The one who's pushing everyone in such a sordid direction."

"That's something good, at least. So what went wrong?"

There was no way in hell he was going to tell her. "None of your business."

"Did you seduce her?" She looked at him closely. "Of course you did. Oh, Benedick, how could you be so cruel! If the woman really wanted nothing to do with getting married again you should have let her be. Unless you really have fallen desperately in love with her."

"I most certainly have not! And I certainly didn't intend...that is, I wasn't going to..." He floundered, then stopped, glaring at her. "I'm not going to discuss this with you."

"You botched it? I'm astonished. I used to hear the maids and the local girls whispering about you, and you were accounted to be a most accomplished lover. Annis used to tell me you..."

"Oh, God," he said weakly. "This is completely inappropriate."

"When have I ever been appropriate?" She grinned. "So you botched the job, she ran away screaming in horror and you're not brave enough to try again. Have I got that right?"

"As usual you're completely wrong. I didn't, as you so delicately put it, 'botch the job.' I was, however, less than...less than kind the next morning. The relationship is quite impossible, and I managed to make that perfectly clear."

"Oh, God, Neddie, your poisonous tongue," Miranda said with a groan. "You could flay a person alive. Were you so afraid of loving her that you had to hurt her?"

He was silenced. She really did know him far too well, better than he knew himself. He closed his eyes, unable to bear the simple truth.

The silence lengthened. And then he heard her slide off the bed, cross the floor and take his unwilling hand in hers. "I'd sit beside you on the floor, the way I used to when I was young," she said softly, "but I'd have trouble getting up again. Oh, Neddie, you've made such a mess of things."

"Yes," he said, not bothering to deny it.

"You can fix this." She gave his arm a little shake. "But first we need to save Brandon, and then we'll see what we can do about you. I want you to be happy, love. You don't need an heir—we've got stuffy old Charles to take care of that, and if it's children you want, I've got babies to spare. Anytime you want to romp with them I'll bring them down to visit."

He finally turned to look at her, a wry grin on his mouth. "You're kindness personified."

"Don't try that with me—I know you adore my children, and they adore you. At times it was my only assurance that you hadn't turned into a cold-hearted fish. We can fix this, Neddie. You can have your happy ending, too."

He wanted to use his poisonous tongue to blister her. But then, Miranda had always been immune to it, and he had no real desire to hurt her. "First things first," he said. "We need to find Brandon."

The Grand Master of the Heavenly Host was feeling well pleased with himself. To be sure, things hadn't gone as smoothly as he might have hoped, but the missteps and danger put a certain piquant edge to the whole proceeding. Who would have thought the Carstairs woman would have been quite so persistent? He'd had her locked in a room, far away from the young girl chosen for the ritual, and so far no one had come looking. If they had, they would find nothing. Ever since the collapse of the north tunnel he'd had the main entrance closed off and another opened in the old stables. He could just imagine the complaints from his congregation, as he liked to think of them. The thought amused him. They would be wallowing in proverbial mud once they reached the caves—they could certainly withstand ancient manure.

They had already begun to gather. The ritual room was set, an altar erected with flowers and fruit and arcane symbols all around, as well as restraints and trays to catch the blood. He was hard with excitement. He'd never killed anyone before, and a young virgin was going to be particularly enjoyable.

The fools who made up the Heavenly Host would *oooh* and *ahhh* and commune in the spirit, wash in her blood, drink it if he insisted. They would do anything he wanted them to do once they drank the wine he'd doctored. He had no idea what the symbols that decorated the altar meant, but neither did any of them. They believed; he did not. That was the difference between power and obedience.

He would have no choice but to kill the much-too-curious Lady Carstairs, but he could enjoy the impromptu nature of the act. Perhaps he'd have one of his followers wield the knife, or perhaps snap her slender neck himself. That was part of his grand plan, after all.

It was gloriously simple. He wanted, craved, power. Power brought you everything you wanted— money, sex, control. And he knew just how to acquire it. By witnessing the deeds he had planned for later that evening, every one of the members would then be culpable. A member of the House of Commons, known for his rants that went counter to sound business practices, could hardly keep his head up when confronted with the knowledge that he'd participated in a ritual murder. A young earl couldn't refuse to sponsor an admittance to an exclusive club or the suit of an unwelcome lover if threatened with exposure. He could have anything he wanted; he would be unstoppable, all by dint of a bit of blackmail.

He considered his choice of Brandon Rohan as executioner to be a particularly brilliant stroke. There was no way he could get someone like Viscount Rohan under his thumb. Rohan wasn't interested in the little games the Heavenly Host enjoyed, and he was impervious to blackmail. But when it came to protecting his baby brother he would do anything. There would be no way in the world he would stand aside and let Brandon Rohan be tried and hanged for murder.

Indeed, it had seemed ridiculously easy. It hadn't required much persuasion to keep Rohan's addiction to opium alive, and his rapid consumption of alcohol was benefitted by the addition of certain substances that had been carefully preserved. Rye ergot gave visions approaching the beatific, or the horrific, depending on one's frame of mind. If they came without warning the effects could be devastating.

He hadn't counted on young Rohan having enough of his brother in him to almost destroy his careful plans. He had set the details out for him last night— he hadn't wanted to tip his hand too soon. There should have been no problem. Young Rohan had killed before; he was a soldier, after all, and there were rumors of a distressing incident with some of the locals that had been hastily covered up. The Grand Master had been unable to find the details but he hadn't given up hope. Sooner or later nothing would be closed to him.

But Brandon Rohan, sodden with drink and dazed with drugs, sat in his chair, staring dully at the ornate blade the Grand Master had had forged for just this occasion, and said, "No. Absolutely not. Not ever," in tones so clear he might not have recently imbibed impressive amounts.

The Grand Master wasn't one easily dissuaded, though, and he simply kept feeding the stuff into his unwilling proxy. All to no avail. He eventually passed out, the flat, monosyllabic word still on his lips. "No."

It was no matter. He would never know the difference. He'd had his servants cart Brandon Rohan's unconscious body to an opium den in the worst section of the east end rookeries—he wouldn't be found for days, if he was even found alive at all. His men had instructions to smear blood all over Rohan's cassock and tuck the blood-stained knife beneath him. As always he'd been prescient enough to have two made. Rohan would awake and be convinced he'd committed the murder he'd refused to do. The Grand Master's only regret was that he wouldn't be there to witness the man's horror.

But he had his own job to do. The cassocks decreed by the Heavenly Host were indistinguishable, and the hoods and cowls assured complete anonymity. All he needed to do was copy Brandon Rohan's dragging gait and everyone would recognize the crippled war hero committing the crime.

Truly, he'd planned it so well he astonished even himself. A quiet giggle escaped, and he slapped his hand over his mouth lest someone hear him. But the only noise was from the trussed form of Lady Carstairs, and he had plans for her.

Very specific plans.

32

Never let it be said, thought Benedick Rohan, that sitting around waiting was any less heroic than charging into battle. It was a damned sight harder. He was trapped in his house, with his meddlesome, far too acute younger sister and her blackguard of a husband, and he didn't dare leave. Eating alone in his room was too childish to be contemplated, so he had no choice but to sit at table with the Scorpion and the woman he'd abducted and forced into marriage, and while nothing could induce him to be pleasant, there was simply a limit to how much boredom he could withstand.

One way to alleviate that boredom was to fleece his brother-in-law out of every penny he had on him. Not that Lucien de Malheur wasn't a practiced gambler, but when it came to faro there were few who could beat a Rohan. Miranda reluctantly served as banker, more as a means to keep them from killing each other than an interest in the game, but the play was alarmingly even, probably because Miranda's husband cheated. The winnings went back and forth, well into the early hours of the morning when once more Benedick consumed far more brandy than was good for him, but this time when he retired to bed he was too drunk and too weary to want to kill the Scorpion.

He woke late, suddenly alert. He dressed hastily, even shaving himself rather than waiting for Richmond to make his appearance, and by the time he was downstairs he'd decided that, wise or not, he couldn't wait in the house any longer. He was going out looking, and be damned to the consequences.

But Lucien sat at his dining room table, drinking coffee and looking perturbed, and Miranda paced the floor. Her face, when she saw him, was far from reassuring, but at least there was news.

"They've found him!" she cried. "In some wretched hovel, and if it hadn't been for Lucien's connections, he probably wouldn't have been found until the middle of next week. If he'd even been found alive."

Benedick felt his heart sink. "Where is he now?"

"They're bringing him," Lucien said, sounding equally grave. "He's not in the best of shape, and my men have orders to be discreet, so it's taking a bit of time…"

"Not in the best of shape?" his wife interrupted him. "He was in an *opium den,* Lucien! Unconscious, and no one could rouse him. Wearing a monk's robe and covered in blood." She started pacing again.

Not good, Benedick thought, but he gave Miranda a reassuring nod. "At least he's found. That's the first step. As for the blood, granted, that's not a good sign. But the actual ritual is set for tonight, so at least we know he's not going to be any part of that particular foulness. We may need to call a doctor to attend him..."

"I've already sent word," the Scorpion interrupted, looking grim. "If my information is reliable, and I have no doubt that it is, he's in very bad shape, indeed. With luck the doctor will be here before Brandon arrives home."

"Dr. Tunbridge seldom comes out that promptly..."

"I summoned my doctor, not yours, Rohan," the Scorpion said coolly. "He's more capable of dealing with this kind of situation. I doubt old Tunbridge has ever seen a case of opium poisoning."

It would have made things so much better if he could have simply slammed his fist into Lucien de Malheur's face, Benedick thought fondly, keeping his hands clenched at his sides. Except for what it would do to Miranda, who was already looking far more distressed than a woman in her condition ought to.

She must have picked up on his hostility, for she shot him a quelling glance. "Don't you dare."

He opened his fists and held them up in a sign of surrender. "I'll behave. Things are bad enough already."

It seemed to take forever. The Scorpion was right, the doctor did arrive before Brandon, but at least he didn't look like the shady quack Benedick was anticipating. Miranda kept herself busy by ordering the preparation of a sick room, sending servants running up and down the stairs, while Benedick took a chair as far away as he could from his brother-in-law, drumming his fingers silently and waiting.

He lifted his head when he heard Miranda come back into the room with tears streaming down her face, and his panic erupted. "What's happened? Have you heard something?"

His wretched brother-in-law stood at the same time. "Is he back, my love?"

She nodded. "The doctor is examining him right now. But it's bad, Lucien. Very, very bad. He's covered with blood, and he was found with a bloody knife, and he won't wake up."

"I didn't even hear them bring him in!" Benedick protested, irrationally furious.

"Because they brought him in the back way," Lucien said in the tones reserved for an idiot. "If he's involved in murder we're going to have to be very discreet. Unless you prefer to have your brother hauled off to jail?"

Benedick didn't dignify that with an answer. "When this is over, you bastard, you and I are going to have a serious reckoning."

Lucien's scarred face curved in a malicious grin. "I'll be looking forward to it. But in the meantime do you suppose we might pay attention to what's important?"

Miranda hadn't exaggerated. Brandon lay on the narrow bed, his color dead white. The doctor had already removed the stained clothes, and Brandon's thin, scarred chest rose up and down, imperceptibly. His skinny, clawlike hands were stained with blood, though Miranda was busy washing them clean.

"You shouldn't be doing that!" Benedick said abruptly. "We should call a servant or something…"

"No!" Miranda snapped. "The fewer people who know about this the better. Besides, I need to be able to do something." She reached out and brushed a shock of his dark hair away from his face. "Poor little baby brother," she whispered, tears in her eyes.

"He's in rough shape, but he should make it," the doctor, a thin man with sad eyes far older than his years, murmured. "The amount of opium he ingested has a depressive effect on the heart, slowing it down, and I feared it might stop beating completely, but it's already coming back, and his breathing is better. Even his color is improving."

Benedick looked at the sickly yellow and white of Brandon's skin. "His color is improving?" he said doubtfully.

"You should have seen him when he first arrived," Miranda said. She glanced up at the doctor. "What can we do?"

"Watch him. As long as he cannot add more opium or anything similar, such as laudanum syrup, then he should continue to come back. Keep any sort of spirits away from him, as well. Tie him to the bed if you must, but don't let him ingest anything more for at least two days. If you can, a full week would be better."

"Two days?" Miranda echoed, incensed. "He's never going to touch that filthy stuff again."

The doctor looked at her sadly. "In my experience, my lady, that's seldom the case. He's a habitual user, and while I imagine he started as a response to the pain of his injuries, he now uses it to shut out the world, and it's hard to bring someone back from that. Apart from his addiction, he's in one piece. No injuries, broken bones or the like."

"And the blood?" Lucien spoke then, and the man lifted his head.

"I saw no blood, my lord," he said calmly.

Lucien nodded. "You'll be taken care of as per usual."

Benedick's annoyance grew. "He's my brother. I'll take care of any remuneration. If you'll tell me where to have it sent, Doctor...?" He waited for the man to supply his name, but the doctor looked from the Scorpion back to him, and shrugged.

"We're better off without names," he said gently. "And the Scorpion knows how to get in touch with me. I leave it to you two gentlemen to sort out who pays." There was a cynical twist to his mouth, before he turned to Miranda and put a gentle hand on her head as she sat beside Brandon, clutching his thin hand in hers. "Don't worry, dear lady. He'll be better soon. And then you may begin the hard work of convincing him to stay away from the opium. I wish you luck."

She smiled up at him, but the man had already vanished, like the ghost he was.

At that point Brandon's eyes fluttered open, just for a moment, and then closed again. Not before Benedick saw the expression of clear panic in his bloodshot eyes.

"He's waking up!" Miranda said, her voice brimming with excitement.

Benedick had to wonder if his brother-in-law had seen that same look of horrified pleading. "You need to come downstairs with me, my love, and have something to eat. You've been pacing and hovering for too long."

"But Brandon needs me!" she cried, mutinous.

"Brandon has Benedick, who is more than capable of providing nursing duties, and most likely better at holding a chamber pot. And you, my dear, need to consider the baby, and eat properly."

"You're not fighting fairly," she shot back.

"Of course not, my love." He held out his arm, and after a moment she rose and took it.

"But I'm coming right back. Do you understand?" she said stubbornly.

"You could do with a short nap. Then you may come back, and by then your baby brother will probably feel better able to withstand so much family and your dauntless enthusiasm." He put his hand over hers, leading her away. "Leave this to Neddie."

Benedick waited until they were out of earshot, stifling his irritation at the Scorpion's mocking use of the pet name only his siblings were allowed to utter. When he turned back, Brandon's eyes were open and full of blinding despair.

"I killed her, Neddie," he whispered, his voice a painful rasp. "I told him I wouldn't. I told him there wasn't anything that would make me do it, but I killed her anyway."

"Hush, now," Benedick said, taking the seat beside him and holding the hand Miranda had abandoned. There was still blood beneath the fingernails, and he hoped Brandon couldn't see it. "Who told you to kill her? And who is she?"

"The Grand Master," he choked out. "No one knows who he is, but we're all sworn to obey. But I told him I couldn't. Not ever. But I must have. There was blood all over me, blood on my hands, the knife…"

"But you don't remember actually killing anyone?" It was faint hope, but worth nurturing. For both their sakes.

There was an almost imperceptible shake from Brandon's head. "Not for sure. But I remember seeing her. Some poor serving girl, barely more than a child. And the things he ordered me to do to her. I couldn't, Neddie. But I must have."

"You were right the first time," he said soothingly. "You couldn't. You don't have it in you. You're not a killer. You don't abuse women."

His laugh had a ghostly quality. "There's where you're wrong, Neddie. You have no idea the things I've done, the horrors I've seen. I lost count of how many men I've killed. As for women…you don't want to know. It's been…I can't live with it. Even the opium won't drive the memory away, not completely. You don't need the memory as your burden, too. I'm a monster, and my face only shows what I really am."

Benedick kept his expression blank. Brandon was right; he didn't want to know, but if his brother needed to confess then he'd hear him. He reached out and smoothed the hair away from Brandon's pale, sweating face, much as Miranda had done. "It'll be all right, old man," he said gently. "Things are never as dark as they seem."

Brandon's ghostly laugh was eerie. "No. They're often a lot worse." He sank back on the pillow, closing his eyes. "Forgive me, Neddie."

For the first time in years he wanted to cry. "Nothing to forgive, baby brother. Trust me. Big brother is going to fix everything."

But Brandon had already drifted into a deep, dreamless sleep. At least, Benedick hoped so.

The housemaid who'd assisted the doctor appeared in the doorway. "You want me to sit with him, my lord?" she whispered.

"Yes, thank you, Trudy." He blessed himself for remembering her name. He wasn't as good as he should be with servants but he was better than most. "Call me if there's any change."

"Doctor says he'll sleep twenty-four hours or more, until that poison gets out of his system. I'll watch him and make sure he rests easy."

Benedick nodded. A deep pall had settled over him, which made no sense. Brandon was back, safe. It didn't make sense that he'd killed the girl—it was too soon for the sacrifice. They would wait until the full moon, which wasn't until sometime tonight.

Which meant some poor child was imprisoned, waiting, and by tomorrow would be dead. And he could sit and do nothing about it, or he could do what he knew he must do. Go to Kersley Hall and stop them.

He heard the commotion as he started toward the first floor, a flurry of voices, and he stopped on the landing, frozen, as he looked into the pale, desperate face of Emma Cadbury.

One of the footmen was arguing with her. "His lordship is not at home to women of your sort, my girl. Go along with you."

Richmond would have known better. "Wait," Benedick said, coming down the rest of the stairs.

The older footman turned. "Your lordship, this woman was found sneaking around the house. She must have got in the servants' entrance, and she says she's looking for you, but Cook says she's one of those scarlet women, and she's got no right visiting a decent gentleman's establishment, less'n he's asked for her, which I figger you didn't, as you were worried about your brother, and…"

"Your brother?" Emma Cadbury broke through. "What's happened to your brother?"

"I don't think that's any of your concern," Benedick said stiffly. "Did you sneak in here to see me?"

"I couldn't think of any other way. I knew I'd

scarcely be allowed in by the front door." Her voice was defiant.

He considered her for a moment, then made up his mind. "Come into the library," he said abruptly. "That will be all," he added to the footman, whose name he didn't know. "Keep my sister and her damnable husband away from us."

"But my lord…" the man began, but it was too late. Benedick had already pushed past him and pushed open the door, revealing Lucien de Malheur with his very pregnant wife sitting on his lap, kissing him.

"Shit." It wasn't a word Benedick had ever used in the presence of a woman, but the circumstances more than called for it, and he said it again. "Shit. What are you two doing in my library? Don't answer that. Don't I provide you with a bedroom, albeit against my will? Go there."

"Who's this?" Miranda said, hopping off her husband's lap with surprising grace. The Scorpion rose as Mrs. Cadbury entered the room, ever polite.

"You don't need to introduce me, my lord," she whispered. "I know I shouldn't have come here, but I couldn't think of anything else to do."

"I would suggest you leave it up to me to decide who I introduce my sister to," he said acidly.

"Let me solve the problem and do the honors," Lucien said smoothly. "My dear, I presume this is Mrs. Emma Cadbury, formerly one of the most notorious madams in all of London. Mrs. Cadbury, this is my wife, the Countess of Rochdale."

Miranda gave her a dazzling smile. "But you're so young. That's quite an achievement for one of your youth. And I collect you've retired?"

"Miranda!" Benedick groaned.

"She married me, Rohan," the Scorpion said. "She's used to all sorts of bad hats."

"Is that what I am?" Mrs. Cadbury said wryly. "It's better than some other things I've been called. But Lord Rohan, I really must speak with you."

"You may as well do it in front of my sister and her wretched husband. What has Lady Carstairs done now?"

"That's the problem, my lord. She's gone missing."

33

The day had gone from incomprehensibly bad to cataclysmic, Benedick thought with almost absent precision. What had started with worry over his brother and annoyance with his sister had flipped over into a kind of focused panic. They had Melisande, God help her.

And God help them.

He managed to keep his voice under control. "What makes you think I know anything about it?"

Emma Cadbury gave him a look of withering disdain, something he deserved. "I was hoping you would, sir. I was truly hoping she'd been fool enough to spend the night with you again and simply hadn't bothered to let us know."

"I could only wish," Miranda said wryly.

"But since she'd gone out in search of young Betsey, who disappeared, and she promised she was coming to ask you for help, it seemed odd that she didn't send any word back to us. She never would have abandoned Betsey for some shallow affaire with a hardened rake," she said bitterly.

She certainly had the hard part right, even if the shallow affaire and rake part were far and away off. "I never saw her," he said. "Haven't seen her since two mornings ago."

"When she left here in tears," Emma Cadbury said bitterly. "You bastard."

He blinked in astonishment. He wasn't used to being called a bastard by anyone, much less someone so far beneath him in rank.

Miranda jumped in before he could respond. "Not precisely, but close enough. To make things worse, the damned fool's in love with her and refuses to admit it. I am so weary of pigheaded men and their stubborn natures."

Lucien de Malheur laughed.

"*You're* not exempt, either!" she snapped.

Emma Cadbury looked at Benedick with skepticism. "I don't see any signs of love, my lady. I see a cruel, heartless pig of a man who used her and then sent her away, and…"

"Enough!" he thundered, and all was mercifully silent. "I do not appreciate being called names in my own house. I am not a bastard, a rake, a pig or anything else you women might think of. My love life is not open for discussion, no matter how interested you two are."

"Make that three," the Scorpion tossed in, and Benedick sent him a bitter glare. He should have known someone like Lucien de Malheur would offer no loyalty, no male solidarity.

"And beyond that, I believe we should be more concerned about Lady Carstairs. Explain to me what happened," he demanded in a peremptory tone.

"But first, please take a seat," Miranda broke in.

"You don't offer a seat to a brothel-keeper, Miranda," Benedick said.

"But she's retired."

"I don't want a seat. I want to find Melisande and make sure she's safe. I'm afraid she's gone after those men, and she doesn't even have your doubtful company to protect her."

He ground his teeth at the word *doubtful* but let it pass. "When did she leave?"

"Yesterday, in the late morning. She took a hired coach, and the monk's robe we'd made for her, and she said she was bringing Betsey home. And that's the last we've heard of her, or Betsey for that matter."

"You could have come to me sooner," he snapped, a dozen horrifying scenarios racing through his mind.

"I assumed she was with you. That's what she told me. I should have realized that something was amiss. Particularly when you consider how distraught she was when she returned home from here the last time."

Another stab to the heart, but he ignored it. "Yes, you should have," he said icily. He glanced at Lucien. "I need to leave. She must be at Kersley Hall, and it's growing late. I don't know if they intend to use her for their nasty ritual."

"I gather she's…er…not a virgin," Miranda offered.

"That's not my fault," Benedick snapped. "She was already a widow."

"Your lordship." Richmond was at the door, a pile of cloth in his hand. "I thought you might be needing this."

"What?" he demanded irritably.

"A monk's robe. I found it among Master Brandon's things and removed it, hoping it might stop his current activities. Not that it did any good."

He wanted to hug the old man, but he simply grabbed the cloth and threw it over his arm. "I have to go," he said again.

"Then go," Miranda said, waving an arm. "Lucien and I will be close behind as soon as our carriage is readied, and I'm certain he can summon some of his less savory acquaintances to assist." She turned to her husband. "Do you know where Kersley Hall is, darling?"

"Generally. We'll find it," he said. "Do you know when this supposed ritual is going to take place?"

"Midnight. And don't even think of bringing Miranda. She's pregnant, for God's sake!"

"You've known her all your life," Lucien retorted. "Do you really think I have a chance in hell of keeping her home?"

"Oh, you're a fearsome creature, indeed, Scorpion."

"Stuff it. Your sister is enough to terrify anyone."

Benedick ignored him, turning to his sister.
"Someone needs to look out for Brandon. I don't
know that Trudy will be fully up to it."

"Mrs. Cadbury can do it. You don't mind, do you,
Mrs. Cadbury? The doctor assures us he'll simply
sleep the next twenty-four hours, but we'd feel better
if someone was keeping an eye on him."

Emma Cadbury looked like a cornered doe. "I
shouldn't even be here… Really, I must go. They'll
be worried…"

"You can send word home. And really, don't you
think Lady Carstairs will want to see you first thing
when Benedick brings her safely home? And he will.
Won't you, Neddie?"

He had no choice. "Yes, please stay, Mrs. Cadbury. It would be a kindness."

She nodded, giving in.

"What are you waiting for?" Miranda demanded,
in full warrior mode. "We'll be there before midnight. How will we find you?"

There was no way to stop her, any more than he
could stop the incoming tide. "Make a commotion.
Some kind of distraction that will draw the attention away from whatever this so-called master has
planned. I suppose your sources didn't figure out
yet who's running the Heavenly Host?" he asked his
brother-in-law.

The Scorpion shook his head. "I'll keep my wife

safe. Mrs. Cadbury will look after Brandon. The rest is up to you."

"God help us," Benedick muttered.

The house was silent. Emma Cadbury sat alone in the Viscount's library, a tea tray by her side. She'd managed to drink a cup, but the sight of the tea cakes, so beloved by Melisande, had her on the verge of weeping with fear, and she had never been a woman to give in to tears. She'd simply covered the plate with a serviette.

He was above stairs, sleeping. Lady Rochdale had assured her that he would be fine—a servant would fetch her if he awoke, but that was very unlikely. She had the direction of a doctor, if he should suddenly get worse, but in truth, all she had to do was wait.

As if things weren't bad enough, she thought, trying for a wry smile and failing. On top of everything else temptation was thrown in her face. She'd wanted to see him so many times in the past few months, ever since they'd whisked him away from the hospital, but there'd been no chance. She'd told herself it was for the best. And now here he was, sick, wretched. Unconscious.

He wouldn't know that she'd looked in on him. He was a boy, despite all the horrors he'd been through, despite the determination with which he was trying to destroy himself. She could pray over him, but she never prayed anymore. She was frightened, more frightened than she'd been since the night she'd run away, terrified that Melisande would have finally walked into a danger she couldn't escape, terrified that poor little Betsey would be slaughtered.

Surely she deserved the one sweet respite of a look at Brandon Rohan's sleeping face? Just to reassure herself.

She moved quietly up the stairs. It was growing dark outside, the late-spring evening coming on quickly. The servants were out of sight, as good servants were supposed to be, even the kindly old man who'd brought her the tea had told her he was going down for his own supper but all she had to do was pull the bell if she needed assistance.

It was as good a time as any.

She moved up the stairs quite slowly, half hoping she'd think better of it, but the closer she came the more she knew she couldn't turn back. His room was at the end of the hallway, and while the door to the hallway was closed, she could see dim light coming from under the door. Lady Rochdale had told her a maid would be stationed outside, but the chair was empty.

She moved up and pressed her ear against the door, only to hear absolute silence. And then a hideous thump.

She slammed the door open in time to see Brandon Rohan hanging from his neck in the center of the room, the chair he'd been standing on kicked over.

She rushed to him, holding him up so the strain on his neck was eased. "You *stupid, stupid* fool!" she cried. "Damn you to hell! Stop this immediately."

He'd fought her for a moment, kicking at her imprisoning arms, and then he stopped moving, and she had the horrifying thought that his neck had already been broken. She looked up, tears streaming down her face, to find he was looking down at her, his dark eyes puzzled, the noose loose around his neck.

She reached out with her foot, blindly, catching the edge of the chair and pulling it over. It took her three tries to get it upright, and she set his feet on it, relinquishing her hold as she pulled out the knife she always carried with her. She climbed onto the chair with him, reaching high over his head to cut the rope, and suddenly realized his arms had come around her, and he was looking at her as if he'd seen a ghost. "My harpy," he whispered.

And then he collapsed.

34

If he rode any other horse but Bucephalus, he would not have made it. He went hell-bent, through uneven roads in the murky darkness, and he cursed the rising of the moon, knowing it only brought disaster closer. But Bucephalus was as sure-footed as ever, with nary a misstep as he raced through the night, so fast that the spring dew had no time to settle on his shoulders.

He pulled up short at the copse where he and Melisande had left the horses the other day, ignoring the stab of fear. It was a good thing his sister and her husband were following, though he could still wish Miranda had stayed at home. He could hardly carry Melisande home on his horse again, much as he'd like to, and there was the young girl, as well. Besides, Miranda could be very comforting to those she wasn't related to, and annoyed with, and there was a good chance Melisande or the girl would need a woman's care. But God, he hoped not.

Brandon's robe fit him well enough. They were

of a height, though Benedick was broader in the shoulder, and he considered limping, pretending to be Brandon if anyone should spot him. Ah, but whoever had set his brother up would know perfectly well he wasn't, and that was the main person he had to beware of. He contented himself with hunching slightly, to disguise his height, and moved through the night like a ghost.

There were perhaps a dozen robed figures wandering the empty paths of Kersley Hall, but to his surprise they weren't heading toward the entrance in the old dairy. The building was pitch-dark, the doors shut and barred. Instead they were heading toward the stable, in the midst of muffled laughter and drunken conversation pitched too low for him to hear. He had no choice but to follow them, back into the deserted stable where a man held a lantern aloft. Each acolyte who passed him and disappeared into the stall had to suffer torchlight on his face, and Benedick drew back, ducking into one of the darkened stalls. He could hardly expect to gain admittance if he had to show his face. He had no history with this new, more secretive version of the Heavenly Host, and given Brandon's recent involvement he'd definitely be persona non grata. There were too many people around to stop him if he tried to force his way. At least he could be relatively sure that nothing had happened yet. Whoever the mysterious master was, he would wait for a full audience.

He couldn't imagine how people could stand by while a child was slaughtered. He recognized

Elsmere's drunken laugh, and his lady-wife's admonition. They were hardly people he cared to spend time with in the normal run of things, but he couldn't believe they would be a party to something so hideous. He'd believe everyone was mistaken, but he'd seen the blood on Brandon's hands, the torn cassock on the floor with its ominous dark stains. No, this was very real.

It seemed as if he waited forever, but in fact it was probably less than ten minutes. The slow stream of robed attendants came to a halt, and when he lifted his head there were no lights coming from outside. Only the guard at the distant stall remained.

He moved back out of the stall, into the night air, and circled around, satisfying his suspicion that the last of the Heavenly Host had arrived. There was a door at the opposite end of the stable, near the guard, leading out toward the overgrown woods. They thought no one would approach from that side. They relied on their distance from the city for protection. They were wrong.

He would have liked nothing more than to beat the guardian monk to a pulp, but he couldn't afford the time. He made do with a manure shovel, smashing it over his head so the man went down in a sprawl of limbs. He recognized the face—some pimply-faced young squire up from the country, no doubt looking to join the ton. He took the robe belt off him, noticing in disgust that he was naked underneath. It only made sense—he was expecting an orgy. Benedick tied the boy's arms behind his back, looped the rope around his ankles and left him trussed like a chicken. For good measure he took his handkerchief from his pocket and shoved it in his mouth to keep him quiet before depositing him in one of the other stalls. And then, picking the lantern up in a calm hand, he started down the steps into the tunnels.

He held the lantern aloft, looking around him. This entrance was past the one they had used a few days ago, and he assumed they would be gathering in the large central room. He peered into the dark behind him, but there was no trace of light, and he moved forward, as quietly as he could, in case there were any latecomers.

The tunnel opened out into a room, one they hadn't seen before. It was lit by a few smoking torches, the shadows adding to the ominous feel of the place. The room was smaller than the gathering hall, with lower ceilings and numerous alcoves arranged for licentious purposes. Long, low tables were set out, laid with cold meats and breads, wines and ale, and another with a bizarre arrangement of fruit and vegetables as a centerpiece, consisting mainly of grapes and something pale. And then he caught his breath.

The centerpiece festooned with grapes was indeed something pale. It was the completely nude body of a woman, a familiar, gorgeous body.

Melisande.

He leaped for the table, half-afraid he'd find…

But she was alive. Breathing. In one piece. Her arms and legs were bound, tied to the table, and they'd put her on a huge platter with bits of greenery around her, and dark purple grapes placed at strategic places on her. Her eyes were open and she was staring up at him in mingled fury and entreaty, and he realized they'd gagged her.

Never a bad thing, he thought, half-giddy with relief as he began unfastening the restraints. Melisande had struggled so hard the knots were impossible to undo, so he simply took his knife and cut through, hoping he wouldn't slice her as he did so. The moment her arms were free she sat up, pulling the gag from her mouth and throwing it, while he cut through the leg shackles. And then she launched herself at him, ignoring the knife he still held in his hand, almost knocking him down.

He caught her, all that lovely, naked flesh, pulling her into his arms and crushing her against him, kissing her, openmouthed and hungry. She was shaking all over, her eyes wide and shocked. "I thought you wouldn't come," she whispered. "I was so afraid."

He wanted to reassure her, but he was too busy kissing her. And she was kissing him back, her hands pushing the cassock away, fumbling with his clothing. He caught her wrists, frowning down at her, but she simply struggled.

"I need you," she said, her voice thick with tears. "I need you to…they touched me. They put their filthy hands on me, and I can't stand it. I need you to wipe out the feel of those awful hands. Please, Benedick."

He was past rational thought. Fury at her words

washed through him, as well as lust that he knew he should ignore. But her hands were desperate, and he'd been so frightened, and he pulled her back into the shadows, into the darkness, and pushed her up against the wall.

There was no time, no need for preparation. She was wet, he was hard, and he simply released himself from the breeches, lifting her up and bracing her against the wall before he thrust into her with a grunt of satisfaction, feeling her tight around him.

He wanted to slow down, afraid he might hurt her, but she dug her fingers into his shoulders. "No," she whispered in his ear. "Don't stop. I need you. Hard. I need you to take me. Harder."

He knew what she wanted. Something to blot out the horror of what she'd been through, something to drive her into oblivion and beyond. She had no use for tenderness right then; she needed domination, and he gave it to her, slamming into her, and she absorbed each thrust with an inner clutching, wanting more, needing more.

He felt the climax sweep through her, hard and fast, followed by another, but he wasn't ready to stop, wasn't ready for her to finish. He put his hands between them and touched her, covering her mouth with his. He'd wanted to make her scream with pleasure but this was the wrong time and place. He needed to fuck her in silence, swallowing her cries, and he did, sweating, his body shaking, his legs wanting to give way, her own wrapped so tightly around him that he wanted to die from the pleasure of it.

Her final climax was his undoing, and he let his seed spurt inside her, reveling in the feel of it as he had the time before, not worrying about the consequences. Breaking all the rules he held so fiercely and not caring. Needing to fill her, own her in the most primitive manner.

Still clutching her, he collapsed against the wall, leaning his forehead against hers while he tried to get his breathing under control. Her own was coming really fast, and her heart was still slamming against his. He could feel the stray shudders dancing through her body, squeezing him, and he knew if he stayed like that he'd get hard again. And that was one indulgence he didn't dare claim.

He moved his mouth to her ear, biting the lobe with just a faint nip, and she came again. He wanted to laugh, lighthearted at such a desperate moment, but if he did he'd slip free from her, and he wanted to stay locked together for just a moment longer.

"Are you all right?" he whispered.

He felt her momentary hesitation, but the fear had left her, the shock and disgust. "Splendid," she said dryly. "At least, slightly splendid."

He smiled against her face. "I'll never think of grapes in the same way."

She shoved at him then, and he withdrew, letting her down carefully. She was glaring at him, and he was relieved as well as distracted. He quickly rearranged his clothes, telling himself to stop thinking

of her like that. At least she didn't have the vulnerable, frightened expression. He much preferred her
as a virago.

"Give me your robe," she whispered.

"I can hardly infiltrate them dressed like this. And
they're expecting you to be naked. Of course, I can't
figure out why they would have trussed you up and
just left you. An army of them must have walked by
and barely seemed to notice you."

"They're drugged," she said briefly.

"That explains it. No competent male would
ignore a woman like you."

It wasn't working, and he knew it. "Give me the
goddamn robe."

He'd been about to relinquish it but her tone made
him stop. "I need it more than you do. Why don't you
hop back up on the table and lie still? With luck they
won't see you on the way out, either."

Her hand caught the rope belt, yanking him
against her. "If you think I'm in the mood for this,
you're wrong. Give me the robe."

He relinquished it reluctantly, not so much because he needed it but because the sight of her naked
body was something normal and beautiful in this
eerie, evil darkness. He was dressed in dark clothes,
usual for him, and he blended into the shadows well
enough. "You need to go back up. I'll find Betsey
and bring her up, as well."

"You don't even know her," Melisande whispered.

"How many children will they have trussed up
and ready to sacrifice?"

"I really don't know."

His momentary good humor, thanks to the release of sex and the assurance that Melisande was safe, vanished. He looked down at the woman who somehow mattered to him in ways he wasn't going to think about, and frowned. "You're not going to leave and head for safety, are you?"

"Not when someone's life is at stake."

"I assure you, the person most likely to die a horrible death tonight will be whoever started this whole mess."

"Wasn't that your ancestor?"

"The original organization was a far cry from the cruelties and mad plans of this current group. Whoever's behind it isn't going to make it through the night. He's convinced Brandon he murdered a young woman. He's done everything to push Brandon over the edge. And I'm going to kill him for it."

She surveyed him for a long moment, then sighed. "Lovely," she said in a caustic voice. "Before you avenge your brother could we please rescue Betsey?"

He'd done something wrong again; he knew it with dismal certainty but he couldn't afford to stop long enough to figure it out. Another female on his coattails, another female he wanted safe at home, in bed, in his bed. Another female he cared too much about, try as he might to drive her away.

"I don't think so," he murmured. And before she realized what he was doing he clipped her across the jaw with a perfect fist, dropping her like a stone.

He caught her before she landed on the hard-packed floor. Years of training in the pugilistic arts had finally paid off with the best hit of his life. If she hadn't caved, he didn't think he would have been capable of hitting her again, even to save her life. He'd never hit a woman in his life, would never have even considered it. But to save her life he'd do anything.

He held her in his arms for a moment, looking down into her peaceful face. "I'm so sorry, my darling," he whispered, brushing his mouth against hers. "But I refuse to risk your life. You can kill me later."

Holding her tight against him, he moved to the farthest alcove, laying her down on a bunch of cushions clearly marked for more licentious activity. He should probably take back the robe, but he couldn't see leaving her naked and defenseless. He only wished there was enough time to get her back outside again, but he daren't take the chance.

He took the rope belt and wrapped it around her wrists, loosely, so that she could untie herself if he didn't come back. There was no guarantee he'd be successful, but sooner or later his sister and the Scorpion would show up with reinforcements. He might despise his brother-in-law, but he had absolutely no doubt that Lucien de Malheur would make hash of these aristocrats and their putative master.

She looked so peaceful, and he wished to God he could just take her and run, leave the rest to Lucien. But he couldn't. He'd promised her, and even if he hadn't, he could scarcely leave a child to such monsters.

He drew back. And then, before he could change his mind, he turned and strode out of the room, down the endless warren of tunnels to the quiet buzz of noise that was slowly growing louder.

She waited until his footsteps died away, and then she opened her eyes. She knew she should be angry enough to kill, but at the moment she was past that. She sat up, reaching her bound hands up to her jaw, wiggling it a little. It hurt. He'd hit her hard, and she hadn't been feigning her collapse. By the time he'd caught her she'd gathered her disordered senses, smart enough to know that fighting him would be a losing battle and only delay him from getting to Betsey. So she kept her eyes closed as he carried her into this place and tied her wrists. Kept her eyes closed as he'd kissed her, so sweetly, with more gentleness than he'd shown her so far.

He'd called her "my darling." Did he mean it? She didn't have time to consider that, either. If he loved her, she'd forgive him for trying to knock her out. If he didn't, she was going to kill him.

She tugged at the rope around her wrists, then used her teeth, pulling it free with surprising ease. So he would avenge his brother and probably ruin his own life, but he didn't give a damn about her, trussed up like a Christmas goose. She'd been forced to lie there as they pawed her, and she'd been desperate for anything to get the feel of their hands off her. He'd done the job, quite effectively, and even now, beneath the enveloping monk's robe, she could feel his seed sticky on her legs, and she wondered if she would go through another ritual scrubbing when she finally got home. Or whether she would let it remain, knowing it was the last time he would touch her.

She managed to scramble to her feet, only the slightest bit shaky. She knew she couldn't indulge that shakiness, and she started after him, her bare feet cold on the hard stone floor. As she passed the table they'd trussed her to she realized she was starving, and at the last minute she plucked a bunch of grapes to take with her. No one, no one could crush her, no matter what they did. She might fall apart momentarily, but she was ready to fight once more, and she wasn't going to let a perverted group of randy aristocrats terrorize her.

She didn't bother to consider why he'd come after her; she could only be glad he did. The monk's robe still retained his body heat, delicious around her chilled skin, and his spicy scent lingered. She wouldn't give this back, she thought, even though it symbolized everything horrific about the group she was determined to wipe out. It smelled like Rohan, and like a lovesick adolescent she wanted to hold on to it, cling to it for safety.

She could hear the noise of the chanting from a distance. There was no sign of Rohan, and she felt an icy chill sweeping through her body. Had they caught him so quickly? Was he now lying trussed up as well, one more offering to whatever strange god they seemed to worship. She held her breath, praying it wasn't too late. She'd been insane to stop long enough to…what would he call it? To fuck him, that's what it had been, plain and simple. Well, perhaps not so plain and not so simple, but it had hardly been making love. Her fear and need had blinded her to the much more important task. Saving Betsey's life.

By the time she reached the hallway approaching the large gathering room the myriad candles were sending out bright pools of light into the darkened corridors, and she could see Benedick ahead of her. He'd set the lantern down, pressing against the side of the cave, disappearing into the shadows. He was so busy concentrating on the scene in the vast room beyond that he hadn't noticed her arrival.

She stopped where she was, flattening herself against the wall. She had to face the unpleasant fact that he was, at least this time, right. She needed to be out of the way so she didn't distract him. The odds were bad enough without her getting in the way.

She held her breath, waiting. And then she closed her eyes and began to pray.

35

Benedick leaned back, not moving. The chanting was loud and mindless, in some kind of Pig Latin. He could only hope his sister and the Scorpion had moved quickly. Things were rapidly getting out of hand, and if he didn't get out of here alive then someone would need to rescue Melisande. At this rate time was running out.

"Has someone joined us?" A smooth, oddly familiar voice carried from the chamber beyond, and Benedick cursed beneath his breath. Scratch that. The time had come. And without another word he strode into the center of the great hall, grateful at least that Melisande was safely out of the way.

The chanting didn't stop when he walked into the room. They didn't even seem to notice, though their faces, hidden in the depths of their hoods, were turned upward to watch as they knelt around the perimeter. But he wasn't interested in the mind-addled mad monks. It was the center of the room that caught his attention.

The young girl lay spread out on what could only be an altar. She was wearing a lacy white dress and her hair was clean and flowing around her peaceful face. He could only hope that whatever drug the so-called Grand Master used on his acolytes had been given to Betsey, as well. She'd be a lot easier to deal with if she were unconscious.

The man stood alone in the middle of the room, cowled, hidden like the coward he was, an ornamental dagger in one hand. There was something that resembled a tray surrounding the platform where the girl was placed, presumably to catch her blood, and he didn't want to think what they planned to do with it.

"I was expecting you," the man said, moving around so that the altar lay between them. He was limping badly, and it took Benedick a moment to realize why. He was pretending to be Brandon, wrapped in the enveloping monk's robe and hood, so that his drugged followers would believe in his brother's guilt. "Though I suppose you released that tiresome woman. I would have thought you'd had your fill of her by now."

For an opening salvo it was a weak one. "I don't think that's possible," he said evenly, determined not to let the man bait him. "But you wouldn't understand that, would you?"

"The sentimentality of love?" The Grand Master's voice was mocking. "I have been spared that particular embarrassment. I would have thought you would be, too, brother. You could always take her back to the banquet hall. Feed her some wine and she'll do anything you tell her to. By the time you come back this will be over and done with, and you won't even be a witness."

He didn't turn around. He had the sudden, unbearable suspicion that Melisande had managed to escape his makeshift bonds, but he couldn't afford to waste his time considering it. "We found Brandon in that hellhole you left him. These idiots might think you're my brother but I know better."

"Yes, but you see, they can't hear so well. They're in an altered state, thanks to the drugs I administered to their wine and the advanced practice of mind control. When they awake they will only remember what they think they saw. Which is your crippled brother slashing the throat of an innocent girl and splashing them all with her blood."

He heard a strangled noise behind him, but he kept focused. Damn the woman. "But I'm not drugged. And I know who you are."

He was rewarded with a familiar giggle over the maddening chant. "Of course you do, old man. I wouldn't expect anything less."

"I have people coming, you know. You can't really expect to get away with this. Let her go. If you left now you could get to the continent and no one would come after you."

"Why should I do that, when I'm about to have everything I want?" his old friend said smoothly. "You won't turn me in. Too many reputations are a stake. None of these impossibly highborn people want to admit that they were part of anything so shameful, but if you're the one to betray them then I'm sure they will all testify that your brother killed this young girl. As for your so-called reinforcements, you don't have any. Most of the people you call friends are already here. Accept it, Rohan. I've won. And I'm only beginning."

He raised the knife high over his head, and his cowl fell back just far enough for Benedick to see Harry Merton's smiling face.

"No!" Benedick shouted, leaping forward and vaulting the altar, but not all the monks were as mindless as they appeared to be. Harry sidestepped him adroitly as two cowled figures came up behind Benedick, pinning his arms behind him. He didn't bother to struggle—he kicked at the man on his left, hard behind the knee, and the man went down in a yelp of pain, leaving only the second man to face Benedick's fury. He smashed a fist beneath the enveloping hood, directly into the man's face, and he felt the crunch and splinter of bone, the spurt of hot blood, the skin split on his own hand as the second man let out a howl, pushing back the hood. It was Pennington, shrieking in fury as he fell back, and then it was only Harry Merton, watching him from a short distance away, calm, a cheerful light in his eyes, the ornamental knife in his hand.

He was closer to the body than Benedick was, and he doubted he could move quickly enough to stop him. "Come on, Rohan, old friend," Harry crooned. "You've taken out my two best men. Surely you aren't going to give up now. Or do you realize I'll have this child gutted before you even move, and that will signal a bacchanalia that not even you can stop. You'll be pulled down beneath my followers, washed in her blood, and I can promise you, someone will slip a knife between your ribs before you have any idea what's happened."

"I'll take you with me, you bastard," he said, leaping for him, ready to rip his throat out. He heard her scream from a distance—Melisande—but he didn't stop, simply kept moving when the world exploded.

36

Melisande screamed, unable to keep still any longer. It sounded like the wrath of God or the end of the world, and she buried her head as the ceiling disintegrated, dirt and stones and rubble pouring down around them. Something hit her hard between the shoulder blades, knocking the breath from her, and she coughed, struggling, trying to get to her feet once more, trying to reach Benedick.

Slowly the tumbling rocks and sliding dirt halted. And so, thank God, did the ghastly chanting, though the garbed monks didn't move, still kneeling around the tableau. She finally lifted her head, her eyes searching for Benedick, but there was no sign of him, just a huge pile of rocks and dirt, and she felt hysteria rise in her throat. If he was dead…if he was hurt…

And then a movement caught her eye, and she turned her head to see him at the altar, covered in dust as he rose to his full height, brushing the debris from Betsey's body. He'd covered her, Melisande realized in shock. In the last minute he'd leaped forward to try to save the innocent girl he insisted didn't matter, and it made her want to cry.

She looked around for Harry Merton, but there was no sign of him. And then she saw the legs sticking out from beneath the pile of rubble, and she breathed a sigh of relief. It was over.

She started toward the altar and began to unfasten the leather straps, then stopped, looking overhead to the night sky above. A very pregnant young woman was looking down at them. "Is everyone all right down there?"

Benedick looked at Melisande for a long, silent moment, and then he moved away from the altar, peering upward. "That was a bit more effective than I expected, sister mine," he drawled, sounding only slightly rattled. "Deus ex machina, indeed."

"We didn't know this was directly over you, Neddie," the woman said in an apologetic tone. "Is anyone hurt?"

"Only the right people. Harry Merton is dead."

Miranda let out a shriek. "God, no!"

"Thank God, yes. He's the Grand Master." He moved to the sloping side, refusing to look at Melisande. "Find Lucien. I want to get the women out of here, and the cave leading to the stairs has collapsed in the explosion."

His sister disappeared, and Benedick came over to the altar, moving Melisande aside with gentle hands, before he finished unfastening Betsey's bonds. Ignoring Melisande, he scooped Betsey up in his arms and carried her to the side of the cave-in. Someone had found an old ladder, and it was lowered down. Benedick climbed the first few rungs with Betsey over his shoulder, passed her on to waiting hands and then turned back to Melisande, finally looking at her.

She raised her chin. "What are you going to do about the Heavenly Host?"

"Leave it to us. You don't have to be responsible for everything." He held out an impatient hand to her. "Are you coming?"

"No, I thought I'd stay here with the degenerates and the dead body," she said, angry once more. She slid off the altar, ignoring his hand and headed for the ladder. She was halfway up, with him directly behind her, when she remembered she was wearing nothing beneath the enveloping monk's robe, and he could see directly beneath it.

Tant pis, she thought. It would give him something to remember her by.

The hands that caught her were strong and rough, and in the bright full moonlight she found herself surrounded by what appeared to be a gang of criminals. The pregnant woman had her arms around Betsey, wrapped in a blanket, and she was talking to her gently, soothing her, and for a moment Melisande stood still, feeling useless.

"Lady Carstairs?" A rich voice came from beside her, and she turned to look into the scarred face of an otherwise handsome man. He clutched a cane, and she knew who he was.

"Mr. Brandon Rohan?" she inquired.

He shuddered. "God, no. Though I suppose we might as well be bookends, given our similar injuries. No, I can thankfully say that I have none of the wild Rohan blood in me. Only in my children. I'm Rochdale, and that very pregnant woman is my wife, the only female Rohan. Allow me to escort you to our carriage...."

"Take your hands off her, Scorpion!" Benedick's voice was deadly as he emerged from the collapsed tunnel.

The man's smile was angelic. "I didn't touch her, old man. But I thought you didn't want her."

"I..." His voice trailed off, and Melisande felt the last of her elation vanish.

She turned to Rochdale, or the Scorpion, or whoever he was. "I would appreciate the kindness of a ride home, Lord Rochdale. I find I'm quite exhausted."

The woman had brought the dazed Betsey over to her. "She's all right," she told Melisande. "She doesn't remember much, but she was worried about you."

"Oh, Betsey," Melisande murmured, pulling her into her arms. "And I promised you'd be safe."

"Not your fault," the Scorpion's lady-wife said cheerfully. "And she won't remember much of it anyway." The woman looked her up and down, assessing. "So you're the woman my brother has fallen in love with. So much for the best-laid plans." She peered at her more closely. "You poor thing, you look done in. Let's get them back to town, Lucien. Benedick can follow after he's made arrangements for the cleanup."

Her husband nodded. "What do you suggest we do with the Heavenly Host?"

"My thought would be to fill in the hole and leave them to rot," Benedick said, coming up behind them. "But I don't suppose that would go over too well. And if it weren't for our parents' unwise involvement with the Heavenly Host we might not be here." He looked at Melisande. "I need to talk to you."

"Not now, Neddie," Miranda said firmly, taking Melisande's arm in one hand and Betsey's in the other. "It can wait until you get back to London."

She wasn't going to see him when he returned to London, Melisande thought fiercely. She wasn't ever going to talk to him again. He could jump in the hole with the rest of those degenerates and stay there, he could...

She found herself handed up into a luxurious carriage, with Betsey coming after her and the ungainly Lady Rochdale following. "You might stay and keep an eye on Benedick, my dear," she said to her husband. "See that he doesn't tarry too long. I suspect Lady Carstairs's patience is running thin."

The man looked resigned. "Is there a horse for me to ride?"

"I'm sure Jacob's men would have come prepared. We'll be waiting for you when you get back."

The carriage started with a jerk, throwing Melisande back against the squabs. Betsey immediately curled up on the seat beside her and fell back into a sound, drugged sleep, and Benedick's sister looked at her across the darkened carriage. Neither of the lamps had been lit, but the fitful moonlight danced by her face, bringing it in and out of the shadows, doubtless doing the same to her own, Melisande thought. It was a strange way to hold a conversation she didn't want to have.

And Lady Rochdale didn't appear to be interested in sparing her. "I gather my brother has made a hash of things."

She tried to stop her. "Lady Rochdale, I've just been through an exceedingly trying few days. I've been hit on the head, abducted, abused and watched a man die. Perhaps we could continue this conversation another time."

"You aren't going to want to hold this conversation another time, Melisande. I imagine I'll get nowhere near you. Might as well have it out now, while the wounds are still raw. I'm Miranda, by the way. Much easier than Lady this and Lady that, particularly since we're going be sisters-in-law."

That was enough to jerk Melisande out of her determined torpor. "Don't be ridiculous!" she snapped, all her customary good humor and good manners vanished in the extremity of the moment. "He's done nothing that would force him into marrying me."

"What an odd way to put it," Miranda replied. "And I'm afraid you're wrong. He certainly has done something that would force him to marry you. He's fallen in love with you."

Melisande mentally counted to ten in a vain effort to regain her shattered self-control. "I must warn you, Lady Rochdale, that I am very close to screaming, and I wouldn't want to disturb Betsey."

"Miranda," Benedick's sister corrected, undeterred. "As I said, he made a hash of it. Perhaps I might explain. It's tedious of him and very male. Men don't admit weakness, nor examine their feelings. They simply blunder, or in my oldest brother's case, snarl their way through life, pretending that nothing touches them, when it's hardly the case. It's his wives, you see."

She didn't want to hear this. But short of putting her hands over her ears and singing loudly like a stubborn schoolchild, there was nothing she could do to stop her. "He's still mourning his dead wives. Yes, I can imagine."

"That's not it. Annis's death took the joy from him, Barbara's death finished it. But he mourned them and released them. He's simply terrified that it will happen again. That he'll fall in love and marry and his wife would die in childbed once more."

Melisande laughed mirthlessly, on the edge of hysteria. "I don't believe it! He was all set to propose to Dorothea Pennington, for the sole purpose of creating an heir. He seemed perfectly willing to do that."

"Because he didn't love Miss Pennington."

Melisande was struck dumb. "That's rather awful," she said finally.

"Yes, it is. I never said my brother was a kind

man, though compared to my husband he's an innocent lamb. However, to be frank, I don't think I could bring myself to mourn Dorothea Pennington overmuch myself."

The countess's frank words startled a laugh from Melisande. It was rusty, odd, but it was definitely a laugh, when an hour ago she would have wagered she'd never laugh again.

"That's better," said the countess. "You, on the other hand, he couldn't bear to lose. So he drove you away. I won't ask how, but I expect it was with his nasty tongue. As I said, stupid of him, but at times all men are stupid. Particularly when they are in love."

"Would you stop saying that!" Melisande begged. "He's not in love with me."

"Allow me to know my brother better than you do. He's most pathetically, desperately in love, even if he refuses to admit it. And I expect you love him, too, or you wouldn't be so hurt and angry."

"I'm annoyed," Melisande said stoutly. "Apart from that I simply don't care."

"Liar," said the countess. She peered at her closely. "Or perhaps I'm wrong. I love Benedick so much, know his strengths and his frailties so well that I assume anyone with discernment would love him, too."

"I have no discernment whatsoever."

Miranda smiled then, the doubt in her face vanishing. "You need to punish *him,* not yourself, Melisande. The only way you're going to get a chance to do that is to marry him."

37

Melisande slept. She awoke when the carriage pulled to a stop. Dazed, she realized the door was being opened from the outside and the steps let down. Betsey was handed out into liveried arms, and she knew they were in Bury Street. She stayed where she was. "I would prefer to be returned home."

"I don't think Betsey can handle much more at this point. She needs a bed and a period of sleep." Indeed, Betsey was making fretful, sleepy noises like a fractious child. Which indeed, right now, she was. "And your friend is waiting for you here."

"My friend?"

"Mrs. Cadbury," Miranda clarified.

"Emma would never come here."

"She did when she knew you were in danger. I prevailed upon her to wait for you, and to keep an eye on Brandon. He's in bad shape, poor lad, from the opium and whatever else that beastly Harry Merton pumped into him. If you insist, I'll summon the carriage to take you all home again. But first, please come inside for a bit. Benedick is still in Kent—you don't need to worry about running into him."

That, at least, was true. And she had already discovered that it was almost impossible to fight the countess of Rochdale. To her shame her legs felt weak as she climbed the front steps, and it was the very pregnant countess who supported her, not the other way around.

Once inside, the countess immediately became efficient. "Richmond, would you have a nice warm bath poured for Lady Carstairs? She's covered with soot and she's had a trying night. And is there any chance some of my old gowns might still be here? I'm afraid her ladyship has lost her clothes."

The elderly butler bowed, his seamed face impassive, but she remembered him, and his kindness. "It will be the work of a moment, your ladyship. And I believe I might interest you in good hot tea and sugar cakes, might I not? His lordship has required that Cook keep a supply of them on hand since your first visit."

Melisande looked at him for a moment, uncomprehending. And then finally, finally, she began to cry, as the countess folded her into her arms and the butler beat a hasty retreat. "There, there, my pet," she murmured, her pregnant belly a third party between them. "It's been dismal, I know. But a hot bath, fresh clothes and tea will make all the difference. By the time Benedick returns you'll have the upper hand, and he'll have to grovel. It will be delicious."

Melisande managed a watery laugh.

"Richmond, where is Lady Carstairs's friend?"

"She went back to the Dovecote…that is, back to Carstairs House, my lady. She left a note for Lady Carstairs, said she'd understand."

"How odd," Miranda said. "And Master Brandon?"

"He had a fall. Not sure how it happened, but Mrs. Cadbury found him, and we brought the doctor back in. He's a bit the worse for wear, but getting better, though he's a bit banged up."

Melisande could feel the tension in Miranda's arms. "Then I'd best go sit with him myself," she said calmly. "See to Lady Carstairs, please. And find a nice warm bed for the stray lamb over there." Betsey was sound asleep on one of the chairs in the hallway.

"Yes, madam."

"I should go home…" Melisande began once more, but the countess stopped her.

"Enough!" she said. "It's been a trying night for me as well, and in case you didn't notice, I'm in an interesting condition. Indulge me in following Richmond. He'll take most excellent care of you."

She stopped arguing. The countess, of course, was right. The warmth of the bath was restorative in the extreme, soothing away not just the grime and dust from the cave-in but the aches in her muscles, and the remnants of that fast, rough coupling in the empty room at Kersley Hall. She knew she should rush through her ablutions, dress and force her way home before Viscount Rohan returned, but she couldn't bring herself to move, staying in the tub until the water grew cool.

It was the countess's personal maid who helped her dress in the clothes that were a bit too tight. Melisande was taller than the countess, and more robust, and had no interest in being tightly laced, but still, being properly dressed helped enormously. There were no shoes that would fit her feet, but that was the least of her worries. Things had been so desperate she hadn't even considered her ankle, but it was swollen and throbbing after the abuses of the past twenty-four hours, and she had no intention of walking very far.

She took the tea and sugar cakes in solitary splendor in the bedroom, once the bathtub had been removed and the maid returned to her mistress. Emma's note was on the tray, but it made little sense, just a bunch of vague excuses and a promise to explain everything once she returned home. It should have galvanized her into leaving. She poured herself another cup of tea.

Eventually, she heard his footsteps on the stairs, taking them two at a time. They could belong to no one else—the earl limped, and the servants would take the back stairs even if called upon to hurry. She knew who it was, and she braced herself as he slammed open the bedroom door and stood there, glowering at her.

He was covered with soot and dirt, though he'd made an effort to wash his face. He smelled of night air and horse and sweat; he smelled of spices and warm skin and everything she wanted. She sat there, waiting.

"No children," he said abruptly.

She blinked. "I beg your pardon?"

"I'm only considering this because presumably you're barren. There'll be no children. Do you understand?"

She understood, the countess's words coming back to her with blinding clarity. She should make it easy for him, help him. But in his case her charitable instincts had long dried up. "Considering what?" she said calmly.

He ran a hand through his hair and was rewarded with a shower of dust on his filthy jacket. "Marriage. It's the sensible thing to do."

"Sensible? Hardly. You need an heir. I can't provide you with one. I've already told you it makes a great deal more sense for me to be your mistress."

"Absolutely not. You're going to marry me, and the hell with an heir. I have two brothers and a nephew who could inherit the title. An heir doesn't matter."

"Then what does?"

For a moment he didn't say anything. And then he moved so swiftly he shocked her, crossing the room and sinking to his knees in front of her, yanking her into his arms with a fierceness that belied the fact that his strong arms were shaking. "You'll marry me," he said, his face buried against her shoulder, "because I love you, damn it. Against my better judgment, against my will, I adore you, every square inch of your perfect pink skin, every word from your mouth, every foolish, pigheaded thing you do. I've done my best to drive you away, but I can't keep my hands off you, and on top of everything else you make me laugh. I love you, and I'm tired of fighting it."

"But what if I don't love you?"

He lifted his head, looking honestly astonished, and she laughed at his utter incredulity. "Don't worry. I love you," she said. "I just thought I'd torture you for a moment."

He kissed her then, full and hard and deep, his tongue against hers, heat and desire rushing through her. He threaded his hands through the curtain of damp hair that hung around her shoulders, and he broke the kiss to bury his face in it, groaning. "I'm so filthy," he said. "I stink of dirt and horse and sweat, and you're so clean and sweet..."

"I can always take another bath," she murmured, reaching up to unfasten his buttons.

Epilogue

It was a rough night in Somerset. Benedick, Viscount Rohan, was being forcibly held down on a sofa in his study as his father poured him another tall glass of good Scots whiskey. He handed it to his son-in-law, better known as the Scorpion, a man tolerated because his daughter adored him, and eyed him warily. "Whiskey's the only thing for it," he said.

"Indeed," Lucien replied. "So I've discovered. Drink up, man," he said to Benedick. "It'll be over soon enough."

The storm was howling outside. Inside, Benedick was wild-eyed and desperate, but there was no way his father or Lucien would let him leave the room, and he knew he could simply ride Bucephalus over a cliff come morning. No, he wouldn't do that to such a fine beast. He'd hobble him and then jump himself. It didn't matter how. If he had a sword, he'd fall on it, in fine Roman fashion. But for now all he could do was get as drunk as he possibly could.

"How bad is he?" Charlotte, Marchioness of

Haverstoke stuck her head in the door. She was a fine-looking woman even at her age, her red hair streaked with gray, her eyes full of compassion as they surveyed her eldest son.

"I expect he's a sight worse than your daughter-in-law," Adrian replied, smiling at her.

Charlotte nodded. "He looks it. Won't be long now."

Momentary concern crossed Adrian's face. "The girl…she's all right, isn't she?"

"Strong as a horse," Charlotte assured him. "Just keep on with the whiskey."

It was near dawn when the door opened once more. Benedick, stubborn bastard that he was, had simply refused to pass out, but he was sitting there mumbling, planning all the ways he would end his life now that he was certain his wife was gone. "He's pathetic," Miranda observed as she walked over to the fire.

"Don't be so harsh on him, darling one," Lucien said. "He's had a hard history."

"Not anymore," she said briskly. "She popped him out easier than I do." She touched the light swell of her eighth and, she hoped, final pregnancy.

"Him? It's a boy then?" Adrian lifted his head. He'd imbibed his own fair share of the whiskey, as had Lucien, and none of them were in any great shape.

"You have a grandson. Charles Edward, after your brother who died young."

For a moment Adrian blinked, and it had to be the

whiskey that brought the tears to his eyes. "Whose idea was that?" he said gruffly.

"Oh, Melisande's. Benedick wasn't going to come up with a name—he was that certain he'd be burying her and the little one."

"And they're healthy?"

"Listen for yourself," Miranda said, holding the door open, and a loud, lusty wail came down the hall.

Benedick lifted his head, suddenly, astonishingly sober despite all the Scots whiskey he'd ingested. Miranda smiled at him. "Come along, my brave one. Your wife and son want to see you."

* * * * *

Turn the pages for your
exclusive free read

THE WICKED HOUSE OF ROHAN

by

Anne Stuart

1740, Venice

Miss Kathleen Strong was so hungry she could have eaten three of the pigeons that normally fluttered through St. Mark's Square, raw. The only problem being that they were wily little creatures, and every time she got close they flapped away, knowing that a scarecrow like her wouldn't be providing bread crumbs.

But today it was pouring rain. There were no tourists. The pigeons had deserted the place.

Still, she could be glad of the rain. It kept her awake and alert enough to make her appointment with Sir Wesley Marblethorpe. She hadn't had a bed in two days, and sleeping in an alleyway had its drawbacks, like rats and other nighttime predators. She had no weapon apart from a particularly nasty hairpin about six inches long, fairly suitable for jabbing a miscreant in the eye. She was long past being squeamish.

She was reasonably clean, thanks to the presence of water everywhere. Her serviceable gray dress was stained, to be sure, but she'd gotten most of the darker spots out, and she'd even managed to plait her hair in severe braids, affixing them to the base of her neck with the hairpin cum Excalibur. She knew that Sir Wesley would see her just as she was, a proper British governess, down on her luck, admittedly, but starched and proper enough; presuming he didn't look too closely, she would qualify for whatever form of employment Sir Wesley was offering.

If she got the job she might even have enough nerve to request an advance on her salary and she could liberate her meager belongings from Signora Montalba, the beady-eyed landlady who'd kicked her out two days ago. The very idea of asking such a boon made her shrink with shame, but her last meal had been a withered apple, and that was a day and a half ago. If she didn't get something to eat soon she was going to end up facedown in the Grand Canal.

Palazzo del Zaglia was up ahead, on one of the less busy campos. There were none of Venice's omnipresent cats around, and Kathleen wondered idly if she'd ever eat one. Probably not. She *liked* cats.

In truth, there was no way to tell for sure if this large, crumbling building was indeed Palazzo del Zaglia. She should have approached it from the water side, but she hadn't enough money for a gondola.

She would just have to hope for the best. The steady beat of the rain had turned her bonnet into a sodden mass that hung limply around her face, and her hair was plastered to her head beneath it. She would look unprepossessing indeed, but the advertisement said Sir Wesley was quite desperate. As was she. Surely a match made in heaven.

She climbed the cracked stone steps to the intimidating door and pulled the bell. Next she'd have to face a superior servant, who might just send her off with a flea in her ear. She had no idea what she'd do in that case.

But the man who opened the door was a far cry from a servant. A bit on the short side, with a little too much paunch and a simple bag wig set askew on a balding pate, he wore a well-trimmed goatee and had the smallest, meanest eyes she'd ever seen.

"Miss Strong?" He had a high-pitched, almost effeminate voice. "Miss Kathleen Strong?"

She wondered if she was supposed to curtsy. If she tried she might very well pass out at his feet, which would hardly improve matters. She managed a slight dip. "Sir Wesley?" she said hopefully.

"Indeed. But my poor Miss Strong, you're soaked! Please come in out of the rain and dry off. My friends won't mind waiting."

"Your friends?" she said doubtfully, relinquishing her bonnet and reticule into the hands of the supercilious servant she'd been expecting.

"Marcello, please take Miss Strong into the dining room or whatever the hell Alistair is calling it. Miss Strong, I'll be joining you in a moment."

Her brain hadn't melted in the Venetian rain, even if it felt like it. She knew, immediately, that this was not the kind of employment she was seeking. She should say she'd made a mistake, turn and get out of there as fast as she possibly could.

But where could she go?

Sir Wesley must have read the indecision on her face, and he smiled winningly, like a chubby, naughty little boy intent on mischief.

She'd dealt with naughty little boys and she knew just how to handle them. The grown version couldn't be so different.

"Just hear us out, Miss Strong," he said with the right amount of earnestness and charm. "I just know we can be of service to each other. Please, go with Marcello."

The absurdity of her suspicions hit so hard she laughed. Venice was filled with the most beautiful women in the world. No one would have any use for a skinny spinster nearing thirty years of age. She was being ridiculous.

"This way, miss," the servant said, and, consigning her doubts to the Adriatic, she followed his stiff figure down a series of passageways, hallways and salons. They were in the same declining condition of every single palazzo she'd seen since she'd arrived in this beautiful, curst city. The palazzos must be built already disintegrating.

She heard the voices well before they reached the room, and her irrational misgivings came back. Men's voices, loud, slightly drunken.

Courage, she reminded herself. There were almost as many courtesans as there were pigeons in Venice. They didn't want her for *that*. Nobody did.

Marcello pushed open the door, and the noise and heat spilled forth, accompanied by the unmistakable smell of cinnamon and chocolate. Maybe they'd feed her even if they didn't hire her—if she just had a decent meal she might be able to attend to her desperate problems with a fresh perspective.

She stopped in the doorway, unsure what to do. And then she saw him.

He sat at one end of the table, long legs propped up on the scarred surface, and for a moment she stared. He was jaded, beautiful, dissolute, and his faint smile was dangerously seductive. All the other men in the room seemed to fade into the shadows, and Kathleen stared at him as if she'd seen a ghost.

And ghost he was. The ghost of her girlhood, when she was young and hopeful and daydreamed with her sister about the man who would be her true love.

He'd looked very much like that man, from the tousled wave of thick brown hair, the piercing blue eyes—the mouth perfect for kissing. A knight on a white stallion, come to rescue her.

Madness. He caught sight of her, and his mouth curved in a smile so cynical that for a moment she was crushed.

"I believe we have a guest, gentleman," he announced in a lazy voice, and the sudden silence was shocking. "A little gray wren has come to visit us. Let's make her welcome, shall we?"

She wasn't sure what she would have done next. This announcement was greeted with such raucous enthusiasm that she almost turned and ran, but Sir Wesley had come up behind her, taking her arm in his and escorting her into the room as though she were an honored visitor.

"This is the woman I told you about. Miss Kathleen Strong, may I introduce to you our little organization, the members of the Saving Grace?"

"I thought we decided on the Heavenly Host," a drunken voice called out.

The man at the table spoke again, his voice low, pleasant. Implacable. "What is she doing here, Marblethorpe? I thought we discussed this."

"We came to no consensus. And Miss Strong is in dire need of employment. Aren't you, Miss Strong?"

She had a hard time pulling her gaze away from the man's eyes. They were a golden color, like dark honey, and that made her think of toast and tea and rich pastries... She forced herself to look at some of the other men. All expensively dressed, albeit their fine clothes were in sad disarray after what was presumably a night of carousing. "Yes," she managed to say in a low voice. "I'm in need of employment."

"I don't like it," her hero said flatly, forcing her to look at him again. He'd discarded his neckcloth and if he'd worn a wig it was long gone. His white shirt was open, exposing a quantity of beautiful golden skin, more skin than she'd ever seen on an adult male.

And she really was losing her mind. She glanced back at Sir Wesley. The movement of her head was too swift, and for a moment blackness started to close in.

"You might get Miss Strong a seat if we're going to continue with this nonsense," the beautiful man said, and her heart sank. She'd already been judged not qualified for the position. She found herself settled into a large wooden chair, just moments before she took a header onto the none too clean marble floors of the Palazzo del Zaglia.

And she drifted into the golden-honey-colored eyes, as the voices flowed around her.

Alistair Rohan was annoyed, at Wesley Marblethorpe, at his dozen or so drunken boon companions, fellow intellectuals and degenerates, but most of all with himself.

He'd called this meeting of the nascent organization they'd dreamed up one drunken night. It was an organization dedicated to excess and debauchery, to questioning the status quo of faith, the existence of God and the devil, and the limits one could go to in search of pleasure. They'd taken their motto from the ancient Abbey of Theleme—DO WHAT THOU WILT—and Marblethorpe and the others were ready to jump in with enthusiasm.

Alistair was already bored with the notion. But then, he grew bored easily, particularly nowadays. What had seemed like a brilliant idea when he was roaring drunk now seemed tawdry and childish by the light of day. He didn't need the approval of his friends to plumb the depths or heights of his erotic nature. He wasn't interested in dressing in costumes or playing at blasphemy. He believed in nothing, therefore there was nothing he needed to flout. In truth, he had always done what he wished, from the time his bastard of a father died and left him his sole heir. There was no title—his cousin was the English Viscount Rohan—and all he'd inherited had been a crumbling castle in Ireland and enough money not to have to live there. He'd rented this moldering palazzo and availed himself of the myriad pleasures Venice had to offer, and there had been an impressive number of them, and never looked back.

In fact, it was because he'd finally run out of diversions that he and Marblethorpe and his friends had come up with this ludicrous idea of the Heavenly Host, and he hadn't sobered up enough over the past few weeks to talk the others out of it.

He looked at the girl—no, woman—who'd been ushered in. She looked as if she might faint, which would have been an annoyance. He'd gotten her a chair because he didn't want her smashing her skull on the floor—the marble was cracked and stained already and blood was the very devil to clean up. At least, his servants had never managed it well.

"So who the hell is this, Marblethorpe?" His voice was lazy, though he already knew exactly what this pathetic creature was.

"You know perfectly well, Alistair," Wesley said in a stiff voice. "Miss Strong can provide the one element we need to make our revels complete. Indeed, she's probably the only one in Venice, unless you're willing to involve children, and I believe you all overruled me on that?"

"You're a sick bastard, Wesley," Alistair said evenly, turning to look at the woman. She'd started at the mention of his name—clearly his reputation preceded him, even among little gray wrens. She seemed oddly familiar, but he was certain he'd never seen her before.

"Miss Strong," Wesley said, and the woman looked up, slightly dazed. She was pale, but her bone structure was lovely, he thought dispassionately. Too thin for the optimal sensual pleasures, but there was still something indisputably appealing.

There were no fresh glasses on the table, and he didn't want any of his servants bothering them, so he refilled his own glass of wine, rosé, and sauntered over to stand in front her. It took her a moment to look up, and when she did so, he noticed she had particularly lovely eyes. A warm brown, almost like rich chocolate, though at the moment she could barely focus. He wondered if she were a laudanum addict—they often were too thin and had that dazed look.

He put the wineglass in her cold, gloveless hand. "Here," he said, "Drink this. You'll need it before you hear Wesley's proposition."

"I shouldn't," she said, and it was no polite demurral. She really thought she shouldn't.

He didn't care what she thought. "Drink it."

She did, and a faint blush of color rose to her pale cheeks. She started to thank him, but he turned away, taking his seat once more, ignoring the astonished looks from his fellow rakehells.

He shrugged in response to the unasked question. "She's just so damned pathetic," he said.

She raised her head at that, and her brown eyes sharpened. So, she was more alert than she seemed. Well, she *was* pathetic. Pale, thin, half-drowned.

He waved a hand at Marblethorpe to continue, and he did so with a portentous clearing of his throat.

"As I was saying," he continued, his high, nasal voice only slightly slurred. "Miss Strong is a virtuous gentlewoman fallen on hard times. She arrived in Venice four months ago as the governess to the children of Mr. and Mrs. Brandon. After two months she was summarily turned out for improper behavior. She was able to secure another post, which lasted less than a week once Mrs. Brandon paid her new employers a visit. Since then she's been eking out a living with English and Italian lessons and the occasional fine needlework. As you can see, the perfect impoverished English gentlewoman."

Marblethorpe was like a cat with a mouse. He liked to torture any poor creature he managed to capture. Usually Alistair didn't mind. In fact, he didn't mind now, he told himself, watching her.

"Would you tell us why you were dismissed, Miss Strong?" Jasper Fenton was slightly less drunk than the evening's ringleader and therefore able to form a coherent sentence.

She'd ducked her head again, her shoulders bowed, but she looked up at that. "Gross immorality, sir," she whispered.

"Demme, Wesley, we need a virgin, not a blasted soiled rose," Lord Maxwell protested.

"Hush, Maxwell," Marblethorpe said. "Give the upright and pure Miss Strong a chance to defend herself. Were you, in fact, guilty of these immoral transgressions?"

"No, sir." Her voice wasn't much more than a whisper. She'd drained his glass of wine, Alistair noticed, and she was clinging to the empty glass so tightly he thought it might snap. It would cut her hand if it did, but he decided he'd used up his full allotment of Christian mercy for the next decade, so he waited.

"So you are, in fact, a virgin?" Maxwell continued.

She looked at Marblethorpe then, and he'd never seen anyone look more defeated in his life. "I was inquiring about a job as a governess to your little sister, Sir Wesley. I assure you that despite Mrs. Brandon's unfortunate misapprehensions I am more than capable of providing a moral and challenging education for your sister."

"A bit late for that," Wesley said cheerfully. "Elspeth's married with two brats, and she's been having affairs since she got back from her honeymoon. I expect every man in this room has had her at one time or another."

There was a chorus of drunken assents. Alistair said nothing. He'd been the first, seducing her away from her older husband out of boredom. If he hadn't, the next man would have, he thought, still watching the drowned kitten before him.

No, that wasn't quite it. A drowned cat. There was a flash of real fire in her eyes. "Then if you aren't in need of a governess, why, pray, am I here?"

"In fact, we are in need of a virtuous woman," Wesley announced. "A virgin, in fact. And it sounds as if, rumors to the contrary, you qualify?"

She said nothing, waiting.

"Well, then," Wesley continued, only slightly ruffled by her lack of response. "We both appear to have problems that are easily solved. You're in need of money to discharge your debts and pay passage home to London, am I right?" He didn't wait for an answer. "And you have a commodity that interests us, one we're willing to pay highly for. Your virginity."

She tried to rise, but Marblethorpe dropped his hand on her shoulder, pushing her back down.

Alistair rose then, ambling across the room, and removed Wesley's thick hand. "If we're doing this, and apparently we are, she needs to agree to it without any coercion from you. Look at me, Miss Strong."

She didn't move, her head and shoulders bowed.

"Look at me!" he snapped, and she jerked her head up. Her eyes were no longer a dull brown, they were blazing with rage. "That's better," he said in his coolest voice, the one his mistress once complained could freeze hell. "Do you understand what Sir Wesley is asking of you? What we're asking of you?"

"A-all of you?" she stammered.

He glanced back at Wesley. "No, not all. One of us. We're asking you to offer up your virginity in return for financial security and a swift trip home."

"A few short hours," Wesley broke in eagerly. "No restraints, no whips. Just coitus."

"Penetration and the breaking of your maidenhead," Alistair continued. "With an audience."

He wouldn't have thought she could turn any paler. She looked up at him with such hatred in her eyes that he was taken aback. What had he ever done to hurt her that she would despise him so? It was Marblethorpe who had lured her here under false pretenses. And then the animation left her eyes. "Yes," she said in a voice so low he couldn't believe he'd heard it.

"Louder, Miss Strong. We need everyone to hear your assent." His voice was like a lash, trying to sting her. He was furious, and he couldn't imagine why. Despoiling a willing virgin as part of their silly gathering was harmless. He was a firm believer that any excess was permissible so long as those involved were in agreement, and when Marblethorpe had proposed the notion of the ritual breaking of a hymen, he'd found the idea vaguely erotic. Still did, if he looked at Miss Kathleen Strong, though he wasn't sure he'd like an audience for it.

"I said I agree," she said in a stronger voice. "On one condition."

"Name it," Marblethorpe said eagerly, but she didn't look away from Alistair.

"That the man chosen isn't you."

It shocked Alistair, when he thought he was past being surprised by anything. And then he laughed. "It shall be as you wish, though I do need to tell you that you're rejecting a true master of the erotic arts. Be that as it may, how shall we decide who gets this particular treasure?" His voice was sarcastic, almost cruel, surprising himself. Had the wretched creature actually offended him? Apparently she had.

"I found her, I should get her," Marblethorpe said eagerly.

"Not fair!" Jasper protested. "I say we wager for it."

"Then do so," Alistair said in a bored voice. "Take your prize and go away. I'm in need of a nap if I'm going to be up for a certifiable orgy tonight."

"Tonight?" the woman whispered.

He glanced down at her. "Tonight. Don't worry, Miss Strong. The sooner it's done the sooner it's over, and you can be on your way back to England and forget this ever happened."

She said nothing, and he turned his back on her, washing his hands of the whole tedious situation. He'd done his best for the wretched creature, God knew why, when he himself had the irrational urge to bed her. An hour ago, after a vigorous night, he thought he'd never want sex again.

But he did. With her. And he didn't want anyone else to have her, which was ridiculous. He'd always shared his lovers. The whole situation made no sense.

"You can see yourselves out," he said. And he walked away from them, closing the door behind him.

Kathleen heard them talking. He was gone, and her last bit of strength left her.

"What's wrong with Rohan?" one man said. "He hasn't changed

his mind about all this, has he? It isn't like him."

"Of course not," another man said. "He's been setting a prodigious example for all of us in his drinking and wenching. I imagine he's worn out. I'm just demmed sorry he's not going to have the virgin—I would have liked to observe his technique. I'm betting he could have made her climax."

"I'm certain any of us are capable of doing the deed," Marblethorpe said. "Come, let's go to my place and play cards for her. Or shall we use the dice?"

"What will we do about her in the meantime?"

Oh, please God, feed me, she thought wearily.

"Leave her here. We'll be gathering here tonight anyway and if we take her with us we might misplace her. Alistair won't touch her, rules and all that."

"An excellent idea. I'll have Marcello keep an eye on her, make sure she doesn't bolt."

Their voices were fading away, but she was scarcely aware of them. The eventual silence was so blessed she almost wept.

Alistair Rohan. Why hadn't she known him immediately? She'd never seen eyes that captivating color on anyone but her brother's friend.

She'd been fifteen, he'd been twenty, sent down from Oxford with her brother Jack for some prank involving chickens and the dean's office, much to her father's annoyance.

She'd taken one look at him and fallen madly, desperately in love, as only a fifteen-year-old can love. Of course Rohan had barely noticed Jack's gawky little sister, though he lightly flirted with her when they'd been thrown together.

He left, and she'd never seen him again. Jack had served in India and, like so many before him, died there. Mary had died in childbirth, and their parents were already gone. She was alone, and she'd had no qualms about becoming a governess, and proved to be an extremely good one. She'd leapt at the chance to travel to Venice with the Brandon family, and then disaster fell.

Leaving her destitute, and now a whore, facing her childhood crush. She pushed herself out of the chair and went to survey the littered table, hoping there might be a scrap of food left behind.

Apparently the members of the Saving Grace or the Heaven Host or whatever they were calling themselves were only interested in drink, and that one glass of wine had been a very bad idea.

Death before dishonor. It was a lovely sentiment, but she didn't want to die. If she had the chance to go back to England then she didn't fancy a grave as an alternative. They buried the dead on a separate island here—she didn't want her body dumped on a barge and carried over there with the other paupers.

An hour or two in exchange for getting out of this country. She had no sure idea what would await her in England, whether Mrs. Brandon's slander would follow her there, but she had good enough references from other families. And no one would ever need know of this.

She would think of it as a medical procedure, close her eyes and endure. At least no one would cut her open, and the pain would be marginal and quick, or so her sister had told her.

She moved over to the window seat, curling up against the bolted shutters. If Marcello showed up she'd ask him for food, which he'd probably refuse, but starvation had its own compensations. She was already so muzzy-headed she'd probably barely notice what they did to her.

She had drifted off to sleep when the door opened and Alistair Rohan came in, heading purposefully toward the table. His head was wet, and clearly he'd just bathed. She would have killed for a bath.

She sank back into the alcove. A mistake, because her movement caught his attention and he turned to stare at her for a long moment, clearly surprised.

"What are you still doing here?" he asked in that lazy voice she remembered so well.

Somehow she found she was able to answer. "They were afraid they might misplace me."

He gave a short, sharp laugh. "You look like you're starving," he said abruptly. "Can I offer you some food, or will you throw that back in my face?"

"Food...would be very nice," she said in a faint voice.

He nodded, more to himself than to her. "Come with me."

She followed, determined not to fall over, trailing behind the straight, tall back that she'd once sighed over. The room he brought her to was small and cozy, with a blazing fire to fight off the damp Venetian chill. She stood there, uncertain what to do.

"Go. Sit by the fire," he said irritably, and disappeared.

She did as she was bid. The chair was cushioned, the fire so hot that her hands and feet finally began to warm, and she could see steam rising from her sodden garments. She ought to be embarrassed, but it was nothing compared to what was coming later that night.

She didn't know how long he was gone. She had probably drifted off to sleep again, because when he appeared, the supercilious Marcello was with him, carrying a heavy tray.

She almost cried then. But she swallowed back the tears as Marcello set the tray down on the table beside her, then moved it in front of her. Soup, baked eels, cold chicken, hard cheese, bread, sweet confections. She couldn't believe the food there, and she didn't know where to start.

"If you think I'm going to hand-feed you you're wrong," Alistair said, throwing himself down in the chair opposite her.

"Don't…don't you want any?" She'd stab him if he did.

He shook his head. "I've been eating regular meals. Clearly you haven't."

It was all she could do not to fall on the food like a ravenous savage. She forced herself to eat slowly, knowing she'd make herself sick if she shoved it all in her mouth, knowing he was watching her out of those heavy-lidded, honey-gold eyes. She was past feeling self-conscious. When she finally finished she sat back, her stomach pleasantly full for the first time in weeks.

She had no choice—she'd been brought up with manners. "Thank you."

He raised an eyebrow. "No longer wanting me dead? Though I can't imagine what I've done to earn your enmity. I was trying to save you from the worst folly imaginable."

"Why? Oh, I remember. I'm just so damned pathetic," she said.

He grinned at that. "I can tell you're feeling better already. I've had Marcello prepare a room for you and a bath. You look as if you haven't had a good night's sleep in weeks, and you're going to need your strength if you expect to get through tonight's festivities."

"A bath?" she echoed. "I've changed my mind—you can have me after all." It was meant to be a joke, but it was a poor choice of words.

His eyebrow lifted again. "Kind of you," he murmured, "but I think I'll decline the sacrifice."

She could feel her face redden. "I was being facetious," she said stiffly. "But the thought of a warm bath is quite…wonderful. Thank you."

"My pleasure," he said. "Or not, as the case may be."

"When…when do things start tonight?" He was wrong. The better she felt the more difficult it was going to be. An hour ago she'd been numb. She was coming back to life now, and the thought of what lay ahead of her was daunting.

"Late. I believe your part involves the thrust of midnight, so to speak." He ran a careless hand through his thick brown hair, frowning at her. "You know they won't let you change your mind. They'll hold you down if you tell them no."

"I won't change my mind." She had no choice. Back out to wander the streets of Venice like a lost soul? She'd end up raped or dead.

He shrugged. "So be it. Marcello is waiting for you. Don't let him give you any trouble. He's a surly bastard."

She was being dismissed. She rose, no longer as shaky as she had been, and he stayed where he was, watching her. She'd already gotten used to the fact that gentlemen didn't rise when she did. As a governess she was only slightly higher than a servant, but it still felt strange to have him lounge there insolently.

He was no longer the same man, she reminded herself, moving past him. But then his hand caught her wrist, halting her, and heat ran through her entire body, like an electric shock. She looked down at him, schooling her expression.

"You really don't know what you're doing, Miss Strong."

"No, I don't. If I had experience of all this I'd be of no use to you and your degenerate friends."

He released her, and she resisted the impulse to rub her wrist. It had been a light touch, and it burned. "Get some rest, Miss Strong," he said. And turned away from her to stare into the fire.

Marcello was beyond surly. He was more like a guard than a servant, and when he ushered her into the dark dressing room he was clearly impatient. But the copper bath was there, steam rising from the water, and she didn't care, barely noticing that he locked the door behind her.

There was a bright fire blazing in the fireplace, and the room was positively warm. She pulled off her clothes, her fingers clumsy in her hair, dumping them on the floor. Everything, including her chemise, when she usually kept that one for bathing. It wasn't until she slid into the hot water that she put her face in her hands and wept.

She stopped as quickly as she could, stiffening her shoulders. She didn't want to waste the warm water with foolish regrets. There was rose-scented soap, and she ducked her head under the water then scrubbed her hair with the soap. She washed every inch of her body twice over, until the water was growing cool, and then she lay back, resting her head on the edge of the tub and closing her eyes. She wanted to stay there forever.

She heard the lock in the door, but she was too sated with pleasure to pay attention, until the door opened. She started to sit up in panic, then realized that her breasts would be exposed if she did, so she sank lower in the tub, glaring as Alistair Rohan strolled into the room, closing the door behind him.

"I thought you would have been done by now," he murmured.

"If you'll go away then I'll finish," she snapped.

He leaned back against the door, surveying her lazily. "Oh, don't mind me. It's nothing I won't be seeing in full in about twelve hours."

"Go away."

"No," he said in a sweet voice. "But I'll give you a towel."

She put out her hand, trying to keep the rest of her under the rose-clouded water. He pushed away from the door and came to stand over her, and she suddenly felt hot, so hot she wondered if the water would start to heat up around her once more. She took the towel and waited for him to move back.

He didn't. She glared up at him. "Go away," she said again.

"Don't waste your breath, my love. I'm not going anywhere. Here, I'll hold the towel for you."

Even in the shadowy light he could see her glare, and he laughed. "Very well, I'll back off. A few feet. But we're going to have to talk, sooner or later."

He really would stay there until she gave in. It was difficult, holding the towel in front of her as some kind of blanket, then trying to angle herself out of the tub without getting her hair wet all over again.

She slipped, and he was there to catch her, lifting her out, the towel a thin layer between them, his hands on her naked back as he held her.

He looked down at her, surprise clear on his face. A moment later it was gone, replaced by the sardonic languor she was fast growing accustomed to. "You're much too thin," he observed. "I can feel your ribs." His cool fingers stroked her heated skin. "But I find you're much more interesting with your clothes off."

She yanked herself out of his arms, wrapping the towel around her. He caught her arm before she could move completely out of reach, and he picked up a thick strand of her hair. Once she'd washed it she'd let it hang over the edge of the tub and it was almost dry, its familiar strawberry-blond color warm in the firelight. "And your hair is quite lovely. Such an unusual combination— chocolate-brown eyes and strawberry hair."

She froze. Fifteen years ago he'd teased her, flirting with her, telling her she had chocolate eyes, and it had been a joke between them. She allowed herself a brief, searching look at him, but he didn't appear to have made any connection. He'd probably seen any number of women with *chocolate* eyes.

"The bed is in the adjoining room," he said.

"Wh...what?"

His smile was wry. "You were going to take a nap, remember? Unless you've changed your mind?"

"Please release me," she said in response. She couldn't think straight when he was touching her. Even the simple hold on her wrist sent waves of heat through her body, to places she didn't even want to think about.

"Why?"

She yanked, but he didn't let go. "If you bruise me your fellow degenerates might complain," she said bitterly.

"I expect they'll bruise you far worse than I will. Why do you want me to take my hand off you?"

"Because I don't like you."

"Try again. Don't you have any idea why you shiver when I touch you?"

"Revulsion? Extreme dislike? Nausea?"

His slow smile widened until it was absolutely wicked, and he trailed his other hand up her bare arm, to the base of her neck, letting his fingers dance over her racing pulse. "No. But then, you wouldn't be likely to recognize it. Try this."

And before she realized what he was going to do he'd leaned forward and brushed his mouth against hers, a light, clinging kiss, pulling away before she could react.

She stared up at him in consternation. "Why did you do that?" she whispered.

"To make a point. It's called sexual attraction, my innocent one. It's a powerful force when it hits this hard. It's animal instinct, the mating urge, and for some bizarre reason it exists between you and me."

"Ridiculous." She barely managed to get the word out.

He was trailing his hand up and down her arm while his other one captured her wrist. "Not at all. It's perfectly natural. It's just surprising it's so powerful between us. You're hardly my type."

Her heart was thudding against her breast, so hard she thought he might hear it. The touch of his mouth had been devastating, and he was right, she wanted more.

"Let. Go. Of. Me."

He smiled ruefully. "Of course," he said, and released her, stepping back. "There are clothes waiting in the other room, though I have to admit I'd rather you didn't put them on."

"Whore's clothes?"

"On the contrary. You're missing the point. They want you because you're innocent. For all I know they'll dress you up like a nun."

She slammed the door behind her, then looked for a key. Of course there wasn't one, but he didn't seem to be interested in following her. The clothes that lay across the bed were pristine and lovely—fresh white batiste undergarments, modest and understated, with nothing to cover them. She dressed quickly in what they'd left her—shift, drawers, petticoat and light corset. She laced it loosely, then climbed up onto the bed. She wasn't going to think about it, wasn't going to think about anything. She was going to fall asleep, immediately.

Which she did. But as she drifted off she remembered his mouth on hers, his hand brushing against her neck, and she wanted to weep.

Alistair Rohan stared at the closed door for a long moment. This was quite the most interesting day he'd had in a long time, perhaps years. It wasn't the birth of the Heavenly Host after months of drunken planning, it wasn't the incipient erotic events coming up. It was his own reactions that astonished him.

He wanted her. That pathetic little dab of a thing—who wanted anyone but him—and he was more aroused by her than by the most experienced, beautiful women in Venice, Paris or London. She was too thin, she was absolutely ignorant of any kind of pleasure, and, while her eyes brought back some hazy sense of a long-lost happiness, they weren't enough to account for this powerful attraction.

He'd like to believe it was her animosity, but there were any number of women wise enough not to want to have anything to do with him. His reputation was widespread—most women with sense would keep their distance.

Perhaps it was because he felt her strong attraction to him, the attraction she was too innocent to recognize. She was so untutored that she had no idea that it was sexual longing raging in her pure veins.

He could have her later. After Marblethorpe or whoever had finished with her, he could soothe the hurt and show her what love was like. He was sick of this city—he could take her back to England himself. Or even Ireland, to the crumbling old castle that was hardly as bad as this crumbling city.

He was out of his mind. Yes, he wanted to have her. He wanted to stretch her out on the bed and taste every bit of her; he wanted to push inside her, so deeply; he wanted to hear her cry out her release in his ear. He wanted her mouth on him, he wanted to…

Damn, he was hard just thinking about her. It was absurd. She'd sold herself to the Heavenly Host for a pittance and a ticket home, and the sooner he stopped thinking about her the better.

Except he'd put her in his bed. Her skin was warm and pink from the bath, smelling like roses. His sheets would smell like roses.

Marcello was waiting outside the door, the ring of heavy keys in his hand. Despite the munificent sum he paid him, Alistair was perfectly aware that Marblethorpe paid him more. "Don't lock her in," he said.

"No, sir," Marcello said. And Alistair no more believed him than he would have believed Sir Wesley Marblethorpe.

He held out longer than he would have thought. It was late afternoon, and she'd slept at least four hours, while Alistair tried to distract himself with anything he could think of. In the end he gave in. He sent his valet out with instructions, poured an ewer of cold water over his head, and went to his bedroom.

She was locked in, of course. He didn't bother with Marcello— there were other ways. There was a narrow balcony overlooking the canal that ran along the side of the palazzo, one in front of each of the main rooms, with a few feet between them. He simply jumped across to the one in front of his bedroom.

He'd done it before, dead drunk. Sober, it was admittedly easier, and he landed lightly, then pushed open the windows.

She was a small lump in the middle of his bed. She hadn't done anything with her hair—it spread around her, and he wanted to wrap himself in it. She was still asleep. The fire had died, but the room was still warm, and he pushed the windows closed behind him, moving toward the bed.

Kathleen heard him come into the room, and she didn't move. She'd already realized that this was, indeed, his private bedroom. Perhaps he'd just come in search of something and would leave the way he'd come.

And perhaps pigs could fly and Venice had roads. She knew why he was here, and she'd been unconsciously waiting for him. Wondering what kept him so long.

She'd even been able to sleep, which astonished her. But when she slept she dreamed of Alistair, and not the sweet, innocent hero of her childhood. She dreamed of the beautiful, dissolute rake, his hands on her breasts, between her legs, his body naked against her skin. She dreamed of heat and sweat and sex without even knowing what she was dreaming of, and when she awoke he was looking down at her.

"You're not doing it," he said. "Marblethorpe will have to find somebody else."

"I have to," she said wearily, as if to a recalcitrant child who wasn't paying attention. "I have no other options."

"I'm taking you back to England. My valet has secured passage for us on a packet ship that leaves tomorrow morning."

She wasn't sure whether she felt despair or elation. "So I get to be your whore instead of a virgin sacrifice? How is that any better? With the other, I only have to put up with it one time."

"Wretch," he said in his lazy voice. "Move over."

"Now?" Her eyes widened.

"No," he said patiently. "You don't have to put up with anything you don't want. I told Simpson to book two rooms. If you don't want to share mine then Simpson can."

"You're telling me you'll save me even if I don't become your mistress?"

He sat down on the bed, next to her hip, and she scuttled over, afraid to touch him. "I'm telling you…" he began, then stopped, staring down at her. "Why do you look so familiar? Why do I suddenly feel as if I have to take care of you whenever I look at you, when frankly I don't feel the slightest bit of responsibility for anyone else? Which makes life very difficult, because I also want to fuck you, and the two don't go together."

She flinched at the ugly word. What would he say if she told him the truth? Would he remember? After all these years?

And if he did, what would happen? He probably had enough decency left in him that he would leap from the bed in horror that he'd talked that way to Jack Lunning-Strong's little sister.

It would be revenge. It would be rescue. It would be despair.

She'd come this far. She lay in his bed, practically naked, and even the touch of his eyes made her skin warm. If she told him the truth she'd get home safely, her virginity intact, and she'd die that way.

"Make up your mind," she said, looking into his dark amber eyes. "What is it you want to do?"

He stretched out beside her, and his hand slid down her throat, brushing across the top of her breast, and she wanted to arch into it. "I want to render you unusable for Marblethorpe's little game. I want to get in bed with you and make love to you until you weep with pleasure, and then I want to do it all over again. And the thing is, my innocent little angel, that you really want it too. You just don't recognize it." He pushed her hair away from her face in a gentle caress.

"You're wrong."

He leaned over her and pressed his lips to the corner of her eye, a light, butterfly kiss. "Of course you'd say that." His smile was self-deprecatory.

"I do recognize it."

He froze, as if he couldn't believe what she'd said. It was no wonder—she couldn't believe it either. All she knew was that if he pulled away from her now she would die.

"Well," he said after a long moment. "Then what are we going to do about this, Miss Strong?"

She reached up and cupped his face between her hands. Bad things had happened to him since she'd once fallen in love with him, turning him cynical, but in truth she was a constant soul. When she fell in love it was forever, and in fifteen years the one thing that hadn't changed were her feelings for him. If this was the only way she could have him then she'd take him this way. "I think we are going to render me unusable for tonight's ceremony."

For a moment he didn't move. And then he leaned over and kissed her softly at first, and she wanted to cry from the sweetness of it. And then he deepened the kiss, his mouth open, and he used his tongue, shocking her, arousing her. Her hands were clutching his shoulders, and she touched his tongue with hers, shivering in response. Her breasts felt swollen, sensitive, and she was wet between her legs. She didn't know why, all she knew was that she wanted his hands on her, all over her. He touched her breasts, his thumbs rubbing against her nipples, and the heat inside her began to build. He slid her shift down, so that her breasts were exposed in the cool night air, and then he bent down, his tongue dancing across one breast, and she heard a quiet moan, one that had to have come from her.

"You're beautiful," he whispered against her skin, untying the corset and pulling it from her. "But I need to feed you more."

"I like to eat," she murmured.

"I was hoping you'd say that," he said with a soft laugh, then moved to her other breast, sucking it into his mouth, and her moan was louder this time. "But we'll save that for another time. Tonight we'll concentrate on you."

She had no idea what he was talking about, but whatever it was sounded wicked and wonderful. The petticoat was off her now, and all that was left was her shift and her drawers. And then they were gone as well, and she was naked beneath him, as he moved his mouth down her body, letting his tongue dip into her navel. "You taste like roses," he murmured. "I like that."

"Good," she said in a strangled voice, as he slid his fingers into the curls between her legs. Of course he was going to touch her there—that was how it was done. But she knew she was wet, and she suddenly felt very shy.

But he'd already slid his hand lower, and she felt his fingers lightly touching the most secret parts of her, and it was too late. "You're wet," he said, rubbing his face against her stomach. "I *love* it."

All right, she thought. Then maybe the wetness wasn't a bad thing. He slid one finger into her, and she arched up, understanding why. He brought it out and put two in, spreading the moisture around, touching her, stretching her, getting her used to the feel of his hand, before she got used to the feel of his penis.

His thumb brushed against something, and she cried out in surprise as a rush of pleasure surged through her. She reached for him then, pulling at his shirt. She heard his chuckle, and he pulled it over his head and tossed it, then rolled over on top of her, still wearing his breeches, settling between her legs. She could feel that part of him, that thick, insistent bulge against her, and she shivered in reaction, arching up for him, wanting him, needing him.

He bumped against her, gently, and she cried out, trying to pull him closer. "Slow down, my angel. I want to make this last."

"I don't," she said in a choked voice. "I want you now. I need you."

He laughed against her throat, and his fingers moved between her legs again, three now, moving deep into the dampness, stretching her as he stroked her. "I know you do. And I could take you this minute and lose myself in you. But you need to know the pleasure if you're going to take the pain." His fingers trailed upward, touching that secret place that made her shiver and cry out. "I want you to unfasten my breeches," he whispered, as he slid, and then rubbed, and slid, and rubbed, until she thought she'd go mad with it, and she fumbled with his breeches, practically ripping them off him, releasing him.

She was afraid to touch him, but he took her hand and placed it on his erection, and for a moment she was terrified. That would never fit inside her, it would rip her apart. But he moved her hand on him, cupping her fingers, sliding her fist up and down the way her body would grip him, and the excitement built again, wiping out her fear. This had been happening since the dawn of time, and the parts were made to fit together, even if it seemed unlikely. She ran her fingers over the head, and felt his dampness as well, and she wanted more.

"Please," she said, stroking him, pulling gently at him, marveling at the hardness beneath the silken skin, and he muttered a low curse.

"You're being difficult," he chided her. "And if you keep doing that I won't be able to hold out."

"I don't want you to hold out. I want you…"

"Where do you want me, Miss Strong?" he whispered in her ear, taking the lobe between his teeth and biting lightly.

She groaned in unexpected pleasure. "Inside me," she said.

"Then let's get this virginity done with, shall we?" he said with a laugh, and he pushed her legs apart, settling down, the head of him resting against her. He pushed in, just a little bit, and she knew a slight burning along with exquisite pleasure. Yes, this was what she wanted. This was where he belonged, the joining that would stay forever in her heart. He pushed deeper, and the pain increased, as well as the joy. She put her arms around him, sliding her hands up his sleek, beautiful back, and then she tugged at him, lifting her hips.

"More," she said.

"Oh, God," he moaned, and thrust deep, breaking through the barrier and coming up hard against her.

It hurt. She couldn't help it, she cried out, and for a moment the pain was searing. And then as quickly as it came it began to recede, not completely, but to a point where it was simply a reminder that this was part of the price.

He was holding very still, looking down at her. "Are you all right?"

"Yes."

"Did I hurt you?"

"Yes."

"Do you want me to stop?"

"God, no," she said, holding him tight against her. There was more, she knew it, and it was just out of reach, but already she was feeling waves of pleasure, the feeling of rightness. "It feels…wonderful."

He began to move then, a slow, gentle withdrawal and surge to get her used to the feel of him. He did it again, and it felt better. "More," she said, and he laughed, thrusting deeper, and she took it without pain, glorying in the feel of him tight inside her, filling her, joined so tightly they might never be truly apart again.

She felt her body begin to loosen, adapting to his, and she caught the rhythm, moving in answer to his thrusts. He made a guttural sound, deeper still, and she felt a shudder run across her body.

"More," she whispered, and he moved faster, harder, and he took her hands and wrapped his own around them, his mouth on hers.

Strange feelings were rippling through her body, and she fought it, afraid. "Let go," he whispered in her ear, arching over her, staring down at her as his hips pumped, his thick, hard penis sliding deeper and deeper. "Just…let…go."

She shook her head, distressed, unable to speak as something dark and terrifying seemed ready to sweep over her. She didn't want it, she wanted safety, she wanted…

"Let…go…" he said. "Don't fight it. Let…go."

"Don't…want…" she gasped, and then it was too late. She seemed to explode, as her body went rigid and darkness shut down around her. Wave after wave shook her, and as each one died another took its place. Then he slid his hand between their joined bodies, touching her, and she cried out, as she felt him fill her with his seed. When she fell back, weeping, he collapsed on top of her, panting, unable to catch his breath.

Reality came back, slowly. He pulled away from her, getting up, and she was afraid he was leaving her, but he was back in a moment, a wet cloth in his hand, and he lay back down beside her and began to clean her, with gentle, loving hands.

And then he gathered her into his arms, holding her against him. His heart was still racing, his hold on her tight and protective. "I think," he said after a few minutes, "that we should get the hell out of here. Marblethorpe is not a pretty sight when he's thwarted, and I really don't feel like killing him."

She rubbed her face against his chest like a kitten. "Aren't we locked in?" she murmured sleepily. "I don't know if I can climb across the balconies like you did."

"Oh, you saw that, did you? I should have known you weren't really asleep. The thing is, I'm a very resourceful man. Marcello may have taken possession of the household keys, but I have one tucked away in here just in case I wanted to keep people out. I never thought anyone would be trying to keep me in." He sat up, reaching for his discarded clothes. "Simpson has already packed and taken enough of my clothes with him to tide us over until we reach England, and if I know my valet he'll have been able to provide something suitable for you as well. Simpson's a most excellent valet."

She sat up in the bed, her hair covering her, and watched him. "Am I going to leave in my underwear then?" she asked, pulling on her shift as he tossed it to her.

He glanced at her. "I think you're going to need to be totally indecent and wear some of my clothes."

"I'm not going to look like a boy—my hair is too long."

"This is Venice, my love. No one will care."

My love. It was a casual endearment—surely he didn't mean it. "And what about your organization of degenerates? What will happen to them?"

"Clearly there'll be no midnight ritual deflowering of a virgin, unless Marblethorpe can find another. In Venice it's unlikely," he said with a grin. "As for the Heavenly Host, I bequeath them to Wesley and his friends. Whether I like the idea or not, I expect to be quite busy enough with you." He tossed her a pair of blue satin breeches and a loose white shirt.

She looked at him. "You don't like the idea? You certainly don't need to feel obligated…"

He moved back to her and pulled her off the bed, into his arms. "The only obligation I ever listen to are my own desires. I realized something when I was deep inside you."

His words made the heat start forming again inside her, and she wanted to touch him again, go to him. Instead she reached for the breeches, pulling them up and over her shift. They were tight on her, but then, men had no hips. She pulled the shirt over her head, emerging with enough calm to say, "And what was that?"

"If you lust after someone and have an absurd and overwhelming need to protect them, then the best way to deal with the situation is to marry the person."

She froze, looking at him. "Besides," he said with a rueful smile, "Jack would have killed me if he knew I'd despoiled his beautiful baby sister with the huge crush on me."

She felt the color flood her face. She swallowed. "How long have you known?" Of course he'd insist on marrying her. He was basically decent beneath it all. And she had no choice but to refuse.

"About halfway through the whole process. If I had even a shred of honor I would have stopped, but I'm afraid I'm quite impossible. You're going to have your hands full with me."

"I won't marry you."

"Of course you will," he said. "Why wouldn't you? You followed me around like a puppy dog all those years ago, which was pure misery, because I wanted nothing more than to toss you down in the straw and despoil you, and you were too damned young. Back then I had scruples. Fortunately, nowadays I have none."

"Then why do you want to marry me?" she said, shoving her hair away from her face.

"I have no idea," he said idly. "I expect I love you. Nothing else could account for such bizarre behavior on my part. I imagine the captain of the packet ship can perform the ceremony. Are you ready?"

She didn't move. She couldn't marry him, and she needed shoes, and she wasn't sure which was the more important to argue about.

"Oh, shoes," he said, noting the obvious. "I have a pair of boots that will do. If you have trouble navigating, I'll carry you."

"Through the streets?" she said, aghast and amused.

"It's Venice," he said. He reached over the bed and produced a key. "Shall we go, my love?" He held out his arm for her.

She hesitated for just a moment. "Oh, what the hell," she said, and ran into his arms, feeling them wrap tightly around her. He kissed her again, kissed her until she was breathless, and then unlocked the door.

"We'll live in Ireland, I think," he mused as they left the palazzo, wandering down one of the back alleyways. "You'll like it."

She looked up at him. "I still love you," she said.

"I know you do," he replied with a cheeky grin. "I think we'll have horses." And they strolled down the narrow alley, across St. Mark's Square, heading for the docks, and no one looked twice.

After all, it was Venice.

The House of Rohan

If you liked this story, be sure to read more scandalous stories about the Heavenly Host in the House of Rohan trilogy by Anne Stuart!

RUTHLESS
(August 2010)

RECKLESS
(September 2010)

BREATHLESS
(October 2010)

"Anne Stuart proves once again why she is one of the most beloved and reliably entertaining authors in the genre. Every book she writes is witty, inventive, dark and sexy—a wild adventure for the mind...and the heart."
— No.1 *New York Times* bestselling author Susan Wiggs on The House of Rohan series

Read for an excerpt from *Ruthless*...

Paris, 1768

The visit with the lawyer had not gone well. Elinor Harriman arrived home just as her sister, Lydia, had finished dealing with their landlord, and she ducked out of sight so the old lecher wouldn't see her. Monsieur Picot had no patience for either her or her mother, but her baby sister was a different matter. All Lydia had to do was let tears fill her limpid blue eyes and make her Cupid's bow mouth tremble and M. Picot was destroyed, awash with apologies and assurances. He didn't realize he was being played until the door was firmly closed behind him and Elinor could sneak up the stairs, grateful that she hadn't had to defend Lydia's honor if M. Picot got carried away.

He never did. None of the landlords and butchers and greengrocers ever took advantage of Lydia's delicate beauty. She radiated such an exquisite innocence that no one would dare. Even in this less than felicitous area of town, no one would even think of offering her an insult.

"Told you," Lydia said with an impish grin far removed from her Madonna smile. "It works every time."

Elinor flopped into the nearest chair, letting out a groan as an errant spring poked her backside. During their last enforced move they'd had to relinquish all but their most wretched of furniture. The tiny parlor on the edge of one of the least savory neighborhoods in Paris held three chairs and a meager table that served as a desk, a dining surface and a dressing table, and the chairs were barely functional. The bedrooms were as bad. One sagging bed in the first room held their mother's snoring body, in the other there was only a shared mattress on the hard floor. She refused to think about how Nanny Maude or Jacobs the coachman slept in the back area that served as kitchen and servants' quarters.

And how absurd it was to have a coachman when it had been years since they'd even had a horse, much less a coach. Not since their very first days in Paris, when their mother had been in love and the two sisters had reveled in their new adventure. But Jacobs had come with them from England, under Lady Caroline's spell as most men were, and nothing, not even a total lack of wages, could induce him to leave.

The lover and the money had disappeared quickly, to be replaced by someone almost as wealthy. In the last ten years Lady Caroline Harriman had been working her way down to a state Elinor couldn't bear to consider. At least right now her mother was too ill to cause trouble, to go looking for another bottle of blue ruin, another game of chance, another man to finance her more important needs, which had never included her daughters.

"So how much time have we got?" she asked, reaching for her knitting. She was a wretched knitter—her handwork was atrocious but she convinced herself she could do something useful, even if her socks and vests were full of dropped stitches. Nanny Maude had taught her, but as usual she was proving less than adept.

Lydia sighed. "He'll be back in a week, and I don't think I'll be able to put him off again." Sweet Lydia was perfect in everyway, pretty and darling and clever, and her handwork was flawless. She could dance perfectly with only the cursory lessons their mother had once paid for, she could paint a pretty picture, sing like a bird, and any man who met her became her willing slave, from Jacobs, their elderly manservant, to the wealthy young Vicomte de Miraboux whom she'd met at the lending library. For a brief time Elinor had hoped their problems were solved, until the Vicomte's family caught wind of what was going on and the Vicomte had been swept away on a grand tour of Europe.

They'd offered her money, Elinor thought, rubbing her chilled hands, and she'd probably been a fool to throw it back in their smug faces. As if a Harriman would ever stoop to being bribed. But at that moment, with M. Picot just walking away, she suddenly thought she could do almost anything if it ensured safety for Lydia and their little family. Even for their reckless mother.

Lady Caroline had been too ill to cause trouble recently. They had no money for a doctor or medicine, and the flush that had covered her body and disordered her never-clear mind was a mixed blessing. Ill as she was, at least for the time being she was bedridden, unable to get them deeper in debt.

"So tell me about the lawyer, Nell," Lydia said, calling her the pet name only she used. "Has our father left us some vast fortune to ease Maman's final days? Or at least a minor pittance?"

"He's left us something, though a vast fortune might be too optimistic," Elinor said morosely. "His title and estates have been left to a Mr. Marcus Harriman, and another, undoubtedly smaller amount for us. He probably wouldn't have left us anything if he could have helped it." She carefully avoided the fact that whatever inheritance existed belonged, nominally, to her. Lydia's parentage was cloudy, but most definitely had nothing to do with Elinor's father, and everyone knew it. Though British law declared a child born within a marriage to be the legal offspring of the husband, her father had been infinitely inventive in denying either child or his ex-wife any kind of support.

Lydia sighed. "Perhaps M. Picot would be put off another week if I allowed him a few liberties. A kiss would hardly compromise my soul if it kept a roof over our heads."

"No!" Elinor dropped another stitch, and tossed her knitting aside in frustration. She looked up at her sister. "The lawyer definitely said our father had left us something, though apparently there was some ridiculous stipulation that I would have to go to England to receive it. I just wish we'd known of his death sooner— we could have put this in motion months ago. I expect the death notice would have gone to our former residence, and since we left in the middle of the night with our bills unpaid they would have been unlikely to pass along any correspondence that might have showed up. I'm sure it won't be too miserable an amount. He wouldn't let his daughters starve."

Lydia's brief smile was wry. "Don't try to sweeten things for me. He always said he wanted nothing to do with the spawn of the harlot he'd had the misfortune to marry. Why should he change his mind on his deathbed?"

"Well, he was still angry. It was only a few years after mother had left him, and he was the laughing stock of London. Sooner or later he must remember that we are his blood and he has some responsibility to us."

"I thought he claimed we aren't actually his children, didn't he?"

Elinor could barely remember their father. He'd been a tall, singularly unpleasant man with little interest in anything but his horses and his women. It had always seemed patently unfair to Elinor that his wife had been denounced for following similar interests, but she'd learned fairness had little to do with reality. "Of course we're his children," she said. At least Lydia had never suspected the truth about her own parentage. "I'm as tall as most men, and I have his wretched nose."

"It's a very nice nose, Nell," Lydia said gently. "It gives you character, whereas I'm just a pretty little nothing."

"There are times when I would have given a great deal to be a pretty little nothing," Elinor said morosely.

"No, you wouldn't. I don't really think you want to be anyone but yourself, if truth be told," Lydia said.

Elinor forced a laugh. "You're probably right. I always was wretchedly strong-minded. I'd like to be exactly as I am, only fabulously wealthy. That's a reasonable enough request, isn't it? Unfortunately the only way to obtain a fortune is to marry one, and The Nose precludes that."

"A very good man would appreciate you, elegant nose and all," Lydia said firmly. "And I have every intention of marrying someone fabulously wealthy, so you don't need to worry about it. You will be free to marry for love."

Elinor snorted in disbelief, a very unladylike reaction. "A lovely thought, dear. But how are you going to meet this very rich man when we're living on the edge of the Paris slums? The next move will put us in the heart of them. It's going to come to that, eventually, and I'm not quite sure we'll survive."

"I have faith," Lydia said simply. "The answer will be provided when we need it." On top of everything else Lydia was a devout Christian, whereas Elinor had lost her faith years ago, when she'd met Sir Christopher Spatts, and now she accompanied Lydia to church only as a matter of form.

"I think the answer is long overdue," she grumbled. "If you could make it hurry up I'd appreciate it."

She heard the commotion coming from the back of the apartment, and Jacobs burst into the room, his hat in his hand, his weathered old face creased with worry, Nanny Maude close behind him.

"She's gone, miss," he announced.

There was never any question who he was talking about. "What do you mean, gone?" Elinor said, jumping up. "Is she dead?"

"No, Miss Elinor," Nanny said, her voice thick with worry. "Your mother managed to find the last of the money I'd had for food, and she put on her fancy dress and left."

"Oh, dear God. How did she manage that? I thought she could barely move," Elinor said, chilled. "We can find her, can't we? She can't have gotten far."

"I almost caught her, miss," Jacobs said miserably, crushing his hat with his big, strong hands. "I thought I recognized her running down the streets, but she got in a coach before I could catch her."

"A coach? Are you sure it was my mother? I didn't realize she still knew anyone with a coach."

"It was her," Jacobs said grimly. "And I recognized the coach. Even in the streetlights I could see the crest."

"Oh, Lord," Elinor moaned. "What new disaster has she gotten us into? Whose was it?"

"St. Philippe."

"Bloody hell," Elinor said. "Don't look at me like that, Nanny Maude. I know you raised me better, but if any occasion deserved a curse then this one does. You know who St. Philippe's friend is, don't you, Jacobs?"

"I don't," Lydia piped up, her blue eyes shining with curiosity.

"You don't need to know," Elinor snapped.

"It's that devil, isn't it?" Nanny said, her voice grim. "She's gone and taken herself off to the devil's lair, where there's orgies and such, and she'll lose the tiny bit of money we have left and probably end up sacrificed to the dark one."

"I don't think they do sacrifices, Nanny," Elinor said in her most practical voice, trying to ignore her own racing heart.

"They do," Nanny said, nodding her head so vigorously her lace cap slipped off her silver hair. "Women go in there and are never seen again. They kill virgins and drink their blood."

"Well, if it's virgins they kill then I think our mother's safe," Elinor drawled, determined to take the terrified look off her sister's face. "And I doubt anyone will be so besotted with her that she'll disappear. She'll gamble away the money and then come crawling home, sick and helpless."

"You don't understand, miss," said Nanny. "It's the only money we have left. And she took the diamond brooch."

A cold chill ran down the center of Elinor's body. It was the last thing of value they owned, a poor piece with tiny, flawed diamonds that was worth very little, but she'd kept it hidden for an emergency that didn't involve their deliberately self-destructive mother. She straightened her shoulders. "Then I'll simply have to go after her."

She ignored Nanny's howl of protest. Jacobs said nothing—he knew there was no other choice. Lydia rose. "I'm going with you, Nell."

"You certainly are not. If I walk into that den of iniquity I know I'm safe. They'd be on you like a pack of ravening wolves."

"I think you overestimate my irresistibility," Lydia said with a grin.

"And I think you underestimate it. Nanny said they drink the blood of virgins, remember?" she said with just enough lightness to allay her sister's fears.

Unfortunately Lydia could see right through her.

"You're a virgin too, darling, unless you've been keeping something from me. They'll drink your blood too."

Elinor didn't even flinch. "They won't be drinking anyone's

blood. They thrive on scandal and secrecy, but I suspect they're not nearly as dangerous as they pretend to be," she said in a matter-of-fact voice.

"They murder babies," Nanny contributed helpfully.

"Hush," Elinor said. "I'm hardly a baby. Jacobs will take me to the house of the Comte de Giverney and we will extract our mother and be back before midnight."

"Begging your pardon, miss, but they were heading out of town," Jacobs said. "I think they've gone to his château."

Elinor remained calm. "And how far away is that?"

"Not far, miss. An hour out of town if we hurry."

"Then we'll be back by dawn," she said. "Safe and sound, and this time we'll tie mother to the bed when we can't watch her."

"And how do you intend to get there?" Lydia said. "Last I heard we had no coach, nor horses, nor money to rent them. Are you intending to walk?"

Elinor shared a knowing glance with Jacobs, who backed out of the room without another word. "Jacobs will handle it," she said smoothly. "In the meantime I'm counting on you to make certain Mother's room is clean and ready for her. We'll probably have to use the restraints we had from the time she was raving. It will depend on how much gin she's drunk and if she's been fed anything else dangerous."

"I don't want you going there alone."

"I'll go with her," Nanny said, bless her elderly heart. She was so crippled with the rheumatics that she could hardly walk, but she'd fight a dragoon of soldiers for her babies.

"No, Nanny," she said gently. "I need you to look after Lydia." She met Nanny's gaze for a moment, and a world of understanding passed between them. If by any bizarre chance Elinor didn't come back Lydia would need someone, and Nanny was their only choice.

Nanny nodded her head, and Elinor could see tears shining in her eyes. "Don't be ridiculous, you two. I'm not walking into the gates of hell. The Comte de Giverney is just a man who throws decadent parties, not Satan himself, and I'm hardly the type of female to inflame his darker passions. Besides, Jacobs carries a pistol, and he'd shoot the first man who tried to harm me. I'll go in, ask for my mother, and they'll probably be happy enough to get rid of her. So there's nothing to worry about."

"Except the diamond brooch," Nanny said grimly.

If Elinor had been closer she would have kicked one of Nanny's painful shins. The old lady had a very gloomy outlook on life, and right then Lydia needed to be hopeful. She didn't need to learn their last hope of rescue had vanished, and if the jewelry was lost they were well and truly doomed.

The World of Mills & Boon®

There's a Mills & Boon® series that's perfect for you. We publish ten series and with new titles every month, you never have to wait long for your favourite to come along.

Blaze. Scorching hot, sexy reads

By Request Relive the romance with the best of the best

Cherish™ Romance to melt the heart every time

Desire Passionate and dramatic love stories

 Browse our books before you buy online at
www.millsandboon.co.uk

M&B/WORLD

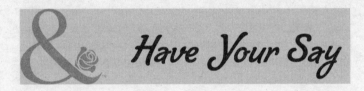

Have Your Say

You've just finished your book.
So what did you think?

We'd love to hear your thoughts on our
'Have your say' online panel
www.millsandboon.co.uk/haveyoursay

- ❧ Easy to use
- ❧ Short questionnaire
- ❧ Chance to win Mills & Boon®
  goodies

 Visit us Online

Tell us what you thought of this book now at
www.millsandboon.co.uk/haveyoursay

YOUR_SAY